Headcase
By Keith A Pearson

For more information about the author and to receive updates on his new releases, visit…

www.keithapearson.co.uk

Important Author's Note

Headcase is the fourth instalment of a series. You'll appreciate (and understand) the story to a greater degree if you've read the first three novels in the series:

1. *Who Sent Clement?*

2. *Wrong'un*

3. *Clawthorn*

All three novels are available from Amazon in ebook, paperback, and audiobook format.

If you've already read those three, welcome to Clement's latest adventure…

1.

After a twenty-minute journey, the van's heater had only just begun to blow warm. Steve, the driver, flicked the indicator stalk and turned into a side street.

"It's down here somewhere," he mumbled.

His colleague, Jimmy, replied with an unenthusiastic grunt from the passenger's seat.

The van edged slowly forward while Steve peered left and right, looking for the destination address. As they rounded a bend, he spotted two men in fluorescent green jackets; deep in conversation at the rear of a building which had seen better days.

"Must be over there."

Slowing the van to near walking pace, Steve edged towards the two men and opened his window.

"I'm looking for Martin Featherstone. We're from Abacus."

"You're late," the older of the two men replied.

"Rush hour traffic. Sorry."

Martin Featherstone frowned and then ordered Steve to reverse onto a patch of weed-ridden tarmac at the rear of the building.

Steve complied.

"He's a miserable bastard," Jimmy complained, as the engine fell silent.

"It's a shit-awful Monday morning in January, and it's freezing out there. Do you blame him?"

"'Spose not."

"Come on. Let's get this over with."

The two men exited the van. Featherstone strode straight past them towards a reinforced steel door; shackled with a heavy-duty padlock and chain.

"That's a bit over the top for an empty shop," Steve commented.

"It's designed to keep the bloody squatters out. We had problems with a similar building over in Guildford and it took almost a year to evict the bastards."

After wrestling with the padlock, he then tugged hard at the door three times. On the third attempt, it sprung open.

"Everything is stacked in crates," Featherstone said to Steve. "I need it cleared as quickly as possible. We've got a demolition crew arriving at lunchtime."

"No worries."

"Come and find me when you're done. I'll be over in the site cabin."

With that, Featherstone left them to it.

"You heard the man, Jimmy. Let's crack on."

Steve rolled open the rear shutter of the van and grabbed one of two rechargeable lamps, which he passed to Jimmy.

"No electricity and the front windows are boarded up."

Jimmy took the lamp and his boss grabbed the other. Steve switched his on and led the way.

He stepped through the doorway into a wall of damp, frigid air; his own breath clouding in the light of the lamp.

"Looks like a staff room," he said, teeth chattering.

"How long has it been empty?"

"Dunno. Couple of years, I think."

"Places like this give me the creeps."

The two men then checked the doors: one leading to a toilet, and the other to an empty storeroom. They found what they were there to collect beyond the third door.

"Ah, shit," Jimmy groaned.

Ahead of them, over a hundred plastic crates, stacked in the centre of the floor. Steve stepped across to the nearest stack and snapped the lid open on the top crate. He found exactly what he expected inside — piles of second-hand books. He pulled out a paperback, flicked through the pages, and then sniffed it.

"Thank Christ they're not damp," he said. "Otherwise we'd be heading straight to the tip, and you'd be heading for the dole office."

Inwardly, Steve felt relief. He'd only taken this job on because business was typically grim in January and he had bills to pay. Clearing the contents of an old bookshop for a few hundred quid wasn't likely to pay those bills, but Abacus

Clearance Solutions made a reasonable profit from selling whatever they salvaged from jobs. Steve already had a buyer lined up for today's haul.

"Come on then," he said, placing his lamp on the floor. "This lot won't shift themselves."

The cold became a non-issue as the two men then ferried crate after crate from the shop floor to the back of the van. Working silently and efficiently, it took just fifteen minutes to complete their task.

"We done?" Jimmy asked, panting hard as he returned from the final trip to the van.

Steve glanced around the shop. Beyond the empty display shelves and a counter, it was virtually a shell.

"Yep, we're done."

"Can we get going?"

Jimmy picked up the lamp to stress how little he wanted to remain in the shop. Steve followed his colleague back out to the van.

"You lock up and I'll go tell Featherstone we're done."

A minute later, Steve returned.

"All set?"

"Yep."

They clambered into the van.

"Have we got time to stop for breakfast?"

Steve glanced at the dashboard clock.

"It'll take us at least an hour to get to Edgware and we've got another job at eleven."

"No, then?"

"Sorry, mate."

Steve entered the address into the sat-nav. He hated driving anywhere close to London, but he hadn't been able to find a local dealer willing to take thousands of second-hand books in one single consignment.

Like it or not, London beckoned.

ONE WEEK LATER ...

2.

Samuel Johnson famously once said: When a man is tired of London, he is tired of life.

I'm exhausted.

When I stepped off the train at King's Cross eleven years ago, it felt like I was heading into an exciting new wonderland. True, it began with a buzz of anticipation, and it remained a blast for a while. Then, I hit a peak, and that's when I should have left, but I didn't. I carried on hoping to catch that first wave of excitement again. It never came, but circumstances changed and I stayed anyway. Now I'm weary of the people; tired of the noise and the constant chaos.

That is London. That is my life: a party I wish I'd left a long time ago.

"Mr Nunn?"

"Yes."

"I'm Simon Crawshaw-Smith."

I stand up and shake his hand.

"I'm sorry to have kept you waiting," he says, taking a seat behind the desk.

It's been sixteen minutes since I walked into the estate agent's office.

"No problem," I chirp.

He turns to look at a computer monitor.

"I understand you've got a few issues with your flat?" he says.

I retrieve the sheet of paper from my pocket and hand it to him.

"Oh, you've a list."

"Yes, sorry."

He takes a cursory glance at the list and drops it into a tray.

"Leave it with me Mr Nunn and I'll talk to the landlord."

"May I ask when?"

"As soon as I have a chance."

"Can you be more specific?"

"The landlord is a busy man so I can't be sure."

"Every one of those issues will worsen the longer it's left. There's mould in the bathroom, the bedroom window won't open, and there's an awful smell coming from the kitchen sink."

"I understand. As I say, leave it with me."

"Okay."

I get to my feet.

"Before you go, Mr Nunn, I should remind you there's a rent review due next month."

"Again? We only had one last year."

"We review the rent every year, as per your tenancy agreement."

"And are you likely to review it in a downward direction, just for once?"

"Highly unlikely."

"Right," I sigh.

"Supply and demand, Mr Nunn," he smirks. "If you're not happy with the rent, you could always seek alternative accommodation."

Sadly, not an option. Flats with garages are rarer than hen's teeth in London, and Crawshaw-Smith knows it.

"No, I'm sure we'll cope. Somehow."

I flash a parting smile and walk away.

Outside, the bitter wind instantly penetrates my overcoat and every layer beneath; the kind of cold that stings your skin and chills your bones. It's only just gone five but the sun clocked-off an hour ago. The sky might be dark, but London never is. Never dark, never silent, never still.

I don a pair of gloves and cross the street.

Our flat is only a short walk from the centre of Kentish Town; the location of the estate agent's office. It's one of our capital's more affordable districts but the term 'affordable' is relative. As a mental health counsellor I'll never earn enough to live comfortably in London and my plight is exasperated by my wife's sporadic income.

I married Leah seven years ago and, for the last three years, I've suggested countless times we might try living somewhere which doesn't constantly suck money from my bank account and joy from my soul. My wife, being a born and bred Londoner, has a differing view.

We met at a pub in Camden nine years ago. There was an open-mic night for budding stand-up comedians; the same night Leah unleashed her free-spirited comedy on an unwitting audience — one of her many fleeting fads as I later discovered. It didn't go well although I watched on, mesmerised. Her comedy career started and ended that night but, after I plucked up the courage to ask her if she fancied a drink, it became the start of us.

Only when we'd been dating for three months, and I'd fallen hopelessly in love, did she tell me the real reason behind her quirky nature. Irony of ironies, the woman I loved suffered from borderline personality disorder; a condition she'd endured most of her adult life and still lives with today. Maybe she gravitated towards me in order to have her own private counsellor on tap. I never asked but I still wonder.

"I'm home," I call out, wiping my feet on the doormat.

The central heating is set to maximum and my cheeks burn at the sudden change in temperature.

"I'm in the kitchen," comes the reply.

I hang my coat up and navigate past the rows of boxes stacked up along the hallway wall.

"What on earth?"

Leah is at the kitchen table, surrounded by piles of junk, or stock as she likes to call it.

"Freddy was having a clear out. He offered me a deal."

Freddy owns an antique shop in Holloway and Leah often buys his unwanted tat for her market stall.

"How much did you buy?" I ask, while trying to edge past a new pile of boxes occupying the limited floor space.

"Not much. Just a dozen boxes."

"But honey, the flat is already fit to bursting. Shouldn't you focus on selling the existing shi … stock first?"

"It's January, David," she replies with a frown. "Money is tight, and the weather is awful. I'm stocking up for the spring."

This is a conversation we've had more times than I care to remember. It typically ends with a claim I don't understand her business model, and tears — there are nearly always tears. As best I can tell, Leah's business model involves compulsive hoarding and an occasional stall at a market or craft fair where my wife will earn barely enough money to pay the heating bill.

I've had a long day, and I'm not in the mood for an argument.

"Okay, but can we at least agree to keep the kitchen table clear? Please."

"I'll pack this lot away once I've finished the inventory."

I lean over and kiss her forehead.

"Great. Thank you."

She looks up at me and smiles. It's virtually the same expression which greeted me when I asked her for a drink nine years ago. Most days, Leah possesses an almost child-like charm; a sweet-natured innocence. However, it masks an obstinate streak and a hair-trigger temper.

I risk mentioning a well-worn subject.

"If it's too cold for a stall, maybe now is the time to consider selling online?"

Her expression changes in a heartbeat.

"Not this again," she huffs. "I keep telling you, I'm not willing to boost the profits of some tax-dodging multinational corporation."

"But, you'd clear your stock backlog in a few weeks."

"I don't care. I'd rather sit on my stock until the end of days than sell online."

If The Four Horsemen of the Apocalypse turned up at our flat, they'd take one look at the hallway and turn around on health and safety grounds.

"Fair enough. What's for dinner?"

"I have been busy, you know. I've not had chance to think about dinner."

I swerve past the boxes and open the fridge.

"Or go shopping," she adds.

My shoulders slump as I stare at the near-empty shelves.

"Have we got any eggs left?" I ask.

"In the cupboard."

"Cheese omelette?"

"Yes, please."

I wasn't offering to be chef, but it's less hassle than the alternative — asking my wife to suspend her inventory and cook for a change.

It hasn't escaped my attention I'm married to a woman who personifies the city in which she was born — Leah and London share many similar traits. They're both erratic, disorganised, frenetic, and complex. In fairness, there have been occasions when they've also shared positive traits. I've seen glimpses of my wife's beauty when strolling through Hyde Park on a crisp autumn morning. I've experienced her compassion on the occasions I've witnessed kind-hearted souls helping the homeless. And, I've been captivated by similar flashes of brilliance while visiting the capital's museums and galleries.

They are also both prone to swinging between extremes. From light to dark, from joyous to enraged, from captivating to infuriating.

As a rule, I try not to counsel my wife because she sees her own therapist once a month, alongside the medication she takes. However, during her darker moments when I've no choice but to intervene, I've told Leah what I tell my clients: we are all broken to some degree.

I live in hope that one day, she might accept that living in this damn city is part of the problem with her mental health. Her denial is much like those who've suffered in an abusive relationship — victims who struggle to accept that leaving is the first step. However, too many stay when promises of change are given, and then broken. On one level, that remains my wife's problem. London is the abusive partner, and she needs to leave.

"Can you have a look at the van after dinner?" she asks.

"What's wrong with it this time?"

"It's making a strange noise."

I crack the last of the eggs into a bowl.

"You'll need to be more specific, honey."

"Like a grinding noise, whenever I press the brake pedal."

"The pads probably need replacing."

"I think the whole van needs replacing," she says while examining a garish vase.

What I should say at this point is that selling some of the junk occupying our flat might generate enough funds to buy a new van.

I don't.

"I'm afraid it's a case of make do and mend for the moment."

"Bloody van," she mumbles under her breath.

"Presuming it is the pads, it's beyond my limited mechanical skills. I'll get someone to look at it."

"When?"

"When I can. It's not as though you're using it for work at the moment."

"I'll need a new Oyster card, then. I don't want to be stuck here all day with no way of getting around."

I draw a sharp intake of breath.

"You've spent all your money on stock?"

She nods while I recall a story about cows, markets, and magic beans.

"Fine. I'll transfer some money into your account."

We're no different from most couples in that strained finances are a good starting point for a guaranteed argument. Not long after we married, I decided it would be best to have separate bank accounts after an unfortunate incident rendered us near-destitute. Leah received an email stating she'd won five million pounds on the lottery, and the funds would be transferred into our joint account within twenty-four hours. All she had to do was email them back with her debit card details. Back then, my wife had only just started using the internet and I should have warned her about email scammers.

I can still remember the excitement in her eyes when I arrived home that day; can still taste the Veuve Clicquot champagne she'd bought to celebrate. Only when I asked where she purchased the winning ticket did my wife stop to consider if she actually had purchased a ticket. She hadn't.

13

We both learnt a valuable lesson that day but online scammers aside, our finances wouldn't be so strained if we lived just forty miles outside of London. It seems whatever we argue about, living in this Godforsaken city is nearly always the root cause. Frustration usually ensues so I rarely bring the subject up these days.

"Can you set the table, please?" I ask, while trying not to grate my knuckles alongside the remaining morsel of cheese.

She huffs like a sulky teenager and tosses a hardback book into one of the boxes. I've only been home fifteen minutes but all signs suggest this is not one of Leah's better days. I need to lighten the conversation.

"So, have you found anything interesting?" I call out over my shoulder.

"Everything is interesting in its own way."

"Right."

"I did find a beautiful little tobacco tin," she adds in a lighter tone. "It's probably not worth much, but it's inscribed."

"Nice. Can I see it?"

My interest in the tobacco tin is minimal but I want to nurture her enthusiasm. Leah loves objects with a story; even if that story evolves from her own imagination.

She sidles up next to me at the hob and presents the battered tobacco tin.

"What do you think?"

"It's … lovely."

"Let me read you the inscription."

She turns it over and squints at the bottom.

"For my darling William. Yours, always. Emily."

"Very sweet."

"I wonder who they were. William and Emily?"

She looks up at me as if I might have an answer. I don't, but I look back at her and it serves as a reminder why I'm willing to live this life. Based on physical appearance alone, we're completely incompatible. At thirty-two, my wife is only a year younger than me but we've aged at a different rate. Perhaps it's because I've carried the stresses of our time together. Her hair

14

has the colour and sheen of chocolate ganache while I've noticed a few strands of grey developing at my temples. Her skin is flawless while my crow's feet are developing crow's feet. Her pale blue eyes remain lustrous and bright while I avoid eye contact in the bathroom mirror.

"If William loved Emily half as much as I love you, I'm sure they were blissfully happy … whoever they were."

I'm rewarded with a kiss on the cheek and a smile. She then skips back to the table and clears enough space for two plates. Nine years, and perhaps I'm close to understanding the inner-workings of my wife. I'm probably kidding myself — Leah is a complex work in progress and the best I can do is play my part in keeping her ship steady. Until her next storm, that is.

3.

I wake up to a chorus of clunks and gurgles — courtesy of our antiquated central heating system — thirteen minutes before my alarm is due to sound. Pointless going back to sleep but too cold to get up. I settle on lying back and listening to the radiator creak as the cold metal fills with hot water.

Beside me, Leah stirs. She scratches her nose and rolls over.

Last night, when we came to bed, she initiated one good reason I should count my blessings. My wife is a different person when we make love and it's the one and only area of our lives where she takes the lead. It's not that I'm particularly submissive; more Leah has — shall we say — a greater breadth of experience. She also possesses a voracious appetite. Nine years together and we still ruffle the bedsheets three or four times a week.

Alas, our frequent liaisons are for pleasure rather than the purpose of procreation. Leah had a backstreet abortion at fifteen which almost killed her. She recovered but her reproductive system didn't. I don't know if motherhood would have made her or broken her, but it's academic, and not a subject I dwell on. As she says: it is what it is.

I sit up and my eyes are drawn to the pile of boxes stacked across the back wall of the bedroom. Leah and I reached an agreement last year where she promised to keep her stock contained to the garage. Weeks later, a couple of boxes appeared in the kitchen and, over time, more followed. Now, every room has its own collection of battered boxes in various shapes and sizes. Our home now resembles the storeroom of a charity shop and there's a constant dank hum about the place. I need to formulate a strategy before it gets completely out of hand. There are only so many times a man can stub a toe on the way to the bathroom.

On that note, I get up and slip into my dressing gown.

Once I've dealt with my bodily functions, I manoeuvre my way through the kitchen and put the kettle on. I then check the bread bin but there's only two slices left, which I leave for Leah. She won't get up for another hour so I won't be around to witness the tantrum if there's nothing in the flat to eat, but I'll certainly hear about it when I get home. While I wait for the kettle to boil, I open my banking app and transfer fifty pounds into Leah's account so she can buy an Oyster Card and hopefully, some groceries. I try to avoid looking at my balance but it flashes up in the centre of the screen when the transfer is complete.

"Christ," I mumble.

I hate money. No, I hate never having enough money.

When I left University, I knew I'd be following a career path which would never lead to riches, but I hoped I'd earn enough to live comfortably. I know I sound like a whiney millennial but the system doesn't work for those, like me, who pursue a vocational career. It's not a case of being entitled, but the experience at the estate agent's yesterday highlighted the perilous predicament of our finances. I've no doubt the rent will increase significantly next month whereas my salary will see a meagre inflationary rise. If I tighten my belt any further, I risk cutting myself in half.

The sixty-third reason why moving out of London makes sense.

I make a cup of tea and drink it at the kitchen table. Beyond the window, I can just make out a slither of ashen sky above the house next door. Checking the weather forecast on my phone, it tallies with the foreboding view; rain or sleet for much of the day. It's this kind of day at this time of year when demand for mental health counselling peaks. Post-Christmas blues they used to call it; short, gloomy days, and a lack of money. It harks back to a time when those suffering mental health issues were simply told to cheer up or pull themselves together. If only I could genuinely help my clients with a quick pep talk and a slap on the back.

As my tea cools towards a drinkable temperature, I waste five minutes checking the news. The headline is now so familiar it looks like a cut and paste: another stabbing in London last night and another teenager dead. Another family decimated and another young life soon to be ruined when the police charge the perpetrator. As I read the report, it confirms the attack happened in Camden; barely a mile up the road. As close to home as it is, we've seen at least a dozen stabbings in Kentish Town over the last twelve months, and God-knows how many muggings and assaults.

I shut the app. Way too depressing.

People sometimes ask how I cope with life's lows. Those who work in mental health aren't immune, and when you spend every working day with people at their lowest ebb, it's not possible to switch off completely. We are human and prone to the same negative thoughts as anyone else, which is why we're regularly assessed to ensure we're not venturing into the same dark place many of our clients occupy.

It's particularly challenging in my case as I have a wife at home who also suffers with her mental health. Fortunately, I'm blessed with the ability to compartmentalise. Work is work, home life is home life, and Leah is Leah; each filed in their own folder and separated from one another. That's my coping mechanism, and on the whole, it works.

It also helps I enjoyed a well-balanced upbringing in rural Oxfordshire.

My parents are about to celebrate their fortieth wedding anniversary and still live in the same house I grew up in. They're both now retired but Dad was Head of Social Services for the local council and Mum a Senior Nurse. When we were old enough, both parents would regularly tell us about cases they'd encountered at work. They ensured my older sister, Katie, and I understood how fortunate we were. Whinging about homework or chores wasn't tolerated and, in fairness, we rarely did. As Dad often pointed out, our stresses and woes paled into insignificance when compared to kids living in abject poverty or facing a terminal illness. We had it drummed into us, we should count our blessings, and we did. Still do.

Katie now works as a teacher for a charity; helping to educate young girls in some of the poorest parts of Africa. As for me, I wanted to make a difference to those who have nowhere else to turn. Most of my clients only seek help once they've hit rock bottom and the charity I work for is often their last resort. I spend much of my working day in conversation with those suffering depression, anxiety, addiction, and all manner of overwhelming issues. Put simply, these people are trapped in a hole and it's my job to help them climb out, or at least learn to live in that hole.

Leah wanders into the kitchen; wrapped in a fluffy yellow dressing gown.

"Oh, morning. You're up early."

"Couldn't sleep," she yawns, flopping down on the chair opposite.

"What have you got planned for the day?" I ask.

"Finish my inventory and then I might go to the library."

"I've put some money in your bank account. Can you pick up some groceries?"

"Guess so."

She folds her arms and then stares at the table. Leah isn't at her best in the mornings and I know better than to expect in-depth conversation.

"I should get ready for work. The kettle has just boiled if you want tea."

I receive a grunt in reply.

It takes twenty minutes to shower and dress. When I return to the kitchen, Leah is still in the same chair but now sipping from a mug.

"Don't forget to sort out the van," she says. "There's an indoor market in Crouch End on Saturday. I remembered last night."

"That's good. I'll see what I can do."

"Promise?"

"I promise I'll try."

She smiles up at me. It's early, but I think today might be a good day.

"Right, I need to make a move. If there's anything ..."

"Yes, David, I know the drill. Call if I'm having a bad day."

"Sorry."

I lean over and plant a kiss on her forehead.

"I love you."

"You too."

I grab my keys and make for the front door.

Outside, it's bitterly cold but at least it's not raining yet. I scuttle up the pathway which leads to the main road and turn back to check if Leah is at the window to wave me off as she sometimes does. She's not there so, rather than my wife's beautiful face, my parting vision is the ugly block of flats. It's hard to imagine how bad a day the architect was having when he designed such a dreary block of brick and tile. Still, at least we have a home, even if it is a fair take on Orwell's dystopian nightmare.

To stave off the cold, I move at a brisk pace; faster than the vehicles crawling along beside me. Why people bother driving through central London in rush hour is beyond me. I get that some people have no choice if they're carrying goods or tools, but I pass too many cars with a single occupant in business attire. Is this a good use of their time? Surely not. Then again, I've been on the tube during rush hour and it's no fun.

I reach the centre of Kentish Town and pass the estate agent's office. They're not open yet, but I guess they don't have to be. If profits are down, they only have to hike rents to rake in more cash. It's a racket.

I cross the street and pass a row of businesses which provide an eclectic range of products and services to the residents of Kentish Town: groceries, haircuts, carpets, Indian food, and funerals. I've personally used three of the businesses, but thankfully I've never stepped foot in the undertakers. Sadly, I know too many people who have.

Turning the corner, the traffic is at a complete standstill. In the distance, the siren of an emergency vehicle wails, but it's so commonplace in this part of London I've become desensitised to the sound; not least because our flat sits on a busy road and I'm used to hearing sirens every hour of every day.

I reach the offices of RightMind and enter my access code to unlock the front door.

"Morning, Debs."

As a charity, we don't have the budget for a receptionist so my colleague, Debbie Marlor, works from the reception desk. Debbie is employed as our chief administrator — a grand title considering Debbie is our only administrator. She's also adopted several other roles we can't afford to fill: funding coordinator, human resources manager, outreach liaison officer, and chief bottle washer. Beyond her long list of titles, she's a remarkable, selfless individual, and the glue which holds our charity together.

"Good morning, David."

Unsurprisingly, she's multi-tasking, and flashes the briefest of smiles before turning her attention back to a computer monitor. Equally unsurprising is her attire this morning. Debbie doesn't believe in the fripperies of fashion and wears a black trouser suit with a white blouse every single day. One less decision she has to contend with, apparently.

"Can I get you a tea?" I ask.

She looks up at me, over the rim of her spectacles.

"I'm good, thanks, but you could do me another favour."

"Sure."

"Mark has called in sick and he had two new clients booked in today. Could you take one on?"

"Err, probably."

"That's the right answer. I'll email you his file."

"What time is he due in?"

"Half-eleven. I checked your schedule and you've got space."

"Lunch at my desk it is, then."

"You're lucky to get lunch," she sniggers. "I can only dream of finding five spare minutes to snatch a sandwich."

It's a response I should have expected. Whenever any of us complain about our workload, Debbie reminds us she works longer hours for less pay. It's a fair argument, and Debbie also misses out on the primary perk of the job — seeing a client leave our offices for the final time with a changed outlook on life.

"I'll grab you a sandwich when I get mine," I reply.

"And I'll probably eat that sandwich on the loo."

21

"Always the multi-tasker."

"Yep."

She returns her attention to the screen and I head to my office.

It would be lovely if we were able to separate our work space from where we see clients, but there isn't room in the building. My office is no larger than a typical lounge but it houses a desk, three filing cabinets, and a couple of chairs which sit either side of a coffee table. The furniture has seen better days and the pale yellow paint on the walls is peeling in places. The vast majority of my clients don't notice, or care.

I am fortunate to have an office with a window though, although the view of a litter-strewn yard at the back of the building is hardly inspiring. I'm also fortunate to earn a salary, meagre as it is. Most similar charities rely upon volunteer counsellors who each offer a few hours of their time, for free. We also utilise volunteer counsellors but three of us work full-time — two counsellors, and Debbie. I joined RightMind five years ago; not long after a generous benefactor bequeathed our building, and the two either side, in her will. The rental income from those properties, plus a number of grants and charitable donations help us cover the running costs. Just.

After hanging my coat up, I sit down at the desk. Like so much of our equipment, my computer is second-hand, and came courtesy of a company who updated their machines a few years ago and donated their castoffs. It's showing its age and takes an age to boot up. I switch it on and wander through to the poky staff room to make a cup of tea.

The computer is just about awake when I return. I check my schedule and find it's typically rammed. We give each client a forty-five minute slot with a break in between to prepare for the next. The length of that break depends on how busy we are, and today, Debbie has shuffled my appointments so I've only got fifteen minutes between each one. Nowhere near enough time but needs must.

After checking my emails, I open the case notes for my first client of the day. Alisha is nineteen years of age and lives in a one-bedroom flat with her two young children; their father serving an eight-year sentence for dealing drugs. I'd like to say Alisha is an exception to the rule but her circumstances are sadly too common. Poverty, crime, poor education, and the lack of a support network are the typical reasons people like Alisha end up with mental health issues. Living on a sink estate and surviving on state handouts and food banks, it's no wonder she's clinically depressed.

Today is her third session, and I think we're making headway.

My ten o'clock slot is with Oswald Dennis — a fifty-six-year-old bus driver with a severe gambling addiction. Oswald had a good life until he placed his first bet two years ago. Some people are more prone to addiction than others and when Oswald attended a casino for a friend's birthday, little did he know it would awaken an addiction which had lain dormant his entire life. Within a year, he'd lost his marriage, his home, and most of his friends and family. Like many people suffering with gambling addiction, his biggest challenge was accepting he had a problem. That landmark reached, Oswald is slowly beginning to realise no one ever finds hope at a roulette table.

I finish my tea just as Debbie pokes her head around the door.

"Your first appointment is here."

"Thanks."

I catch the sound of a baby crying in the reception area. Alisha couldn't arrange childcare, it seems. Not an ideal way to ease myself into the working day. Saying that, it's not exactly ideal for Alisha, either.

It always pays to keep a little perspective in this job. Even on dreary winter mornings.

4.

I shake Oswald's hand at the door to my office.

Our session went well, and I've put him in touch with an organisation that provide long-term support for gambling addicts. As with most addictions, there isn't a cure, as such, but counselling helps folks like Oswald manage their addiction.

As for Alisha, her problems are more complex.

We try to provide a holistic approach to mental health; one which focuses on the cause and the symptoms. With someone like Alisha, the depression is often rooted in personal circumstances and, unless we can help improve those circumstances, no amount of counselling will ever help. For that reason, we liaise with dozens of other charities from homeless shelters to Citizens Advice. It's a popular misconception that therapy alone can fix someone, but it can't. We help clients develop their own tools to cope with the symptoms of their illness, but we often require the help of third parties to provide solutions to the problems which triggered the issue in the first place.

With that, I've booked Alisha an appointment with Citizens Advice in the hope they can address her financial plight. If that can be eased, it'll go a long way to helping her cope with the depression. Sometimes, it only takes a glimmer of hope to drag a client away from the dark edges of despair.

All in all, a productive morning so far. I've enough time to reward my endeavours with a cup of tea before the next client arrives.

I make it halfway to the staffroom when Debbie catches me.

"Sorry, David. Slight change of plan."

"Oh?"

"We've got a walk-in. Would you mind seeing him?"

"But, didn't you want me to see a new client at eleven-thirty?"

"Mark has just arrived so he'll take that client."

"I thought Mark was ill."

"He's got man flu. I promised a constant supply of chicken soup and a hot water bottle if he struggled in."

"We should award him a certificate to mark such bravery. What a hero."

"Hmm … didn't you have man flu just before Christmas? I seem to recall you were at death's door."

"It was a particularly nasty case of man flu."

"Aren't they all?" she chuckles.

"Changing the subject, what do you know about the walk-in?"

"Very little as he's in a bit of a state. I've coaxed out a name — Cameron Gail — but that's about it. He's just mumbling a lot and repeatedly stating he needs help."

"Okay. Give me a minute and I'll come out and meet him."

"Thanks, David."

Debbie scoots off and I make a quick cup of tea before heading back to my office. I suspect I won't get around to drinking it but I place the mug on my desk and a notepad on the coffee table. Time to meet our latest walk-in.

The reason charities like RightMind exist is because demand for mental health services way outstrips supply. The NHS waiting list is long and it can take many weeks, or even months to secure an appointment with a counsellor. We provide service on demand which, in practical terms, means our door is always open whenever someone needs help; much like The Samaritans.

It seems one young man has reached the straits of desperation this morning.

I make my way through to the reception area. Debbie is in conversation with, I guess, my new client.

"David, this is Cameron."

I hold out a hand towards the dishevelled young man. He looks near-feral; nervy, with wild eyes, and jet-black hair long overdue a wash.

"Hello, Cameron."

He doesn't accept my handshake. Not uncommon.

"Would you like to have a chat?" I ask. "Nothing more. Just a chat."

25

Eventually, he nods.

"Great. Come this way."

He glances at Debbie for reassurance and her smile seems to do the trick.

Knowing precisely nothing about the young man, or what brought him to our door, I offer a seat and begin with a casual introduction.

"So, Cameron. My name is David and I'm a counsellor here at RightMind. My job is to listen and identify ways we might be able to help folks who are struggling. At this point, it really is just a casual chat and don't feel you have to discuss anything you're uncomfortable with. You can tell me as little or as much about your situation as you like. How does that sound?"

"Okay," he sniffs.

"Good. Now, do you feel like telling me what brought you here today?"

His skittish body language suggests some level of paranoia.

"I'm … someone's after me," he says in a low voice. "I need to get away."

I'm a little taken aback by his accent which is a long way from the usual working-class London accent I hear most days. It's more the tone of a middle-class upbringing.

"Do you know who this person is?"

He nods but doesn't offer a name.

"Is this person threatening you?"

"I … I don't know. It's the … I've taken so much. My head …"

"You mean drugs?"

Another nod.

"Are you a regular drug user?"

"I'm not a user … I … I …"

He leans forward and puts his head in his hands.

"Take your time."

With no immediate answer, I need to bring him back to basics.

"Do you live locally, Cameron?"

He looks up, and eyes me with suspicion.

"Why do you want to know?"

As with many of our clients, not having friends or family to turn to — or not wanting those friends or family to know they're in trouble — is often a problem in itself. Feelings of isolation have a tendency to magnify every issue, and it's clear Cameron wandered into RightMind because he has nowhere else to turn.

"I'm just trying to establish your circumstances. Nothing more."

"I … I'm staying in a bedsit in Camden."

"Okay, and do you have family living locally?"

A shake of the head.

With the limited knowledge I have, Cameron's story is likely one I've heard before. Youngsters get involved in drugs and before they know it, they've developed a habit. They steal to feed that habit, often from parents, and there begins the downward spiral. As much as any parent loves their child, there's only so much they can cope with. Inevitably, the addict is ostracised from the family home — often to protect younger siblings. I understand why parents get to that stage, but it only exasperates the problem.

"Do you feel comfortable talking about your drug use?"

"You … you wouldn't understand. I need rehab."

"I'm willing to try, if you're willing to explain."

My suggestion is met with silence. Knowing his preferred narcotic might aid a course of action.

"Can I ask what drugs are you using?"

"Kimbo."

There are at least twenty drugs in common use; each with as many different names. I'm well versed on those names, but I've never heard of Kimbo before.

"That's a new one on me. Is it based on cocaine, or cannabis …"

"It's synthetic," Cameron interrupts. "And no one has heard of it."

There was a time where most drug use led back to a variant of either cocaine or cannabis. Those days are long gone with the advent of drugs created in a lab, like Spice; a synthetic cannabis

27

which is highly addictive and leaves users in a zombie-like state.

"How long have you been using Kimbo?" I ask.

He finally looks up and holds eye contact.

"Twenty-two days."

Strangely specific.

"I see. And, did you come in today hoping to get some help with your drug use?"

"I need help … yes."

"When was the last time you took Kimbo?"

"What day is it?"

"Wednesday."

"I … I'm not sure. I can't stop …"

"You can't stop?"

"If I stop taking it … I'll die …"

"Just try to relax, Cameron. Sit back and take a few deep breaths."

I've met my fair share of drug addicts over the years and on the whole, they're rarely compliant. Cameron immediately sits back in the chair and closes his eyes. He then draws several deep breaths.

Part way through one of those breaths, his eyes suddenly pop open and he stares straight at me.

"What's your name?" he asks, frantically.

"David."

"I need rehab, David … today."

"Let's just take one step at a time."

"Can you get me into rehab?"

"It's not that simple …"

He gets to his feet and before I can finish my sentence, he's out the door. I follow but by the time I reach the reception area, he's gone. I tug the front door open and scan the street. No sign of him.

"Everything okay?" Debbie asks from behind the desk.

I close the door.

"Not really. He asked about rehab and ran off as I tried to answer."

"Did you work out what his problem is?"

"I got the gist but not really, no. I only got as far as asking a few basic questions."

I pause for a moment and replay my brief conversation with Cameron.

"Have you ever heard of Kimbo?"

"Nope. What is it?"

"A drug, apparently. I haven't heard of it either."

"Have you checked the database?"

"Not yet."

"Why the interest?"

"Cameron mentioned it, and … forget it. It's not important."

The phone on Debbie's desk rings so I leave her to take the call.

Returning to my office, I make the most of a rare moment of free time, sipping lukewarm tea and staring mindlessly into space. The temporary peace breaks when I remember a promise to Leah. I open the desk drawer and search for a business card a former client gave me a few months back.

I don't make a habit of staying in touch with former clients but a number make the effort to tell me how they're doing. Denny Chambers suffered from acute anxiety and panic attacks, linked to stress when his business went under. The last time I saw him, he popped in to give me a bottle of whisky and to say thank you – we're not supposed to accept gifts but if a client is insistent, what can you do? He also gave me a card for the new business he felt confident enough to launch. Fortunately for me, Denny is now a mobile mechanic.

I call the number and Denny answers after a few rings.

"Hi, Denny. It's David Nunn, from RightMind."

"Ello, David," he says cheerfully. "How you doing?"

"I'm well, but more importantly, how are you doing?"

"Couldn't be better, mate. Business is going well and I've not had any other problems with … you know."

"That's good to hear. It's actually your new business I'm calling about."

"Yeah? What can I do for you?"

"It's my wife's van. It needs a new set of brake pads, I think. They're making a grinding noise."

"What's the make and model?"

"It's a Ford Courier. The 2004 model."

"No worries. When did you want it done?"

"As soon as you can, ideally."

"I'll need to pick up a set of pads but I could do it tomorrow early evening if you're around?"

"That would be great. Dare I ask how much it'll set me back?"

"The pads are only about thirty quid. No charge for the labour."

"Oh, that's very kind of you, Denny, but I can't ask you to work for free."

"I wouldn't be working at all if it weren't for you, mate. Fitting a set of brake pads is the least I can do."

After an admittedly half-hearted attempt to change his mind, I accept Denny's kind gesture and give him our address. It's still money I can ill-afford to spend but significantly less than a garage would charge. I text Leah the good news so it doesn't play on her mind.

One problem solved. I've got twenty minutes to grab an early lunch before the next one arrives.

5.

After saying goodbye to my final client of the day, Debbie summons me to her desk.

"What's up?"

"I did a little research on that drug of yours?"

"My drug?"

"Kimbo."

"Oh, that. Why?"

"I have a curious mind and if there is a new drug on the scene, it's best we get ahead of it. Remember when we first met a client in the throes of a Spice episode?"

"Remember?" I snort. "I'm still having flashbacks."

Two years ago, we received a visit from a young guy with drug-related problems. Unbeknown to me that young man smoked a joint laced with Spice minutes before his appointment. While sitting in my office he suddenly slipped into an unresponsive state: eyes open but very little happening beyond those eyes. We had to call an ambulance as we couldn't pull him out of his trance. I've seen drug users overdose before, but I've never seen someone so completely catatonic.

"Anyway," Debbie continues. "Do you want to know what I discovered?"

"Sure."

"I discovered absolutely nothing. There's no mention of Kimbo on any database."

"Maybe it is new, but I reckon it's just a street name. Either way, I have an inkling we won't be seeing Cameron Gail again."

"I'm not so sure."

"I'll bet you lunch we don't."

"You're on, but can you still ask around, please?"

"Sure, but I wouldn't lose any sleep over it."

She replies with a half-smile but the look in her eye implies sleep will be lost.

The reason Debbie works so tirelessly for RightMind is deeply personal. Her younger brother, Dominic, died over twenty years ago after a battle with depression which led to a chronic addiction to heroin, and a fatal overdose on Christmas Eve. Debbie blamed herself for not recognising either the signs of depression or her brother's descent into drug addiction. Since Dominic's death, she's devoted her life to helping others; a responsibility which can sometimes be a little overbearing.

I return to my office and put my coat on.

Five minutes later, I'm ruing my forgetfulness as I cower against the sleet; my umbrella in the hallway at home. My head bowed, I hustle along the pavement with the traffic moving at a pedestrian pace. I stop to cross over and catch a flash of blue light some three hundred yards up the road. Inconveniently, a double-decker bus slows down, blocking my path and view. I continue on with the bus driver seemingly keen to keep his vehicle in the way. It's another hundred yards before it comes to a halt and I can cross. As I pass the bus, the blue lights flash with increased vibrancy and I can see the source — a police car parked part-way on the pavement opposite; worryingly close to our flat.

I dash across the road, almost colliding with a cyclist, and jog up to the police car. There could be scores of reasons a police car might be parked within yards of my flat, but its presence peaks concern. I hate Leah being at home all day on her own, and she still hasn't replied to my earlier text about the van.

A policeman emerges from the narrow road which runs down the side of the flats; giving access to a block of garages at the rear and leading on to a public footpath. He looks around and then makes for his car.

"Excuse me, officer."

"Yes, sir?"

"Can I ask what's going on?"

"Nothing for you to worry about."

"But I live there," I protest, pointing to my front door.

"Ah, I see. You are?"

"David Nunn."

He opens the car door and grabs a roll of tape.

"There's been an assault, Mr Nunn," he says.

32

My heart misses a beat.

"Is the victim male or female?"

He looks at me like I've asked a question I've no right to ask.

"Male," he replies flatly. "Why do you want to know?"

"My wife is at home."

"I'm sure your wife is perfectly fine, unless you're married to a male in his late teens."

"Err, no. Is the victim okay?"

A siren screams from further up the road. I turn around to see an ambulance fighting its way through the traffic.

"Does that answer your question?"

It does.

"One of my colleagues will call round later," the policeman then adds.

"Why?"

"In case your wife saw anything. It's standard practice to canvass residents."

"Okay. I'll let her know."

The ambulance nears and I take my cue to leave.

Entering the flat, I call out Leah's name.

"In here," she replies, to my relief.

After hanging my coat up, I head through to the kitchen. Leah is at the table, sorting through the same boxes of junk she started yesterday.

"How's your day been?" I ask.

"Not bad. I'm sorting out what stock to take on Saturday."

"You didn't reply to my text message."

"Oh, sorry. I forgot to turn my phone on."

She then scans the kitchen for a phone which could be anywhere. Losing either her keys, her phone, or purse provides a daily game of hide and seek, inevitably one which ends in a hissy fit.

"I'll look for it later," she says dismissively. "What was the text about?"

"The van. A chap is popping over tomorrow evening to replace the brake pads."

She leaps to her feet and throws her arms around me.

33

"I do love you," she whispers. "And I'd be lost without you."

Much like her phone. Still, it's nice to feel appreciated.

"Love you too."

We sit down at the table and I dare to ask a question I fear will ruin the mood.

"Did you get a chance …"

"Yes, David. I bought some groceries."

"Thank you."

"You don't have to thank me," she frowns. "I know it's my responsibility."

Her attention then shifts to a notepad as she chews the end of a pen. Probably best I forewarn her about the impending visit from the local constabulary.

"Oh, did you know there's a police car out on the main road?"

"No, what's happened?"

"I think someone was assaulted in the side road."

"Are they … are they okay?"

"Not sure. I spoke to a policeman briefly, and he said someone will probably knock on our door later."

"Why?"

"I guess they're hoping to find a witness."

"I've been in here most of the afternoon, and I didn't see a thing."

As our kitchen has one window with a view of a brick wall, it's no surprise Leah didn't see anything.

"Oh, well. It'll be a short conversation then."

"They didn't say what time they were calling round?"

"Nope."

"Best I start dinner then."

I'm pleasantly surprised by Leah's offer to cook. She gets up, opens the fridge, and then withdraws two packaged ready meals.

"Chicken korma okay?"

"Lovely," I smile through gritted teeth.

When both meals have taken a turn in the microwave, Leah decants the contents onto plates, and dinner is served.

"There we are," she says proudly. "It smells great, doesn't

it?"

It smells like plastic — an opinion I keep to myself.

"Thanks, honey."

As it turns out, the korma tastes better than it smells. We sit and eat while Leah babbles on about her stock choices for Saturday. I have little to offer in the way of advice — I'm just pleased we might have three or four fewer boxes cluttering the flat.

We finish and Leah transfers the plates to the sink.

"I bought you a surprise for pudding," she declares on her way.

"Wow, pudding too. I am being spoilt."

The doorbell rings.

"Guess it'll have to wait."

I pad down the hall to the front door and open it to a male police officer, burdened by the masses of kit they have to carry on their person these days.

"Evening, sir."

"Hi. I guess you're here about the assault?"

"I am. Have you got five minutes?"

"Sure. Come in."

The officer has trouble navigating the assault course of boxes in the hallway but eventually follows me into the kitchen.

"I'm David. David Nunn," I confirm, offering the policeman a seat. "And this is my wife, Leah."

"I'm PC Shah."

"Can I get you a cup of tea, or coffee?" Leah asks.

"That's very kind but I'm strapped for time, thanks."

Leah and I join PC Shah at the table as he opens his notebook.

"I spoke to one of your colleagues earlier," I confirm. "Any news on the victim?"

"He's in a bad way, but he'll live."

"Let me guess: a gang-related squabble over turf?"

"What makes you say that?"

"I'm a counsellor at the charity, RightMind, so I get to see the fallout from drugs, gangs, and knife crime all too regularly. I

35

know the problem is at epidemic levels."

"I see."

He scribbles in his notepad.

"In this instance," he continues. "We're not sure the attack was gang-related. Did either of you see anyone acting suspiciously around five o'clock?"

"I was at work."

"And I was in here," Leah says. "As you can see, there's not much of a view."

"You didn't hear anything? Raised voices?"

"I'm afraid not. I tend to have the radio blaring when I'm sorting out my stock."

Whenever Leah is nervous, she babbles. PC Shah listens patiently as my wife tries to recount each and every item she listed around five o'clock. I intervene with a random question to save the poor officer.

"What makes you think the assault wasn't gang related?"

"Because it doesn't fit with the profile of a typical gang attack. We found the kid with a large stash of pills in his pocket, and these gang members nearly always use a knife. Well, that or a gun. Our victim was beaten senseless; not stabbed or shot. Besides, this wasn't a one-off attack."

"Really?"

"It was the fifth attack of this nature in the wider area over the last month or so. On all five occasions, the attacker beat the living daylights out of the victim but they were all found with a large amount of cash or drugs on their person."

"That's odd."

"It could be a tactic to lead us down a blind alley but the lack of a weapon is a twist, though."

"Great," I sigh. "Just what we need on our doorstep."

"For what it's worth, Mr Nunn, we're just about to launch a new initiative to address the ongoing issue of gang-related crime so you can expect to see more officers on the street over the coming weeks."

"Reassuring."

"In the meantime, please don't worry. These incidents have a tendency to stop as abruptly as they started."

The policeman flashes a smile at Leah and gets to his feet.

"If you hear anything, no matter how insignificant it might seem, please give the station a call."

He hands us a card.

"We will."

"Thanks for your time. Enjoy the rest of your evening."

Unlikely, considering what we've just heard. I see him out and return to the kitchen.

"You alright, honey?"

She smiles up at me and nods, apparently nonplussed. I guess a lifetime of living in London has a desensitising effect, whereas it took me several years before my paranoia eased to manageable levels. Even so, knowing some poor soul was beaten senseless just fifty yards from our home is deeply disconcerting; not that I want Leah to recognise my concern.

"Now, didn't you mention something about pudding?"

"Oh, yes. Sit down."

I do as I'm told. Leah returns to the fridge and pulls out another packaged product.

"Bread and butter pudding," she declares. "Your favourite."

I've yet to establish where Leah got the idea I love stodgy stale bread and raisins, but I don't want to appear ungrateful.

"That's very sweet of you. Thanks."

The microwave is set to work again and my favourite pudding is served. From experience, I know it'll be stone cold in places, and hotter than the surface of the sun in others. I nudge it around the bowl with my spoon.

"I was thinking, maybe we could visit my parents next weekend, seeing as we didn't get to see them over Christmas."

"If you like."

A notable lack of enthusiasm.

"You don't seem keen."

"Do you blame me? You should work for the Oxfordshire Tourist Board."

"Sorry?"

"Every time we visit, you constantly bang on about how

37

lovely it is in the countryside, how fresh the air is, and how there's hardly any traffic."

"Do I? I didn't realise."

"Yes, you do, David."

"I'm sorry. You should have said something."

She releases her spoon and it clatters into the bowl.

"You told me I was being over-dramatic."

"That doesn't sound like something I'd say."

"You didn't say it … not exactly. But you gave me a funny look."

"Perhaps you'd like to take a photo next time. I wouldn't want to use the same expression again."

"Are you being sarcastic?"

"Maybe, a bit."

She snatches her bowl up.

"I'm going to the bedroom. I'd like to be left alone."

"But …"

"Don't, David. Just don't."

She storms off, slamming the kitchen door behind her.

"Happy New Year, David," I mumble to myself.

6.

Last night ended in a confession from my wife — a confession I've waited a long time to hear.

An hour after dinner, as I waved the white flag at the bedroom door, I found her crying. We talked, and she confessed her reluctance to visit my parents had little to do with my love of the countryside, and a lot to do with her past.

Leah's upbringing was not a happy one. Her father absconded his parental duties when Leah was only five, and her mother then embarked upon a long and painful journey into alcoholism before Social Services finally intervened. For the next six years they shoved Leah from foster home to foster home before allowing her to live with her mother again. Six months after she moved back home, Leah's mother jumped from the fourteenth floor of a multi-storey car park.

Contrast my upbringing to my wife's and we have our problem — Leah can't bear being reminded of what she never had.

I place a mug of tea on the bedside table.

"Thanks," Leah croaks, having just woken up.

"How are you feeling today?"

"Much better. Sorry again for being such a drama queen."

"I don't need an apology. It's forgotten."

I kiss her goodbye and head off to work.

The short walk offers an opportunity to digest last night's conversation with Leah. So much talk of the past, but once again, no mention of the future. How much longer can I stay on this hamster wheel? I'm thirty-three, and most of my friends from uni are living settled lives with a future mapped out. Where will I be in three, five, or ten-years' time? The thought of walking the same pavement to the same office and listening to the same woes isn't one which fills me with delight.

Actually, it fills me with dread, if I'm being honest.

The last time I saw my parents I had a long chat with Dad about my situation. Whilst my father is a compassionate man, he's not one to shy away from a few home truths; bluntly so, sometimes. I guess his attitude stems from his career. Being the head of Social Services meant balancing the needs of the community with a financial budget and finite resources. At some point, I'm sure Dad had to say no when his conscience said otherwise.

The other issue is he doesn't see me as a thirty-three-year-old man, nor a professional counsellor. He sees me as his son; a son who isn't happy but remains unwilling to do anything about it for fear of upsetting his wife. In his opinion, I should tell Leah we're leaving London, whether she likes it or not. My dad might be enlightened man, but he's still a man of a certain generation; one where men are men and women do as they're told. I'd never accuse him of sexism, but some of his views err on the simplistic side.

"That wife of yours needs a strong hand," he once said. "For her own good."

Of course, I defended Leah and accused my dad of lacking sensitivity, or a basic grasp of mental illness. Rather than accept my view, Dad accused me of being too idealistic, too much a martyr. To make his point, he used a well-worn analogy: sometimes you've got to remove a wall brick by brick, slowly and carefully. Other times, a sledgehammer works best. In his opinion, I don't use the sledgehammer nearly enough, particularly where Leah is concerned.

I love and respect my father, but on the subject of my wife he's wrong. Alas, an alternative, realistic answer continues to elude me.

I arrive at the office just after eight-thirty and Debbie is already at her desk.

"Morning, Debs."

"Yes it is," she replies flatly.

"Everything okay?"

"Not really. The tenants next door have given notice."

"Oh, dear. Did they say why?"

"They don't have to, and it doesn't really matter. What matters is we can't afford to have that building empty for long."

There's a knock on the door. I turn around, expecting to see one of the volunteer counsellors but there's a stocky, middle-aged guy the other side of the glass.

"Can you see what he wants?" Debbie asks.

"Sure."

I open the front door.

"Good morning," the man says crisply.

Dressed in a black suit with an expensive-looking overcoat, he's not our typical visitor but it pays not to judge. Our client base is broad, and mental illness doesn't discriminate against social class.

"What can I do for you?"

"May I come in? It's a little brisk out here."

"Oh, sorry. Of course."

I step aside and hold the door open. He confidently strides in and removes a pair of black leather gloves while his eyes wander around the reception area.

"Did you know this building used to be a tobacconist?" he asks.

"I didn't."

"A long time ago. Bourke & Sons were renowned for their range of cigars ... Cuban, Ecuadorian, Honduran ..."

He sniffs the air, as if the scent of tobacco might still linger in the air.

"When did it close?" I ask.

"Must have been thirty years ago," he replies wistfully. "I bought my first ever cigar here ... I think I was about seventeen or eighteen at the time. These days I have to schlep to a place in Tottenham."

I don't like to judge but, on first impressions alone, I'd say our visitor is a man who enjoys the trappings of an affluent lifestyle: fine wines, expensive restaurants, and fat cigars.

"Anyway, I'm sure you don't have time to hear my reminiscing."

"Um, it's fine."

"I'm actually here on a mercy mission."

"Right."

"I'm looking for my nephew and a reliable source tells me he paid your organisation a visit yesterday."

We adopt an almost obsessive policy on client confidentiality, and that includes never confirming or denying any individual has utilised our services.

"I'm afraid, Mr …"

"Kingsland. Fraser Kingsland."

"I'm afraid, Mr Kingsland, it goes against our confidentiality policy to disclose any client's name."

"I just want to know if he came in here, or not. Surely you can tell me that?"

"I'm sorry."

Mr Kingsland stares directly at me. Outwardly, his expression appears friendly but his light grey eyes have all the warmth of a frozen pond.

"His name is Cameron Gail," he adds.

I can't stop myself and my eyes flick to the left, towards Debbie. In poker parlance I've just revealed my tell.

"Ahh, so he did come in yesterday," Kingsland gleefully confirms.

"As I said, we can't tell you, even if he did … although I'm not saying he did."

"Understood, but may I ask a favour?"

"Possibly."

"My nephew is not in a good place, mentally, and his poor mother is worried sick. I said I'd do whatever I can to track him down before he does something silly. All I ask is you give him my card if he should turn up. Tell him it would be in his best interests to call me."

He extracts a business card from his coat pocket and holds it out.

I take the card — jet black with just his name and mobile number in white serif text.

"If someone of that name should drop by, I'll pass on your message."

"Much appreciated."

He holds out a hand.

"Sorry, I didn't get your name?"

"David Nunn."

"Nice to meet you, Mr Nunn."

I shake his hand; his grip the uncomfortable side of firm. He then nods towards Debbie and leaves.

"I didn't like him," she remarks, the second the door swings shut. "Arrogant sod."

My mind is already elsewhere. Cameron said he didn't have any family living locally, let alone a worried mother or an apparently concerned uncle. I glance at the business card again. Who has a business card which doesn't state who you work for or what you do? And, in this day and age, why no reference to an email address or website?

"He knew Cameron had been here," I mumble.

"You're a terrible liar. I've always said that."

"You make it sound like it's a negative trait."

"No, but it comes in handy when you need to hide the truth."

"I suppose, not that it matters. As I said yesterday, I don't think we'll see Cameron Gail again."

"And if he shows up?"

"I'll give him the card."

Noticing the time, I leave Debbie to get on, and head to my office. I turn the computer on and then wander through to the staffroom.

With a cup of tea in hand, I return to my desk and check today's schedule. My first appointment isn't until nine-fifteen which allows me an extra ten minutes to prepare. As I mindlessly sip tea, I can't shake off the brief meeting with Fraser Kingsland, and Cameron Gail's plight. The obvious option would be to do nothing but that doesn't sit right. Clearly the young man needs help, and he has a family willing to offer help. The very least I can do is make Cameron aware his uncle is searching for him.

The motive is sound, but the method an issue. He left without registering his personal details yesterday so I've no idea how to get a message to Cameron Gail.

I sit forward and open Facebook on my computer. A quick search for the name Cameron Gail reveals how rare a name it is

43

— only two results. The first of those results is for a young man in Colorado, but the second profile has Surrey as the user's location — not a million miles away. The profile photo is of a young man with a passing resemblance to the one I met yesterday, albeit without the gaunt features, pale skin, and lank hair. I click the profile link.

"Bugger."

The information on the page is scant, with most of the content restricted to the user's friends. The only information visible confirms this Cameron Gail is studying chemistry at Oxford University.

Perplexed, I stare at the screen. On closer inspection I'm sure it's the same young man, but how does anyone go from being a student at one of the world's greatest universities to the life of a drug addict, living in a Camden bedsit? I've born witness to the destructive nature of drugs countless times, but if his Facebook bio is to be believed, Cameron Gail's fall from grace appears tragically spectacular.

Unfortunately, there's little else on the page to hint at his possible whereabouts. I can't see his list of friends, his posts, or any personal information. At the top of the page, a message suggests I send him a friend request to see what he shares. With little else to go on, I do exactly that. Presuming he accepts, I'll let him know his uncle is looking for him and then terminate our virtual friendship.

One thing I've learnt over the years is how easy it is to get obsessed with helping a particular client, and how bad an idea it is. Not long after I took up my first position in London, a colleague had to resign after he let a homeless young woman sleep on his sofa for a few nights. I know his intentions were honourable but the optics weren't good. We have a duty to keep our distance, so whilst I could spend days chasing down Cameron Gail, I already have enough clients queueing up for my help.

I slip Fraser Kingsland's business card into my in-tray and close Facebook.

The day progresses in the usual see-saw of good and bad.

Some clients don't turn up, some have made progress, and a few require help I have to outsource. There are a growing number of people who worry about their job being taken by a computer utilising artificial intelligence, and I know some businesses are already trialling AI in their customer service centres. Based on my typical day, I don't think it's a concern for the counselling profession — I'd love to see a computer cope with a seventeen-year-old wannabee rap artist with attention deficit hyperactivity disorder.

Just before five, my phone chimes: a message from Denny Chambers, saying he'll be at the flat in an hour. I reply to confirm and keep my fingers crossed all the way home he doesn't discover any other problems with Leah's troublesome van.

7.

I open the front door to an unexpected aroma. Taking my coat off, I try to identify it. Food, obviously. Savoury? Definitely.

It seems my wife is cooking dinner, and I mean actually cooking rather than just lobbing a tray of processed mush in the microwave. I make my way to the kitchen where Leah is at the hob.

"Hey, honey."

She turns around and her face lights up.

"Thank God you're home. I was worrying dinner would be ready before you got here."

"It smells divine. What are we having?"

I ease up behind and put my hands around her waist.

"Fillet steak," she replies. "With triple-cooked chips, mushrooms, peas, and tomatoes."

"Wow. I'm …"

I could say delighted or grateful, but I'm not feeling either of those emotions. I hate to admit it, but I'm a tad annoyed.

"I bet those steaks were expensive," I remark, trying not to let my irritation show.

"They were, but I thought you deserved a treat. You do so much for me and I just wanted to show you how grateful I am."

Talk about conflicted feelings. It's so sweet of Leah to show her gratitude, but I fear she's blown our grocery budget for the next few days on this one meal. I revert to crossing my toes the van needs nothing more than a set of brake pads.

My wife orders me to sit at the table, and dinner is served.

During the meal, Leah casually drops the price of the steaks into the conversation. They were on offer; a snip at just twelve pounds. I manage to overlook the cost and focus on the taste, and admittedly it's a delicious meal.

I offer to wash up but the doorbell rings before I make it to the sink.

"That'll be Denny."

"Who's Denny?"

"The guy fixing your brakes for thirty quid, hopefully."

"Oh, great. Can you do me a favour while you're in the van?"

"Sure."

"I left a packet of tablets in the glove box. Can you grab them, please?"

"No problem."

I pluck the van keys from a hook and make for the front door. Opening it, I'm taken aback to see Denny looking several pounds heavier than the last time I saw him.

"Hey, Denny. You're looking well."

We shake hands.

"Yeah, I am well. As you can tell, I've got my appetite back."

He pats his stomach and chuckles. He's certainly put on some timber but looks a lot healthier than the stress-ridden skeleton who wandered into our offices last year.

"Great to see. Where are you parked?"

He gestures towards the side road where his own van is blocking the junction; hazard lights flashing.

"If you drive thirty yards on, there's a turning on the right which leads to the garage block."

"Righto."

He waddles off to his van while I cut down the pathway which leads to an expanse of poorly lit tarmac and eight garages behind our flats. As I pass through the gate, the headlights of Denny's van swing into view; illuminating the eight garage doors in various states of neglect. I point to the last garage in the row and step aside. The van pulls past and comes to a stop. Denny gets out and I wander over to our garage with the keys at the ready.

"Sorry, there's not much in the way of light," I remark, removing the padlock.

"No problem. I've got a halogen lamp."

He opens the back door of the van as I prise open the garage door. I'm met by the rear of Leah's van — I should have guessed she wouldn't have reversed in.

"There's no way this stomach is fitting in that space," Denny sniggers.

"Do you want me to drive it out?"

"Ideally."

Denny hops into his van and backs up. I squeeze into the driver's seat of Leah's and reverse out. Then, I have to conduct a ten-point turn before I can reverse back into the garage; leaving the front end of the van poking out.

As the temperature continues to drop, Denny gets on with his work. Placing a lamp on the floor, he slides a jack under the front of the van and levers it up. The right-hand wheel is off in minutes.

"You've done that before," I remark, jokingly.

"Yeah, once or twice."

I feel like the proverbial spare part. Ideally, I'd like to head back indoors where I'm less inclined to die of frostbite but it seems rude leaving Denny out here on his own.

"What's the prognosis?" I ask, as he inspects the hulk of filthy metal in the wheel arch.

"Yep, the pads are shot. You've also got some rust issues in the ball joints."

"Is that bad?"

"It won't get better, and you might find it's picked up on the next MOT."

"That's a problem for another day. I'm hoping the lottery fairies pay me a visit so we can get a new van."

"I'll keep my fingers crossed for you, mate."

Denny gets on with replacing the pads and we swap small talk about nothing in particular; neither of us keen to go over the old ground which brought us together in the first place. In no time at all, he replaces the pads on the right and the same process begins on the left wheel.

"Had you thought about leasing a new van?" he asks. "There's some cracking deals around at the moment."

"To be frank with you, Denny, Leah's business isn't exactly a roaring success at the moment so any van is likely beyond our budget."

He does that tradesman's air sucking gesture after removing the left wheel.

"I'd give it some thought if I were you," he says, shaking his head. "The rust is even worse this side."

I puff a resigned sigh and a cloud of frozen breath drifts through the lamplight.

Denny deals with the left-hand brake pads in the same efficient manner while I jig on the spot to retain some warmth. It's a huge relief when the left-hand side of the van drops as the jack is lowered.

"All done, mate."

I help him return his tools to the van and hand over three ten-pound notes.

"Money is a bit tight at the moment, Denny, so you're a lifesaver."

"Temporarily. The brakes are good now, but you should plan for a new van. The old girl is on life support, mate."

"Noted."

I see Denny off with a handshake and confirm I'll be in touch to discuss options for dealing with Leah's van at some point. I hope to Christ that point is many months away.

With hypothermia setting in, I quickly reverse the van back into the garage and slam the door shut. My hands are so numb I can barely fix the padlock in place. What I need is a long soak in a hot bath.

I return to the flat with that very intention. Leah greets me in the hallway.

"Everything okay?"

"You now have a shiny set of new brake pads so no more grinding."

Probably best not to mention Denny's long-term prognosis.

"Thank you for sorting it out. Hopefully, I'll make enough money on Saturday to pay you back."

"Let's hope you make more than thirty quid, honey."

"I'll try," she smiles.

"Good. Now, I need a hot bath. I'm frozen to the bone."

"I'll run it. You go sit and warm up a bit."

She turns to enter the bathroom and then stops.

"Oh, did you get my tablets?"

"Bugger, I forgot. Do you need them now?"

"Um, I do. Don't worry, I'll go get them."

No part of me wants to venture back out into the cold, but I'm not about to let my wife head out to the garages on her own.

"No, I'll get them."

"Are you sure?"

"I'll be back in a tick."

With much reluctance, I open the front door and retrace my steps back down the path towards the garage block. Just as I open the gate, I catch the sound of raised voices. After yesterday's events I have every right to be paranoid and take a step back. Cautiously, I then peek around the gate towards the source of the voices. Maybe twenty yards away, two figures in padded jackets are face-to-face in the light of a street lamp.

As my eyes adjust to the gloom, I can just identify the figures as white males but not much else. They're clearly having some kind of dispute as the male nearest me is highly animated; his body language nervy. The second male then dips a hand into his jacket pocket. A moment later, the two men appear to shake hands but I suspect it's not a cordial gesture as I've seen this scene many times before — a dealer and an addict. Their handshake is a method used to disguise a transaction; a small bag of drugs for cash.

Deal done, the nervy male turns and scoots away. Twenty minutes from now, he'll be holed up somewhere; off his face on whatever hideous substance he could afford. The other male turns to walk towards the public footpath which skirts the side of the garage block. He suddenly stops and pulls a phone from his jacket pocket. A call from another desperate addict, I'd wager.

After a brief conversation, the dealer ends the call and takes a couple of steps towards the footpath. A figure emerges from the dark and blocks his route forward. Both men stare at each other and words are exchanged; too quiet to hear. Whatever those words were, the dealer's reaction is to retreat a few steps backwards. In an instant, the scene takes on a sinister edge as he suddenly pulls a knife from the inside of his jacket. My mind immediately turns to the conversation I had with PC Shah in our kitchen yesterday.

Frantically, I pat my pockets looking for a phone which is back in the flat.

"Shit," I hiss under my breath.

Helpless, all I can do is adopt the role of primary witness.

The newcomer takes a few steps forward. As he moves into the light of the street lamp, the sheer bulk of the man becomes apparent. He stands at least eight inches taller than the dealer and his black donkey jacket would probably fit a carthorse; never mind a donkey. However, his size isn't his most intimidating feature — that would be his expression. I've seen men gripped by rage, by anger, but this guy looks like he's ready to tear the drug dealer in two.

I'm not the only one to realise the magnitude of the threat and the dealer waves the knife left and right. With absolutely no warning or fear for his own safety, the big man suddenly snaps out his left arm and grabs the dealer's wrist. The snatch is bear-trap fast, and the dealer looks genuinely shocked to find his hand locked in thin air.

The big man takes one step forward and leans in. For a second, it looks like he's about to whisper something in the dealer's ear. He doesn't. My stomach threatens to eject six quid's worth of fillet steak as a savage head-butt is duly administered.

The dealer collapses to the floor where he receives a boot in the ribs to silence his screams.

I gulp hard not wanting to witness what I fear is about to follow. If this assault continues, there won't be any need for an ambulance; they'll need a mortician's van. I have no time for drug dealers but I can't stand here and do nothing.

The big man circles around the dealer's prone body mumbling words I can't make out. Another boot to the stomach results in a pained cry.

"Stop!" I yell, stepping beyond the gate.

Without doubt, I'm no match for the big man but I have one advantage. A keen track athlete in my uni days I reckon I could easily outpace him in a foot race.

I take a dozen slow steps forward; my palms raised to show I'm no threat.

"Please," I beg. "You're going to kill him."

I get within six feet and stop. The big man eyes me with disdain.

"So?" he grunts.

If ever there was an ideal time to test my conflict resolution abilities, this is it.

"Whatever he's done, I think he's probably learnt his lesson, wouldn't you say?"

He glares at me and shakes his head. His focus then turns back to the dealer, and he continues to circle the battered young man. The next words to leave my mouth could literally mean life or death. I turn my attention to what those words might be.

In the mere seconds I take to ponder, the situation changes. I've barely time to engage my leg muscles, let alone run, when the big man suddenly leaps forward with astonishing speed. I manage to turn and take one step when a hand grabs the collar of my coat. Like a seatbelt snapping in a collision, I'm tugged backwards with such force it's all I can do to stay on my feet. That is, until I clatter into a metal garage door.

Winded, I drop onto all fours. This was not a good idea … what the hell was I thinking?

An inability to draw breath results in sudden panic. I try to scramble to my feet but, as I look up, the big man is right over me. He grabs two handfuls of my coat and slams me against the garage door; his face just a foot from mine. I have no option but to stare straight into the eyes of my assailant; cold, dead eyes which offer no hint of mercy, or humanity.

Long seconds pass as he stares at me in much the same way a lion might look into the eyes of a wounded gazelle — before ripping its throat out. The cold and fear grip my body while the stench of cigarettes fills my nostrils. My eye line is full of a gnarly face adorned with broad sideburns and a thick moustache; part hipster, part serial killer.

Finally, he speaks.

"You should learn to keep your nose out of other people's business, sunshine."

His accent is rooted in the dark underbelly of London; the tone akin to pea shingle being poured into a garden shredder.

"I'm … sorry," I gasp, still struggling for breath. "Please … please don't hurt me."

"Who are you?" he asks.

"Nobody. I'm nobody."

"You've got a name, dickhead. What is it?"

"David," I gulp.

"You a fan of drug dealers, Davy Boy?"

"God, no … but … but, you were close to killing him."

"Everyone's entitled to a hobby. Kicking the shit out of scum happens to be mine."

"Okay. Can I ask why?"

"Let's just say I've got unresolved anger issues."

That much is clear, not that I'm stupid enough to confirm it. Besides the violent assault I just witnessed, I suspect the man pinning me to a garage door is probably responsible for yesterday's attack.

"Are you going to hurt me?" I ask.

"Depends."

"On?"

He removes one hand and pats my jacket. The patting stops when he finds the pocket containing my wallet, which he then pulls out.

"There's only a tenner in there, but you're welcome to it."

"I don't want your money."

He flicks the wallet open and studies my driving licence.

"You live in those flats?" he asks, nodding towards his right shoulder and the block beyond.

As he's just seen my driving licence, there's no point denying it.

"Yes."

"Now I know your name and where you live, it'd be a good idea if you kept your gob shut about what just happened."

"I won't tell a soul … I swear."

He takes a long glance at the contents of my wallet, as if memorising all my personal details.

"What's a mental health counsellor do?" he then asks, holding up my business card.

"I help people who are experiencing issues with their mental health."

"Like a shrink?"

"Kind of, but I'm several years shy of the training you need to become a psychiatrist."

To my surprise, he releases his grip on my coat and takes a step back. Seeing as he still has my wallet and knows exactly where I live, an escape attempt might not be sensible.

"You help people, though?" he presses. "Folks who might be a bit fucked in the head?"

"Well, I wouldn't put it quite like that, but yes, I help people who are struggling to deal with a variety of mental health challenges."

He closes my wallet and hands it back to me.

"I could do with a bit of help."

That's an understatement.

"I work for a charity and our door is always open."

A long, uncomfortable stare follows.

"Guess I'll be seeing you then, Doc."

"Okay, but I'm not a doctor, and ideally you need to make an appointment."

"You'll see me when you see me. I don't do appointments."

With that, he turns and strides away, casually lighting a cigarette on the way.

Speechless, I watch him go. Only then do I notice the drug dealer had the good sense to limp away while he still could.

Left alone in the dark, an uneasy sense of foreboding arrives. I really don't want to see that man again.

8.

Problems rarely seem as bad once you've slept on them. That's what I tell my clients, but this morning I'm not sure I believe it.

I returned to the flat in a fluster last night and hid in the bathroom for almost an hour while I processed what happened by the garages. I went to bed with the intention of calling the police this morning but lying here at half-seven, I'm not so sure it's a good idea. I've been threatened many times by many clients, but no one has shaken me like the big man in the donkey jacket. If I lived on my own, it might be a different story but I've Leah to think of. If that thug were to discover I'd reported him to the police, I've no doubt he'd seek retribution. If that retribution arrives while I'm at work ... I don't want to even think about it.

I get up and pad through to the kitchen.

By the time I've made a cup of tea, I've reached a decision: I should put last night's events behind me. Even if I called the police, it's not likely the drug dealer reported his attack so what's there to gain if there's no victim? Besides, whatever injuries he suffered, he got away so they can't have been that severe.

"Rusty ball joints," I mumble to myself.

Everyone has problems to contend with but coping with them is a matter of perspective. I'd rather focus on a problem which, in the grand scheme of life, isn't so troublesome. If the van fails its MOT, it'll cost money to fix and money worries have become a constant in recent years. There's some comfort in familiarity.

After finishing my tea, I get ready for work and kiss Leah goodbye. Sometimes she barely stirs and sometimes she'll try to pull me back to bed. This morning I receive a semi-conscious mumble. There was talk of preparing for her stall tomorrow so hopefully the lie-in won't stretch on too long. I'll call her in an hour, just to be on the safe side.

I set off for work, reminding myself I've got one more day

and then I've the weekend to look forward to. Kind of.

Stepping through the front door of the offices, Debbie is just finishing a call.

"Morning."

"Morning, David."

I pause for a moment.

"Debbie, I might receive a visitor over the next few days. I'd rather you didn't let him into the building."

"Oh, why not?"

"He's a dangerous man."

"In what way?"

"Dangerous, as in a threat to our safety. I bumped into him last night and … let's just say I have no wish to meet him again."

"I'm not with you," she frowns. "Why would he come here?"

"He told me he's dealing with anger issues, and might drop by for a chat."

"Since when did we turn people away? If he has anger issues, surely he needs our help?"

"Trust me on this — he needs locking up, not our help."

"You're the counsellor," she concedes. "What does he look like?"

"White, maybe six-five, six-six, and built like a truck. He's got quite a distinctive moustache and sideburns."

"And what am I supposed to say if he turns up?"

"Tell him we're not taking on any new clients, but whatever you do, don't let him into the building."

"Noted."

I have an inkling the big man is unlikely to seek help — his type rarely do — but should we receive a visit, there's some comfort knowing our main door is always locked and visitors have to speak through an intercom. We also have security cameras and a panic button in every office.

Debbie declines my offer of tea, and I head to my desk.

Once I've woken the lazy computer I check my client roster for the day. Nothing too taxing today; assuming I don't have any unexpected or unwanted visitors. I prepare my notes for the first client and with fifteen minutes to spare before he arrives, I kill time by researching the cost of replacing Leah's van. As I expected, we're unlikely to get much change from four grand. I could get a loan but our monthly disposable income is already stretched too thin as it is.

I could ask my parents but I can already guess their response. Dad doesn't understand why Leah can't get a proper job and pay her fair share. I have explained her condition makes it difficult holding down a job because most employers don't want to deal with her mood swings. She's also prone to making rash or naïve decisions.

It's been three years since Leah last had a proper job. She worked as a cleaner in a large office block in Belsize Park, and up until her sixth day, she appeared to be doing well. On that sixth day, her supervisor asked her to vacuum an office she hadn't cleaned before. Leah couldn't find a free plug socket so she pulled out a random plug, did the vacuuming, and put the plug back as she found it. That plug was for the company's main server and it took their entire network offline for a morning.

That experience destroyed whatever remained of Leah's confidence, along with her future job prospects. Her only real option proved to be self-employment and having worked in a market as a teenager, Leah liked the idea of running her own stall.

We discussed stock ideas, and initially the plan was to sell vintage clothing. That then morphed into objet d'art and items with a retro theme before Leah's inventory broadened further. A year later, she secured a regular pitch at a twice-weekly market, but by then her stock had a distinct car boot sale vibe: everything from bric-à-brac to books, jewellery to jigsaw puzzles. In fairness, she did okay and most months made close to a thousand pounds profit. Unfortunately, she then took too much of an interest in acquiring stock and not enough interest in selling it. The Market Inspector eventually gave her pitch to someone else and Leah went from three or four outings a week to three or four a month.

I still haven't worked out how I can stoke her original enthusiasm, but until I do, I can't rely on my wife to contribute financially, particularly at this time of the year. If it were just our finances at risk, I might not be too concerned but if Leah loses the van, I fear she'll descend into a depressive state. We all need a sense of purpose in life, which is why so many people suffer mental health issues after losing a job.

Asking my parents for money is a last resort. The best I can do is hope the van lasts until the summer when Leah is earning more.

Debbie raps on my door.

"Jean Campbell is here."

My first client. Time to put my problems to one side.

I get up and wander through to the reception area where Jean is waiting. Looking at her, she's a picture of normality; a slightly overweight fifty-six-year-old mother and grandmother with greying hair and a friendly disposition. The year before last, Jean's son gifted her an iPad for Christmas, and he introduced his mother to the app store. Six months later, Jean innocently downloaded a bingo app she'd seen advertised on television. No harm playing a few games a week, she thought. It didn't take long for Jean to form an addiction to that app and, after losing thousands of pounds, she sought our help last month.

Jean's session goes well, as do most of the seven other sessions throughout the day. My last client, Andy, has made such good progress we're able to wrap up his session within half-an-hour. Once he's left, I sit back in my chair and puff a long sigh. Days like this are rare, but they're the reason I do this job. Conversely, there are some days it's a battle getting my clients to even turn up for their appointments. It's best to celebrate the victories whenever and however they come.

I decide to wind down the clock by checking Facebook. I don't get to see my sister, Katie, often but she regularly posts updates on Facebook; mainly for the benefit of my parents. As my page loads, a red notification bubble pops up at the top of the screen. I click it and a chat window opens up. It appears Cameron Gail has connected with me and sent the briefest of messages: a single question mark. I'm guessing he wants to know why I sent him a friend request. I type a reply, confirming his uncle paid us a visit yesterday and appears keen to track him down. I hit the send button.

Within a second, three dots appear in the chat box to indicate Cameron is already typing a reply. It arrives: *My uncle?*

Perhaps I should have confirmed which uncle. I reply to confirm the uncle in question is Fraser Kingsland. His reply is almost instant: *Need to meet, it's urgent? 6pm at the Duke of Wellington. PLEASE!*

I ask why. His answer is succinct: *Kingsland is NOT my uncle. Meet me, it's important.*

I'm about to type another question when Cameron goes offline.

It goes without saying we have a duty of care to our clients but technically, Cameron Gail is not my client. He got up and left my office without registering, or booking a follow-up appointment, so I bear no responsibility for his troubles.

Why then do I find myself reading his messages again? Why am I so perplexed Fraser Kingsland claimed to be Cameron's uncle? What's so important he wants to see me?

Curiosity is, in a way, like a drug addiction. It starts as an itch but the longer you try to ignore it, the greater the need for a hit. I can ignore Cameron's request but I guarantee my curiosity will peak later this evening and I'll be craving answers.

I drum my fingers on the desk.

Grabbing my phone, I ping a message to Leah to say I'll be an hour late tonight. I suspect she won't be preparing steak so it's no drama; at least I hope she's not preparing steak.

I shut the computer down and slip my coat on. Time to scratch that itch.

9.

The Duke of Wellington isn't a pub I'd typically frequent, not that I frequent many pubs these days. Leah doesn't drink alcohol at all, on account she's borne witness to its worst effects, and even a small glass of wine can mess with her medication.

I push through the door into the public bar.

The Duke, as it's more commonly known, has a reputation as a hang-out for the less savoury elements of society but the overall atmosphere this evening seems convivial. I guess most of the customers have finished work for the day and are beginning their weekend.

I make my way through the crowd to the bar and wait to be served. Scanning the room, there's no sign of Cameron but it's not quite six yet.

A heavily tattooed barman eventually serves my sparkling water and I move around to the far side of the bar where it's not so crowded. The reason I tend to steer clear of The Duke is because some of my previous clients are patrons. For that reason, I maintain a low profile while watching the door for Cameron.

At five past six, a thin, dishevelled young man enters. He scans the room and I raise my hand to catch his attention.

Looking even more nervy than when he wandered into RightMind, he keeps his head down and scurries over.

"Evening, Cameron."

"You came."

"I'm a slave to my curiosity. Drink?"

"Coke," he mumbles.

I place his order.

"How are you doing?" I ask. "You left my office in quite a hurry on Wednesday."

"I wasn't … I'm not in a good place."

"Are you feeling better today?"

"I'm functioning, but it won't last."

His Coke arrives. I pay, and make for the only free table. There, Cameron slumps down while I hang my coat on the back of the chair opposite.

"So, Cameron," I say, taking my seat. "What is it that's so important?"

"I need help. Urgent help."

"You do understand I'm not here in my capacity as a counsellor, right? As far as anyone is concerned, we're just two casual acquaintances having a drink but if you need my professional support, you must book an appointment at RightMind."

"I get it."

"Good, what do you need help with?"

"I need to get into rehab … in the next day or two."

"Okay, and what makes you think I can help with that?"

"I researched your charity. You've helped people in the past."

"Well, yes, we have, but only after exhausting other options, including counselling."

"I haven't got … you don't understand. I need to get away, and if I don't get into a rehab programme, I'm a dead man."

I take a sip of water and attempt to shake off my irritation. It's difficult enough securing a rehab place for those who genuinely have no other option, and there are no shortcuts for the self-entitled.

"I can't help you with rehab, Cameron, but I'm willing to help you deal with your addiction through counselling."

"Counselling won't help," he snaps. "I'm too far gone, and … if he finds me, it's all over, anyway."

"If who finds you?"

"Fraser Kingsland."

"The gentleman who claimed to be your uncle?"

"He's no uncle. He's … he's the reason … I wish I'd never met him."

"You'll have to fill in a few blanks for me here. Who is Fraser Kingsland if he's not your uncle, and why is he looking for you?"

"I … I can't tell you, but I'm in serious trouble."

"Is this related to your drug problem?"

61

"Yes ... no ... kind of."

"If you're in trouble, you should go to the police."

"No, I can't," he snaps. "He knows people in the force ... they'll tell him."

Cameron might not be in the grip of a drug-induced stupor, but he appears just as edgy and distracted as the young man I spoke to on Wednesday. I need to calm him down and then maybe I might get some straight answers.

"Shall we start at the beginning? Assuming we're just two strangers getting acquainted, tell me about Cameron Gail."

He ignores my request and stares intently past my left shoulder towards the far side of the bar. His eyes suddenly widen.

"Fuck!"

Before I can turn to see what spooked him, Cameron is on his feet. He frantically scans the bar and then darts towards the nearest door; the gents' toilet. As I sit confused, two men in dark clothing stride purposefully past my table and through the door Cameron just left by. Were they the reason he bolted? I only caught a fleeting glance, but they both had that loan shark look about them. The circle of debt, and drugs, and crime is a common one which many addicts find themselves trapped in.

Come to think of it, Fraser Kingsland didn't come across as a man who earns a living working for a traditional lending institution.

Christ, what do I do?

I'm still processing that question when the two men barge back through the door and move quickly towards the nearest exit. I leap up and head to the gents' toilet.

Cautiously opening the door, I'm met with the familiar stench of urinal blocks, and cheap air freshener struggling to mask a less fragrant odour.

"Cameron?"

There are two stalls opposite the urinals; both doors slightly ajar. I nudge the first one open with my foot — empty. The second one is empty too, but there's an open window above the cistern. It's only twelve inches high but just about large enough

62

for someone of Cameron Gail's frame to escape through; an obvious conclusion as there's nowhere to hide in here.

Stepping onto the toilet, I poke my head out of the window to check if Cameron is hiding on the other side.

I'm met with a view of a small car park but there's no one around. Then, beyond my view, an engine screams at high revs, accompanied by the squeal of tyres. Within a few seconds the revving fades into the general thrum of ever-present urban noise.

I climb down from the toilet and slam the cubicle door shut on my way out.

I'm annoyed with Cameron for dragging me into his troubles, but I'm more annoyed with myself for playing along. I should know better, and Cameron isn't even my client. This was a mistake.

Ruing my poor judgement, I return to the bar.

The only consolation is my coat is still on the back of the chair. I slip it on. I'm about to set off when I catch a flicker of light from beneath the table. Curious, I squat down and immediately establish the source — a mobile phone lying on the carpet beneath the chair Cameron abandoned. In his haste to leave it must have slipped from his pocket.

I pick it up and tap the screen. It lights up with a photo of a young couple; two happy faces smiling back at me. I'm looking at a photo of Cameron Gail; his complexion radiant and his hair clean, shorter, and meticulously styled. It's always a bittersweet experience seeing pre-addiction photos of drug addicts. I've often used such photos to remind clients of who they really are, but in certain cases, that person is lost for good. The girl in the photo looks equally vibrant, with butter-blonde hair and dazzling blue eyes. Together, they're the model of youthful happiness, untainted by life's burdens.

"Damn fool," I mumble to myself, slipping the phone into my pocket.

I'll send Cameron a Facebook message when I get home, and he can collect his phone from the office on Monday. Assuming he shows up, I'll also confirm there won't be any further meetings in pubs, or discussions about rehab unless he commits to counselling.

I send Leah a message to say I'm on my way home and head out into the bitter evening air.

To my relief, I arrive home to the fusty odour of boxes rather than filet mignon, roasted partridge, or some other delicacy we can't afford.

"I'm home," I call out, hanging my coat up.

Wandering through to the kitchen, Leah is at the table sorting through a large cardboard box.

"How's it going?" I ask.

"Nearly done. I've got fourteen boxes prepped for tomorrow."

"That's brilliant."

"I only hope I don't come back with twelve of them. I'm worried no one will have any money at this time of the year."

I sit down and put my hand on hers.

"True, people are hard-pressed in January, so what better time to pick up a bargain. I think it'll be busy."

"Do you really think so?"

"Yeah, I'm sure of it."

I find a reassuring smile which seems to do the trick.

"What's for dinner?"

"Fish and chips."

"Great."

I glance at the oven which isn't switched on.

"Shall I do the honours?"

"Would you mind? I just want to get this last box sorted."

I switch the oven on and set the timer. While Leah completes her stock inventory, I ping a message to Cameron confirming I have his phone. I hope he has some other method of checking his account otherwise he'll never see the message. Worst-case scenario, I'll have to drop it off at the police station as I've no other way of contacting him.

Once we've eaten dinner and I've helped Leah stack all her boxes in the hallway, we settle down on the sofa to watch television. The evening passes by in a dull haze of forgettable shows; many of which are interrupted by my wife as she tries to talk herself out of going tomorrow. I use every tool in the box to kindle positive thoughts, and we go to bed at ten with her mind made up – she's going, thankfully.

The only downside is I won't get a lie in. Still, I've a day to do whatever I like, as long as it doesn't cost anything.

I drift off to sleep with a thought I haven't considered since I was a student; the thought of getting a weekend job to make ends meet.

Not the future I envisaged back then, that's for sure.

10.

I wake up in some weird parallel universe as Leah places a mug of tea on the bedside table.

"Morning," she smiles. "I made you a tea."

"Thanks. What time is it?"

"Half-seven."

My wife is already dressed and seems to be in a chirpy mood, considering the ungodly hour.

"Would you mind helping me load the van?" she asks. "I need to get going soon."

I knew there had to be a catch. The tea is a bribe.

"Sure," I rasp. "Give me a minute to get dressed."

Besides the constant traffic congestion in London, there is another good reason I don't own a car: parking anywhere is near-impossible. Every square inch of tarmac is protected by red or yellow lines and a dozen cameras. Consequently, Leah can't move the van closer to our front door to load. The venue she's visiting today provide loading bays and trolleys, but we have neither luxury. It's a brutal way to start the day — lugging boxes eighty yards to the garage in sub-Arctic conditions.

Once the final box is loaded into the van, I kiss my wife goodbye and wave her off.

When Leah first started her venture I offered to help on the stall but she declined, stating I wouldn't be able to help if she had a regular job, so why should the stall be any different? I considered that a perfectly reasonable response, which is why I try not to get involved, unless she asks. This morning, I'm particularly pleased about my wife's independence as I can return to a cosy flat while Leah faces the loathsome London traffic and eight hours of haggling over tat.

The only issue I face, once I've had breakfast, is boredom. You'd think there would be plenty to do in our capital city, but once you've done the museums, the libraries, and all the sights, every other form of entertainment requires money. When I first moved here, I used to watch the occasional Arsenal game at the

Emirates Stadium but nowadays my paltry budget wouldn't cover the cost of a programme and a half-time beverage. Still, when you can't afford champagne, sometimes you have to settle for cider, so once or twice a month I'll watch the nearest non-league team, Hendon. It's a far cry from the Premier League, but in many ways I prefer it; particularly the cost of entry.

I check the Hendon FC website and I'm pleased to see they're playing the mighty Gosport Borough at home today. That's my afternoon sorted, at least.

With nothing else better to do, I sit at the kitchen table and check Facebook to see if Cameron has replied to my message. The app confirms he hasn't even read it. I wander through to the hallway and retrieve his phone from my coat pocket. If it isn't locked with a password or fingerprint, I might be able to find an alternative phone number. I prod the oversized screen on the iPhone but there's no photo of Cameron and his smiley friend this time; the battery dead.

Leah and I both switched to Android phones a few years back, mainly for reasons of cost, but I think we might still have a charging cable somewhere. I return to the kitchen and place Cameron's iPhone on the table while I search the drawers.

The search is cut short when the doorbell rings. I pad down the hall to the front door and open it.

"Good morning, Mr Nunn."

I stare back open-mouthed at the suited, middle-aged man on my doorstep.

"What are you doing here? This is …"

"I apologise," Fraser Kingsland interrupts. "I wouldn't have called around unless it was important."

"How did you get my address?"

"The electoral roll."

"I'm sorry, Mr Kingsland, but I don't appreciate uninvited guests turning up at my home."

"I understand, but as I say, it's important. We've managed to get Cameron into a rehab clinic, but he's having a hissy fit because he can't find his mobile phone. He said the last time he remembers having it was in the pub last night … when you met him."

"Yes, I found his phone. He dropped it under the table."

"Oh, good," he smiles. "If you'd like to go fetch it, I'll leave you in peace."

"I'm afraid that's not possible."

"I'm sorry? Why not?"

"Because it's Cameron's phone. If he contacts me and gives his permission, I'll gladly give it to you but I'm not willing to hand it over to just anyone."

"I'm not just anyone," he replies, his expression and tone sour. "I'm his uncle."

"But you're not though, are you?"

Kingsland frowns.

"I beg your pardon?"

"Cameron told me he doesn't have an uncle."

"He told you that?"

"Yes."

"And what else did you discuss with him?"

"That's between the two of us. Now, if you don't mind Mr Kingsland, I've got …"

"Go get the phone, now," he demands. "Before this situation gets out of hand."

"Are you threatening me?"

"I'm asking you nicely. Give me the phone and I won't have cause to bother you again."

"Bother me again and I'll call the police."

I slam the door but it doesn't close as a polished leather brogue meets it half way.

"Mr Nunn," Kingsland hisses. "This is your final chance. Give me the phone or the next time we meet, I won't be so civil."

I pull my phone out and tap the screen three times. The operator answers almost immediately.

"Police, please."

The call does the trick as Kingsland removes his foot. As I wait to be connected, he glares at me before finally walking away. I apologise to the woman who asks the nature of my emergency and end the call.

I shut the door and return to the kitchen.

Bloody Cameron. Whatever mess he's got himself into, I want no part of it, and I certainly won't be bullied by the likes of Fraser Kingsland. I guess it would have been easier to hand the phone over, but I learnt enough from my conversation with Cameron to establish he and Kingsland aren't the best of friends, and they're definitely not uncle and nephew.

I think it would be better all-round if I drop the damn phone at the police station. Cameron Gail and Fraser Kingsland can squabble over it there.

To distract from the annoyance, I grab my Kindle and play some classical music on the stereo in the lounge. I've got a couple of hours to kill before the match and losing myself in a good book should fill those hours nicely.

As it happens, I get so lost in a Dan Brown thriller I lose all track of time. At just after two o'clock, once I'm wrapped up like a polar explorer, I leave the flat and make my way to the tube station. Half-an-hour later, I push through the turnstiles at Silver Jubilee Park and make straight for the refreshments hut. If ever there was the ideal weather to be sipping on a cup of hot Bovril, this is it. I then make my way to the stand and hunker down with the few dozen other fans willing to brave the wintry conditions.

The first half is a drab affair and ends goalless. Another cup of Bovril is in order.

As the second half gets under way, Leah sends a text message to say she's packing up for the day. No mention of how well she's done, which doesn't bode well. I reply to confirm I'm at the football and I'll help unload the van tomorrow. I've got a horrible feeling most of the boxes I lugged to the van this morning will make the return trip tomorrow morning, albeit at a more civilised hour.

The match livens up and Hendon score twice. With only a few minutes remaining, I prepare to depart and Gosport Borough score a late consolation goal. It makes for a nervy ending but Hendon hang on and the final whistle is greeted by an enthusiastic cheer from the few hundred spectators. Under an ink-black sky, I make my way to the tube station; barely able to feel my toes.

I arrive home just after half-five and Leah calls out from the lounge.

"Good game?"

"Not bad," I call back. "But I think I've got frostbite."

She appears at the lounge doorway.

"Would an Indian takeaway help? Something nice and spicy will warm you up in no time."

"Um, I'm a bit strapped …"

"My treat."

"Oh."

"I've had a brilliant day," she beams. "I took just over three-hundred quid."

"That's … wow! Well done."

I am pleased, but more than a touch guilty for presuming the worst.

"I'm really proud of you, and yes, I'd love a curry. Thank you."

"And you were right about people being in the market for a bargain. It was packed most of the day."

"And as a bonus, I don't have to lug all those boxes back into the flat tomorrow."

"Well, not all of them. And, I might have spent some of the money on extra stock."

I knew it was too good to be true.

"How much extra stock?"

"Just a few crates of books a dealer was looking to clear. Both crates only cost thirty quid and there's over a hundred books in each one. If I only sell them for a quid each, it's a tidy profit."

"Hmm … and when are you planning your next outing?"

"There's another market next Saturday. If I have another day like today, I should clear at least a dozen boxes."

She pads over and puts her arms around me.

"Anyway, let's not worry about my stock tonight. I'll order dinner shortly but I think we should discuss dessert."

There's no mistaking the intonation in her voice, or the mischievous look in her eye.

"What did you have in mind, Mrs Nunn?"

"Do you want to know, or would you prefer a surprise?"

"You know I love surprises."

With that, Leah places her hands at the back of my head and pulls me into a long, slow kiss.

"That's just the starter," she then purrs. "I'll go order mains."

This day is definitely ending on a better note than it began.

11.

Those of a particular mind-set insist every day is a gift. I think Mondays are a gift most of us would be happy to return.

"Honey, wake up."

Leah mumbles a few profanities.

"Please, wake up."

My wife finally blinks into consciousness.

"What?" she groans.

"I left a mobile phone on the kitchen table. Have you seen it?"

"I … what? I don't know."

The last time I recall seeing Cameron Gail's phone was on Saturday morning. I should have put it back in my coat pocket, but it kind of slipped my mind after the visit from Fraser Kingsland. As Leah was sorting out stock at the table yesterday, I've a suspicion the phone may have inadvertently found its way into her inventory.

"I'm running late. Can you have a look for it when you get up, please? It's a black iPhone."

"Yeah, yeah."

She tugs the duvet tight around her and rolls over.

"Bye, then."

No response.

As I still haven't heard from Cameron, I had intended to take his phone to the police station today but that's not happening now.

I take one last envious look at my wife, snugly cocooned in the duvet, and head off to work.

A brisk walk helps to make up the lost time and stave off the worst of the cold. I arrive at the office dead on half-eight, enter my access code on the lock, and push the door open.

Debbie isn't at her desk but the half-drunk mug of tea suggests she's in the building. I get on with my usual routine; finally sitting down at my desk and checking the day's schedule. Friday was a good day and I hope that roll continues.

It doesn't.

Three clients over three hours; each of them a challenging mess of tears, tantrums, and general testiness.

Last year, a local newspaper asked if I'd do an interview for a feature relating to the increase in mental health problems amongst the young. During that interview, the reporter asked if I ever encounter clients who don't respond to counselling. I answered honestly — plenty. The human mind is almost unfathomably complex, and it's naïve to think I, or any counsellor can address every client's issues through talk alone. Some require medication, some require clinical psychotherapy, and far too many just give up when we can't provide a magic cure. Our therapy requires a need from the individual; a willingness for that individual to help themselves.

This morning, there's been a distinct lack of willingness.

With a forty-minute gap before my next client I take the opportunity to nip out for a sandwich.

"Just popping to Greggs," I inform Debbie, as I pass the reception desk. "Can I get you anything?"

"I'd love a sausage roll."

"What happened to the New Year's resolution? I thought you were trying to lose weight."

"It's Monday. Everyone is allowed to break resolutions on a Monday … it's enshrined in law."

"Is it indeed?"

I flash her a smile and head out the door.

The bargain bakery is a five-minute stroll away but the cheapest place to buy lunch. After a frustrating wait in the queue, I make the return journey with a hot sausage roll and tuna salad sandwich. Halfway back to the office, I rue not buying two sausage rolls; the scent is tantalising.

I unlock the office door and hurry in to find two men stood in the reception area. They don't look like clients.

"David, these two gentlemen are here to see you." Debbie says, her tone of voice oddly strained.

I turn to the two men. Both in their forties, I'd guess, they carry a distinct air of authority, despite their casual attire. The

73

slightly taller of the two steps forward, flashing his warrant card.

"I'm Detective Sergeant Turner and this is Detective Constable Greenwood."

Most people have very little to do with the police and therefore a surprise visit might be unsettling. In my line of work, I get to speak to the police more often than I'd like.

"What can I do for you, gents?"

"Can we have a word, in private?"

"Sure. Come through to my office."

I hand Debbie her sausage roll and the two detectives follow me through the corridor. Inviting them in to my office first, I pull the door shut and make for my desk.

"Please, take a seat."

"We're okay, thanks," Detective Turner replies with no hint of emotion in his voice. "This won't be a long visit."

"Oh?"

"David Nunn, I'm arresting you on suspicion of rape. You do not have to say anything. But, it may harm your defence …"

"What?" I blurt. "Is this some kind of joke?"

Turner continues reading my rights but my mind has other priorities and I don't take in a word. The allegation is so preposterous I can't begin to formulate, let alone ask, the obvious questions.

"Do you understand, Mr Nunn?" Turner asks.

I stare back at the detective, still stunned.

"No, I don't."

"The exact details of the allegation will be explained during your interview at the station. Now, I'm sure you'd rather avoid being handcuffed so shall we do this in a civilised manner?"

I'm being falsely accused of a heinous crime — where is the civility in that?

"I haven't done anything. This is …"

"You are under caution, Mr Nunn."

Caution or not, I appear unable to form a coherent sentence, anyway. Nor am I able to shake off the shock as I'm guided back through the corridor to the reception area. Debbie is on the phone but stares up at me with a look of confusion. I turn to Detective

Turner.

"Can I explain to …"

"We've already informed your colleague what's happening," he confirms before I can finish my sentence.

The next thing I know, I'm in the back of a car, travelling through the streets of Kentish Town. To the police officers it's just another day and I'm just another suspect but for me, every aspect of the experience is terrifying. We arrive at the station where I'm booked in, and then subjected to the humiliation of being fingerprinted, photographed, and a swab of my DNA is taken. I have the right to make a phone call but who would I call, and what would I say?

Eventually, I'm led to an interview room. I'm joined by both the arresting detectives. Turner confirms I'm still under caution and anything I say will be recorded, and might be used in evidence. Formalities sorted, they pose the first question.

"Can you recall where you were on the evening of the twelfth of February last year?"

"No idea."

"Think carefully, Mr Nunn. It's important."

"Can you recall where you were? It's a ridiculous question."

"It has been alleged you visited an address in Camden around eight o'clock, and there you raped Chantelle Granger."

"Who?"

"Chantelle Granger. That name doesn't ring any bells?"

"Not at all."

"Are you certain?"

"Yes. I've never heard of her, and I'd like to categorically state I'm a happily married man. I wouldn't dream of sleeping with another woman; much less forcing myself on anyone."

"To be clear, you deny having ever met Chantelle Granger?"

"I categorically deny it."

The detective swaps a glance with his colleague and opens a folder on the table.

"Miss Granger knows you, Mr Nunn. In fact, she was a patient at your clinic."

"Firstly, it's not a clinic, and secondly, we don't have

patients as we don't provide medical services. We're a charity and I have clients I counsel."

"My apologies. Nevertheless, it is Miss Granger's assertion you were her counsellor, and after making lewd suggestions during one of your sessions, you later visited her flat. After rebutting your advances, Miss Granger claims you became aggressive, trapping her in the bedroom and then raping her."

"Absolute fiction."

"Which part?"

"All of it."

The detective flips a page in the folder and turns it around. He then makes a remark for the benefit of the tape.

"Do you recognise that card, Mr Nunn?"

I glance at the sheet of paper.

"As you can see, it confirms Miss Granger had an appointment with you."

"I … I have no recollection of meeting her. You have to understand, I see hundreds of clients every year."

"We checked with your office, and they confirmed Miss Granger had two sessions with you."

"Again, I've no recollection of our sessions and I definitely wouldn't have visited her flat."

"But you accept you have met the victim?"

"What? No … I, might have, but I can't say for certain."

Declining legal advice suddenly feels like a bad idea. I did so because I am innocent and therefore there cannot be any evidence against me.

"I'm wondering, Mr Nunn, if other events have slipped your mind."

"You think I raped one of my clients and I've just forgotten?"

"Some individuals blank out their crimes, particularly when they're in denial."

I've had enough. I've tried to be compliant, and I assumed my compliance would demonstrate innocence. It's not working.

"Let me make it absolutely clear, Detective, I never made any advances towards Miss Granger, nor did I visit her flat. And, I certainly didn't rape her. I have no idea why she's made this dreadful allegation, but it is completely false. I won't be answering any other questions so unless you have any actual evidence, other than the word of a deluded woman who needs help, I'd like to get back to work."

Despite my statement, the detective continues to pose questions. My response to each one is the same: no comment. This goes on for another half-hour before he calls a halt to the interview.

"Can I go now?"

"Not just yet. We'll take you to the cells and a decision will be made on your detention."

"You're going to lock me up?"

"It won't be for long."

"I don't care if it's for five minutes — this is outrageous."

"I'm sure you can appreciate we have to take this allegation seriously, Mr Nunn. Like you, we have protocols and processes we have to follow."

"We don't lock up innocent people."

He gets to his feet and, despite my protestations, I'm led to a cell. There is no more damning a sound than a heavy metal door being slammed; no more depressing an experience than being locked in a twelve foot square room with no proper window and a stainless steel toilet in the corner.

Left to stew, I pace up and down the tiled floor. My anger switches from the detectives to Chantelle Granger. No matter how hard I try to recall the apparent sessions we had, there's nothing there to recollect. I may well have seen her, but without a face to put a name to, it's a pointless exercise. Whoever she is, I don't understand her motivation. Despite my current incarceration, there is no evidence so there's no likely chance of a conviction — I do have some faith in the criminal justice system. So, why has she done this? The fact she sought help from RightMind implies there might be some mental health issues and maybe those issues have evolved into a deeper-rooted problem.

There is no one more sympathetic to the needs of those with challenging mental health problems, but I'm having a hard time finding any sympathy for Miss Granger at present.

With no watch or phone to check the time, I can't be sure how long I'm left locked up, but it feels like forever. Eventually, Detective Greenwood comes to the door and I'm escorted to the custody desk where my nightmare first began.

"You're being released on police bail," the officer confirms.

"What does that mean?"

"My colleagues will conduct further investigations. You're to return in two weeks."

I'm handed a piece of paper outlining the terms of my release.

"This is beyond ridiculous," I mumble. "Surely you can see that?"

"It's not my job to determine anyone's guilt or innocence, sir."

There's nothing to be gained by venting at the custody sergeant so I just stand and seethe. My personal possessions are returned, and I'm then seen off the premises.

I check my watch. Three bloody hours, wasted. Technically, it's RightMind's time being wasted, but it's still time I could have spent helping someone worthy, rather than two police officers investigating a fairy tale.

Keen not to waste another minute, I stomp back to the office. I get halfway there when my phone rings.

"David Nunn," I answer sharply, the caller's identity not in my contact list.

"Afternoon, Mr Nunn."

"Who is this?"

"Fraser Kingsland."

"How did you get my number?"

"Does it matter?"

"Yes, it bloody-well does. I thought …"

"Stop yapping," he snaps. "I'd strongly recommend you listen."

"I beg your pardon."

"I'll be sending one of my associates over to your flat early evening, to pick up Cameron's mobile phone. Make sure it's ready."

"I told you, I'm not willing to hand it over to anyone other than Cameron himself."

"And I told you, I'm not someone you want to mess with, Mr Nunn. If you don't hand over that phone, your problems with the local constabulary will likely worsen."

I stop dead and scan the immediate area, looking for signs I'm being followed. With scores of people on the streets there's no way of telling.

"How do you know where I've just been?"

"I have eyes and ears everywhere. Now, that allegation against you will go away once I've got the phone. However, if you want to be bloody-minded, one or two other young women might come forward with their own allegations."

I don't know how, but I think it's clear who encouraged Chantelle Granger to falsify the claim against me.

"This is preposterous, and I'll be reporting this phone call to the police."

"I wouldn't do that if I were you, Mr Nunn. One of the young ladies I've got lined up claims you interfered with her when she was just fourteen. Imagine how her allegations will go down with the police, your colleagues, your family … and your wife."

"You … you're sick."

"You know what they say: there's no smoke without fire, and I'll burn you to the fucking ground if you don't hand that phone to my associate."

He hangs up.

12.

Standing motionless in the centre of the pavement, people pass by but few seem to notice my state of inertia. They don't know my temporary paralysis is born partly from anger, partly from fear. The two emotions are trying to drag me in different directions. The anger wants me to return to the police station to report Kingsland's threat. The fear wants me to go straight home and check on Leah.

Fear edges ahead and I call home.

"Honey, it's me."

"I know."

"Everything okay?"

"Yes. Why wouldn't it be?"

"No reason. No reason at all."

"I'm a bit busy at the moment. Did you want something?"

I hear voices in the background.

"Where are you?"

"At the charity shop on Kentish Town Road."

"Please tell me you're not buying more stock."

"Actually, I'm not," she huffs. "Quite the opposite."

"Eh?"

"I thought I'd take your advice and try to clear some of the stock in the flat."

"Isn't the idea to sell it, rather than give it away?"

"I'm only donating stuff I've tried to sell before, but nobody wants."

"Oh, okay. Did you … did you find that mobile phone?"

"You didn't look very hard as it had fallen onto the chair. Anyway, whose is it?"

"It belongs to a client … well, a kind of client. He dropped it when I saw him on Friday."

"Right, well, it's no longer lost."

"Thank you. I'll see you in a few hours."

Within a heartbeat of ending the call, I've reached a decision — I'd rather be beholden to anger than fear. I shake off the paralysis and continue on towards the office. It's only a short walk but sufficient time to ponder Fraser Kingsland's threat. I know nothing about him or what he's capable of, but I do know I've just spent a couple of hours being interrogated by the police on the back of a false allegation. One spurious allegation is bad enough, but if more were to follow, my innocence becomes less relevant than the narrative.

I arrive back at RightMind with my mind made up. He can have his precious bloody phone.

"What happened?" Debbie asks, the second I walk through the door.

"A misunderstanding. It's hopefully done and dusted now."

"Oh, good. I should warn you …"

"Hello, David."

Gerald Duff approaches with a clipboard in hand.

"Oh. Hi, Gerald."

Gerald is the Chairman of the trustees committee. A retired civil servant, he's a mildly pompous but diligent custodian of our charity. He's also a little too fond of popping in whenever it suits and interfering with matters beyond his remit.

"Thought I'd drop by and say hello, see how you're coping with the usual New Year influx of clients."

His timing couldn't be worse.

"I'm running behind schedule, Gerald, so you'll have to excuse me."

"I was hoping we could have a word."

"About?"

"Just a trifling policy matter. Nothing to worry about."

I glance at Debbie and she avoids eye contact. It's safe to say she's already told Gerald I disappeared with two police officers earlier. In any other work environment, covering for your colleagues is expected. Those expectations are rarely found in professions such as ours: admittedly for good reason.

"Shall we go through to my office?" I suggest.

"Yes, let's."

I close the door and Gerald takes a seat without waiting for an invitation.

"How are things?" he asks, as I flop down in my chair opposite.

"Things?"

"Anything the trustees should know about?"

I know precisely what he's referring to.

"You'd like to know why the police wanted to speak with me?"

"You are contractually obliged to disclose any dealings with the police."

"It was nothing. They released me without charge."

"They arrested you?"

He peers at me over the frame of his glasses; an expression twixt disapproving and judgemental.

"Yes."

"On what charge?"

I can't lie, but the short, four-letter word is so damning I can't bring myself to say it.

"It was a false allegation which will be withdrawn within the next twenty-four hours. You have my word."

"That wasn't my question, David. What did they arrest you for?"

"Rape," I mumble. "A former client I can't even remember meeting, apparently."

Silent seconds pass as my sordid revelation sinks in.

"My word," he finally sighs, shaking his head. "This puts the charity in a difficult position. This isn't a speeding fine or some other misdemeanour we can ignore."

"I know, but there's no foundation to it, whatsoever."

"Have they exonerated you?"

"Well, they're conducting further investigations but there isn't a shred of evidence because it's a blatant lie."

"So, you're on police bail?"

"Yes, but not for long."

"But you are currently on police bail with a rape charge hanging over you. Do you not see how that might look?"

"To who? Besides the two officers, no one else knows."

"That's hardly the point. What if a tabloid journalist got hold

82

of the story? Just the whiff of a scandal could see our donations dry up overnight."

"It's not likely, is it?"

"Maybe not, but what happens if this allegation leads to a court case?"

I glare back at Gerald, dumbfounded.

"You think I'm guilty?"

"My opinion is irrelevant, David. On balance, I'm almost certain you are innocent but we have to work with absolute certainties to protect the charity. I've seen good organisations torn to pieces by the behaviour of one individual, so we have to play Devil's advocate in these situations."

"While ignoring the word of a long-serving, loyal employee with a faultless record?"

"What would you do if the roles were reversed? Would you put the entire charity at risk on instinct alone, or would you do everything within your power to play by the rules and mitigate that risk?"

"I'd … I'd be willing to wait twenty-four hours."

"We have rules for a reason. I'm sure you're right and this will blow over within twenty-four hours, but the rules are clear: you shouldn't be here, and you definitely shouldn't be seeing clients."

"You can't be serious? Why should my clients suffer because of some random woman's bullshit?"

"Language, please," he frowns. "The policies are designed to protect the charity. Surely you understand that?"

"You want to protect the charity I've given so much to by kicking me out?"

"Don't be so melodramatic," he says dismissively. "No one is kicking you out. It's a temporary suspension while the police conclude their investigation."

"Can I appeal?"

"You can. It won't change what I now have to do, though."

"Namely?"

"I must ask you to leave the premises. I'll get the Secretary to confirm your suspension in writing but I assure you as soon as the bail situation is addressed, you'll be able to return to work."

"I can't believe this," I huff. "It's so unfair."

Gerald gets to his feet.

"Just think of it as an unexpected break. Silver linings, and all that."

"Whatever."

I grab my mouse with the intention of shutting down my computer but Gerald intervenes.

"Sorry, David, but I must insist you leave immediately."

For the second time this afternoon, I'm escorted from my office. Gerald takes my keys and asks Debbie to change the door code. I can't deny it had crossed my mind I might try accessing Chantelle Granger's file. That option is no longer on the table.

I now have a dilemma.

If I head home, Leah will want to know why I'm earlier than usual, and I'll have a similar problem tomorrow morning when I'm still in bed at eight o'clock. I'm deeply uncomfortable lying to my wife but telling her the truth will open a Pandora's box of problems. Leah can be prone to occasional bouts of paranoia and even the tiniest seed of doubt could quickly blossom if she's in the wrong frame of mind. I can almost hear her questions now; each one more accusatory than the last until she works herself up into a state.

Needing time to think I head to the nearest coffee shop.

Rather than deal with an explanation for Leah, I spend the first fifteen minutes staring out the window and working through the residual self-pity. I'm not so much irritated by my suspension — I understand measures must be in place to protect our clients — but the spurious reason for that suspension. Then again, I can't deny Gerald did the right thing. Kingsland couldn't have got his patsy to allege any worse a crime, apart from the one he subsequently threatened me with.

What a vile human being.

I compartmentalise the negative emotions relating to Kingsland and return to the reason I'm supping tea in a coffee shop mid-afternoon — an explanation for my wife. I need to protect her from the truth which means concocting a white lie.

It takes another half-hour to devise a bullet proof excuse. With that, I begin a slow traipse home.

When I open the front door, I'm taken aback to find an absence of boxes in the hallway. Not wishing to startle Leah, I yell out that I'm home before making my way through to the kitchen.

"What the …"

I'm sure there are worse scenes a husband could come home to; particularly those involving an infidelity.

"What are you doing here?" Leah blurts. "You're early."

"Have we been burgled?"

"This is all that's left after my trip to the charity shop. I was about to tidy up, before you start complaining."

The table, every inch of work surface, and most of the floor is littered with my wife's stock. If there's some inventory system in play, it isn't evident.

"Do you need a hand?"

"No, it's fine."

"Okay, I think I'll go sit in the lounge."

"Wait. You haven't told me why you're home early."

I let my eyes drift over the mess.

"We'll talk about it when you've finished. It's nothing to worry about."

If Leah is concerned, there's no obvious reaction, and she turns her attention back to the chaos which is our kitchen. A thought then occurs.

"Please tell me you put that phone somewhere safe."

"What phone?"

"The one I asked about this morning and mentioned earlier when you were at the charity shop."

A blank stare is returned.

"Oh, yes," she then declares. "Sorry, I'm having a scatterbrain day today. I put it on top of the fridge for safekeeping."

I can't get near the fridge, but at least it isn't buried in the junk pile.

"Thank you."

I leave her to it and wander through to the lounge. Knowing one of Kingsland's stooges will be at our door any time I switch the television on to provide a distraction. A game show provides a little light relief, but I won't feel completely at ease until that bloody phone is out of our flat. Why he's prepared to go to so much trouble for a phone is beyond me but I pray he sticks to his word once it's in his possession. I could, I suppose, tell him I won't hand over the phone until he gets Chantelle Granger to rescind her preposterous allegation but it would require levels of nerve I sadly don't possess. Besides, I've already established what happens when you say no to Fraser Kingsland.

The game show ends and I get up to draw the curtains.

"All done," Leah chirps from the doorway.

"Oh, great."

"Come and see."

She takes my hand and leads me back into the kitchen.

"Better, eh?"

A usable kitchen has been returned. There are still several boxes stacked up in the corner but nowhere near as many as before.

"Much better."

I show my gratitude with a kiss.

"What's for dinner?" I ask.

"Meatballs and pasta okay?"

"Sounds good."

"Right, you sit down and I'll cook. And, you can tell me why you came home early."

The doorbell rings.

"I'll, err, explain in a minute. That's probably the guy wanting his phone back."

I make for the fridge and snatch at the black object on top. Only when I've got the phone in my hand do I realise I've got a problem.

"This isn't an iPhone," I snap at Leah.

Not only is the phone in my hand noticeably smaller than Cameron's but it also bears a Motorola logo on the back.

"What?"

"This is … it's just some crappy old Android phone. Where's the iPhone I left on the table?"

"You said you lost a black phone."

"No, I said a black iPhone. Where is it?"

The look of panic on Leah's face almost certainly mirrors mine.

"I … um … I don't know."

The doorbell rings again.

13.

My wife possesses some kind of trip switch. In moments of high stress she just shuts down.

I could ask her the whereabouts of Cameron's phone a hundred times but I won't get an answer of any kind, let alone a useful one.

The doorbell rings for a third time; quickly followed by a series of sharp knocks.

"Shit," I mumble under my breath.

I don't know what to do but doing nothing is unlikely to improve the situation. Taking a second to compose myself I decide on the only option available. I'll just answer the door and calmly explain we've got a slight problem locating the phone.

"I'm coming," I yell, as I dash up the hallway.

I open the door to a man who looks vaguely familiar. Six foot tall with close-cropped hair and the kind of grizzled face only a mother could love. He looks a lot like one of the men who chased after Cameron in The Duke.

"David Nunn?" he confirms flatly.

"Yes."

"You're expecting me. I believe you have something my employer wants."

"Ah, yes. There has been a slight problem."

"Have you got it? Yes, or no?"

"Um, yes, kind of."

"Go fetch it, then."

"That's the thing. It's been mislaid temporarily. If you could pop back in a day or two, I'm sure we'll have found it by then."

"Mislaid, you say?"

"I can only apologise."

"Not to worry," he smiles. "Let me give you my number and you can call whenever it turns up."

"Oh, great," I reply with a relieved sigh. "Let me just grab a notepad."

I've barely turned around when the man suddenly steps

forward and administers a hefty shove. Taken by surprise, I stumble awkwardly, until I trip over my own feet. The hallway carpet does little to soften the impact as I crash to the floor.

The man steps into the hallway and looms over me. Judging by his scowl I don't think his initial patience was entirely sincere.

"Where's the fucking phone?" he spits.

"I … I told you. It's been mislaid."

"You've got thirty seconds to find it.

"But I don't know where it is."

He takes another step forward until he's virtually on top of me. A boot then comes to rest on top of my splayed hand.

"Jesus," I wince, as the man transfers more weight to his right leg. "You're hurting me."

"I haven't even started. Are you going to find the phone?"

More weight is applied. I bite hard on my lip to prevent a yelp. The last thing I want is for Leah to appear, and offer this lunatic an alternative victim.

"Please," I beg. "I just need a few hours to find it."

I look up, hoping to see some sign of concession in the man's face. There is none; just a face lined with deep creases.

"I'll give you five minutes," he sneers down at me. "Then, I'm going to …"

From nowhere, an arm swings into view and wraps around the man's neck like a huge black python. He repositions his feet to maintain balance, freeing my hand from his boot. As the shaven-headed man struggles to remove the arm around his neck I grasp the opportunity to clamber to my feet. Only then do I get to see the face of whoever is throttling my unwanted visitor.

"Evening, Doc."

"You?"

"Yeah, me."

I now have two violent men loitering in my hallway; one in the process of choking the other to death. The big man who attacked the drug dealer then drags the other man backwards to the front door. Once he's beyond the threshold he releases his arm from around the smaller man's neck. The shaven-headed man gasps for air but the respite is brief as the big man slams a punch into his ribcage. I can't be sure, but I might have just heard the sound of ribs cracking.

My assailant crumples to the floor and his assailant snarls a question.

"Want some more?"

The shaven-headed man, gasping hard, scuttles backwards beyond my line of sight — I presume he didn't want any more of whatever was on offer. The big man then turns to me.

"Think we need to have a chat, Doc."

"I …"

He steps back through the door; closing it behind him. I seem to have lost one uninvited guest and gained another.

"Please, I don't want any trouble."

"You ain't gonna get any from me. You've got my word."

"What do you want then?"

"As I said, just a chat."

I look up at the monster I've now met twice. On both occasions he's almost killed someone. Not the kind of man you want in your home, but not the kind of man you want to rile either.

"Can you at least tell me your name?"

He holds out a hand large enough to excavate foundations.

"Clement."

Hesitantly, I accept the handshake. It's firm but not overly so.

"What did you want to chat about, Clement?"

"We just gonna stand here, are we?"

"Um, sorry."

I open the door to the lounge and wave him in.

He steps through the doorway; ducking down to avoid the top of the frame. I follow him in but stay close to the open door.

"You just moved in?" he asks, noting a pile of Leah's boxes stacked in the corner.

"No, they're my wife's stock."

"Alright if I sit down?"

"Sure."

He flops down in an armchair not designed for a man his

size.

"Oh, hello."

I turn around to find Leah in the doorway. This is a complication I really don't need.

"I'm so sorry," she says to Clement. "It's not David's fault."

I realise she probably thinks the big man is here to collect the missing iPhone.

"Err, don't worry about it, honey. I'm just going to have a quick chat with Clement here, and then we can sort dinner."

"I'll set another place at the table," she replies.

My wife has misunderstood. I'm about to correct her when our guest replies.

"Very kind of you, Doll. What we having?"

"Pasta and meatballs."

"Triffic. Don't 'spose there's any chance of a brew?"

"Yes, yes. I'll go put the kettle on."

"Nice one."

Clement winks at my wife; a gesture which puts a smile on her face. She dashes off back to the kitchen. I can't quite believe I've just stood by and let this situation develop around me, to the point we're set to have dinner with a possible psychopath.

"That your missus?" the possible psychopath asks.

"Yes."

"You've done alright for yourself there, Doc."

"Thank you … but please don't call me Doc. I'm not a doctor."

"Closest thing to a doctor I've met in a while."

"That's as maybe, but … wait, is this chat about your issues?"

"Issues?"

"The other night you mentioned something about anger management."

"Oh, that," he says dismissively. "Nah. I've got a proposal for you. That's why I popped round."

"I'm listening."

"You gonna stand there like a spare prick, or you gonna sit down?"

91

I sit on the sofa opposite.

"That bloke in the hallway — I'm guessing he weren't here to read the gas meter?"

"No."

"You got yourself into a spot of bother, Doc?"

"Nothing I can't handle."

"You didn't look like you were handling it too well when I turned up."

"No, but … it's all a bit of a mess, if I'm being honest."

"You wanna tell me about it?"

"With respect, it's not really anyone's business but mine."

"What about your missus? Is it her business if some dickhead turns up and beats the crap out of her husband?"

An uncomfortable counter-argument. Perhaps time to move the conversation along.

"You mentioned a proposal."

"Yeah, I did. I think you're in deep shit; you just ain't willing to admit how deep that shit is. I can help."

"You'd like me to pay for protection? If that's your angle you've come to the wrong guy because I'm broke."

"Who said anything about money? I'm talking about a trade."

"A trade of what, exactly?"

Leah pops her head around the door.

"Sorry to interrupt. Do you take milk and sugar, Clement?"

"Milk and three sugars please, Doll."

My wife hesitates for a second and then attempts to engage our guest in conversation.

"I've never met someone called Clement before. It's such an unusual name."

"Cheers," he replies with a smile. "Can't take any credit for it, though."

"I'll go fetch your tea."

Leah returns to the kitchen and I return to my question.

"You suggested a trade?"

"That's right. I'll help you out of this hole you're in, and in return you can help me."

"Help you with what, exactly?"

He sits forward in the chair.

"You're covered by some kind of oath, ain't you?"

"Oath?"

"Yeah. You're not allowed to judge patients, right? Do no harm, or something?"

"I think you're referring to the Hippocratic Oath which applies to medical practitioners. As I've said, I'm not a doctor so I'm not covered by that oath but I would never judge a client."

"Even those who might be a bit mental?"

"Err, you really shouldn't use that term, but no, I'd never judge someone with mental illness."

"You can help me, then."

"I'm deeply uncomfortable with that suggestion, Clement. If you do have concerns about your mental health, your first point of call should be your doctor."

"Don't have one."

"Why not?"

"Long story, but I can't go see a quack, alright."

"Okay, well, there are various helplines you could …"

"It ain't a friendly chat I'm after," he scolds. "I need someone to tell me if I'm a headcase or not, and it's gotta be you."

"Why me?"

"That's the thing, Doc. There's a voice in my head, telling me."

"One cup of tea," Leah announces. "Sorry, David, I forgot to ask if you wanted one."

"Eh? Err, no. Thanks."

She hands Clement a mug.

"Cheers, Doll."

"You're very welcome."

Leah skips off. Clement sips at his tea before placing the mug on the coffee table.

"You're hearing a voice in your head?" I confirm.

"In a nutshell, yeah."

"And what is that voice telling you?"

"All manner of shit," he shrugs. "But it's more a whisper

93

than a clear voice. Most of the time it makes no sense."

"How often?"

"It can go quiet for months, and then it just starts again. That's why I know you're in shit."

"I'm sorry?"

"It only happens when I meet someone who's got a problem. See, that's what I do — fix problems."

This is way beyond my pay-grade. Based on what little I know, Clement appears to be displaying several symptoms common to schizophrenia: hostility, irrational behaviour, and delusions.

"I think it's great you recognise a need for help, Clement, but I'm just a counsellor. It would be wrong for me to assist with your diagnosis; let alone treatment. Dangerous and criminally wrong; to be frank. With fear of repeating myself; I'm not a doctor."

"I ain't ever gonna see a shrink so you're my best bet for sorting my head out."

"I'm really not. Sorry, but there's nothing I can do for you."

"Fair enough," he says, suddenly getting to his feet. "I'll leave you to deal with your shit."

He then digs a hand into the pocket of his donkey jacket and pulls out a basic mobile phone.

"No one has rung this in months," he says. "Don't even know the number."

He hands it to me.

"Can you get the number from it?"

"Err, probably."

I unlock the screen and click on the contact list. There are just two names: Clement, and Emma.

"Who's Emma?" I ask. "A friend?"

"She was."

"You can't talk to her about your concerns?"

"Tried that," he replies solemnly. "Didn't end well."

"Right."

"You gonna write my number down?"

I grab a notepad and scribble Clement's number. I don't

envisage ever calling it.

"I promise you something, Doc — it might be tomorrow, the day after, or next week, but you will need my help soon enough. Give me a bell and we can talk about that trade again. You might see things a bit differently if your problems continue."

"I'll bear it in mind."

"Apologise to your missus for me. Ain't got much of an appetite after all."

He then stoops back through the door into the hall. A second or two later, the front door latch clicks.

I stare at the notepad for a second, and then at the empty armchair. Clement might have left the room, but the scent of cigarettes still lingers.

"He's gone?" Leah asks.

I look up from the sofa.

"Err, yes. He said to apologise about dinner."

"What a shame. Anyway, it'll be ready in five minutes."

"Great."

"You okay?"

I stand up and hug my wife.

"I'm fine, honey. It's been a bit of a day."

"Come through to the kitchen and you can tell me all about it."

I do as I'm asked and sit at the table while Leah busies herself at the hob.

"Why the early finish today then?" she asks.

"I had a particularly challenging experience with a client. Gerald suggested I should take a day or two to get my head straight."

"Do you want to talk about it?"

"Thanks, but I'd rather not."

"Does that mean you're off tomorrow?"

"Yep."

"We could spend the day in bed."

"That sounds like a splendid idea."

Leah turns her attention back to the hob while I consider what Kingsland will do next. Clement might have thwarted one visit but he won't be here the next time one of Kingsland's associates arrives. I really need to find that bloody iPhone.

"Here we go."

Leah places a plate in front of me.

"Thanks, honey."

She sits opposite.

"How long have you known Clement?"

"I only met him last week."

"He seems a nice guy."

"You think?"

"Yes. I like him. He has a certain aura."

"He's a violent man with a ton of issues, Leah. Just to be clear, if he turns up and I'm not home, do not let him in."

"Is he likely to turn up again?"

"Hopefully not. I don't want the likes of him in our home."

"I thought you're supposed to help people with issues?"

"Not people like Clement."

"You really don't like him, do you?"

"It's not a case of liking him. I can't say I particularly like a lot of my clients but that doesn't stop me helping them. Clement is … he's not someone we want in our lives."

"If you say so, David," she replies with a dark stare. "Far be it from me to form my own opinions."

I sense an argument brewing. I don't have the energy, and I need to keep my wife grounded if I've any hope of finding Cameron's phone.

"Sorry," I mumble. "Just ignore me."

We eat in silence, although my recent guest isn't the only one lacking an appetite.

"Something wrong with it?" Leah asks.

"No, not at all. I'm just concerned about finding that mobile phone. The guy who owns it desperately needs it back."

"We can look for it after dinner."

"Thank you."

I force down the rest of my food and clear the plates. Keeping her word, Leah makes a start on one of the dozen-odd boxes stacked in the corner. After washing up, I join in the search. Once those boxes have been emptied, checked twice, and repacked, we scour every inch of the kitchen, even pulling out the fridge in case the missing phone has inadvertently fallen behind it.

It's almost nine o'clock when the search finally ends.

"I'm so sorry," Leah professes.

"Could it have found its way into one of the boxes you took to the charity shop?"

"I don't think so but … maybe, I really can't say."

My phone pings to signify an incoming message. I pluck it from my pocket and press the screen. The message is from the same phone which called me this afternoon on the way back from the police station. Kingsland's demand is clear: *Bring the phone to The Duke of Wellington at noon tomorrow or your life won't be worth living.*

"Problem?" Leah asks.

"It's nothing."

"It's about the phone, isn't it? I've caused you a real problem."

I try not to let the inner dread reach my face. My final option is to visit the charity shop first thing in the morning, and hope to God the phone is there. If it isn't, I'll have no choice but to report Kingsland's threats to the police. At least I have his message as evidence now.

"I'm sure everything will be fine."

The second time I've lied to my wife today. She appears to believe me — I don't.

14.

I woke up at six and couldn't get back to sleep. The second my brain latched on to the day ahead, it would never let me rest.

At eight o'clock, I kissed my still-slumbering wife goodbye and left the flat with a growing sense of dread. My destination: a charity shop on Kentish Town Road.

The shop in question doesn't open until half-eight, but I want to be the first person they see at the door.

As I pound the icy pavements, I'm trying not to think any further ahead than the search for the phone. Being optimistic, I'm hoping they haven't already sorted through Leah's donation, and in one of those boxes I'll find Cameron Gail's elusive iPhone. I can then meet Kingsland at noon and put this sorry saga to bed.

Optimism, however, requires grounding in realism. You can be optimistic about the weather in January, but that won't save you from freezing your arse off. As much as I'm keeping my fingers crossed, I'm also pondering what I'll do if I can't find the phone. As I see it, there are only two options: I either explain to Kingsland the phone is lost and hope he realises the futility of further threats, or I head straight to the police station and report those threats.

I arrive at the charity shop still undecided which of those options is the least palatable. The front door is locked but the lights are on. I peer through the glass at the rails of clothes and shelves bursting with an eclectic range of second-hand goods. The scene doesn't look too dissimilar to my kitchen when I arrived home yesterday.

There's no sign of anyone in the shop itself, but I chance a knock on the glass. Seconds pass until a white-haired woman steps through a doorway. I throw a friendly wave but the woman glances at her watch and frowns.

"Five minutes," she mouths.

Seeing as I need her cooperation, I smile back and wait.

There's nothing else to do other than dance on the spot and

rub my hands together to keep warm. On the fourth check of my watch I hear a lock click behind me. I turn around and the white-haired woman is at the door. She then pulls it open.

"Someone is keen," she says. "We've never had a queue before."

I don't think one person constitutes a queue but keep that observation to myself. I catch sight of the woman's name badge: Faith — Manager. The irony of her name isn't lost on me.

"Morning," I reply, stepping through the door into the warm shop. "I'm actually here on a mercy mission."

"Oh?"

"My wife dropped off some boxes yesterday afternoon and we think a friend's mobile phone might have found its way into one of those boxes."

Her expression alone dents my optimism.

"Do you know what those boxes look like?" she asks.

"Box-like?"

My humour doesn't hit home as Faith's frown deepens.

"Come with me," she then orders.

I follow her back through the doorway to a large storeroom. At least twice the size of the shop itself, there are six rows of shelves which stretch from floor to ceiling, and run the entire length of the room. Every single shelf is rammed with boxes.

"We've been meaning to sort out the stockroom for months," Faith says apologetically. "Unfortunately, we're so short of volunteers we just don't have the time."

"Err, are you saying my wife's boxes could be anywhere in here?"

"Not quite. We always try to stack newer stock near the back door so we can check through it, but sometimes it gets put where there's space."

My eyes slowly drift along the nearest shelving unit. Five shelves, each housing roughly a dozen boxes. A quick bit of mental arithmetic confirms the worst: give or take, there must be over three-hundred boxes here. Allowing four minutes to check each box, it would take me twenty hours to go through them all. I have a shade over three hours before I'm expected at The

Duke.

"Would you mind showing me the most likely contenders please, Faith?"

"Not at all."

She leads me to the end of the furthest row; adjacent to the back door.

"This section is your best bet."

There are still a lot of contenders, but it's not three-hundred.

"Would you mind if I checked through them?"

"Can I see some identification first? You have an honest face but one can't be too careful."

Why anyone would want to steal from a charity is beyond me, but I willingly oblige.

"My drivers licence and my business card. As you can see I work for a local charity myself."

She squints at my business card.

"My late husband was called David," she remarks.

I adopt an appropriately sympathetic expression.

"I'm so sorry to hear he's no longer with you."

"I'm not. He was a bone idle shit."

"Oh."

"Anyway, I'll leave you to it as I'm on my own in the shop until ten. Good luck."

"Thank you."

Faith shuffles off and I grab the nearest box. Only when I pull that box from the shelf do I realise there's another layer behind.

"Crap."

I open the first box; almost with a treasure hunt sense of anticipation. Rather than just delving in without thoroughly checking, I carefully remove every item, until I can see the bottom. It's a slow process but necessary. The first box is a bust, not unsurprisingly, but my four-minute estimation wasn't far off.

By the tenth box it no longer feels like a treasure hunt. It feels exactly like what it is — wading through unwanted junk with increasing desperation. I'm only distracted from my dwindling optimism when I stumble across a donation which beggars belief: a jar of pickled walnuts, a half-used toilet roll, a Thermos flask with no lid, and countless VHS video cassettes.

Some people have no shame. I just hope my wife isn't one of those people.

I press on, and by ten o'clock I've checked twenty of the boxes nearest the door. There are probably another half-a-dozen contenders left before I'll be creeping into the regular stock — all three-hundred boxes of it.

My phone rings.

Glad of the break I snatch it from my pocket. Leah's name is on the screen.

"Hi, honey."

"How's it going?"

"No luck so far."

"Oh, I thought you'd found it."

"What made you think that?"

"The flowers."

"What flowers?" I ask wearily.

"I've just taken delivery of a dozen black orchids. I thought you'd sent them to … you know, to say sorry."

"Sorry for what exactly?"

"Snapping at me last night."

"Leah, I didn't send you any flowers, okay. Is there a card with them?"

"Err, I didn't check. Hold on."

Some men might feel concerned at their wife being sent flowers but the poor door signage in our block means we frequently take delivery of goods meant for our neighbours; ranging from parcels to post to pizzas.

"You still there?" Leah asks.

"Yes."

"There is a card. Shall I open it?"

"If you want to ensure the flowers find their rightful owner, yes."

"Okay."

There's a moment of silence followed by the tear of paper. I

101

really don't have time for this.

"It says: time will tell if our condolences are premature. Tick tock."

"What? Read that again."

She does, and it does nothing to ease my racing pulse.

"Is there a signature?"

"No, but there's a name at the bottom."

"What is it?"

"The Duke. Who's he?"

"I … err, no one. Just put them in the bin."

"Why? They're so lovely."

"Please," I snap. "Just put them in the bin."

"David, what's going on? You're scaring me."

I draw a breath and attempt to strip the panic from my tone.

"There's nothing to worry about, honey. I think it's just a prank; albeit in bad taste."

"Are you sure?"

"Positive. If you want to keep the flowers, it's fine."

"Really? You don't mind?"

"I'd better get on. I'll be home shortly, I promise."

"Okay. Love you."

"Love you too."

I end the call and stand motionless. What do I do? There's no doubt Kingsland sent the flowers, and the threat is equally obvious. Should I go to the police?

Looking at the shelves I'm suddenly struck by the hopelessness of my quest. Cameron Gail's iPhone is lost and there's virtually no chance of finding it. The only question I need to focus on now is what I do about it. I return to my two options. Perhaps they're not choices to make but steps to take. Not one or the other, but one before the other. I should meet with Fraser Kingsland and explain the situation. If he still doesn't back off, then I contact the police.

I dart back to the shop.

"Have you found it?" Faith asks.

"Afraid not, but I've run out of time. Can I leave my business card just in case it turns up?"

"Of course, but can you jot down on the back as much detail as possible? We receive a lot of mobile phones."

"Sure."

I scribble down the make, colour, size, and the only identifying mark I noticed: a smudge of yellow residue near the button at the bottom of the screen.

"You know," Faith says. "If you wanted to come back — maybe as a volunteer — you could help us sort out the stockroom while looking for your friend's phone."

"I might take you up on that offer. I'll get back to you."

The look in Faith's eye tells me she doesn't expect our paths to cross again.

"Well, you know where we are."

"I do. Thanks."

After a dash back along still-icy pavements, I arrive home. Leah is waiting for me in the lounge. Also waiting for me is a vase with a dozen black orchids — the symbolism clear.

"Where's the card that came with them?" I ask.

"On the kitchen table. Are you sure it's okay to keep them?"

"Sure."

I head through to the kitchen and snatch the small envelope from the table. Nervously, I extract the card inside and read it. I had hoped maybe Leah had misread the text but now, seeing it with my own eyes, the message is clear. It's also clear how highly he prizes that mobile phone. Not exactly a death threat but a strong hint of what might happen should I fail to deliver the phone.

"Damn you, Cameron," I spit.

I toss the card back on the table and grab my phone. The original message I sent to Cameron is still unread but I need to vent so I add a short but concise follow-up: *Where are you? We need to talk NOW!*

I hit the send button and stare at the screen. Seconds turn to minutes but there's no activity.

Frustrated, I grab my laptop. People of Cameron's age don't use Facebook nearly as much as other social media platforms, so perhaps I might have better luck contacting him via Instagram, or Twitter, or WhatsApp.

I invest an hour scouring the pages of every popular social media website but find nothing. Leah wanders in.

"Cup of tea?"

"Please."

"What are you doing?"

"I'm trying to find someone."

"Who?"

"Just an old client."

"Don't you have their records at work?"

"It's complicated, but no."

Detecting my reluctance to chat, Leah quietly makes the tea while I stare at Google's home page and an empty search box. Time to face facts: I've no idea how to contact Cameron and time is not on my side.

"One cup of tea."

"Thanks."

"Are you okay, David? You seem on edge."

"Just this case at work getting under my skin. Ignore me."

"It's not like you."

"I know. I've got a meeting in a half-hour and hopefully that'll help."

"A meeting with who?"

"Just … a friend of that client."

"I hope it goes well. If not, maybe I can put a smile on your face this afternoon?"

She leans in and whispers in my ear how that smile might come about. Her suggestion sounds delightful, but it depends on both my testicles returning home with me after the meeting with Fraser Kingsland.

I drink my tea and leave, not sure I'll be able to keep my parting promise.

15.

I arrive at The Duke a few minutes before noon.

Pushing open the door to the main bar I'm immediately struck how different the atmosphere is to Friday evening. There's no jovial chatter or sporadic laughter, just the quiet mumblings of a dozen wizened patrons who don't work, can't work, or live their lives by pub opening times.

I make my way to the bar and order an orange juice from a barmaid who already looks tired, barely an hour into her shift.

There's minimal conversation over the transaction. I pay and turn to scan the room for a man I wish I wasn't here to meet. Then, the main door opens and Fraser Kingsland enters as if he owns the place. The already hushed atmosphere drops a few decibels further.

"I like a punctual man," he remarks when his gaze stops on me.

Without a word from Kingsland a tumbler of amber liquid is placed on the bar.

"Cheers, darling," Kingsland snorts towards the barmaid.

"Afternoon, Mr Nunn."

He offers his hand. I consider refusing the handshake on a point of principle, but fear is a strong motivator, and it's only now I realise just how scared I am. This is a bad idea; a bad situation to have put myself in.

We shake hands and Kingsland orders me to follow him. We make our way to a booth in a gloomy corner.

"Put your phone on the table," he then demands.

"Why?"

"I don't trust you. Don't take it personally — I don't trust anyone."

I do as instructed and Kingsland checks I'm not about to record our conversation. He's either paranoid or smart, as he then pats me down to ensure I've no other recording device on my person.

"Glad to see you're a sensible man," he says. "Have a seat."

I comply, and Kingsland sits opposite; resting his arms on the table. Being in such close proximity I catch a lungful of his overpowering cologne.

"Let's start with a nice easy question, eh? Who attacked my associate when he called round your flat?"

"No idea," I shrug. "He just invited himself into my home because he heard I help people with mental health issues."

"If you see him again, tell him he's a dead man."

I nod.

"So, have you got the phone?" he then asks, his tone flat.

"I'm afraid not."

"Where is it?"

"That's the thing — I don't know."

"You had it, and now you don't know where it is?"

"It's … it's been mislaid."

He slowly nods.

"That is unfortunate because I really need that phone."

"I'm willing to buy a replacement if it helps?"

He laughs at my suggestion.

"How much do you reckon it's worth?" he asks.

"Um, four or five hundred."

"You're a bit out, Mr Nunn. That phone is worth about fifty million, possibly more."

I almost choke on my orange juice.

"I beg your pardon?"

"It's not the phone, it's what's on the phone."

"Oh, I see. Surely Cameron backed his data up?"

His thin lips curl downward as if he's just caught a bad smell.

"You tell me, Mr Nunn. Did he?"

"How would I know?"

"I have an inkling you know a lot about Cameron Gail."

"I hardly know him."

"You were his counsellor, and I know how people like to bare their soul to your kind."

"Mr Kingsland, I think you've got the wrong impression about my relationship with Cameron Gail. I only had one session with him, and then we met up here last Friday. We only talked

106

for a matter of minutes before he shot off."

"He didn't tell you anything during either meeting?"

"Well, he told me a few things."

"Such as?"

"You know I can't discuss that with you."

"Oh dear," he sighs. "I thought you were an intelligent man, but it seems you're not as smart as you look."

He then sits back in his seat and puts his hands behind his head.

"About that young lady you raped."

"I didn't rape anyone."

"That's not what the police think."

"They can think what they like — there's no evidence because it's a malicious lie."

"There's no evidence yet. However, I meant what I said on the phone. I've got a long line of young women willing to come forward and make similar allegations. Besides the lengthy and public police investigation, I wonder how your wife would feel, knowing she married a prolific sex offender."

I've spent much of my career trying to coax the truth out of people, to the degree I know when the person opposite me isn't being sincere. Fraser Kingsland means what he says.

"Why are you doing this to me?"

"Because you have something I want."

"But, I don't. I told you I can't find the damn phone."

"And I believe you."

"You do?"

"Yes, which is why I'm prepared to offer you an alternative solution — bring Cameron Gail to me."

"What?"

"He trusts you, which puts you in a particularly exclusive club, Mr Nunn. All you need to do is get him into your flat and my colleague will come collect him. Do that and all this unpleasantness with the police goes away."

"I don't know where he is."

"You'd better start looking, then. I'll give you five days."

"You're crazy. I could spend five months looking and still

not find him."

"That's all I'm offering. Five days to bring me either the phone or Cameron Gail."

"And if I don't?"

"More allegations will be made against you; enough the police won't offer bail. And, while you're locked up in a cell, poor Leah will be home alone. This is a rough city, Mr Nunn … bad things happen to innocent folks every day. Know what I mean?"

His lips curl in the opposite direction.

"This is madness. Can't you just hire a private detective to find him?"

"He's a smart lad, young Cameron, and I guarantee he'll have covered his tracks. The only person he'll come out of hiding for is you."

I've nowhere else to go, nothing left in my defensive locker.

"And just so we're clear," he adds. "If you speak to the police about our arrangement that would be a mistake … a fatal one as far as your wife is concerned."

He stands up and necks the amber liquid from the tumbler.

"Be in touch on Sunday, Mr Nunn, unless you find what I'm looking for beforehand. For your sake, I hope that's the case."

He slams the tumbler down and walks away.

There isn't much I don't know about controlling panic attacks. I've studied them at length and helped hundreds of clients establish coping mechanisms. I've never experienced one, but I recognise the signs.

I clutch the table edge and draw in long, slow breaths. Still, the walls continue to close in, as my heart thumps with such force I swear it's about to explode.

"You alright there, love?"

I look up at the barmaid as she collects Fraser Kingsland's empty tumbler.

"Want some advice?" she asks.

Instinctively, I nod.

"Whatever he wants, give it to him. If he's offering, don't take it."

She runs a cloth across the table twice and returns to the bar.

I stare at the glass of orange juice as time passes. I've no idea how long; nor do I care. My thoughts are dominated by a simple question: what in God's name do I do next? If I were giving advice to someone in the same situation, I'd likely advise they go straight to the police. Easily said when you're not the one who's just been warned not to, and it's not the woman you love being used as a bargaining chip.

The situation calls for pragmatism. I need to think through my options before I do anything rash.

I get up and leave The Duke.

The walk home takes twice as long as the outbound journey. Shuffling along, I work through a series of scenarios, in the hope one of them leads to a satisfactory resolution. The obvious solution would be to find either the phone or Cameron Gail, but I've already tried the former, and I don't have time to sift through hundreds of boxes at the charity shop; assuming the phone is even there. As for finding Cameron where would I even start?

I should speak to the police. It's the only sensible option, but is it the right option?

More questions follow as I cover the final few hundred yards of pavement. Is Fraser Kingsland's threat genuine? I've met his kind before and there's a world of difference between those who threaten to kill and those with the necessary mind-set to carry out the threat.

I hang my coat up and wander into the lounge where Leah is on the sofa, watching television.

"How'd it go?" she asks.

"I made progress."

Another effortless lie.

"Oh, good," she replies, patting the seat next to her. "Come and sit down."

Wearing a dressing gown and her hair damp, I'm guessing my wife is fresh from the shower. I know if I sit down, Leah's original plan for our afternoon will come to fruition. Ordinarily, I'd love nothing more than to spend the afternoon in bed with my wife but this is no ordinary afternoon. The vase of black orchids on the coffee table serve as a reminder.

"I'm sorry, honey, but I've got a lot of work to get through this afternoon."

"Suit yourself," comes the haughty response.

She grabs the remote control and aims it towards the television. I make my escape before her strop develops into a full-blown sulk.

The kitchen clock rather than my stomach confirms I'm overdue lunch. I've no appetite and settle on a cup of tea. I then sit down at the table with my mobile phone, laptop, and a notepad laid out in front of me.

"One hour," I whisper to myself.

Setting a deadline for problem resolution is a technique I've recommended to clients who suffer from indecision. A set period in which you'll forensically dissect the problem and brainstorm all the possible solutions. Having a deadline aids focus and stops the inevitable mind drift which happens when you haphazardly dwell on your problems.

Ten minutes pass, then twenty. Inert, I stare at the laptop screen; hypnotised by the blinking cursor. Another ten minutes pass before I realise this isn't a problem — it's a gamble. Do I invest my time searching for Cameron in the hope of finding him, or do I go to the police and hope they'll protect us from Fraser Kingsland? While I try to calculate which is the shortest bet a memory of my second conversation with Cameron comes into play. Did he say something about Kingsland knowing people in the force? Was that just paranoia, or did he have credible evidence?

The odds continue to fluctuate. My frustration mounts.

"Get back to the problem."

Determined to follow my own advice, I flick open the notepad and ready a pen. The blank page isn't completely blank — a phone number scrawled at the top.

It raises another question.

My career is largely based upon offering different perspectives. Words alone will never change anyone's situation, but they can help an individual's perspective of that situation. It's the classic glass half-full, half-empty test of how someone sees the world, and my job is to change that viewpoint.

I glance at the clock and then back at the notepad. I've invested forty minutes and I'm nowhere further forward.

I need another perspective; someone whose worldview is the polar opposite of mine. Who, though? I possess enough self-awareness to know where my train of thought is heading. The number on the notepad belongs to a man who shouldn't be anywhere near my thinking, but there aren't many other candidates.

I get up and return to the lounge.

"Honey, can I ask you something?"

Leah reluctantly turns away from the television and glares up at me.

"I'm not in the mood now."

"No, it's not … that. It's about our guest last night."

"Clement? What about him?"

"What was your first impression?"

"I liked him."

"Why?"

"Because he … as I said: he had an aura."

"Can you be more specific?"

"Not really, it's just a gut feeling. Unlike you, I don't feel the need to pigeon-hole every person I meet."

"That's harsh."

"Don't take it personally. It's just what you do."

"Care to expand on that insult?"

"It's an observation, not an insult. I think you spend so much time with people who need fixing, you struggle to see the human beyond their condition."

"And you think there's more to our guest than just the imminent threat of violence?"

"I do. He had kindly eyes."

"Funny, because I thought his eyes looked dead."

"And that's where we differ, dear husband. You look for the flaws in people while I look for the good."

I step across and kiss my wife.

"Thank you."

"What for?"

"Helping me with a decision I didn't want to make."

She turns her attention back to the television and I return to the kitchen table.

Clement prophesied I might need his help sooner rather than later, and I get the impression his brand of thinking might not be along the same straight lines as mine. I grab my phone and dial the number but stop short of hitting the call icon. If I'm to take this desperate measure, it has to be on my terms. I give myself a minute or two to decide what those terms are, and then make the call.

16.

The phone rings and rings. I'm about to give up when the tone comes to an abrupt end.

"Ello."

"Is that Clement?"

"Who's this?"

"It's David Nunn."

"Who?"

"David … Doc."

The line goes silent until I hear a long puff of air — most likely laced with cigarette smoke.

"When do you want to meet?" he asks.

"What makes you think I want to meet?"

"'Cos you need my help, right?"

"I need some advice, if your offer still stands?"

"Do you know Deckers Cafe, in Camden?"

"Err, I think so."

"I'll meet you there in half-hour. You're buying."

There is no further discussion as he ends the call. I close the laptop and stare at the notepad. What am I doing?

Avoiding the temptation to argue with myself, I return to the lounge and tell Leah I'm popping out. She's so engrossed in the programme I get little in the way of questioning, and that's fine by me.

I tuck the notepad into the inside pocket of my jacket and check the whereabouts of the cafe on my phone. It's only fifteen minutes away, but I'd rather take a slow walk and arrive early than sit at the kitchen table a minute longer.

As it is, I stretch the journey out to eighteen minutes and spend two minutes stood outside the miserable-looking side street establishment that is Deckers Cafe. Clement could already be inside, but I've no way of telling as the plate-glass window is misted with condensation. Judging by the tatty sign above I've a sneaking suspicion the owners won't have employed the services of an interior designer.

I push open the door.

Being mid-afternoon it's near empty besides an old guy sipping from a cup by the window. He glances over but appears disinterested.

"What can I get you, mate?"

I turn to the counter where an overweight man with receding hair is fiddling with his phone.

"Can I get two teas, please?"

"Grab a seat. I'll bring 'em over."

He drapes a tea-towel over his shoulder and turns away. I sit down at the nearest table and flick through the menu while I wait. Everything with chips, but it's cheap.

With no other customers to wait upon the service is efficient. Two mugs are delivered to my table within a minute and the overweight man asks if I want anything else. Having skipped lunch, I'm almost tempted, until I notice his nicotine-stained fingers. I decline.

The tea is strong and admittedly better than the much pricier brew I had in the coffee shop yesterday afternoon. I'm about to check my watch when the door opens. A hulking man in a black donkey jacket enters. This is the third time I've met Clement and the impact of his presence hasn't lessened.

"Alright, Doc."

He sits down opposite.

"That mine?" he asks, nodding at the mug of tea.

"Yes."

Four sachets of sugar are duly dispatched. After a quick stir and a slurp, he smacks his lips.

"Always get a decent cuppa in here."

I nod in agreement.

"So, our trade is on?"

"Um, before we start, I just wanted to clarify why I'm here, and the scope of our conversation."

"You're here 'cos you're in deep shit, right?"

"You could say that, however, I'm only seeking general advice and that's all I'm offering in return. Any discussion regarding the specifics of your condition are off the table. I'm not qualified to offer a clinical prognosis or treatment, understood?"

"Yeah, yeah. I get it. You wanna cover your arse."

"No, I'm saying you should speak to a doctor."

"And I told you: that ain't happening. Tell you what, though, why don't we say I'm asking on behalf of a mate?"

"I can work with that."

"Good, so do you wanna tell me what's up?"

It's unlikely either of the other two men in the cafe care about my woes, but I sit forward and explain the situation in a hushed tone.

"And there you have it," I conclude. "I've got five days to find this young man, or his phone."

"And you ain't told the Old Bill?"

"No, not yet. You said you fix problems so I'm interested in how you'd fix one like mine, generally speaking."

"What's this bloke's name again? The one making the threats?"

"Fraser Kingsland."

"Name don't ring any bells. What do you know about him?"

"Almost nothing."

"Shit, Doc. Some bloke threatens you and your missus, and you ain't even bothered finding out who he is?"

"Um, no."

"Can't you look him up on your phone? Do that googley thing?"

"I could, but I'm not sure how that helps."

"'Cos you need to know who you're dealing with. He could be a serious player, but he might be a no-one and you're getting your knickers in a twist about nothin'."

"Fair point."

I extract my phone and enter the name Fraser Kingsland into Google's search box. The first set of results are vague and yield nothing worthwhile so I use a few modifiers to hone my search. Even then, there are no results: no social media profiles, no news reports, no genealogy results.

"That's odd."

"What is?"

"There's no mention of the name Fraser Kingsland in any context."

"Is that unusual?"

"Highly unusual. If you google any name, there's almost always a mention of it somewhere online."

To prove my point I ask him his surname so I can conduct a search.

"Ain't got one."

"How can you not have a surname?"

"I thought we were talking about this Kingsland bloke? Why's it odd you can't find his name?"

I drop the questioning and search my name in Google. I then hold my phone up for Clement to see.

"As an example, there are thousands of results for people called David Nunn. I could enter any number of names and there would be pages and pages of results."

"Except for the bloke we're interested in. Ain't much help then?"

"Not really."

"What does he look like?"

I explain as best I can.

"And you say he's middle-aged?"

"Come to think of it, I remember he mentioned buying his first cigar when he was eighteen, and that was thirty years ago. That would put him in his late forties."

"I can ask around but I don't have the contacts I used to."

"Used to?"

"Most are dribbling in a nursing home, or dead."

"Right, so for now we'll have to assume Fraser Kingsland's threats are genuine."

"Why ain't you told the Old Bill, then?"

"Two reasons. Firstly, he made a point of stressing the consequences if I did, and secondly, I'm worried about something Cameron Gail said."

"What?"

"Kingsland knows people on the force."

"Bent coppers?"

"Possibly, or just a few friendly officers willing to tip him off."

"Same thing. Either way, I don't reckon it'd be sensible grassing the bloke up until you know who you're dealing with."

"Which I don't."

Clement then sits back in his chair. Raising one of his meaty hands, his moustache receives a couple of strokes while he appears to ponder my dilemma.

"You've only got one choice, Doc — find the kid."

"How on earth am I supposed to do that? I'm a mental health counsellor not a private detective."

"That's where I come in. I'll help you find him."

"No offence, but what qualifies you to make such an offer?"

"Experience."

"What kind of experience?"

"I've helped a few people out of some serious scrapes over the last four years. Finding some dipshit kid should be a breeze by comparison."

"Cameron Gail is no dipshit. He's studying chemistry at Oxford … or at least, he was."

"I couldn't give a shit if he's studying chemistry at Oxford or woodwork in Wandsworth. If he's out there, we'll find him."

"We?"

"Yeah, we."

His eyes bore into me with the same ferocity as the night we met.

"Way I see it, Doc, we do this together and you can help me as we go. I'm guessing you ain't gonna deal with my shit over a cup of tea."

"Putting the 'we' question aside for one moment, what exactly is the crux of your shit, as you so eloquently put it?"

"My mate's shit?" he replies with an exaggerated wink.

"Oh, yes. Your mate's shit."

The moustache receives two long strokes.

"Alright, you ready for this, Doc?"

"As I'll ever be."

"This mate of mine, well, he thinks he's dead."

"Dead? In what way?"

"How many ways are there to be dead?"

"Plenty. He could be emotionally dead, morally dead …"

"Nah, Doc. The bloke is dead dead."

"You mean literally dead, as in deceased?"

"Exactly."

Unquestionably, one of the more interesting conditions thrown my way over the years.

"You might need to give me a little extra detail."

"He was murdered back in the seventies and, for some reason, he's now alive again. Been that way for a few years."

"Let me get this straight. Your friend claims he was murdered at some point in the seventies, and now he's alive again?"

"You got it."

"Okay."

Clement's claim adds further weight to my initial suspicions — he, or his mate, is suffering from acute schizophrenia. I've read case studies on the condition where the sufferer experiences somatic delusions: a person believes their body is affected by an abnormal condition, despite overwhelming contradictory evidence. Granted, believing you died decades ago is a particularly abnormal psychosis.

"Sounds fucking crazy, don't it?"

"I never judge."

"Come off it, Doc. If you told me you used to live on the moon, I'd think you had a screw loose."

"Your mate believes it to be true, though, and that's the issue."

"And it can be fixed, right?"

"There are treatments available for most mental illnesses, but that brings us back to my original position — your friend needs to seek professional help."

"And what if he ain't ill?"

"I'm not with you."

"What if he's telling the truth?"

"You mean, he did actually die and by some miracle he's alive again?"

"More or less."

"We both know that's impossible, Clement. You die, and that's it."

"Unless it ain't," he shrugs. "That's why we're gonna look for this kid together; so you can work out if my mate is telling the truth or if the men in white coats should take him away."

It's my turn to fix Clement with a hard stare. It's exceptionally rare for people suffering from schizophrenia to possess meta-awareness of their condition. They believe their delusions are real and therefore there's no logical reason in their mind to consider an alternative theory. Everything to them is real; in the same way we all accept our own version of reality. We don't question what we know to be true.

"I don't think men in white coats cart off the mentally ill these days," I remark, unsure how else to respond.

"The world has changed, Doc, and not for the better."

"According to you or your friend?"

"I'll let you work that one out."

He then looks over my head towards the counter and orders two more teas.

"You hungry?" he asks.

"Not really."

"And two rounds of bacon sarnies, Grog," he calls out.

"Grog?" I question.

"That's his name."

"It suits him. Anyway, I did say I'm not hungry."

"And I heard you. The sarnies are for me as you're paying."

"Do I have a choice?"

"We all have choices and you've now gotta choose which way you go with your problem. We can help each other out, or you can take your chances with Kingsland and the Old Bill."

Grog delivers two mugs of tea and confirms Clement's sandwiches will be ten minutes.

"What's it gonna be then, Doc?"

Choices maybe, but they're all of the dreadful variety. I don't want to deal with Kingsland or risk reporting him to the police, but neither do I want to spend the next few days in the company of a man gripped with schizophrenic delusions while we try to locate a kid who doesn't want to be found.

"What I really want, Clement, is to get away from this Godforsaken city and live a normal life. I didn't ask for any of this."

"Yeah, well, we all get dealt a shitty hand from time to time. No point bitching about it."

I realise I sound like one of my own clients.

"Sorry. I'm just venting."

"I'm guessing you don't get to do much of that in your line of work?"

"No. I'm paid to listen to other people's problems."

"And who listens to yours?"

"No one, really. I tend to keep them to myself."

"That can't be healthy."

"I manage."

"Until you can't."

"Sorry?"

"I know fuck all about you, Doc, but I do know when someone needs help. And, whether you want it or not, it's bleedin' obvious you need mine."

He puts his mug down and offers a handshake.

"We got a deal?"

It's an instinctive reaction to reach out whenever you're offered a handshake; born from good manners. This is different; which is why I'm not immediately placing my hand in Clement's. The handshake commits me to the least-worse option, but one with all the ingredients of a bad idea.

Ignoring professional ethics — check.

Partnering with a man who is no stranger to violent outbursts — check.

Indulging someone with an obvious mental illness — check.

I would be the one worthy of sectioning if I shake his hand. It is madness.

However, it's not complete madness. I've got five days

before Kingsland expects me to deliver Cameron Gail or his phone, and even if I enter this partnership for twenty-four hours, I've still got time to change course should it bear no fruit. It's a risk, but a calculated one.

I'm kidding myself — it's a desperate one. I accept his hand. "Deal."

17.

A bundle of letters flop onto the doormat just as I exit the bedroom. Wearily, I gather them up and deposit them on the kitchen table on my way to the kettle. I'm so tired I'm only able to function on a basic level until I've had breakfast. As the kettle rumbles away, I slide two slices of bread into the toaster.

Once my nutritional needs are in hand, I sit down at the table and flick through the post. In amongst the usual bills and junk there's a plain white envelope bearing a stamp. I tear it open and immediately recognise the bright green logo on the letterhead. The letter does little to lift the early morning gloom; confirming my suspension from RightMind until the police officially cease their investigation.

Seeing it in writing jars; not least because a copy of it will now reside in my personnel file. A permanent stain on my career. I've no idea who would have filed that copy, but I wonder if they snuck a peak at the contents. Would they have presumed my innocence or did they tut under their breath and think ill of me? One allegation is bad enough, but if Kingsland fulfils his threat, it'll ruin me no matter what the outcome — my reputation will be damaged beyond repair.

I made a decision late yesterday afternoon and subsequently spent all evening ruing it. The letter has changed my mind again. Agreeing to a visit from Clement at nine o'clock this morning no longer seems such a terrible idea. I've got to sort this out and as much as it pains me to admit it, I made greater progress in a twenty-minute conversation with him than I've achieved on my own in days. Besides, if I'm to follow the advice I offer my clients, acknowledging you need help is the first step in finding a solution.

I finish breakfast and head to the bathroom.

It's just gone eight as I pull on a sweater in the bedroom. Leah stirs beneath the duvet.

"Morning sleepyhead."

"Ugh … what time is it?"

"Five past eight. Are you getting up?"

"Already?"

"You do remember we're expecting a guest at nine?"

She sits up.

"Shit. I forgot."

My wife then scurries off to the bathroom demanding a cup of tea on the way. I head back to the kitchen and put the kettle on for the second time today. I have a suspicion it won't be the last. While I wait, I file away the letter from RightMind along with the bills I'd rather avoid. For today at least, I've got bigger issues to contend with than those of a financial nature.

Tea made, I carry two mugs through to the lounge and put the television on. From the hallway, I hear the bathroom door squeak open.

"Your tea is in here," I call out.

"Thanks."

Showered and dressed in jeans and a sweater, Leah joins me on the sofa.

"Remind me again: what is it you're doing with Clement?"

"He's helping me find a client I'm worried about."

"The same client who's upset you?"

"He hasn't upset me, honey. He's just … it's complicated."

"Too complicated for my feeble mind?"

"No, that's not what I meant. It's complicated because you know I'm not allowed to discuss clients."

"But you can discuss them with a relative stranger?"

"As I said, Clement is just helping me find a young man who's in some bother. The reason he's in such bother is confidential, and I won't be sharing that with anyone. Okay?"

Seemingly satisfied with my response, Leah switches her attention to the mug.

"What have you got planned for the day?" I ask.

"Not much. I might check through those boxes I picked up on Saturday."

"No plans to go out?"

"Is that a question or a suggestion?"

"I was hoping I could ask a favour."

"Go on," she says, eyeing me suspiciously.

"Would you mind popping back to that charity shop for me; just to see if you recognise any of the boxes in the stockroom?"

"I'm not sure I would recognise them."

"I know it's a long shot, but I really need to find that phone."

I can tell by her face she doesn't want to go, and I'm not confident she'll have any luck but I decided last night I have to cover all my bases. Being honest, it'll also keep her out of the way so I can talk freely to Clement when he arrives. I don't want Leah knowing the full extent of my troubles.

"If you speak to the manager, Faith, I'm sure she won't mind you having a look."

"Okay," she sighs. "When do you want me to go?"

"No time like the present."

"Are you trying to get rid of me?"

"No, not at all."

The doorbell rings. Too late.

"I'll get it."

I pad down the hallway and open the front door.

"Mornin', Doc."

"Clement. You're early."

"Worms to catch."

He wipes his feet and steps into the hallway.

"Stick the kettle on," he then demands. "I'm bleedin' parched."

"Yes, sir."

As I turn around, Leah appears in the lounge doorway.

"Good morning, Clement," she coos.

"Mornin', Doll."

I can't be sure, but I'm sure my wife just fluttered her eyelids at our guest.

"Come through to the kitchen, Clement."

As he follows, the hairs on the back of my neck stand up. It's like being followed by a silverback gorilla with a hair trigger temper.

"Have a seat. I'll get you that tea."

"Ta."

124

He unbuttons his donkey jacket to reveal a sleeveless denim jacket over a black t-shirt. He looks no less intimidating; perhaps capable of whipping a silverback gorilla in an arm wrestling contest.

Leah wanders in.

"I'll be off in a minute," she says.

"Great. I do appreciate it."

"Have you offered Clement breakfast?"

"I'm sure he …"

"That'd be smashing," our guest interjects. "Anything but rabbit food."

"Scrambled egg on toast?" Leah suggests.

"Perfect."

Despite my protestations Leah insists on cooking Clement's breakfast before she leaves. I sit down at the table and scribble a demand on the back of an envelope: *Don't talk about what we're doing while Leah is around.* I then slide the envelope across the table. Clement nods.

"So, what do you do for a living then, Doll?" he calls across the kitchen.

"I run a stall. Buying and selling stuff."

"Nice. What kind of stuff?"

"Crap mainly," I mumble under my breath.

"Oh, just second-hand gear, really. Anything I can get my hands on."

"I used to have a mate who ran a stall at Camden Market. Helped him out a few times."

"I've worked at Camden Market loads of times. What's your mate's name?"

"I doubt you'll know him, Doll. It was a long time ago."

"Oh, okay. What about you — what do you do for a living?"

I glare at Clement and shake my head.

"I'm in personal insurance," he answers.

"Really? You don't look the type."

"I deal with the more troublesome policies, don't I, Doc?"

"Um, yes."

"Is that why you're helping David?"

"Yes," I answer on our guest's behalf. "Clement's speciality is finding missing policy holders. Isn't that right?"

"Yeah, it is."

"Well, I hope you find this guy he's been looking for. David has been in a right grump over the last few days."

"I have not," I protest.

"Yes, you have. You even turned down an afternoon in bed with your wife."

"I … um, not in front of our guest, honey."

"You can buy pills for that now," Clement suggests. "Lack of sex drive, floppy cock … seen the ads on TV."

"I don't have any problems in that department, thank you, and please mind your language in front of my wife."

"What did I say?"

"Floppy cock," Leah sniggers, placing a plate of toast on the table.

She then shoots a frosty glare in my direction.

"I'm not a child, David. I've heard a lot worse on the stall."

"Sorry," I mumble.

My wife skips back to the hob and returns with a bowl of scrambled eggs. She unceremoniously dumps the stodgy mess on top of the toast.

"I'm not a great cook," she concedes.

"Nah, it looks triffic, Doll. Cheers."

I leave Clement to demolish his free breakfast and escort my wife into the hallway.

"Best you get off, then," I say, grabbing her coat and handbag from a hook on the wall.

"What's the hurry?"

"I'm concerned someone at the charity shop might find the phone and put it on display."

"Ah, okay. Will Clement still be here when I get back?"

"I'm not sure either of us will be here. Depends how we get on."

"I'll just say goodbye then."

She does exactly that, and returns to the hallway with a grin on her face.

"He's quite a character, isn't he?"

"Yes, he is. I presume you're walking to the charity shop?"

"Yep."

"Good. I might need to use the van at some point."

"Just make sure you fill it up."

"You have my word."

I peck Leah on the cheek and see her out the door.

Returning to the kitchen, Clement has already worked through two slices of toast and most of the scrambled egg. He looks up.

"Missus gone?"

"Yes, thankfully."

"Why don't you want her knowing what we're up to?"

"Without going into detail my wife has a tendency to fret over minor issues. I don't think she'd react well, knowing the real reason you're here."

"Mums the word, eh?"

"Very much so. Anyway, shall we make a start?"

He finishes the last forkful of scrambled egg and sits back in the chair, mug in hand.

"What do you know about this kid?"

"Not a lot. His Facebook page says he's studying chemistry at Oxford but that might be out of date. For all I know, he might have graduated by now, or dropped out. Judging by the state of him my money would be on the latter."

"That's it?"

"Er, more or less. Oh, and there was as a picture of him and a girl on his phone — a girlfriend, presumably."

"What's her name?"

"I don't know."

He shakes his head.

"Tell me again what he said when you met. Word for word."

I think back to the conversation in my office, and the brief chat we had in The Duke.

"There's not a lot to tell, really. The first time I met Cameron, he just wandered in to our charity, saying he needed help. I sat him down in my office and he appeared to be in the grip of a drug-induced episode. He'd taken something called Kimbo; a synthetic drug he'd been using for twenty-two days. I thought it odd at the time."

"Why?"

"Drug users aren't renowned for diarising their usage."

"And what's Kimbo when it's at home?"

"No idea. I know most of the drugs in common use, and the variety of street names they go by. My colleague checked the database and there was no mention of a drug called Kimbo."

Clement takes a moment to slurp slowly from his mug; cogs whirring somewhere behind those malevolent eyes.

"What are you thinking, Clement?"

"I'm thinking there's only one lead."

"And that is?"

"Oxford Uni."

"I don't follow."

"How does a kid smart enough to get into a top uni end up doing drugs and living in some shithole in Camden?"

"Drugs wreck lives, and sometimes with alarming efficiency."

"Yeah, but the kid was studying chemistry. Don't you think it's bleedin' odd he'd get hooked on drugs made in a lab?"

"Granted, you'd think he'd know better than anyone."

Clement gets to his feet.

"Come on then," he orders. "Let's get going."

"Where?"

"Oxford. You got a motor?"

"My wife has a van, but hold on a moment. What's the point in going to Oxford if Cameron Gail is living a mile down the road?"

"Unless you wanna go bang on the door of every gaff in Camden we need to find out exactly who we're looking for."

"I don't see how going to Oxford will help us find Cameron Gail."

"It probably won't but you're missing the point. This ain't just about finding the kid — it's about finding out why he's so important to Kingsland."

"Does that matter?"

"Course it does. You can't stop a bloke like that unless you understand what his game is. If you ain't found the kid or his phone by Sunday, what you gonna do?"

"I haven't thought that far ahead, but I won't deny I'm terrified at what he might do. I'm already on police bail."

"Think of it another way, Doc. Kingsland is a snake, and he wants you to feed him. You can spend days searching for food but if you don't find any come Sunday, you'll be his supper. Unless you wanna be eaten alive we better find a knife in case we need to cut the bastard's head off."

"And information is that knife?"

"Yeah, if you like. We go to Oxford and ask around; see if anyone knows your kid and if they've heard any whispers about what he was up to."

There is some logic in Clement's thinking but it still feels like a waste of time. I might have more luck standing on the street and waiting for Cameron Gail to wander past.

"Besides," he adds. "It'll give you a chance to hear about my mate's problem."

I smile but I'm inwardly scouring my mind for a plausible excuse to say no. Oxford is a ninety-minute drive away, and that's about eighty-eight minutes longer than I want to be trapped in a van with Clement and his psychosis.

"What's the matter?" he asks.

"Err, nothing. I'm just considering alternative options."

"You dick around any longer and the only options you'll need to consider will be granite or limestone."

"Eh?"

"Your wife's gravestone."

A troubling point, succinctly delivered. I've been so busy considering the implications for my career I've selfishly overlooked the threat to Leah's safety.

"I'll get my coat."

129

18.

It is exactly one week today I first met Cameron Gail.

One week.

Now, I'm in the driver's seat of a beaten-up van, crawling through the West London traffic towards the motorway, with a mentally ill freak of nature in the passenger's seat. If it wasn't for the blaring horns and stench of fumes leaking into the cabin, I could almost convince myself this is just a bad dream.

It never ceases to amaze me how quickly one's fortune can turn for the worse. Even so, this is ridiculous.

"Where do you wanna start then, Doc?"

"Start?"

"You know, helping my mate out."

Now ridiculous and absurd. This is not how I do my job, nor what I'm trained or qualified to do. I should at least hear him out, though. I owe him that much.

"Err, would you like to talk about your friend's apparent death?"

"It's your call."

"I'm interested to hear what he remembers about it. Perhaps his death wasn't literal."

"Meaning?"

"Perhaps he experienced some kind of traumatic event and as a consequence, his mind shut out all previous memories; leaving behind a distorted version of his past. It's been known to happen in cases of PTSD."

"What's that?"

"Post-traumatic stress disorder; common amongst service personnel. You can only imagine some of the horrific scenes they have to witness."

I glance across. Clement is staring intently at the queue of traffic ahead.

"Do you think he remembers anything?" I ask.

"Bits."

"Do you feel like talking me through it?"

"He was in this boozer … The Three Monks in Camden. Ain't there no more. He'd just finished playing cards and wanted one for the road, and he was chattin' to the barmaid …"

"Does he remember her name?"

Asking him to focus on minor details is a way to push through the false reality.

"Babs," he replies immediately.

"What did Babs look like?"

"Blonde, early thirties, with tits you could park your bike between. She wore this perfume which always reminded … my mate … of strawberry bonbons."

A crude but interesting perception.

"So, he was chatting to Babs, and then what happened?"

"Empties his glass and says goodbye … nah, wait. Babs asked if he wanted to hang around until closing time … he thought she might be up for a bit of fun."

"Fun?"

"Use your imagination, Doc."

"Ah, okay."

"Anyway, he said no. Early start the next day."

"Carry on. What did he do next?"

"He walked across the bar and out the door."

"What was the weather like?"

"It'd been pissing down as there were puddles everywhere."

"Did he turn left or right?"

"Turned right and then right again, down an alleyway. Bit of a shortcut back to his digs."

"What happened next?"

"He takes a dozen steps and then … he pats his jacket pocket looking for his fags. They ain't there … must have left them on the bar. He stops, and just as he turns around he catches sight of a cricket bat swinging through the air. Split second later he's out for the count."

"Did he see who was swinging the bat?"

"Yeah, he did."

Blue lights suddenly flash in the wing mirror followed by the whoop of a siren.

"Bugger."

"What's up?"

"I think we're being pulled over."

"Triffic."

I pull part way on to the kerb and come to a stop. Staring intently in the wing mirror, I lower the window as a police officer gets out of his car and approaches.

"Morning, officer. Is there a problem?"

"You've got a brake light out, sir."

"Oh, right. I'll be sure to get it sorted today."

"Ensure you do, please."

The policeman then looks beyond me, towards my passenger. Clement continues to stare straight ahead; no acknowledgement.

"I'll let you get on your way."

"Thanks, officer."

I close the window and pull away.

"Where were we?" I ask.

"Let's just leave it for now," Clement replies. "We need to decide what we're gonna do when we get to Oxford."

"Fair enough."

"You ever been there before?"

"Plenty of times. My family live in a village about seven miles west of Oxford."

"So, you know the university?"

"I know there is a science faculty and a chemistry research lab. Once we get close, I'll check the exact address but I know roughly where it is."

He nods.

"You ever been to Oxford?"

"Probably. Can't remember."

"Because it was so long ago?"

"Yeah."

"Can I ask how old you are?"

"Forty-something. I stopped keeping track."

"Are you married? Family?"

"No, and no?"

I get the distinct impression Clement isn't one for idle chitchat. I'm not one for sitting in silence.

"Do you mind if I ask you a question?"

"Why do people say that? If you wanna know something, just ask. Don't fanny around asking permission."

"Okay, okay. It's about that night by the garages."

"Spit it out."

"You said you beat up drug dealers as a hobby. Did you mean that?"

"'Spose."

"Why do you do it?"

"Why not?"

"A ton of reasons, not least because it strikes me as a fairly reckless pursuit. Many of them now carry a knife, and some a gun."

"Don't much give a shit."

"It doesn't bother you: the prospect of being shot dead the next time you decide to beat up a random drug dealer?"

"No."

"And have you questioned your motives? You said you had anger issues."

"That's right."

"What reason do you have to be angry?"

"Same as you."

"Me? What am I angry about?"

He turns to face me.

"You hate living in London, right?"

"Passionately. It's the polar opposite of where I grew up."

"You hate everything about the place?"

"Almost everything."

"So, you know exactly how I feel. This ain't where I'm supposed to be — it ain't my home and I don't wanna be here."

"Where is home then?"

"I don't reckon you want me to answer that, Doc."

"Try me."

"It don't matter. All that matters is I need to leave this place 'cos it's doing my fucking nut in."

"Just leave then, if it's that bad."

133

"Yeah, right," he scoffs. "Like it's that easy."

Having my own valid reasons why I'm trapped in London, I'm not minded to question him on the mechanics of why he can't leave.

"You're angry because you can't leave? Is that right?"

"In a nutshell."

"Is it a worry that this rage might eventually consume you?"

"Nothing worries me, Doc, other than getting back where I belong."

"And what if you can't get back?"

"I'd rather be dead. Anything has gotta be better than this fucked-up existence."

"Are you saying you've experienced suicidal thoughts?"

"Trust me, I've tried. Can't do it."

"I've heard that many times before. People reach a point where they genuinely feel the only way out is to end it all. The only reason they arrive in my office is because the act of ending one's own life is mercifully more difficult than the theory."

"It ain't 'cos I don't have the bottle. Dying ain't as easy as you think."

"No?"

"Last year, I got into a scuffle and ended up falling off a bleedin' cliff. Fell about a hundred feet onto rocks and then got washed away in a storm."

"Christ. How on earth did you survive that?"

"Must have been divine intervention," he sneers. "Weren't my time, apparently. I woke up on a beach without a scratch."

His foolhardy attitude towards his own mortality is perplexing. With schizophrenia, the opposite is usually true and sufferers often become increasingly anxious about death, sometimes to obsessive levels. Obviously, it is human nature to fear our own demise but we all have in-built mechanisms to deal with it. Schizophrenia messes with that mechanism and the fear of death can become overwhelming.

"Would it be fair to say you're not afraid of dying, Clement?"

"It would be fair to say I'm tired of living. That's why I'm here."

"Can you expand on that?"

"I need to fix whatever this is and you can only fix something when you know for sure why it's broken. You're gonna help me work that out."

"I never said I'd help you work anything out. That wasn't the deal."

"Don't get your knickers in a twist, Doc. I ain't asking you to diagnose what's wrong with me. I just wanna know *if* there's something wrong with me."

"I can't make any promises; you know that?"

"Man after my own heart. I ain't expecting promises."

He turns and stares out the side window. I'm curious enough I'd like to ask more questions but I know there's nothing to gain by forcing anyone to talk. He'll tell me more when he's ready.

We finally escape the traffic and close in on the motorway.

"Stick the radio on, Doc."

I prod the power button and the aggressive tones of a rap artist leak from the speakers. Leah's taste in radio station differs greatly from mine.

"What the fuck is this noise?" Clement grumbles.

"You're not a fan of rap music, I assume?"

"This ain't music."

"I agree."

I push a button to change the station.

"Rolling Stones," Clement then comments. "That's more like it."

As the road signs change from green to blue I turn to ask him a question. His eyes are closed and his head lopped to the side. It looks like I won't be hearing much from the other side of the van for the rest of the journey.

Instead, I focus on the grey tarmac stretching into the distance towards a bleak sky. I've made this journey so many times when visiting my parents and usually there's a smile on my face which broadens the further away from London I get. On this occasion I'm gripped by the kind of doleful malaise usually reserved for the return leg.

As the miles pass I try to ignore the reason I'm making the trip. It's not so easy to ignore the slumbering giant next to me as he snores away. It becomes unbearable so, when I pull off the motorway nine miles east of our destination, I try to wake him up.

"Clement. Clement."

No response.

"Clement!"

"What?" he mumbles, his eyes still shut.

"We're nearly in Oxford."

He puffs a long sigh and turns to the window, and the view of open fields.

"I hate the sticks."

"You hate open space, fresh air, and trees?"

"There's fuck all here. Nowhere to buy a pint or pack of fags, and no people."

"The lack of crowds is a key attraction in my book. This is my home."

"Where you all have to marry your own cousins, right?"

"That isn't only an outdated stereotype but highly offensive."

"Your missus is a Londoner, ain't she?" he asks, ignoring his previous offence.

"Yes, and before you ask, no we're not related."

"I know. She's too good looking to be related to you."

"I'm not sure if I should take that as a compliment or an insult."

"Take it how you like," he shrugs. "No skin off my arse."

"Have you always been so forthright in your opinions?"

"Speak as I find, Doc. Ask me a question and you'll get an honest answer, like it or not."

I suppose it's a preferable quality to insincerity or blatant lying. Less can be said of his general language, though.

A tune comes on the radio which Clement appears to like, and he turns the volume up. I focus on the driving as the fields and meadows give way to the semi-urban architecture of Oxford. Once we're within a mile of the town centre I pull over for a minute to confirm our exact destination. It's only seven minutes away which means we don't have long to discuss our strategy.

"What exactly are we supposed to do when we get there?" I ask.

"You're heading to the department where this kid studies, right?"

"The chemistry research laboratory in Mansfield Road, yes."

"Simple enough, Doc. Stroll up to the reception desk and ask to speak to him."

"Speak to Cameron Gail? But, we know he's not there."

"We know bugger all."

"And what if they say he's unavailable? How do I get past that?"

"Just use your loaf," he huffs, shaking his head. "The kid was a patient of yours, right? Just say you've got concerns about him, and you're trying to establish he's not dead in a ditch somewhere."

It's not a million miles away from the truth. I am deeply concerned about Cameron Gail but more for my own selfish reasons.

"Right, and what are we hoping they'll say?"

"Dunno, but it'd be handy to know his bird's name. It's also worth asking if he had any mates who might know where he's got to."

"Okay, but feel free to interject if I forget anything."

"I ain't coming in with you."

"What? Why not?"

"Are you pulling my chain? They'll take one look at me and call security."

"You have a point."

"I'll wait by the van — give me a chance to have a smoke and mingle with the locals."

"Try not to beat anyone up, please."

"I'll do my best, Doc."

I turn into Mansfield Road and slow to a crawl in search of a parking space. Oxford is one of the least car-friendly cities in the country, but thankfully, there are still a few areas where you can park on the street if you're lucky. I find a space and pull in.

Clement clambers out of the passenger's door before I've turned the engine off.

I get out and join him on the pavement as he lights a cigarette.

"I'd offer you one, but I'm guessing you don't smoke, Doc."

"You guess correctly."

"You drink?"

"Rarely."

"We're gonna have fun, ain't we?" he frowns.

"I'm not here to have fun, Clement. I'm not even sure why I'm here."

"To save your arse. Now, you gonna go ask some questions?"

I frown back.

"I suppose so."

19.

Leaving Clement to pollute his lungs, I cross the road and approach the imposing glass and tile building which houses the chemistry research laboratory, according to the blue sign at the main gate. People who've never visited Oxford assume it's all steeples and spires, but there are many contemporary buildings dotted around the city and most of them are less pleasing on the eye. This is one of them.

I follow the arrow which points towards the main reception along a narrow road skirting the side of the building. I'm then greeted by a set of steps leading to a glass-fronted vestibule. With nerves and indecision mounting I push through one of the glass doors.

The interior of the building is more impressive than the exterior. I make my way towards an enquiry desk staffed by two women; one of whom is chatting away on the phone.

"Morning," I chirp to the other receptionist.

She looks up from a pile of papers and smiles. Her spectacles are way too big for such an elfin-like face.

"Good morning. What can I do for you?"

"I'm making enquiries regarding one of your students: Cameron Gail."

"In what context?"

"It's, um, a little sensitive so I hope I can rely upon your discretion."

"Absolutely you can," she replies in a sincere tone.

"My name is David Nunn and I'm a mental health counsellor based in North London."

I pull out my wallet and hand her a business card.

"I've spoken to Cameron on two occasions of late and, without breaking confidence, I'm extremely worried about his state of mind. I've driven up from London this morning in the hope I might be able to check he's okay. I understand he's studying chemistry here at Oxford."

"I can check his attendance record if you like? He might well

139

be in today."

"That would be great; just to put my mind at rest."

She taps a keyboard and then stares intently at the screen behind.

"According to our records, Cameron Gail no longer studies here."

"Ahh, that's a pity. When did he graduate?"

"He didn't. It seems he dropped out in November last year."

"Which year of his degree was he in?"

"His third."

This revelation raises another question. Why study for two long years and then give up in the third?

"I don't suppose it says why he dropped out?"

"I'm afraid not."

"Right."

I think I've just hit a brick wall. If Cameron Gail no longer studies here, it's unlikely any of his classmates will know where he might be.

"I'm sorry I can't be of more help."

"No, I appreciate your time. I guess I'll have to continue the search back in London."

I flash a half-smile at the receptionist. I'm about to turn and walk away when she suddenly calls out to someone behind me.

"Alan? Have you got a sec?"

"You're in luck," the receptionist says to me. "Dr Whiting was one of Cameron's tutors and he might be able to shed some light on the circumstances."

We're joined by a studious-looking guy in a white coat. A good decade my senior and slightly scruffy, he has that generic tutor look about him.

"Alan, this chap has been asking about one of your former students."

I offer a hand and introduce myself.

"Alan Whiting," he confirms, accepting the handshake.

I repeat the conversation I had with the receptionist and issue another business card.

"Basically, Dr Whiting, I'm deeply concerned about

Cameron; hence my visit."

"We should probably talk in private. Come through to my office."

He turns and strides away. I thank the receptionist and scurry after Dr Whiting.

Deep in the bowels of the building we finally come to a stop outside the Doctor's office door. He unlocks it and ushers me in with a degree of impatient urgency.

"Grab a seat," he orders.

Like every tutor's office I've ever been in, this one is just as much a fire hazard due to the excess of paperwork and books.

Dr Whiting sits down opposite and checks his watch.

"We'll need to be brief," he says flatly. "Lecture in fifteen minutes."

"No problem."

"I didn't realise Cameron had issues with his mental health. He certainly didn't give any impression he was struggling."

"Talking in general terms it's not uncommon for people to suffer in silence. Outwardly, you'd never tell they have a problem."

"Well, Cameron hid his problem well and I can't offer you any specific information about his whereabouts. However, I might be able to fill in a few blanks on his time here."

"Anything would be useful. I hear he dropped out in November and I was wondering why?"

"Your guess is as good as mine, Mr Nunn. I spoke to him on the phone and he was decidedly vague about his reasons."

"Was he struggling with the coursework?"

"God, no," he coughs. "Quite the opposite. Cameron Gail was one of the most gifted students I've ever taught."

"Doesn't that make his decision to quit even more puzzling?"

"It happens from time to time, particularly with the brightest and best."

"How so?"

"They're lured away by pharmaceutical companies. There is such competition for new talent, some companies are willing to headhunt the cream of the crop before they've even graduated, rather than wait and risk losing them. They're offered a healthy salary and a promise they can complete their degree on a part-time basis."

"And you think Cameron might have received such an offer?"

"I don't know, but he mentioned an opportunity he wished to pursue. I pressed him on the detail but he wasn't forthcoming."

It's an interesting theory, but it doesn't really help my current plight. However, there is one other plausible explanation why a young student might suddenly drop their studies. It's an explanation one or two love-struck students used in my time when they quit.

"Did he ever mention a girlfriend?"

"He was dating. I met her once when I bumped into Cameron off-campus. Pretty young lady."

"Blonde hair and blue eyes?"

"That makes her sound like a cliché, but yes."

"I don't suppose you know her name?"

"He told me but I've got an awful memory for names. You could ask his friend, Dylan … "

The Doctor's face contorts as he tries to drag the surname from the recesses of a no-doubt busy mind.

" … Riley. Dylan Riley."

"Is he a student here?"

"That's a matter of opinion," he replies with obvious disdain. "He's studying music. A bad influence in my opinion, but that's creative types for you."

The Doctor checks his watch again.

"Should you find Cameron, and presuming he's in the right state of mind, could you try to talk some sense in to him? It's criminal a young man with such aptitude should give up his studies."

"If I find him, I'll pass on your advice."

He gets to his feet and offers a handshake.

"Thanks for your time, Dr Whiting."

I'm ushered back to the reception area where I'm left to make my own way to the exit. I wander back to the van to find

Clement leaning up against the bonnet; arms folded.

"Good news?" he asks as I approach.

"Yes, and no."

I relay what I learnt about Cameron quitting.

"So, he ain't been here since November?"

"Nope, but his tutor mentioned the name of a friend. We could try speaking to him; see if he's heard from Cameron or at least knows his girlfriend's name."

"How do we find him?"

"He's studying music so I guess we head to the music faculty."

"Which is where?"

A quick check on my phone reveals the answer.

"It's less than a mile away, but parking is a real issue in that part of the city."

"You wanna walk then?"

I don't, but neither do I want to spend an hour driving around looking for a parking space.

"Guess so."

I lock the van and double-check our direction of travel: up Mansfield Road towards Holywell Street.

"It's this way."

We walk silently along until we reach the junction and turn right into a narrow street lined with ancient three-storey buildings. The pavement is equally narrow and Clement is forced to follow in my footsteps. Eventually, the vista opens up as we reach the busier part of the city which, even in January, is swarming with students and tourists alike.

"It's a proper old manor, ain't it?" Clement remarks, as he inspects several of the historical buildings we pass.

"Eight hundred years of history."

"Good to see they ain't knocking shit down like they do elsewhere."

"By elsewhere, you mean London?"

"Yeah. Bloody cranes and demolition crews everywhere these days."

"Thankfully, the planners in Oxford aren't so enthusiastic

about redevelopment as they are in London."

"It shows."

As we wander through the streets, Clement seems keen to take his time; drinking in the architecture and seemingly impressed. When we enter the High Street, he dawdles past an antique book store, staring in the window as we pass.

"Do you have an interest in history, Clement?"

"Don't everyone?"

"To some degree, perhaps."

"You don't understand the past, you can't make sense of the future."

"That's rather profound."

"Just common sense," he shrugs.

We press on and take a left into St Aldgate's; home to the Oxford Faculty of Music. The building itself is a few hundred yards along and we arrive a minute before noon.

"What's this kid's name?" Clement asks, as we loiter by the front gates.

"Dylan Riley."

"Hold on."

He then approaches two young women who have just left the building and are making their way down the path towards us. They glance at each other before one of them says something to Clement. Words are exchanged for a good minute or so before he wanders back down the path.

"What did you say to them?" I ask.

"I asked if they know the kid we're looking for. They've just stopped for lunch and he'll be out shortly."

"They told you that?"

"Yeah, and what he looks like."

"You didn't threaten them, did you?"

The two young women pass by; both seemingly unscathed by their ordeal if their smiles are anything to go by.

"What do you reckon, Doc?"

"Sorry."

"Yeah, you should be. I don't know what's wrong with me

144

but I ain't no sociopath."

"Okay, message received and understood."

Clement frowns before he turns his attention back to the path.

"This could be our kid," he mumbles. "Best you speak to him."

Clement's suspect is a tall, thin guy with neck-length black hair; his attire styled on an Edwardian dandy. Even if I hadn't just seen him leave the music faculty, I'd have guessed he's studying one of the arts. I step in front of him as he passes the gates.

"Dylan Riley?"

"Maybe. You are?"

"My name is David Nunn. I'm trying to track down Cameron Gail."

"I couldn't be less interested," he replies dismissively.

He turns and walks away. Clement nods I should follow.

"Excuse me, Dylan," I say, catching up with him. "It is rather important I track Cameron down. Have you spoken to him recently?"

"Go away. I'm in a rush."

"Please, I need to find …"

Blanking me he crosses the road without another word.

"Fuck's sake," Clement mumbles. "Come on."

We cross the road and catch up with Dylan just as he's passing a campus clothing store. Clement ups his stride until he's three paces ahead of the pompous student. He then stops and turns around, blocking Dylan Riley's path.

"My mate asked you a question," Clement growls. "I'd suggest you answer him."

Dylan turns to me.

"Tell your boyfriend to get out of my way."

To our immediate left, a narrow, cobbled lane leads away from St Aldgate's. Before I can respond to Dylan Riley, Clement grabs his upper arm and yanks him into the lane. There, he shoves the young man to the ground.

"Clement," I hiss. "What are you doing?"

"Having a chat with this gobby little fucker."

He steps over to the stunned student and orders him to get up. Dylan Riley complies; the look of sneering contempt gone.

"Last chance, dickhead. You gonna answer our questions?"

Clement steps ominously forward and Riley steps back until his shoulder blades meet the wall behind. With nowhere else to go, he nods. This is more an interrogation than a questioning, but at least Riley appears compliant.

"When did you last speak to Cameron Gail?" I ask.

"I don't know. Ages ago."

"Specifically?"

"He came to my father's birthday party in November."

"And you haven't spoken to him since?"

"Only a few text messages. We had a falling out."

"Over?"

"His dim-witted girlfriend said I made a pass at her. She should be so fortunate."

I'm tempted to ask if the claim was true but it's irrelevant. What little I know about Dylan Riley I'd say he's the type who would.

"What's his girlfriend's name?"

"Why is that your business?"

There's a slight air of cockiness in his tone.

"Just answer him," Clement demands.

"I don't know who you two are but Dylan Riley will not be intimidated."

He then looks up at Clement.

"The police station is only a hundred metres down the road. Touch me again and I'll yell so hard they'll be here in seconds."

Confidence restored, he straightens his jacket and slides a step to the right, testing the water to prepare for departure, I'd guess.

Clement puffs a sigh and his body language suggests an admission of defeat. Riley detects a lower threat level and risks another step. He barely has a chance to plant his foot when Clement flicks out an arm. No time to yell, a hand is suddenly gripped around the young student's throat, pinning him against the wall.

"You are starting to piss me off," Clement snarls. "Now, if you ever wanna play whatever fucking instrument you play again, answer the question."

"Clement," I interject. "I don't think he'll tell us anything while you're choking him to death."

He turns to face Riley.

"You gonna play nicely, dickhead?"

Riley manages to nod and Clement releases his grip.

"Kimberley," he then gasps. "Kimberley Bowhurst."

"Do you have her phone number?"

A slight shake of the head as he rubs his throat.

"How can we get in touch with her?"

"She lives in … in Wandsworth … works for the local council in finance, or something."

Clement turns to me.

"Back to London?"

"Guess so."

Just when I think we're done with Dylan Riley, Clement throws another question at him.

"Do you intend to have kids?"

"What? I, um …"

"You tell anyone about our little chat and I'll come back, rip your bollocks off, and ram them down your throat. Clear?"

"Clear," he whimpers.

"Good."

Clement turns and strolls away, whistling to himself.

I'm about to mouth an apology to Riley but, on reflection, I can't muster enough sympathy for the arrogant young man. I follow Clement.

"Spare me the lecture," he says before I've opened my mouth.

"Pardon?"

"We got what we needed. Sometimes you've got to play dirty."

"I know, and just for the record I wasn't going to lecture you. The smarmy little sod brought it on himself."

Clement lights a cigarette and turns to me.

"I'm glad you said that, Doc, 'cos I've got a feeling it won't be the last time I need to get my hands dirty before we find the kid."

"What makes you say that?"

He stares back at me, deadpan.

"Just a niggling voice in my head."

20.

The dictionary definition of normal is thus: *typical, usual or ordinary; what you would expect.*

When that adjective is applied to people, it doesn't sit right. No one individual is ordinary or typical, and I've long since learnt expectations are seldom correct if you pre-judge.

Over the last few days my opinion has been validated. The man next to me in the passenger's seat — the man with no surname — is not normal on any scale. What I can't determine is if he is abnormal: *different from what is usual or expected, especially in a way that is worrying, harmful or unwanted.*

Clement is undoubtedly different from what is usual, and I can't deny his behaviour is worrying, and occasionally unwanted. What I'm yet to determine is if it's harmful, and if so, to who?

The view from the van shifts to a palette of muddy greens and greys again. In the summer the rural Oxfordshire countryside is a sight to behold. Now, there's an undeniable bleakness to it; not helped by a sombre Pink Floyd tune playing on the radio. I turn the volume down.

"Would you like to pick up our conversation again?"

"What conversation?"

"About your friend."

"'Spose so."

"We don't have to."

"I know, but I've been avoiding it for too bleedin' long. Won't sort itself."

"That is true. So, shall we talk about your friend's life, before he … died?"

"Ain't much to tell, Doc. He was just an average bloke."

"Did he have any issues with his mental health? Any bouts of depression or anxiety?"

"Weren't none of that back then. If you were a bit down in the dumps, you'd never tell anyone and you sure as hell wouldn't go see a quack about it."

"It existed, Clement. It just wasn't widely recognised."

"You ever consider folks were better off not knowing?"

"What do you mean?"

"There was this bloke who used to drink in my local. Happy Harry we called him, on account he was a right gloomy bastard … sort of bloke who'd win the Pools but moan about the walk to the bank to cash his cheque. If a doctor had told Harry he was suffering from depression, he'd have probably topped himself."

"Why would he have killed himself?"

"'Cos Happy Harry knew who he was and accepted it; even played up to it sometimes. You tell him he's only that way 'cos his wiring is fucked, and suddenly the bloke don't know who he is anymore."

"But, he might have been able to deal with his condition."

"Not everyone wants a label stuck on 'em, Doc. Ignorance is bliss — ain't that what they say?"

"We'll agree to differ on that point. Do you still speak to him?"

"Nah. He's dead."

"Oh, I'm sorry. When did he die?"

"Either six years ago, or forty-eight years ago … depends if I'm crazy or not."

"Your friend, I think you mean."

"Yeah, him."

"Moving swiftly along. I think we've strayed from the subject."

"What else do you wanna know?"

"Was your friend a religious man?"

"Meaning?"

"Did he have beliefs in a certain religion? Did he attend church, for example?"

"Why do you wanna know that?"

"I'm just exploring the resurrection angle. It would be helpful to know if your friend was a Christian."

"Who said he was resurrected?"

"You told me he died and then miraculously rose decades later. What else would you call it if not a resurrection?"

Clement stares into the footwell and slowly strokes his moustache.

"Ain't ever thought of it like that," he says in a low voice.

I once read a study which suggested about one-third of the schizophrenia sufferers in a sample group were highly involved in religious communities. Indeed, there have been many examples, particularly in America, of preachers and cult leaders suffering from some form of delusional schizophrenia; only diagnosed after they've attempted to organise a mass suicide.

"Would you agree there is some religious connotation here, Clement?"

Rather than answer, he continues to stare into the footwell.

"O child of need, who shall be thy steed?" he then mumbles to himself. "To carry thou on, tho hope be gone."

"Is that from the Bible?"

"It's from *a* bible."

"What does it mean?"

"Couldn't tell you. That's the only bit I remember."

"But you think it has some meaning?"

He looks up and turns to me.

"Why do you listen to crazies all day, Doc?"

"They're not crazy, thank you. And to answer your question: it's my job to help people."

"Yeah, but to what end?"

"I don't understand. It's a vocation, not a journey."

"What if it ain't? What if you're meant to do your job 'cos it's part of a bigger picture?"

"If you're suggesting that picture has a religious frame, you're way off course because I'm deeply agnostic. I believe in people, not Gods."

"And you're nailed-on right about that, are you?"

"I said I'm agnostic, not an atheist. When someone shows me definitive proof of a greater power, I'll happily concede the truth. Anyway, is there a point to your question?"

"Just wondered what you thought. Maybe my mate's job is part of a bigger picture, and that's why he's stuck where he is."

"And what might that job be?"

"Fuck knows."

He turns the radio up again and shuts his eyes.

I turn my attention back to the road, knowing I've only gleaned one conclusion from our brief conversation: Clement is the most anti-social travel companion you could ask for. Everything else just enforces how deeply complex his condition is. If I were a qualified psychiatrist, I could probably make a name for myself writing papers about the denim-clad conundrum.

The motorway miles pass by in a blur of thoughts; perhaps more optimistic than those on the outward journey. We may not have found Cameron Gail yet, but knowing his girlfriend's name, and that she lives in London, is a step forward. The only reason I'm not as positive as I might be is Cameron's declaration about a bedsit in Camden. Why, if he's in such trouble, is he not staying with his girlfriend in Wandsworth?

I still don't have an answer by the time we re-enter the pedestrian London traffic.

"Home, sweet home," Clement yawns.

"Oh, you're awake."

"Did I miss anything?"

"No."

"Thought as much. What's the time?"

"Just gone two."

"No wonder I'm bleedin' famished."

He then looks out of the side window.

"We're near Paddington. I know a decent cafe not far from the station."

"Can't you wait until we get to Wandsworth?"

"'Spose."

He folds his arms and stares ahead.

"I never asked: where do you live, Clement?"

"Here and there."

"What does that mean?"

"It means I live wherever I kip for the night."

"You're not homeless are you?"

"Nah. I always find somewhere."

"It's bloody expensive living in London, don't you think?"

"Depends who you know and what favours you can call in, but yeah. There was a time you could find a flat in a cheaper part of town but those days are long gone. Camden used to be a shit-hole, but a cheap shit-hole. Fuck knows how anyone can afford to live there now."

"I definitely can't. I can barely afford to live in Kentish Town."

"Why don't you move back to the sticks then? Much cheaper out there ain't it?"

"Leah doesn't want to leave London. It's like a security blanket."

"You always do what your missus tells you to?"

"It's complicated."

"What's complicated about it? You wear the trousers, don't you?"

"That's not how our marriage works, Clement."

"Ain't it? Why do you treat her like a kid then?"

"Excuse me?"

"Just sayin' what I see, Doc. You need to be less whiney and more assertive — birds like a proper man, not a bleedin' schoolteacher."

"Thanks for the relationship advice but we're perfectly happy, thank you."

"Yeah, right," he snorts. "Seems I ain't the only deluded mug. Still, it's your life, your marriage — fuck it up how you like."

Annoyed by Clement's crass assumptions, I over-rev the engine and nearly crash into the back of a bus.

"Want me to drive?" he asks.

"No, thank you."

The frosty atmosphere remains for the duration of our journey. It's not healthy and, as I pull into a car park near Wandsworth Town Hall, I offer an olive branch.

"Shall we grab a quick sandwich? My treat."

"Yeah, go on then."

After paying the exorbitant parking charge, we make our way

to the nearest eatery, which happens to be Pret A Manger.
Clement appears less than impressed at the menu.

"Why the fuck does everything have avocado in it?"

"It's popular."

"And what's gluten-free?"

"Free from gluten."

"Yeah, I'm not a complete moron. I meant what's gluten?"

"I'm not entirely sure but I think it's a protein found in wheat."

"What's it taste like?"

"Err, I don't think it tastes of anything."

"Why take it out then?"

"Because some people are intolerant to gluten."

He shakes his head.

"Everyone is intolerant to something these days. Even bloody sarnies."

He begrudgingly settles on ham and cheese with gluten. I choose the same and pay at the counter. A minute after leaving, Clement's sandwich is no more.

"You'll get indigestion," I remark as we walk.

"Don't suffer."

"Lucky you."

We reach Wandsworth Town Hall; an impressive Art Deco building. The council offices, however, are housed in a hideously bland extension attached to the side.

"What were the planners thinking?" I remark, as we approach.

"Like two birds in a nightclub," Clement replies.

"I don't follow."

"It's like when you and a mate go out on the pull and spot a couple of birds. One's always much better looking than the other."

"What a judgemental attitude."

"Marry your missus for her wit and wisdom, did you?"

I reply with a disapproving frown.

"Thought not," he huffs.

Clement follows as I enter the reception area through a set of double doors. Ahead of us there's a desk manned by a twenty-something guy who looks on the edge of a nervous breakdown.

"What's the nature of your enquiry?" he asks wearily.

"I was hoping to speak to one of your colleagues, Kimberley Bowhurst. I believe she works in the finance department."

"Do you have an appointment?"

"Um, no. I didn't know we needed one."

"I'm afraid you'll have to contact the finance department and make an appointment."

"And how do I do that?"

"You can email them, or call. Would you like the number or their email address?"

"But I'm here, now. Can't you just call up and ask if Miss Bowhurst is free?"

"No, you must contact them directly."

"Please, can't you just …"

Clement steps up beside me and stares down at the guy behind the desk.

"Come on mate," he pleads. "Do a fellow Gooner a favour, won't you?"

"You're an Arsenal fan?" the guy replies.

"Forty-odd years. To be honest with you, I don't get along much these days — too expensive, and I preferred Highbury."

"I saw my first ever game at the old Highbury stadium."

"I went and had a look at the old place a few years back. Broke my heart seeing it."

"It's not the same, and neither is the team, unfortunately."

"Lost again at the weekend, I heard."

The guy nods, but then looks across at me.

"Who did you want to see?"

"Kimberley Bowhurst."

"Take a seat. I'll give her a call."

"You're a gent," Clement says. "Cheers."

We retreat to a row of chairs while Kimberley Bowhurst is summoned.

"How did you know he was an Arsenal fan?" I ask.

"The red and white coaster with the Arsenal badge on it was

a bit of a giveaway."

"Oh, right. Nicely done."

"I ain't all about beating the shit out of people."

"Good to know. Anyway, I didn't have you down as an Arsenal fan. I thought you'd be more likely to follow Millwall."

"Do me a favour, Doc."

"I used to watch Arsenal when I first moved to London. Who's your favourite all-time player?"

"Had a few but John Radford was a bloody good striker, and Arsenal through and through. Met him in a pub in Holloway once; a few hours after we beat Spurs one-nil. He scored the only goal so I bought him a pint."

"Can't say I've ever heard of him."

"What about you? Favourite player?"

"I'd have to say Thierry Henry?"

"The French bloke? Never saw him play."

"No, but everyone accepts he's the greatest Arsenal player of all time."

"Yeah, but not my time."

A door swings open and a petite blonde woman hurries up to the enquiry desk. She exchanges words with the guy we spoke to and he points in our direction.

We both stand up as she approaches. I immediately recognise her as the same girl in the photo on Cameron's phone, although the sunny smile isn't evident.

"Kimberley Bowhurst?" I ask.

"Yes. You wanted to see me?"

I introduce myself, and then Clement.

"Alright, Doll."

If I were a woman, I don't think I'd like to be referred to as a 'doll', but Clement seems to get away with it. I don't think I'll ever truly understand women.

"Thanks for seeing us, Kimberley. We're trying to track down Cameron. Cameron Gail."

In a heartbeat, her demeanour changes.

"I've told you I don't know where he is," she hisses. "Why can't you leave me alone?"

"Err, I think there's possibly some confusion here."

"Who sent you?"

"No one."

I retrieve a business card from my wallet and explain how I first met Cameron. The tension eases.

"Sorry," she says. "I thought *he* sent you."

"He?"

Still clearly agitated, Kimberley glances up at a clock on the wall.

"I really don't have time to explain now, but if you're around at five o'clock we can talk then."

"That would be great. Where shall we meet?"

"There's a pub up the road called The Brewers Inn. I'll see you there."

Arrangements confirmed, Kimberley darts off.

"We've got a couple of hours to kill," I say to Clement. "Shall we reconvene in that pub just before five?"

"Suits me. See you then, Doc."

He lumbers towards the double doors and a second later, he's gone.

I pull out my phone and google the player he mentioned before the name slips my mind. I consult three different websites as the information doesn't make sense. They all confirm John Radford played almost five hundred games for Arsenal, from the early sixties to the mid-seventies. Even if Clement is in his late forties, he'd have been pre-school age when Mr Radford was in the twilight of his footballing career. With that in mind, it's difficult to envisage a four-year-old child sipping a pint in a North London pub with his favourite football player.

To paraphrase Yoda from Star Wars: the delusion is strong in this one.

21.

I arrive home to an empty flat. Leah has left a note on the kitchen table to say she had no luck finding the missing iPhone.

Flopping down on the sofa I give my wife a call.

"Hey, honey. You're not at home."

"Well spotted."

"No luck at the charity shop, then?" I confirm, ignoring her sarcasm.

"I tried. Sorry."

"It's okay. Where are you?"

"I'm just heading into the library."

"Will you be long?"

"No idea. I'll be home when I'm home."

"Fair enough. I'm heading out again soon and I probably won't be back much before seven tonight."

"What do you want me to do about dinner?"

"Just grab something I can throw in the microwave."

"Will do. See you later."

She hangs up.

I can't decipher Leah's mood, but as I lay back and rest my weary legs, the mind-set of another individual is a greater cause for concern.

Clement's throwaway remark about the Arsenal player highlight how broken his mind is. Grabbing my phone, I conduct a google search on the condition of pathological lying: where someone lies compulsively with no clear benefit.

As I suspected, several articles confirm there is an overlap between schizophrenia and pathological lying. One article in particular catches my attention. It offers a theory that pathological liars have the opposite ratio of cortisol and testosterone to most people. The imbalance causes them to be highly aggressive without concern for the risks involved. It's a theory which fits with Clement's behaviour.

I wish I had the skills and experience to work this out for myself. It reminds me of the last time Leah's van broke down.

Opening the bonnet, I could see all the parts and I had a vague idea what they all did, but there was little chance of diagnosing the problem as I didn't understand which parts related to the symptoms. The human mind is immeasurably more complex than any engine and I suspect Clement needs more than a new set of spark plugs; way beyond my limited psychiatric knowledge.

The clock on my phone tells me I need to make a move. I'm not willing to endure London traffic just as the rush hour builds, but it'll still take at least half-an-hour to get back to Wandsworth using public transport. It was hardly worth coming home.

I put my coat on and step out the door to a dusky sky. At this time of year it's usually dark by five but never dark enough. When I first moved to London, one of the stark differences I noticed in the urban environment was a lack of visible stars in the night sky. With so much light pollution, the best you can hope for is a view of the moon and a handful of the brightest stars. I miss the rural Oxfordshire sky; the black canvas dotted with hundreds of shimmering white specks. You can sense the scale of the Universe under such a sky, whereas in London, it feels like you're hemmed in from above.

One tube and one overground train later, I emerge from Wandsworth Station and make my way to The Brewers Inn. I arrive at quarter-to-five and push open the door to a large, traditionally themed pub. A big man in a donkey jacket is already supping a pint at the bar. I wander over.

"What can I get you, Doc?"

"A sparkling water, please."

"You're shittin' me, right? Have a pint."

Before I can protest, he asks the barmaid for two pints of lager, and then promptly empties his current glass. Perhaps an injection of alcohol is no bad thing, considering the day I've had, the week I've had.

He hands me a pint.

"Cheers."

"You wanna grab a table?"

Clement follows me to a table near enough to the door we

can spot Kimberley Bowhurst enter, but remote enough we can talk without fear of eavesdroppers.

"What did you make of what Kimberley said earlier?" I ask.

"Dunno, but she seemed nervy."

"I would have thought you were used to people being nervy in your company."

"Only people who piss me off."

"I'll bear that in mind when it's my round."

"You're alright, Doc, even if you are a bit of a drip."

"Gosh, thanks for the character reference."

"You're welcome," he says, flashing a thin smile.

I take a sip of lager. Clement tips half a pint down his neck.

The main door swings open and a blonde woman in an overcoat enters. She stops and scans the bar. I get up and walk over.

"Hi, Kimberley. Can I get you a drink?"

"White wine, please. Better make it a large one."

I hail the barmaid and order a glass of house white. While we wait, Kimberley asks how I became involved with Cameron. Without divulging the full story, I confirm how he suddenly wandered into RightMind last week, and our subsequent meeting at The Duke.

The wine arrives and she attacks it with Clement-level enthusiasm.

"We've grabbed a table over there," I nod.

She follows me over and Clement gets to his feet.

"How you doing, Doll?"

"Ask me in half an hour."

She removes her coat and we all sit down.

"I appreciate you taking the time to speak with us, Kimberley."

"It's okay. I want to find Cameron more than anyone. I'm so worried."

"When was the last time you saw him?"

"Not since November last year. We had a falling out which ended our relationship."

"I'm sorry to hear that. Would I be right in guessing it was

160

because of his drug habit?"

"Cameron doesn't have a drug habit. At least, he didn't."

"That's not the impression I got when he wandered into my office."

"He's a good person, but he's made one or two really bad decisions."

"I gathered. So, you've not heard from him at all?"

"No, that's not strictly true."

She fidgets with a beer mat, perhaps weighing up if the two strangers at the table are worthy of her trust.

"Is there something we should know, Kimberley? About Cameron?"

"I … I don't even know where to start."

"We ain't in a hurry, Doll," Clement suggests. "Start at the beginning."

Whatever Kimberley's story is, her body language implies it's not a happy one.

"Okay. Don't say I didn't warn you."

Another gulp of wine and a puff of the cheeks.

"We met during our first year of college, in Kingston. Two years on, Cameron smashed his grades and got a place at Oxford but I didn't fare so well and decided university wasn't for me. I thought we might struggle with him being away but if anything, it brought us closer together. I honestly thought I'd spend the rest of my life with Cameron."

"What happened?"

"There was this guy he met at college; Dylan Riley."

"The cocky little dipshit?" Clement confirms.

"You've met him?"

"Yeah, briefly."

"We were in Oxford earlier," I add. "Hoping to track Cameron down."

"Oh, I see. I never really liked Dylan, but he got on with Cameron … probably as they were both looking to attend Oxford. Anyway, I think it was in November last year when Dylan invited Cameron to his dad's sixtieth birthday party at some swanky hotel in Weybridge. His family are wealthy and it was billed as the party of the decade, apparently."

"You didn't get an invitation?"

"Nope, but I told Cameron he shouldn't miss out on my account. Dylan's dad had hired a band Cameron really liked and I knew how much he wanted to see them live."

"Okay."

"He got to see the band, but that was as far as his enjoyment of the evening went. Dylan abandoned him to flirt with some girl so Cameron ended up drinking alone in the bar. That's when *he* first approached him."

"Who's *he*?"

"Fraser Kingsland."

She makes no effort to hide her contempt.

"I've met Mr Kingsland myself," I state. "I'm no fan either."

"He manipulated Cameron into giving up his place at Oxford."

"Did he? How?"

"To understand, I need to explain a little about Cameron's background. His dad passed away when Cameron was just fifteen — multiple sclerosis."

"I'm sorry to hear that."

"I never knew Cameron back then, and he rarely talked about it; too painful, I guess. By the time I met him, he'd already developed an interest in chemistry, specifically pharmaceutical chemistry, and that interest had evolved into an obsession by the time he started at Oxford. He formulated this idea; a theoretical drug which might delay the effects of multiple sclerosis — not a cure but a way to slow the degeneration. To be honest, most of what he said went way over my head."

"I spoke to his tutor at Oxford. He said Cameron was one of the brightest students he'd ever taught."

"He was super clever, and he actually made some headway with his research."

"Really?"

"Yep, but as a chemistry student there was only so far he could develop his work. We went away in the summer last year and, by that point, he'd decided to put the project on ice until he graduated. That was that until he met Fraser Kingsland at that party."

"Go on."

"He was sitting alone at the bar and Kingsland strolled up to order a drink, and made a comment about Cameron looking bored. They got chatting and, somewhere in the small talk, Cameron mentioned he was studying chemistry at Oxford. I think Kingsland said something about how proud his dad must be, to have a son at Oxford."

"Understandably."

"The conversation then turned to Cameron's dad, and he told Kingsland about his illness, and how he'd tried to develop a drug which might help multiple sclerosis sufferers. Hindsight is a wonderful thing, but his mistake was telling Kingsland about the issues with the project."

"Such as?"

"The side effects of his initial samples. Cameron said they were horrendous, and every lab rat appeared to experience a twenty-four-hour acid trip. He jokingly told Kingsland he'd set out to create the world's most effective multiple sclerosis treatment but inadvertently created the world's trippiest recreational drug; hence his decision to shelve the project."

"Oh."

"It gets worse. I can't remember the science behind it, but the risk of addiction was off-the-scale. According to Cameron, two lab rats virtually killed one another while fighting over a piece of bread soaked in the drug."

"Christ."

"At that point, Kingsland told Cameron about his teenage daughter, and her own fight with multiple sclerosis. He said he'd lost her the year before, at Christmas."

I glance at Clement. I think he's probably drawing conclusions similar to mine on where this story is heading.

"He gave Cameron a business card and said they should talk. They met up a few days later, and that's when Kingsland made Cameron a once-in-a-lifetime offer: a ridiculously high salary, and use of a fully resourced lab to continue developing the drug.

To Cameron, it appeared they both had the same agenda; to develop and patent a drug which would help millions of people. He accepted the offer and quit uni."

"Which is why he dropped out in November?"

"Exactly, and I can't tell you how much we argued about it. I only met Kingsland once, for about ten minutes, but something about him didn't sit right. I think Cameron saw him as a father figure but I thought he was a sleaze bag and told Cameron as much. We had a huge row about it and didn't speak for a week, during which time I received an unexpected visit at work from Dylan Riley. He offered to act as mediator but rather than a shoulder to cry on, he tried to take advantage and made a pass at me, the arsehole."

"And you told Cameron?"

"By that point we were in a bad place, and he was so busy setting up his new venture with Kingsland he didn't seem to care. We argued again, and that's when he told me we were finished."

"I'm sorry."

Clearly upset, Kimberley seeks solace in her wine glass. As she does, I think back to the last conversation I had with Kingsland, and the obscene price tag he attached to the data on Cameron's phone. I have a vague idea where he got that value from.

"Do you think Kingsland intended to use Cameron and cut him out of any deal when the drug was ready for patent?"

"No."

"Oh."

"There was never going to be any patent."

"Why not?"

"Last Monday evening, two men turned up at my parents' house. Thank Christ they weren't home as the men barged their way in and started making threats. Apparently, Cameron had breached his contract with Kingsland, and gone missing."

"What the hell did they expect you to do about it?" Clement asks.

"They forced me to message Cameron, saying I had to see

him urgently at my house."

"I'm guessing he didn't show up?"

"They waited for almost an hour but I don't think Cameron even read the message. Before they left, one of the men pinned me up against the wall and said if Cameron replied, I had to call him straight away. He also made it clear what would happen if I didn't, or if I spoke to the police — they'd set light to our house while we were all asleep in our beds."

"As I've discovered, Kingsland is keen on levying threats."

"I managed to convince my parents it might be nice to have a few days away and I booked them a hotel in Brighton while I stayed with a friend. I was terrified."

"Did Cameron reply to your message?" I ask.

"Not quite. Two days later, I came out of work to find he'd left a garbled voicemail message."

"Saying what?"

"It was hard to understand him but I gleaned enough to determine Kingsland had no interest in developing a multiple sclerosis treatment."

"I don't suppose you kept that message?"

"Probably. Do you want to hear it?"

"Please."

Kimberley reaches into her coat pocket and pulls out an iPhone. After tapping the screen a few times, she places it on the table. A monotone voice leaks from the speaker, announcing the date and time of a received message.

"Kim, it's me," a frantic voice gasps.

Just a few words but I recognise the desperate tone from my meetings with Cameron Gail.

"I've been so stupid … Kingsland wants …"

The message breaks up. I can only assume Cameron made the call in an area with poor mobile reception.

"… not to treat MS … recreational drug. There's no funded lab … locked in a … in Stratford. The bastard forced me … I'm in a bad way …"

The line fades to static and crackles again.

"… got out through a fire escape … I'm seeing someone later

165

… need rehab. Please, Kim … don't speak to …"

Frustratingly, the signal fades away.

"… dangerous man, and he knows … police. Be careful … it's too dangerous …"

There's another burst of static and the line drops. The monotone voice returns with instructions for saving or deleting the message.

"That didn't sound good," Clement surmises.

"No, it didn't."

"What do you make of it?" Kimberley asks?

"Um, can we hear it again?"

The three of us sit quietly as the message is replayed. I'm first to break the silence when it ends.

"It's hard to decipher but I think we can draw a few conclusions."

Kimberley squeezes her eyes shut for a moment and breathes heavily through her nose.

"Kingsland lied to Cameron, didn't he?" she then suggests. "He had no intention of developing the drug for multiple sclerosis, did he?"

"Based on Cameron's message, it appears not. I think he was duped, and I have to admit it sounds like Kingsland intended to peddle the drug for recreational use."

"What was it he said about no lab, and being locked up?" Clement asks.

We listen to the message a third time.

"Stratford?" I remark. "Where's that?"

"East End," Clement replies.

"But, he said he'd got out through a fire escape," Kimberley interjects, highlighting the only positive element in the message. "And, he was seeing someone about rehab."

"I think that someone was me," I confirm. "He left this message the same day he wandered into my office."

I turn and face Kimberley.

"I'm sorry to tell you, but judging by this message and my conversations with Cameron, I think he's been testing the drug on himself; for twenty-two days if my memory serves correct. It would explain his eagerness to secure a place in rehab."

"He would never have taken it voluntarily … why didn't you help him?"

"If I'd known the full story, I might have been able to help with rehab but Cameron never got the chance to explain."

I decide now isn't an appropriate moment to tell her why he never got the chance.

"Oh, God," she sniffs. "What should I do?"

"Tell you what you shouldn't do, Doll," Clement says. "Speak to the Old Bill."

"Why not?"

"You wanna tell her what the kid said, Doc?"

"Cameron told me Kingsland knows people on the force; people who can't be trusted. I suspect part of his message warned of that."

"I can't just sit around and do nothing," she replies. "He's in trouble."

"I know, which is why we're trying to find him. If we do, I promise I'll do everything I can to help."

"If," Clement huffs. "The kid sounds like he's off his nut."

"That's what scares me," Kimberley says. "He told me just how unstable Kimbo is, and if he's taken it …"

"Kimbo?" I blurt.

"It was his pet name for me; a shortened version of Kimberley Bowhurst. He said he wanted to name his greatest creation after his greatest love."

"That's the name he used in my office. No wonder we couldn't find it on any database — Cameron is the only addict."

Tears follow as Kimberley searches her bag for a tissue. Clement sits forward and puts his hand on her arm.

"You alright, Doll?"

"Not really," she gulps. "I'm so scared of what will happen to Cameron if Kingsland finds him before you do … if that bloody drug doesn't kill him first."

"Do you have any inkling at all where he might be?" I ask. "Anything at all?"

"I wish I did, but his phone is permanently set to voicemail and he hasn't answered any of my messages."

I skip over an explanation about Cameron not being in possession of his phone.

"What about his mum, or other family members?"

"His mum remarried last year, and they emigrated to Canada. Cameron was an only child and there's no one in his family he's close to."

She then asks the obvious question.

"Why were you looking for him?"

It's just as well I've been brushing up on the art of deception lately.

"I was worried. He was in a bad way the last time we spoke."

"You don't think … he's going to be okay, isn't he?"

"He'll be okay if we've got anything to do with it," Clement replies.

Kimberley seems to find some measure of reassurance in the big man's words and empties her glass.

"You want another one, Doll?"

"No, thank you. I need to get going in a minute. I don't like my parents being home alone."

We swap phone numbers and, as Kimberley puts her coat on, I promise to call if I hear anything about Cameron's whereabouts. She makes the same promise and leaves.

"Your round, Doc."

There's no argument because I've never needed a stiff drink so badly. I head to the bar and return with two pints of lager and two whisky chasers.

"This whole situation just goes from bad to worse," I mumble, retaking my seat. "I should have helped Cameron while I had the chance."

"You weren't to know what he was up to. Besides, even if you had helped the kid you'd still be in the same shit. Seems this Kingsland bloke ain't gonna let him walk away without a fight. Too much money at stake."

"Even if Cameron Gail wandered in and joined us, there's no way I could hand him over to Fraser Kingsland; knowing why he wants to track him down so badly."

"So, what you wanna do?"

"I'm screwed whatever I decide. If we continue the search for Cameron and by some miracle we find him, there is absolutely no way I'm willing to facilitate whatever plan Kingsland has in mind for that drug. On the other hand, if I haven't handed Cameron over by Sunday, he'll destroy my life."

"There's only one option, Doc. You've gotta take Kingsland out of the picture."

"Oh, right. And there was me thinking the solution might be difficult."

"Got any better ideas?"

"No ideas, better or otherwise."

"There you go."

"And how do you propose we take Kingsland out of the picture?"

"You deal with him the same way you deal with any jumped-up arsehole. You find his weakness and you use it against him."

"How? We know the sum total of nothing about Fraser Kingsland."

"We'd better find out then, and sharpish."

Clement empties his glass and stands up.

"I'm gonna go ask around. I'll come round your gaff at eight-ish in the morning."

"You don't want me to come with you?"

"Nah, I don't do friendly chats like you, Doc."

"If you're sure?"

"Yeah. See ya tomorrow."

He steps around the table.

"Oh, and I wouldn't say no to a full English for breakfast. Have a word with your missus, will you?"

On that sexist bombshell, he strides away.

22.

How is it possible to suffer a hangover after just two pints of lager and one whisky?

Leah is sleeping soundly as I roll over and try to ignore the pounding headache, to no avail. I'm in desperate need of painkillers and a piss, but not necessarily in that order.

With great reluctance I climb out of bed and make for the bathroom. One issue resolved, I trundle into the kitchen and sift through the drawer where we keep our medicinal supplies. When I locate a packet of ibuprofen, there's only one tablet left.

Half a hangover is better than a whole hangover, I suppose.

It's just gone half-seven by the time I sit down at the kitchen table, nursing a mug of strong tea. In the silence, I slowly piece together yesterday's events in the hope I might have missed some thread of positivity; the thinnest sliver of a silver lining.

A pinging sound emanates from the pocket of my dressing gown. Thinking it might be a text from Clement, possibly with some good news, I pull out the phone and unlock the screen — it's not from Clement. The message is as concise as it is damning: *Three days. Tick tock …*

If the words weren't troubling enough, the sender has attached an image file. I don't want to open it but ignoring the threat won't make it go away. I tap the screen and a photo opens up.

An acidic tang strikes the back of my throat as I stare at a picture of my wife with a phone in her hand, stood outside the library. Impossible to say exactly when it was taken but all available evidence suggests yesterday afternoon when I called. Someone must have been following her.

Panic strikes hard and fast. I get up and pace the length of the kitchen, back and forth on jelly-like legs.

"Calm down," I mumble. "Think clearly."

A few deep breaths and I return to the table. I need to work out my priorities, and deal with them. With that, I grab my phone and make a call.

"Morning, Dad."

"David?" he rasps. "Do you know what time it is?"

"Early, I know. Sorry."

"Is something wrong?"

"Yes, and no."

"Hold on."

Judging by the distant grunts and groans I'm guessing Dad is getting out of bed. I then hear a door close.

"You there, Son?"

"Yes."

"What's up then?"

"I need to ask a favour."

"Go on."

"Would you mind if Leah stayed for a few days?"

"You know you're both welcome. Your mother would love to see you."

"Not me. Just Leah."

"Oh, okay. Can I ask why?"

"There's nothing to worry about but I think it would be in Leah's best interest if she spent a few days out of London."

"And what does Leah have to say about that?"

"She's looking forward to seeing you. It really will do her some good."

"Well, you're the expert so, if you think a spell with the in-laws is in order, you know Leah will always be welcome."

"Thanks, Dad. I appreciate it."

"When should we expect her?"

"Um, probably early afternoon."

"I'll let your mother know. And when will you be gracing us with your presence?"

"I've got a lot on at work at the moment but I promise I'll try to get down in the next few weeks."

"Make sure you do."

I thank Dad and leave him to attend his morning ablutions. One part of the equation dealt with, albeit the easier part, I make another cup of tea and take it to the bedroom.

"Hey, honey," I whisper. "You awake?"

"I wasn't until I heard you mumbling in the kitchen. Who were you talking to?"

She sits up and I pass her the mug.

"Dad."

"Bit early, isn't it? They're okay, aren't they?"

"They're fine, but there's something I need you to do for me. I want you to pack a bag and go stay with my parents for a few days."

"What?"

"They're looking forward to seeing you."

"Me? What about you?"

"No, I'll be staying here."

She puts the mug on the bedside table and folds her arms; an act of defiance.

"Why the hell would I want to stay with your parents?"

I can't tell her the real reason because it'll likely freak her out. The last thing I need this morning is a spousal meltdown.

"Because … it's important. I need you to trust me."

"Why is it important?"

"It just is. Please, honey, do as I ask."

"No," she huffs. "I don't want to. And besides, I've got a stall booked for Saturday."

I forgot about her stall, and it's a valid reason for Leah to stand her ground. As she glares up at me, I need to retreat and regroup. A plausible explanation is required.

"We'll talk about it later. Clement will be here soon."

"How soon?"

"About fifteen minutes."

"Bloody hell. Why didn't you say?"

She leaps out of bed and heads off to the bathroom.

I return to the kitchen and sit at the table. How can I convince my wife that staying in London isn't a good idea without telling her the real reason? I ponder a list of feeble excuses until the doorbell rings.

Leah is still in the bathroom when I open the front door to Clement.

"Morning, Doc."

172

"Quick," I urge, ushering him in. "I need your input on a problem."

He follows me back down the hall and I snatch my phone from the kitchen table.

"This arrived this morning."

I show him the text and the photo.

"That ain't good."

"No, it's terrifying and I need to get Leah somewhere safe which is why I need your help. I've arranged for her to stay with my parents in Oxfordshire but I'm having, um, some difficulty convincing her. Can you think of a plausible reason?"

"Just tell her the truth."

"I can't do that. It'll worry her sick."

"Better worried than dead, Doc."

"It's not an option."

"Alright, leave it with me."

"What? I don't have time …"

Leah breezes in.

"Morning, Clement."

"Alright, Doll. We were just talking about you."

I frown at Clement and hope Leah doesn't notice the slight shake of my head.

"Really?" she replies. "What were you saying?"

"It's a secret," he says. "But seeing as you ain't going anywhere, it's a non-starter."

"Pardon?"

"Your old man was planning a surprise and needed you out of the house for a few days."

Leah turns to me.

"What kind of surprise?"

"It doesn't matter now," I sigh.

"David, tell me," she pleads, like an impatient child.

"Don't waste your breath, Doll. It ain't happening now."

"Why not?"

"'Cos you're here. I was gonna help him sort it out, which is why I'm here at this ungodly bleedin' hour of the morning."

"But, what about my stall?"

173

"I could do it," Clement suggests. "I told you I helped a mate out a few times."

"You'd do that?"

"Yeah, no worries."

Leah skips over and kisses me on the cheek.

"I'll go pack a bag," she says with a smile.

My wife disappears. I hold my hands out in exasperation.

"A surprise?" I hiss. "What were you thinking?"

"Worked didn't it? Why ain't the kettle on and why can't I smell bacon frying?"

He sits down at the table.

"You're unbelievable, Clement."

"And you ain't the first person to say that. Three rounds of toast, ta."

"Right this moment, your appetite is the least of my problems. Kingsland is now making direct threats towards my wife."

"Yeah, but she'll be out of the way soon."

"For a few days, yes, but she'll come back at some stage and then what? I can't live like this, Clement. I never asked for any of it."

"Alright, Doc. Calm down."

More pacing ensues as I work through a decision which was always a last resort.

"I'm going to the police," I declare. "I've no choice now."

"And what are you gonna tell them?"

"Everything. I'll tell them all about Kingsland's plans, and Cameron's disappearance, and the threats made against me and Leah."

"And you've got evidence, right?"

"I've got … I've got the text messages, and the photo. And then there's the flowers, and …"

"And?"

"There's Kimberley. She'll back me up."

"Will she? Funny how she ain't gone to the Old Bill herself."

"She's scared, but I can talk her into coming with me."

Clement sits back in his chair and orders me to sit down.

"Listen," he says calmly. "I did a bit of asking around last night and spoke to at least a dozen people about Kingsland. You wanna know what they all said?"

"Not really, but go on."

"They all said stay well clear. That bloke has built himself a proper reputation."

"A reputation for what, exactly?"

"Someone you don't grass on. I had a long chat with this bloke who used to run a boozer in the East End. A good few years back, Kingsland turned up one evening and said he was offering insurance services."

"He didn't strike me as the type to run a legitimate business."

"Nothing legit about it, Doc — he wanted protection money. This bloke had to pay Kingsland a grand a month so nothing bad happened to his boozer."

"Extortion?"

"Exactly. By all accounts, Kingsland had the entire manor sewn up, and every business was paying him. Then, he moved in on the drug gangs and cleared 'em all out so he could take on the trade. Bit by bit, he's spread his operation across town and fucked over anyone who stood in his way."

"And you believed this former publican?"

"Oh, yeah. I met his missus. She was probably a looker once … before her husband went to the Old Bill and grassed on Kingsland."

"Why, what happened?"

"Two days later, she was snatched off the street on her way home from bingo. Three of Kingsland's men took her to an abandoned warehouse and used her face as an ashtray — fourteen fag burns they counted at the hospital. Poor cow still has the scars."

"And Kingsland? Didn't the police do anything?"

"The landlord pulled his statement about the protection racket and his missus wouldn't tell the Old Bill why her face looked like an overcooked pizza. And trust me, Doc: that weren't the worst story I heard about Kingsland, either. The bloke's a fucking psycho."

I'm about to put my head in my hands when Leah breezes back in.

"All packed," she says.

Snatching the van keys from the table, I get up and hand them to her.

"Probably best you get going then, honey."

"Can't I at least have some breakfast first?"

"Um …"

"Get your arse out of here," Clement pipes up. "As lovely as it is, we've got a surprise to get started on."

"Seeing as you put it like that," Leah replies, blushing. "I'll grab something to eat on the way."

His intervention appears to have worked so I'm willing to overlook the crude statement about my wife's posterior.

"Call me when you arrive."

"I will, but what about the stall? I need to go through everything … and how are you going to get the stock there if I've got the van?"

"A mate will lend me a van," Clement says. "And I'll have a good look through your stock. It's all in hand, Doll."

"Okay. Thank you."

I put my hands on her shoulders.

"I'll let you know when it's safe to return."

"Safe?"

"Oh, just a figure of speech," I chuckle nervously. "I meant, when we're done sorting your surprise."

"I can't wait."

I give her a kiss and she leaves. The relief is palpable, if only temporary. As the front door clicks shut, I return to the table.

"You alright, Doc?"

"No."

"What do you wanna do?"

"I want to grab my wife and get the hell away from this cesspit of a city."

"Why don't you then? You can catch her if you're quick."

"Because, Clement, I'm on police bail and even if Kingsland doesn't find me, they will. God only knows how many other

176

women he's got lined up to lie about me."

"He's got you by the balls, either way. Gotta give the bloke credit — he knows what he's doing."

"You'll have to excuse my lack of respect for a man who thinks it's okay to take whatever he wants, however he wants. He's a piece of shit; the absolute worst kind of human."

"That's more like it. You need a bit of fire in your belly."

"And what am I supposed to do with the fire? You've just told me we're dealing with some kind of arch criminal."

"Blokes like Kingsland come and go," he replies with a shrug. "They ain't … what's the word …?"

"Infallible?"

"Yeah, that's it."

"This isn't a movie, Clement. Kingsland has all the resources, and there's just you and me. In real life, underdogs and good guys rarely prevail."

"Who said I was a good guy?"

He backs up his statement with a cold stare.

"There's still just two of us."

"Yeah, and one of us has got fuck all to lose. I've met the likes of Kingsland before and I ain't ever backed down. I sure as shit ain't gonna start now."

"What do you propose we do?"

"I reckon a spot of breakfast would be a good place to start. I think better on a full stomach."

Being the good host that I am, or a mug, I'd picked up some bacon and eggs on the way home last night, along with a loaf of bread.

"Fine," I sigh, getting to my feet.

I traipse over to the fridge and retrieve the bacon. To my surprise, Clement gets up and fills the kettle.

"What are you doing?" I ask.

"What does it look like? Making a brew. You focus on the grub."

"Err, okay."

"You want one?"

"Please."

As I fry the bacon, Clement whistles to himself while making the tea; a tune which sounds vaguely familiar but I can't place the title.

"What's that you're whistling?"

"Queen, *Crazy Little Thing Called Love.*"

"Ah, that's it. I thought it sounded familiar."

"You a fan?"

"I can't say I know much of their work."

"I'm just catching up with it … kinda missed out on their later albums. There's this second-hand shop near my digs and they flog these compact disc things — you heard of 'em?"

"Compact discs?"

"Yeah, they're bloody amazing. No scratching or hissing, and they're only a quid or two each."

"You've only just discovered compact discs? Have you been living in the Amazon Rain Forest for the last three decades?"

"I ain't a fan of modern technology. Most of it don't make much sense but a friend gave me a stereo with a compact disc player last year. I only had a shitty little radio."

"How very generous of your friend. Why is he a friend when you refer to everyone else as a mate?"

"'Cos he was a she."

"Oh, I see. Emma, by any chance?"

Seeing as the contact list on his phone only contained one name, it's a fair assumption.

He nods.

"Were you close?"

"Rather not talk about it."

His shoulders slump a little; telling. Reading between the lines, I can only assume Clement suffered a relationship breakdown at some point. Perhaps it has some bearing on his mental state and I wish I'd copied down Emma's number when I had the chance. It would be interesting to get her take on his condition as she obviously knows him well. Maybe I'll get the chance to sneak a look at his phone another time — if I'm not banged up in prison or arranging my wife's funeral.

As Clement transfers the mugs of tea to the table and retakes

178

his seat, I crack a couple of eggs into the pan. While they cook, I slide four slices of bread into the toaster. Making breakfast isn't exactly a taxing task but a much welcome distraction.

Five minutes later, I join my guest at the table with two plates of bacon, eggs, and toast.

"Nice one. Ta."

I look down at my plate with little appetite. The nausea from Kingsland's earlier text still hasn't fully abated. I chomp unenthusiastically on a slice of toast and slide the plate across the table.

"Help yourself," I say. "I'm not really hungry."

Clement picks up the plate and slides the contents onto his.

"Cheers."

I try not to watch but he treats his mouth like a waste disposal unit; shovelling food in with greedy efficiency. I've still got a nub of cold toast in my hand as his fork clatters on the empty plate.

"That's better."

"Can we now focus on the issue of my liberty, and Leah's life?"

"Yeah, yeah," he replies before slurping at his tea. "I've got a plan."

"I'm listening."

"Actually, it's more of a punt than a plan but we ain't got a lot to go on. No one seemed to know much about Kingsland, or they were too shit-scared to say anything."

"Right, so what did you find out?"

"He lives somewhere in Chiswick, and he's a huge Johnny Cash fan."

I stare back, dumbfounded.

"Is that it?"

"Pretty much."

"Oh, brilliant," I groan. "What next? Do we wander the streets of Chiswick looking for a ranch-style house; *Ring of Fire* blaring beyond the windows?"

"Course not. Can't you check the voting register on your phone thing? Can't be many people with the name Kingsland

179

living in Chiswick."

"That's a good point."

I grab my phone and google the electoral roll records. One website allows me to conduct a basic search for free so I enter Kingsland's name and confirm the location as Chiswick. The results are disappointing.

"There are six households with the surname Kingsland, but no mention of a Fraser Kingsland, nor an address in Chiswick."

"Maybe he decided not to register. Bloke like him must have enemies and it'd be mad publishing your address for any Tom, Dick, or Harry to look up."

"Fair point."

"But it's gotta be odds on one of those six are related to him."

"Yes, but which one?"

"Only one way to find out. We go knock on some doors."

"And say what?"

"What is it Kingsland wants from you?"

"Err, Cameron Gail."

"Or?"

"Cameron's phone."

"There you go then. We could say we've found a phone and wanna return it to its rightful owner."

"But, we don't have a phone and even if we did, how do we know it belongs to someone with the surname Kingsland?"

"Fuck's sake," he grunts, rolling his eyes. "They ain't gonna interrogate us on the details. All you need to ask is if they know a Fraser Kingsland as you've found his phone."

"So, you're hoping we'll end up on the doorstep of someone related to him?"

"Exactly. We then ask 'em where Fraser lives so we can return the phone."

"And what if they offer to pass it on to him, rather than give us his address?"

"Plan-B. We'll invite ourselves in and make it clear we'd rather know where he lives."

"You mean, threaten his family?"

"He threatened yours."

"I know, which is why I'm acutely aware how awful it is. I'm not comfortable threatening random strangers just because they're unfortunate enough to be related to Kingsland."

"Your call," he says matter-of-factly. "But remember this — when you're tossing soil on your wife's coffin or getting arse-raped in the nick, principles won't count for shit. She'll still be dead and you'll still be some bloke's bitch."

If Clement had reached across the table and slapped me hard around the face, it would have stung less.

"Finish your tea," I gulp. "We need to get going."

23.

While Clement is in the bathroom, doing God-knows what, I reluctantly tap my credit card details into the website so we can access the full address details of the Kingsland clan. It's thirty quid I can ill-afford but thirty quid I've no choice but to spend.

Clement finally ambles back into the kitchen.

"What have you been doing in there? You've been an age."

"Use your imagination, Doc. I'd steer well clear for a while, though."

"I need a pee before we go."

"Don't say I didn't warn you."

Frowning, I head to the bathroom and return two minutes later, eyes watering.

"You could have used the air freshener."

"Shit stinks. Get over it."

"Can we go?"

I grab my keys and Clement follows me out of the kitchen. I hold my breath all the way to the front door. For once, I welcome the fume-filled London air which greets us outside.

"Where's the first address, then?" Clement asks, as we head to the tube station.

I consult the list on my phone.

"Alderbury Road in Barnes."

It's not quite Chiswick, but Barnes is a neighbouring district, south of the River Thames.

"Ain't been to Barnes in years."

"I don't think I've ever been there, although I did once check it out as a potential place to rent a flat. Suffice to say it was a bit beyond our budget."

"Always been a pricey part of town. It's also where Marc Bolan snuffed it."

"Who?"

"Marc Bolan. The band, T-Rex?"

"Never heard of him."

Clement stops dead in his tracks.

"You've gotta be shittin' me? He was one of the biggest names in music back in the early seventies."

"A bit before my time."

"So was Jack the Ripper, but you've heard of him, ain't you?"

"Point taken, and I'll be sure to look up Mr Bolan once I've got my life back."

"You do that."

Clement, perhaps offended by my lack of seventies pop knowledge, doesn't say another word for the rest of our walk to the tube station. We arrive and I consult the tube map on the wall.

"What you doing?"

"Checking the route."

"I know where we're going."

"Oh, okay."

We take the Northern Line to Waterloo and then switch to an overground train for the nineteen minute journey to Barnes. Sitting opposite one another, Clement seems content staring silently out of the window as the filthy urban landscape rolls past.

"Have you always lived in London?" I ask.

"Yeah."

"Never fancied living somewhere a little quieter, cleaner?"

"Like where you grew up? No thanks."

"Nothing wrong with Oxfordshire."

"Didn't say there was but it ain't my cup of tea."

"So, you're intending to live the rest of your days here, then?"

"I bleedin' hope not," he mumbles. "This ain't my town no more, and these ain't my people."

"What do you mean?"

"Take a look around, Doc. You've got terrorists trying to kill folks for no good reason, kids stabbing each other every bleedin' day, and enough poor bastards sleeping on the streets to form an army. This town has always been rough round the edges, but it used to have a heart, used to be about the people. Now, I dunno, it's every fucker for himself."

"Is that your view, or your friend's?"

He puffs a tired sigh and shakes his head.

"We both know I'm talking about the same bloke, so can we dispense with that bullshit?"

"I, um …"

"Doc, we had a deal and if I don't keep up my end, you won't have a job to worry about."

"I suppose not."

"So, let's get down to brass tacks shall we? I don't wanna piss around no more."

"Fair enough."

He then sits forward and clears his throat.

"I died, yet here I am. As fucked-up as that sounds, it's what happened. Now, if I am crazy, I need you to tell me."

"I can't tell you that, Clement. I can only give you my opinion as a layman."

"That'll do, but you gotta keep an open mind, right?"

"You want me to keep an open mind about your apparent resurrection?"

"Call it what you like, but yeah. I'm either batshit crazy or what happened, happened. It's gotta be one or the other, right?"

"Okay, but you have to understand there's no way for me to prove definitively you're suffering a mental illness, or that you're telling the truth. For the umpteenth time, I'm not qualified to provide a diagnosis and I'm definitely not qualified to judge miracles either."

"We'll see, but no more talking about my mate, alright?"

"Understood."

"Good."

He sits back and returns his attention to the outside world.

The only part of our conversation I can whole-heartedly concede is the concern for a potential breach of protocols. At this precise moment, I don't even know if I want to continue my career in counselling, seeing as it's the reason I'm in this hole. I do, however, need Clement — that much is sadly clear.

The train pulls into Barnes Station and we disembark. As we

184

pass through the ticket barrier, I pull out my phone to check the route to Alderbury Road.

"Ah, crap."

"What's up?"

"Alderbury Road is almost a mile-and-a-half away."

"Walking is good for your soul."

"Is it?"

"Fucked if I know. Read it in the paper so probably not."

I can't afford a cab so there's no choice but to nourish my soul for twenty minutes. A few hundred yards and I'm already struggling to keep up with Clement's long strides.

"Can you slow up a bit?" I pant.

"Jesus, Doc. What's the matter with you?"

He lights a cigarette and we continue on at a slightly slower pace; him puffing, me panting. Having never visited this part of London I'm taken aback by the greenery. The road towards our destination is busy with traffic but it's lined with trees and grass verges rather than buildings. Unsurprisingly, the scene changes to terraced housing as we pass the halfway point but they're not the tatty carbon-stained variety common in Kentish Town. Every house is so impeccably presented only the architecture hints at their age.

"How much you reckon these gaffs cost?" Clement asks.

"Several million a piece, I'd guess. Home for the rich, famous, and self-entitled. Whenever you read about some celebrity virtue-signalling about London's poor, they all seem to preach from this part of town."

"What's virtue signalling?"

"It's when someone, usually with a privileged lifestyle, tries to pretend they care about anyone but themselves."

There the conversation ends.

Eventually, the road widens and the houses become grander; several protected by security gates and cameras. We turn left on to Washington Road, and then right on to Boileau Road. The houses aren't anywhere near as grand and the cars parked on the kerb befitting of less-wealthy residents. Another left turn and we reach Alderbury Avenue.

"What number is it?" Clement asks, as we pass number one.

"Thirty-three."

"It's the far end. Typical."

Fortunately, the road isn't long and within a minute we reach number thirty-three; a boxy semi-detached house I suspect was once part of the council's housing stock.

"Are you going to do the talking, Clement, or should I?"

"You sound more honest."

"Thanks."

"That weren't a compliment."

"I retract my thanks. What am I saying?"

"Keep it simple. You found a phone and it belongs to someone called Fraser Kingsland."

"How do I know it belongs to someone called Fraser Kingsland?"

"I dunno," he huffs. "They ain't gonna give a shit, are they? They either won't know our man or won't care — stop over-thinking."

"Okay."

I open the gate and Clement follows me up a narrow path to the front door. A deep breath and I ring the doorbell. Long seconds tick by until a portly, middle-aged woman opens the door.

"Good morning," I chirp. "Sorry to trouble you, but I … we found a mobile phone belonging to a chap named Fraser Kingsland. He doesn't live here by any chance?"

"Fraser Kingsland?"

"Yes."

"Sorry, no. My husband is Martin Kingsland, and our son is Daniel."

"Ah, okay. I don't suppose you know if your husband has any relatives called Fraser?"

"Definitely not."

"Are you sure?"

"We've been married for twenty-five years and I've never heard him mention the name Fraser."

"Right, sorry to have bothered you."

She's about to close the door when Clement throws her a question.

"Excuse me, love. So we're not knocking on doors pestering anyone have you got other family members locally with the same surname?"

"My brother-in-law, Jake, lives in Melville Road, and Martin's Uncle George lives in East Sheen. They're the only Kingsland's local, as far as I know."

"Cheers, love."

She smiles at Clement for a few seconds before closing the door. We beat a retreat back down the garden path.

"You wanna check those names against the list of contenders?"

I open my phone and scroll through the names and addresses I pulled from the electoral roll website. Both Jake and George Kingsland are on the list.

"That's three down. Three to go."

"Where next?" Clement asks.

"There's two addresses in Richmond, and the third is in Isleworth. There are more Kingslands on the list, but they're much further afield."

"Let's get a cab."

"I can't afford a cab."

"My shout."

"That's very kind of you."

"Nothing to do with kindness, Doc. I bought some new pants last week and all this walking is chaffing my knackers. Red raw, they are."

"That's more information than I strictly needed."

Haunted by visions of Clement's inflamed testicles, we make our way back to the main road. Luck is on our side and a black cab passes after a few minutes. Clement waves it down and we climb in.

"Where to?" the driver asks.

"Sheendale Road, Richmond, please."

He taps the meter and we set off. It's a little over three miles and I'm hoping the traffic is kind to us, and Clement's finances.

"Tell me, how do you earn a living as a fixer? It's not the kind of job you see advertised."

"I don't. Not no more."

"So, it's a job you used to do?"

"That's right."

I decide against asking when he gave it up. I'm sure cab drivers hear all sorts of strange conversations, but discussing the career of an alleged dead man in a donkey jacket is probably too much.

"What do you do now, for money?"

"This and that."

"Can I ask you a question?"

He glares back at me.

"Sorry. Force of habit."

"Spit it out."

"This hobby of yours — getting acquainted with the local drug dealers — why didn't you take their cash?"

"How do you know I didn't?"

"A policeman came round one evening after an assault near our flat. He told us there had been a spate of attacks, and all the victims were found with cash on them."

"Weren't mine to take. Besides, I don't mind a bit of dirty cash but I ain't touchin' drug money."

"Very noble, but I still don't understand why you thought it was okay to beat the living daylights out of them."

"Told you. I was pissed off."

"At who?"

"Not who. What."

"Okay. What were you pissed off about?"

"Being stuck here for nearly four bleedin' years."

"Is that when you … came back? Four years ago?"

"Give or take a bit, but yeah."

"What have you been doing in those four years?"

"You wouldn't believe me if I told you, Doc."

"Try me."

"You read much?"

"A bit."

"You ever heard of Beth Baxter?"

"Yes, and I actually …"

Memories of Miss Baxter's tale suddenly flood back. I read her best-selling novel, *The Angel of Camden* a couple of years ago and, from memory, it featured a character called Cliff and he possessed many similar traits to Clement. I wonder if he's read it too. If so, it's entirely possible his delusion has been forged from that character and he now sees himself as Cliff. I need to re-read it to check how far the similarities stretch, but for now, I'd rather we keep our conversation rooted in reality.

"Sorry, I'm getting mixed up with another author."

"You should read her first book. Might help you understand who I am."

"I'll see if it's available at the library. Anyway, you never said what this and that entails."

"Mainly bar work, security, and a bit of wheeling and dealing on the side. Anything that pays cash in hand."

Seemingly bored with the conversation, he turns away and looks out the window. I stare at the meter; watching the fare rise at an alarming rate until we finally pull up outside eighteen Sheendale Road.

"£14.60, please," the driver says.

Clement pulls two crumbled ten-pound notes from his pocket and pays the driver, leaving a forty pence tip.

We stand and watch the cab disappear up the road before turning to face the next hope in the search for Fraser Kingsland — a bay-fronted Edwardian semi.

"Same again?" Clement suggests.

"Guess so."

There's no front gate so I wander up the short path to the door and ring the bell. According to the electoral roll, there's only one resident at the address — Ernest Kingsland.

With no answer, I ring the bell again. Seconds tick by until an elderly, wiry man opens the door.

"Can I help you?"

"I hope so. I've found a mobile phone belonging to a chap named Fraser Kingsland and we're trying to track him down."

"Why are you here, then? There's no Fraser Kingsland at this address."

"Yes, I know, but we checked the name Kingsland against the electoral roll to see if we could find him. Unfortunately, he's not listed, so we were hoping we might find a relative."

The man stares at me with suspicious eyes.

"If this is a scam, you've come to the wrong house, young man."

I pull out my wallet and offer the old man my driving licence.

"It's no scam, sir. We're just looking to reunite the phone with its owner. If it helps, there's my full name and address. I'm trying to do a good deed, that's all."

He squints at my licence.

"Well, Mr Nunn, you've had a wasted journey from Kentish Town, I'm afraid."

"Oh, have I?"

"There is no one named Fraser Kingsland in England; let alone in this street."

"Err, how do you know that?"

"Because I'm an old man with too much time on my hands. I study genealogy, you see, and I know just about every branch of the Kingsland family tree. I've not come across anyone called Fraser in all my research."

"Are you absolutely certain about that?"

"I may be old but I'm not senile."

"Sorry, I wasn't implying you were. It's just that I'm certain the phone belongs to a man named Fraser Kingsland."

"If I were you, I'd take it to the police station. I wouldn't want you to waste your time trawling the streets of London searching for a man who doesn't exist."

24.

The net curtain in the upstairs bedroom twitches. I glance up and catch Ernest Kingsland looking down at us as we stand inert on the pavement outside his house.

"Do you think he was telling the truth?" I ask.

"The old boy seemed sure of himself, and I dunno why he'd lie."

"It would also explain why there's no mention of Fraser Kingsland on the electoral roll, or anywhere on Google."

The moustache receives a few strokes as Clement stares up the road.

"What now?" I enquire.

"Let's go for a wander. No point standing here like idiots."

We head back towards the main road; both deep in our own thoughts. At the junction, Clement takes a right turn and I blindly follow for no other reason than I'm lost, literally and metaphorically.

We reach a seedy-looking pub called The Crown; a tower block of council flats looming large behind it.

"That's handy," Clement comments.

"What is?"

"A boozer. Let's go grab a pint and work out what we're gonna do."

"In there?"

"Yeah, why not?"

On first impressions alone, it does not look like a pub where they welcome non-locals.

"Can't we find a coffee shop?"

"And pay three quid for a cup of lukewarm piss? No, ta."

Clement turns and strides towards the front door. With great reluctance, I follow.

The interior of The Crown lives up to the drab exterior, and the clientele are equally squalid; a dozen or so pale-faced men who all look like they've had a hard life, though not through work.

191

Sticking close to Clement, I edge up to the bar where a tubby man is re-stocking the peanuts.

"Yes, gents?"

"Two pints of lager," Clement replies.

I should interject and request a sparkling water, but I'd bet patrons have been shanked in this establishment for lesser lapses of judgement. Clement pays and we take a seat at a table next to a fruit machine.

I take a sip of a pint I don't really want.

"So, what do we do now?" I ask. "Any ideas?"

"Yeah, I've got an idea but I'm sure you're not gonna like it, Doc."

"Probably not, but it seems I've given up on what I like or want."

"Alright," he says, sitting forward. "We can't find Kingsland so the only option is for him to find us."

"And how do we do that?"

"You've got his phone number, right?"

"Yes."

"Call him and say you wanna meet up."

"For what purpose?"

"Tell him you've found the kid's phone."

"But we haven't."

"Yeah, I know. It's just a ruse to get him out in the open."

I glance at Clement's glass which is three-quarters full. I can discount inebriation as a reason for his crazy idea.

"You're absolutely right," I grumble. "I don't like it … not one bit."

"You ain't got any other choice, Doc. We're pissing in the wind trying to find a bloke who don't wanna be found. Time is running out."

I take another sip of terrible lager; not as terrible as the first sip, or Clement's brainwave.

"Let's just imagine how this might work, shall we? I call Kingsland and tell him I've found the phone, and then what?"

"He'll come and fetch it."

"What if he doesn't? Last time he sent one of his men to

collect it. Don't you recall throttling him in our hallway?"

"If he does send someone else, I'll have to have a chat with him … get some answers."

"Dare I ask how?"

"You got a toolkit at home?"

"Err, yes."

"Gaffa tape?"

"Oh, Jesus. No, I don't."

"It's alright," he says dismissively. "We can pick some up."

"Has it really got to this point? You're seriously suggesting we kidnap one of Kingsland's men and torture him?"

"I wouldn't call it torture. Gentle encouragement."

I put my head in my hands.

"It's only a back-up plan," Clement confirms. "Hopefully, Kingsland will turn up in person."

"Brilliant," I sigh. "And then what? We sit him down and have a chat over tea and biscuits?"

"No need to be sarky."

"Sorry, but I can't see how that'll work."

"It'll work 'cos it's got to. We don't have any other choice."

"Okay, so what happens if Kingsland himself turns up? Short of killing him, I don't know … wait …"

"I ain't gonna kill him. That might help you, but it sure as hell won't help me."

"What then?"

"We sit him down and tell him we know why he wants the kid, and if he doesn't back off, we'll blow the lid on his plans."

"We have no proof of what his plans are."

"So? We bluff."

"And what if he calls our bluff?"

"You ain't gonna be in a worse position, are you?"

He rests his elbows on the table.

"Way I see it, Doc, your missus is out of the way so he can't touch her, and he's already threatening to tell the Old Bill you're a nonce so what have you got to lose?"

"Err, my life."

"If we set this up properly, you'll be fine. I'll do all the talking. All you need to do is make a call and tell him you've found the phone."

"Let me get this straight. If he sends one of his men, you want to torture him until he tells us where we find Kingsland? If the man himself turns up, you want to use evidence we don't have to blackmail him, and hope he doesn't call your bluff?"

"That's about the strength of it."

"Good grief."

I turn towards the fruit machine and watch the lights scroll through a pattern. It's kind of mesmerising and for a moment I'm able to forget the fuck-awful choice I've yet to make.

"Well?"

I turn and face Clement.

"I want your word no one will be seriously hurt."

"Does that include you?"

"Definitely."

"You have my word you'll be fine. As for anyone else, that's out of my hands."

Life is all about compromises. I'll take this one.

"Any suggestions for a venue?"

"Yeah, there's an industrial estate in Archway. Tell him to head past the Royal Mail depot and park at the end of the road."

"Why there?"

"It's quiet, but not too quiet."

"And how are we going to get there?"

"It's only a ten-minute stroll from Archway tube station. Tell him we'll be there in an hour and a half."

I reach for my glass and gulp down as much Dutch courage as I can stomach. Then, I call the number Kingsland used to call me after I left the police station.

It rings twice.

"Yes?"

"Mr Kingsland?"

"Who's this?"

"David Nunn."

"Afternoon, Mr Nunn. I presume you're calling me with good news?"

194

"I've found Cameron's phone."

"Good. I'll send one of my men round to pick it up."

"No, I … um, I'm not comfortable having your thugs in my home. If you want it, I'll text you an address where we can meet."

"Don't dictate to me, sunshine …"

"If you want the phone, Mr Kingsland, I suggest you meet me. If not, I'll hand it in at the police station."

The line falls silent.

"Are you planning a surprise?" he then asks.

"Not at all."

"Let me make this clear, Mr Nunn: if you mess me around, I won't be happy. And, I think we both know that's not in your best interests."

"I'm not sure what you mean?"

"I don't know — maybe you've been a silly boy and had a chat with the police?"

"Considering I'm on bail because of your poisonous allegations, the police are the last people I want involved."

"Very sensible. Text me the details."

"I'll be there in ninety minutes."

He hangs up.

"All done?" Clement asks.

"Apparently."

"Nice one. We'd better get a move on."

Two seconds and his glass is empty. With a sudden queasiness setting in, I risk a final sip from my glass.

We set off and I'm glad to see the back of The Crown, even though our next destination is equally undesirable.

The journey across London from west to north involves a bus and two trains. Clement doesn't appear keen to chat and I can only hope it's because he's plotting and planning the conversation with Kingsland. If he's concerned, it's not reflected in his body language.

We arrive at Archway station and make our way up to the street. Dusk is already setting in and the breeze is brisk enough to skip litter along the gutter as we walk. The urban scene is as bleak as my thoughts.

"Had you considered whoever we're about to meet might be armed?"

"Yeah, but no one is gonna use a shooter."

"Why so confident?"

He points up beyond a fence towards a security camera mounted on the side of an industrial unit.

"Ain't you noticed there are cameras everywhere these days?"

"Yes, but cameras only help in the investigation of a crime after it's already happened."

"Kingsland ain't a mug, Doc. If this drug he's after is worth what you reckon it's worth, he ain't gonna risk shooting someone in public."

"I'm afraid I don't share your optimism. And you're assuming Kingsland himself will turn up."

"Ain't no point frettin' about it. We'll know soon enough."

We turn a corner and follow the path towards the Royal Mail depot Clement mentioned; scores of red vans parked on the road and within the compound itself.

"You know how much a stamp costs these days?" Clement asks.

"Err, I don't, actually."

"Seventy bleedin' pence. They're taking the piss."

"You send a lot of letters, do you?"

"Nah, but I sent a few Christmas cards."

"To who?"

"Folks I knew."

"Knew, as in past-tense?"

"Yeah."

"Folks who you used to know in your former life?"

"How would that work, Doc? Season's greetings from that dead bloke you used to know."

"Sorry. Stupid question."

He shakes his head and we walk on in silence until another question comes to mind.

"If you've been here for almost four years, and know people, why haven't you turned to them for help?"

"Help with what?"

"Your predicament."

"'Cos it wouldn't be right. Things happened that can't be undone."

"Such as?"

"People died," he sighs.

"I … what?"

"You heard."

"You killed people?"

"I didn't kill anyone … not intentionally … but they died 'cos I was there."

"How many people unintentionally died?"

"A few."

I stop walking. Clement takes another three steps before turning around to face me.

"What you doing?"

"You've just told me people died — I don't want to be the next one."

"Those people were bad … rotten fuckers who got what they deserved."

"It's not your place to judge. We have a legal system that decides who's guilty and who's not."

"I didn't judge anyone, and neither did the courts. Smart as you are, Doc, you don't know the half of it."

"You just said they deserved to die."

"Yeah, and I also said I didn't make that judgement."

"Who did?"

"Dunno," he shrugs. "But I ain't gonna let it happen again."

"Is that why you're now estranged from Emma? Did someone die?"

His expression instantly matches our cold, bleak surroundings.

"I ain't talking about her."

"Why not? What happened?"

"I'll tell you what happened, shall I?" he spits. "I showed her my grave."

"Your … your grave?"

"Where they buried my body … decades ago."

If he'd said ice is cold or water is wet, he couldn't have said it with any more conviction. His delusion is off-the-scale.

"I'm sorry," I croak.

The tension in his features eases a fraction.

"You're sorry I died, or sorry I told you?"

"Um, both."

"I'll tell you something: I wish I hadn't told her."

"Emma?"

He nods.

"Thought I was doing the right thing, but …"

The final remnants of tension ebb away as he puffs his cheeks. Quick as a flash, he then refocuses.

"Are we gonna get on with this? He'll be here in a minute."

"Don't you want to talk about Emma? It might help, you know."

"Now ain't the time or place. Come on."

He ushers me to move on. Reluctantly, I put one foot in front of the other and follow.

Once we pass the Royal Mail depot we reach the end of the road. Besides the gates to industrial compounds left and right, there's nowhere else to go but back the way we came. Clement perches on a low brick wall which marks the dead-end. I sit down next to him but with his arms folded and his eyes fixed on the approach road. It appears he's in no mood for chitchat.

Nerves mounting, I check my watch. A few minutes either way but it's more or less the time I told Kingsland I'd be here. I failed to mention I wouldn't be alone.

I join Clement in staring back up the road. A few Royal Mail vans arrive and depart, but otherwise the scene is still.

With daylight fading by the second, I'm starting to think Kingsland has changed his mind. In his line of work, I guess it makes sense to assume a default position of suspicion and doubt.

A car then suddenly appears. From my vantage point, all I can tell is it's a dark-colour saloon. It approaches slowly, yard by yard, until the driver's face is visible. Also visible is the three-pointed Mercedes emblem standing proud on the bonnet. Headlights on, it purrs to a stop twenty feet away from us.

One of the rear doors then opens.

25.

Scarcely able to breathe, I watch on as a suited figure emerges from the car, leaving the door open. With the headlights dazzling, it's hard to see who that figure is, but the silhouette doesn't look much like Kingsland's. Whoever it is, he strides forward until he's level with the front wheel of the Mercedes. Then, I recognise him — the second, shaven-headed man who chased after Cameron Gail that evening in The Duke.

Clement gets to his feet and takes five steps forward. I follow and stand a step short of his position.

"Who are you?" he asks the man.

"I could ask you the same question."

The shaven-headed man appears wary of Clement but not overly intimidated.

"Are you Kingsland?" Clement asks.

Ignoring the question, the man turns to me.

"Where's the phone?"

I pull out my phone and hold it up.

"If Mr Kingsland wants the phone, he can come and get it. After all the trouble he's put me through, I'm not prepared to hand it over to anyone but him."

The shaven-headed man takes a few steps towards me.

"Give it here."

"You heard him," Clement says. "If Kingsland wants it, he can come and get it."

The man smirks and then casually undoes the single button of his jacket. The fabric parts to reveal the grip of a pistol tucked into the waistband of his trousers.

Our bluff has been well and truly called. Frozen on the spot, I don't know what to do but handing over a phone which isn't Cameron's doesn't seem a sensible idea. I slowly turn to Clement in the hope he's got a viable explanation ready.

He takes a step towards the shaven-headed man with his hands raised.

"Listen, mate," he says calmly, while still edging forward.

"We don't want any bother."

"Best you hand over the phone, then."

"Yeah, but …"

Much like that evening by the garages Clement explodes towards his target like a startled rhino. The shaven-headed man catches up with events and moves his right hand towards the pistol, but a brick-like fist is already en route to his jaw. It arrives long before the man's hand reaches its destination.

I'm not a massive fan of boxing, but I've seen enough bouts to know what a knockout blow looks like. However, Clement's fist isn't padded in layers of high-density polyurethane and the man's jaw absorbs the full impact of a bare knuckle punch. He collapses to the ground and emits a sound unlike anything I've ever heard from a human mouth.

Clement then stands over him like he stood over the drug-dealer. There, his actions differ. I'm unable to turn away in time as he stamps down on the shaven-headed man's right hand. Watching Match of the Day, I've heard commentators refer to a bone-crunching tackle. I never thought I'd ever hear actual bones crunching. Belatedly, I turn away and have to forcefully swallow hard to keep the contents of my stomach in situ.

I risk another glance at the fallen man. Whimpering loudly, he's huddled into a foetal position; his one good hand held up in surrender. Clement shows no sign of mercy and takes a step back, and then another, like he's teeing up a penalty kick. There's no ball, but there is an exposed torso.

"Stop!" a voice yells.

Another silhouette appears from the car; one which looks more like the man we came here to meet. Clement lowers his foot and squints as he tries to make out who the voice belongs to. Wisely, perhaps, he takes a few steps back.

Fraser Kingsland edges past the front wheel of the Mercedes; a pistol aimed at Clement. From the other side of the car, the driver gets out and meets Kingsland in front of the bonnet.

"Get him in the car," Kingsland orders, waving the pistol at his stricken associate.

The driver bends down and pulls his still-whimpering

colleague to his feet. Slowly, he then guides him back around the car while Kingsland re-trains the pistol on Clement.

This has not gone well. Not at all.

"Give me that fucking phone," Kingsland screams.

I've no choice now but to do as he asks. My only hope is he doesn't know what kind of phone Cameron Gail owned. Slowly, I step forward with the phone in my outstretched hand. Unsurprisingly, as he has a pistol trained on his chest, Clement stands motionless, staring intently at Kingsland.

I get within a few feet and Kingsland snatches the phone from my hand. He then takes a step back and swings his arm so the pistol is pointing in my direction.

"You'll pay for this," he spits.

Mercifully, I'm afforded a temporary reprieve when he slips the phone into his pocket without confirming ownership. He'll be apoplectic when he realises I've given him my phone. However, that concern takes an immediate back seat, when he cocks the trigger and adjusts his aim an inch.

Suddenly, Clement wakes from his coma and takes two steps to his right so he's stood directly in the line of fire.

"Fucking move or I'll pop you first," Kingsland yells.

Clement puts his hands on his hips and stares his aggressor straight in the eye.

"Get outta my way. I won't tell you again."

The big man takes a step forward in an act of defiance, or suicidal stupidity. There's now barely four feet between the pistol barrel and his chest. I can just about see Kingsland's face beyond Clement's right shoulder. For a man holding all the cards, his furrowed brow would better suit someone caught cheating.

Clement steps forward again.

"Go on. Pull the trigger," he urges. "I fucking dare you."

If ever there was indisputable evidence of Clement's declining mental health, he's just presented it. All that stands between him and certain death is the slightest movement of an edgy man's finger.

He then growls a few words I don't catch; his voice low and

rumbling. Whatever those words were, they have a kryptonite-like effect on Kingsland and he staggers back to the rear door of the Mercedes. As quick as his retreat, he falls into the car and slams the door.

The tyres then squeal as the driver spins the saloon in a tight circle. I watch perplexed as bright red taillights trail back down the road and away.

Clement turns around.

"You alright, Doc?"

I release a breath I've been holding too long. It escapes as a gasp.

Kingsland and his cronies have left, and so it seems has the hideous Mr Hyde — the affable Dr Jekyll stood before me. Split-personality disorder is a condition I've read about, but I've never met anyone able to shift so seamlessly from semi-normal to barbarically violent.

"What just happened?" I blurt.

"I ain't sure, but …"

He doesn't finish his sentence and stares intently up the road.

"Clement?"

"Yeah?"

"What are you staring at?"

"Nothin'. Just …"

"Just what?"

He finally turns to face me.

"This morning. Remember, I whistled that Queen tune?"

"Yes."

"You said it sounded familiar but couldn't place the name?"

"Are you going somewhere with this?"

"Kingsland. He's like a tune in my head … kinda familiar, but I can't work out why."

"You've met him before?"

"I dunno, can't say for sure. There's just something about the bloke which …"

He shuts his eyes and presses his fingertips into his temples as if trying to massage away a headache.

"Nah," he then sighs. "If it's in there, it ain't coming out."

"Now we've cleared that up, what the hell are we going to do next? Within the hour, Kingsland will realise we've duped him and at that point I'm a dead man."

"Ain't you supposed to preach positivity?"

The incredulity catches in my throat.

"What?" I cough. "Please, pray tell, what is there to be positive about?"

"Kingsland has got your phone in his pocket."

"Well spotted. That's precisely the reason I'm not feeling positive."

"Those things can be tracked, though, I've been told. Satellites, or some other bleedin' wizardry, ain't it?"

"Err, yes."

"So, you can track where yours is, right?"

In a fog of gloomy thoughts I'm struggling to see why it's important.

"I don't know … probably. So what?"

"It might tell us where Kingsland lives, or at least where he bases himself."

"And then what? We call in a SWAT team?"

"Do you wanna find the bloke, or not?"

"No, I want to go home, lock the door, and hope to God I wake up in the morning to find this has all been a bad dream."

"If you wanna talk about bad dreams, I've been living one for four bleedin' years. So, cut the self-pity — it's getting on my tits."

His barb stings. I know I'm not perfect but I never considered myself the type to indulge in self-pity. I may have misjudged myself.

"I apologise."

"Accepted. Now, if we know where Kingsland is holed up, it'll give us something to work with, and we ain't got jack-shit else to go on."

"Okay," I sigh.

We set off back along the road past the Royal Mail depot until we reach the main road. Clement then hails a cab and demands the driver steps on the gas. He complies, and we pull up

204

outside the flat within fifteen minutes. My offer to pay is declined, which is no bad thing considering I need to buy a new phone tomorrow.

In the flat I make straight for the kitchen, and my laptop.

"You got any beer in?" Clement asks.

"No, but there's a bottle of whisky in the cupboard by the fridge. Help yourself."

While I log-in to my Google account, my guest pours two large glasses of Glenfiddich; the untouched gift from Denny Chambers. He then joins me at the table.

"How does that work then?" he asks, nodding towards the laptop.

"The website pings the phone, and it responds with a longitude and latitude reference which is then displayed on a map."

"Yeah, but how does the phone know where it is?"

"A combination of satellites and phone masts."

He looks none the wiser.

"Okay, it's sent the signal. I'm just waiting for the phone to respond."

I stare at the screen as a timer icon pulses for what feels like an age. A message in bold letters pops up.

"Sod it."

"What?"

"The phone is offline."

"What does that mean?"

"It's either been switched off, or the battery is dead."

"Shit."

Then I notice another line of text below the damning headline.

"However, it recorded the last known location, and it was only six minutes ago."

"Where?"

"I can't say for sure as it's only accurate to within ten metres, but the phone went offline on Plender Street."

"In Camden?"

I zoom the map out to check.

"Yes, in Camden."

"Shall we get going, then?"

"Don't you think we should work on a strategy first?"

"We already discussed it, Doc. We find Kingsland, and tell him we know about his little plan for the kid's drug. He either backs off or I beat ten bells out of him until he promises to leave you alone."

"Maybe you should have employed that strategy half an hour ago, while we were stood in front of him."

"Not sure if you noticed, but he had a gun pointed in your direction. Weren't exactly the ideal time to chat."

"But you said something to him. What exactly did you say?"

"Nothin' much. I was about to mention his plan but he bolted before I had a chance. Next time, I'm gonna make sure he don't have a chance to point a gun at anyone."

"And what if he does?"

"Trust me, he won't. Let's get a shift on."

He downs the whisky and strides out the door. I close the laptop and I'm quickly at his heels.

"Are we getting a cab?" I ask, closing the front door.

With a frost already settling on the pavements, it's too cold and I'm too exhausted to walk anywhere. Hang the cost — I'll happily pay if it saves me from fifteen minutes of hell.

"Nah. It's only a mile down the road."

"Yes, but we need to get there as soon as possible; before Kingsland moves on."

There's no argument, therefore, and Clement waves a cab coming from the other direction. The warmth in the back is temporary, but welcome.

"How well do you know Plender Street?" I ask.

"Used to know it well, but …"

"It's changed?"

"Yeah, it has."

I shouldn't indulge his delusion but part of me remains curious how far he can stretch it.

"Tell me, Clement: if you've been back for four years, how have you avoided bumping into anyone you used to know before

206

your, um, death?"

"I haven't, as it goes."

"That must have been an interesting meeting."

"Not really."

"Can I ask what happened?"

"I was having a drink in a boozer near Tower Bridge and an old mate came wandering up to the table. He asked how I was."

"Wait … what? Wasn't he mildly curious how his dead friend was having a beer?"

"His son came over and said his dad was senile. The poor sod's head was gone so no one took any notice of what he said."

"That must have been a relief."

"You reckon?" he snaps, turning to face me. "How would you feel seeing a good mate a broken old man? There sure as fuck weren't any relief."

"I, um … sorry. I didn't mean it like that."

Much like when I apologise to Leah for arguments I never caused, I've just apologised for crassly commenting on a situation which couldn't have happened. Maybe I'm the one who needs their head tested. For now, a change of subject might be in order.

"Can I borrow your phone, please?"

"What for?"

"I need to text Leah and let her know I've lost mine. I don't want her worrying."

He pulls his blocky handset from his pocket and hands it over. Then he turns and stares out the window.

With his attention elsewhere, an opportunity arises and I scroll to the phone's contact list. Fortunately, the first five digits are the same as mine and the last six are 500747 — easy enough to remember. Emma's number committed to memory, I send Leah a short text to say I've dropped my phone down the loo and I'll call her tomorrow when I've replaced it.

I hand Clement his phone.

"Thanks."

It's taken without comment. He doesn't strike me as a sulker but I think my previous remarks may have touched a nerve. A

207

slice of empathy might be in order.

"I am sorry, Clement, for what I said. It must be hard with everyone you knew either gone or going."

"Harder than you'll ever know."

"You must get lonely?"

"Are you analysing me?"

"Not really. I'm just interested — if I'm wrong, how many people get to chat to a dead man?"

My attempt at lightening the mood is met with a black stare.

"I'll shut up."

I concede my nerves are probably responsible for the crass humour. I'd rather not think too much about what lies ahead when we reach our destination.

Minutes later, I have no choice but to face reality as the cab deposits us at the corner of Plender Street.

The phone pinged from a stretch of road near a nail salon and I confirm the approximate location with Clement.

"How far is ten metres?" he asks.

"Thirty feet, give or take."

We saunter down Plender Street until we come to the nail salon.

"Now what?"

Clement turns a full circle to weigh up our options. On the opposite side of the street there's an estate agent's office and the New Camden Church; neither a likely location for the phone. On our side, there's a pub, a tapas bar, and the nail salon. Clement noses through the window of the tapas bar but it looks near-empty.

"He could be in the pub," I suggest.

"I'll have a quick gander."

A minute later Clement emerges from the pub, shaking his head.

"He ain't in there."

"Well, he's not getting his nails done or house hunting at this time of the evening so we're out of options."

"Not quite."

He looks up towards twelve windows in the building which

houses the tapas bar and nail salon.

"Could be flats up there," he remarks.

"We know he lives in Chiswick and this doesn't strike me as the kind of area a wealthy crime baron would have a pied-à-terre."

"Only one way to find out. Come on."

I follow Clement along a wide alleyway running up the side of the nail salon. We then reach a door with an intercom and six buttons.

"Must be flats," he confirms. "Now we just need to work out if your phone is in one of 'em."

He presses the first button and a shrill metallic buzz leaks from a speaker. Seconds pass but there's no response.

"One down."

Clement tries the second button, and then the third — neither result in an answer. He presses the fourth and again, it's met with silence. Just as he reaches out to press the fifth button, a voice crackles from the speaker.

"Yeah?"

"Alright, mate. I've got a package to deliver to flat two. Any chance you can buzz me in so I can leave it at their door?"

There's a moment's pause before the lock clicks. Clement pushes the door open.

"Cheers."

I follow him in to the communal hallway.

"How does this help?" I ask.

"We know someone is in flat four, so we'll check five and six and then pay him a visit."

"That voice sounded nothing like Kingsland's. He sounded much younger."

"No harm asking if he's seen our man."

Discussion over, Clement strides up the stairs, two at a time. This feels futile but I traipse up behind him. We reach a landing with two doors opposite each other; flats one and two. We've already established no one is home so we move up the next set of stairs to the second floor, and then the third where flats five and six are located.

Clement raps on the door of flat five and waits. There's no response. He turns one-eighty degrees and tries the door to flat six. After another long pause, a tall, black woman finally answers.

"Alright, Doll."

"Yes?"

"Sorry to bother you but we're trying to find an old mate and we've been told he lives in these flats. Middle-aged bloke called Fraser. Don't suppose you know him?"

"Sorry, no."

"Right, cheers."

She closes the door.

"Now what?"

"We'll go have a word with the bloke in flat four."

"Okay," I sigh.

We head back down to the second floor and I stand at Clement's shoulder as he knocks the door to flat four.

There's a moment's wait, but it opens.

My suspicion proved correct as a pale-faced young man in jeans and a black t-shirt looks up at Clement.

"You alright, mate?" my companion asks.

"Um, can I help you?"

"We're looking for Fraser."

"Fraser?"

"Yeah, you know Fraser, right?"

There's a slightest hesitancy in the young man's response.

"He left half-an-hour ago."

A thick-soled boot is thrust forward and meets the closing door.

"Think we need a chat, sunshine, don't you?"

26.

I've seen the look on the young man's face before. That night, by the garages, the drug dealer displayed a similar expression of helpless dread when he realised his fate.

Clement steps forward and the skinny youth receives a hefty shove to the chest. He stumbles back into the hallway and falls to his backside. The way forward clear, we enter the flat. I close the front door as my partner in crime glares down at the young man.

"What's your name, sunshine?"

"Alex," he whimpers.

"Right, listen to me, Alex. We're gonna have a little chat and if you play nicely, we'll leave you safe and sound. Piss me around, though, and I'll throw your weedy arse out the fucking window. Understood?"

Alex nods.

"Now, get up."

He does as he's told and Clement grabs him by the arm.

"Where do you wanna chat?"

"The … the lounge is through there."

He nods to a door on the right, a few inches ajar.

If Alex intended to bolt for the window himself, Clement thwarts his plan by grabbing a handful of his t-shirt. He then pushes the young man forward through the door. I follow, not because I want to be here but to ensure Clement does nothing stupid — not that there's much I could do to stop him.

The lounge has all the charm of student digs. There's a tatty grey sofa wedged up against one wall, and the carpet is so threadbare in places you can see the tiles beneath. A trestle table abuts the back wall as a makeshift workstation, housing two laptop computers and a smattering of electronic paraphernalia.

Clement shoves Alex down on the sofa and stands in front of him.

"Let's start with a nice easy question, shall we? Where's my mate's phone?"

"I … I don't know. Why would I have it?"

I step over to the trestle table and immediately spot a phone which looks remarkably similar to mine, plugged in to one of the laptops. A brief inspection confirms it is my phone.

"It's here, Clement."

He tuts at Alex.

"Not a good start, pal."

"I didn't know who it belonged to. I swear."

"Why is my phone connected to this laptop?" I ask Alex.

"It's just charging."

I glance at the laptop screen which contains line after line of meaningless code. As I unplug my phone, an error message pings up on the screen: *connection lost — data transfer suspended at 97%.*

"He's lying," I say to Clement. "I think he's been copying all the data from my phone because the man who gave it to him thinks it belongs to Cameron Gail."

Clement takes a step closer to the sofa and cracks his knuckles.

"Start talking," he growls at Alex. "We know who gave you the phone, and we wanna know where he is."

"I don't know."

"Open the window, Doc. We're gonna see if this kid can fly."

"Please, no!"

Alex looks at me in the hope one of his unexpected guests has a modicum of compassion. I shrug my shoulders and step over to the window. It takes some effort to prise the wooden sash open, but it eventually slides upward. The view below is of a yard at the rear of the building and a fall would likely break a few bones.

I turn back to Alex.

"Believe it or not, I'm doing you a favour as he'll throw you out the window whether it's open or not. At least this way you won't get any glass cuts."

His panic mounts.

"I swear I don't know where Mr Kingsland is. Why would he tell me? I'm just … just …"

"One of his lackeys?" I venture.

I step over to the sofa and perch on the arm.

"The reason we're here, Alex, is because another young man, much like yourself, became embroiled with Fraser Kingsland. That young man is now on the run, in fear of his life."

"I don't have any choice," he pleads. "I have to do as he asks."

"And what exactly is it you do for him?"

"I look after his tech. Laptops, mobile phones, that kind of thing."

"Why you?"

He stares at the threadbare carpet for a long while until Clement cracks his knuckles again.

"A year ago I was forced to borrow money from a loan shark after I'd got myself in serious debt. I'd invested everything in a start-up venture that turned sour. I was already struggling with the payments when Kingsland's company bought the debt. He doubled the interest rate and I couldn't afford my flat anymore … ended up sleeping on a mate's sofa. I thought he wouldn't find me, but a few weeks later one of his thugs turned up at my place of work. That's how Kingsland found out what I do for a living, and he suggested I work for him."

"Why didn't you say no?"

"Because I was desperate, and scared. I had nowhere to live and Kingsland made promises."

"Such as?"

"He said he'd clear the debt and pay me ten percent more than I was earning. He also let me live here, rent free."

"Kingsland owns this gaff?" Clement interjects.

"Indirectly. He owns several companies and one of those companies is technically my landlord."

"Right."

Clement's mind then wanders off. His input complete, I take over the questioning again.

"How's it working out for you; this new career?"

"It's not a career — it's a prison. Kingsland has made it clear what will happen if I decide I no longer want to work for him."

"Unfortunately, I've also experienced his threats, but what I don't understand is why he needs someone with tech experience?"

"I … I can't tell you. He'll kill me."

Clement returns from his temporary malaise and steps forward. He then delivers a summary of Alex's position.

"Kingsland ain't here, but I am," he snarls. "You keep answering the questions or he'll be the last of your worries."

"Data," Alex finally sighs. "Kingsland is a dinosaur but he knows the value of data in terms of keeping one step ahead of the police, and any competition."

"And does your skill-set extend to downloading data from mobile phones?"

"Yes," he mumbles. "My previous job involved coding for a digital security company. I was lead programmer in the development of a utility which could bypass the security on most mobile devices."

"And how is that of use to Kingsland?"

"Whenever one of his troops find a rival dealer on their patch, they take their phone and bring it to me so I can download all their data."

"What kind of worthwhile information would a drug dealer have on their phone?"

"You'd be surprised: supply lines, customer contact details, geo-data of their drop-offs, and all kinds of compromising files. It's all useful intel for Kingsland."

It appears our foe is running an efficient operation but little of what we've learnt helps my situation.

"What did Kingsland ask you to do with my phone?"

"He gave me a list of keywords to search. If I found any files or folders containing those keywords, I'm supposed to email them to him immediately."

"When is he expecting you to complete your work?"

"This evening."

"Does he know anything about the phone at the moment?"

"Such as?"

"Who it belongs to?"

"No. There's no way he could determine who the phone

belongs to without gaining access to the operating system."

It seems the decision to get a cab here was a good one. Ten or fifteen minutes later and Alex would have already confirmed who the phone really belongs to. However, it's only postponing the inevitable.

Clement turns to me.

"We need a chat, in private."

He then orders Alex to get up and leads him from the lounge back to the hallway.

"What are you doing?" I ask from the doorway.

Remaining mute, he opens another door and looks inside. He then grabs Alex by the arm and shoves him inside the room.

"We're gonna decide what to do with you," he says to Alex. "You try leaving or make a sound and you're dead. Got it?"

I catch a slight whimper before Clement slams the door shut.

"You've put him in a cupboard?" I ask.

"Nah, the bathroom."

I'm then beckoned back into the lounge. We stand close enough to the doorway so Clement can see the bathroom door but we're out of earshot.

"I suppose it's good news Kingsland doesn't know the phone isn't Cameron's," I say in a hushed voice. "Yet."

"It's an opportunity."

"Is it? How so?"

"I ain't got the first clue what that kid does but somewhere across town, Kingsland is waiting for information from him, right?"

"Correct."

"In which case, we get the kid to send him duff info."

"For what purpose?"

"It'll buy us some time."

"Time for what exactly? Alex doesn't know where Kingsland is so we're no closer to finding him."

"That's where you're wrong, Doc. He owns this gaff, which means there's a paper trail leading somewhere."

"I don't follow."

"Every drum in the land is registered, including this one. On

215

that register, it says who owns a building."

"How is that of any help? We already know Kingsland owns this flat."

"Nah, the kid said one of his companies owns it, and companies have to disclose their trading address."

"Really? How do you know all this?"

"'Cos I ain't been sitting on my arse the last four years feeling sorry for myself. Unlike you, Doc, I deal with my shit."

"What's that supposed to mean?"

"You really wanna get into that now? We need to brief the kid on what he's gonna tell Kingsland."

"No, I want to know what you meant by …"

"That window is open, remember?"

I'm good at reading people but I can't tell if his comment infers a genuine threat or not. I'm not willing to take a chance.

"Okay, okay," I grumble.

"So, what do you suggest we get dipshit to send him?"

"Well, I'm guessing Kingsland hopes Cameron stored notes about the Kimbo formula on his phone. It's the only logical explanation why it's so important to him."

"No point trying to blag that unless you know anything about chemistry."

"Nothing."

"Then the next best thing is the kid himself."

"Eh?"

"We let Kingsland think this Cameron kid has arranged an appointment … I dunno, at the doctors or something. All Kingsland has to do is send his men to pick him up."

"Ohh, I like that idea. It'll also keep him off my back for the moment."

"Exactly. In the meantime, we can dig around a bit more."

"But there is one slight issue with your plan."

"What?"

"How do we know Alex won't tell Kingsland we've sent him false information?"

"Leave that to me."

With that, Clement strides back into the hallway and returns with a still-petrified Alex.

"We've got a little job for you," the big man says, guiding Alex over to the workstation. "Sit your arse down."

Clement then turns to me.

"Tell him what he's gotta do."

"Right, Alex. How do you usually communicate with Kingsland?"

"Always by email. He's paranoid about security so we use an encrypted private server."

"And what is it he's hoping you'll find on that phone?"

"Anything related to the word Kimbo, whatever that is, or information which would locate the phone's owner: appointments, search history, regular patterns from the historic location data, that type of thing."

"Good. So, you're going to email him and say all you've found is an email regarding an appointment."

He looks up at me, open-mouthed.

"You want me to lie to Kingsland? I'd be signing my own death warrant."

Out of the corner of my eye I detect movement from a more immediate threat. I glance across at Clement and shake my head. I'd like to try the carrot rather than the stick.

"Listen, Alex. I'm in the same boat as you in that Kingsland is threatening me and my wife, not to mention the kid he's trying to find. I'm running out of time and unless I can keep that man off my back for a few more days, I'm ... let's just say I don't want to think about the consequences."

"And I'm sorry, but if he finds out I lied, I'm dead."

"How would he know you lied? It's an appointment, and people miss appointments all the time — he can hardly blame you."

"I wish I could help, but the risk is too great."

Clement steps over. I fear the worst.

"Listen, sunshine," he says. "Do you wanna spend the rest of your days working for that arsehole?"

"God, no."

"Then help us. There ain't no risk but if we can find

217

Kingsland and deal with him, you can walk away from all this."

"And how do you intend to deal with him?"

"I have my ways. You've got nothing to lose helping us."

Alex appears resolute and bows his head. Clement then leans over the desk.

"You need to understand something. I ain't a bad man, but that don't mean I'm not prepared to do bad things. I get it; you're scared of Kingsland, but not half as scared as he'll be when I catch up with him."

"I … I don't know …"

"Think about it, Alex," I add. "This could be your chance to escape Kingsland's clutches and make a new start."

A moment of consideration follows. He then looks up at me.

"Alright," he says in a low voice. "I'll compromise. I'll set up the email but you can write it and click the send button. I want plausible deniability."

"Thank you."

He taps the keyboard a few times and gets to his feet.

"All yours."

I sit down in the chair and ponder for a moment. What kind of appointment would a drug-ravaged young man on the run from a deranged crime boss be inclined to keep? The answer is fairly obvious when it strikes, and I paraphrase a fictitious email Cameron Gail sent, confirming an appointment for ten o'clock Monday morning at the offices of RightMind. I then add a few embellishments about how Cameron is desperately keen to discuss a rehab course, and therefore the importance of keeping his appointment is paramount.

"Is this the sort of info Kingsland was hoping to find?" I ask Alex.

"More or less, but you should mention there was nothing else on the phone relevant to his keywords."

I add another couple of lines, confirming as such.

"Is he likely to email a response asking for more information?"

"Unlikely. He trusts that I'm thorough."

I tap a key to send the email and get to my feet.

"I think we're done."

Clement suddenly grabs Alex by the scruff of his neck.

"Just so we're clear," he snarls at the young man. "If you're thinking about telling Kingsland after we've left, you might wanna know what happened to the last person who grassed on me … he can't count to ten no more."

Alex looks too scared to ask why.

"Not using his fingers, anyway," Clement adds.

We leave Alex whimpering to himself on the sofa; counting both his blessings and his fingers.

27.

With my mobile phone recaptured, replacing it is one expense I no longer have to worry about. Nevertheless, I don't want to lavish money on an unnecessary cab fare and suggest we walk back to the flat. Clement grunts an acknowledgement and we make our way back through the streets of Camden, northward towards Kentish Town.

My companion has little to say, but I do.

"Do you think Alex will keep quiet?"

"Dunno. Maybe."

"That's reassuring."

"What do you want me to say, Doc? It's your job to tell folks everything is rosy, even when it ain't."

"That's not what I do."

"No?" he snorts.

"Far from it."

"Don't you ever get sick of it? Listening to folks whine on all day?"

"Not sick of it, but I'm no different from anyone else in that I have good days, and bad."

"Ain't a job I could do," he says, before lighting a cigarette. "Much rather say it as it is."

"I gathered."

"You should try it sometime."

"What? Be more like you? I'm not sure my clients would appreciate it."

"Some might appreciate a few home truths, and your missus definitely would."

"Why do you say that?"

"Has it ever crossed your mind that not everyone needs an arm around the shoulder — some need a boot up the arse."

"Nothing is that black and white," I reply with a frown. "I work to find solutions based on compromise, both at home and in my career."

"And that's your problem. You're too keen on compromise

and compromise don't always work."

"I beg to differ."

"Beg all you like, but I'm right. If we'd compromised with Hitler, the world would be a very different place."

"That's a flawed example. From what I recall about modern history, there were efforts to negotiate peace, but it was Hitler who failed to compromise."

"Nah, you're wrong. Even before the war started, we tried to compromise by entertaining a lunatic … even the bleedin' Royals were at it. We knew what he was up to and we should have just shot the fucker dead the moment he glanced at Poland."

I don't know anywhere near enough about the events of World War II to offer a counterargument.

"And do you reckon you can compromise with Kingsland?" he adds, to reinforce his point.

"Sadly, no," I concede.

"There you go then. Sometimes in life you can sort shit out but other times you've gotta stand your ground."

"Okay, I get it."

"Especially with your missus."

"That is not a topic of conversation I wish to pursue."

"Why? 'Cos you know I'm right?"

"No, because you don't understand."

"Bullshit."

"You know nothing about my wife or my marriage so I'd appreciate it if you kept your crass opinions to yourself."

"Give over, Doc. I've seen enough."

"Oh, have you?" I snap. "Have you heard the countless times she's said her life isn't worth living? Have you seen her sobbing uncontrollably because she feels worthless? Have you seen the list of medication she has to take, just to get through the day?"

"What you saying? Your missus is not right in the head?"

"That's exactly what I'm saying."

I wait for an apology but Clement doubles-down.

"In that case, Doc, you're an even bigger bottler than I thought you were."

"How dare you …"

"You said your missus would be better off living out in the sticks, didn't you?"

"I ... what? Yes."

"Then don't keep pussyfooting around. Do something about it, man. You've got yourself in a rut where you're too bleedin' scared to speak your mind and that ain't doing either of you any good."

"Well, thank you for that insight, Clement. Clearly you know more than me, despite my university education and numerous counselling qualifications."

"And that's your problem," he replies, shaking his head. "If the answer ain't in a book, you're fucked. You keep doing the same thing 'cos that's what you were taught to do. What do they call it ... indoctrination?"

"I disagree."

"You would. Anyway, I've said my piece, and you'd do well to take some of it on board. Maybe one day you'll thank me for it."

I don't respond. It's hard enough living with Leah without adding Clement's deluded advice to the mix.

We negotiate the final few streets in silence and arrive back at the flat just before nine. The two whisky tumblers and bottle of Glenfiddich are still on the table.

"Want one?" Clement asks, unscrewing the bottle without invitation.

"How kind to offer me a glass of my own whisky. Go on."

"You still sulking about what I said?"

"No."

"Good, 'cos we've got work to do. You need to use the interweb thing to get the title details for Kingsland's flat."

I sit down and take a sip of whisky before opening my laptop. The burn in my throat is a reminder why I don't regularly drink whisky, but it takes the edge off my fatigue.

"What am I searching for?"

"Land registry."

I conduct a search and a series of links to the Land Registry website appear at the top of the page.

"Search property ownership, yes?"

"Sounds about right."

I click the link and then navigate through to a page where I'm prompted to enter the address. There's a fee to see the record, but thankfully it's only three pounds. I enter my card details and the website processes the transaction. Once completed, I'm offered a download link.

"Here we go," I say, taking another sip of whisky.

When the file eventually opens up, it confirms what Alex told us.

"A company owns the flat: Folsom Property Holdings Limited."

"Folsom?"

I spell it out.

"Why does that name ring a bell?"

"I've never heard it before. It could be an acronym?"

"Nah, it's … what the hell is it?"

Clement frowns at the table.

"Want me to google it?"

"Yeah, go on."

I return to the web browser and search for Folsom. A Wikipedia page offers a partial answer.

"Folsom is a city in Sacramento County, California."

"That ain't it."

I read on.

"It is commonly known for Folsom Prison; popularised in the song *Folsom Prison Blues*."

Clement brings a fist down on the table with such force the laptop jumps.

"Knew I'd heard it before," he announces triumphantly. "Johnny bloody Cash … I'm sure he recorded an album there."

"Ohh, didn't you say Kingsland was a fan?"

"That's what I heard."

I google Mr Cash's name for clarification.

"My, God," I blurt, as I read the short bio text at the top of the page.

"What is it?"

"Guess where Johnny Cash was born."

"No bleedin' idea."

"Arkansas in America. The town of Kingsland."

I stare across at Clement. He stares back as we both churn over the implications of this information.

"No wonder we couldn't find any record of him," he says first. "Kingsland ain't his real name."

"Seems that old boy was right about his family tree."

It finally feels like we've made some actual progress.

"Okay, so I guess we need to dig into Folsom Property Holdings Limited?"

"Yeah. Ain't there a company register you can check?"

"I think so. Hold on."

A few more taps of the keyboard and I'm on the Companies House website. I enter the details in the search box and strike the enter key. There's one result; the company name listed with a registered address.

"Bloody hell," I groan. "I don't believe this."

"What?"

"I've found the record for Folsom Property Holdings but their registered address is a firm of accountants in Windsor."

"Fuck's sake. Should have guessed."

"Is that legal, using an accountant's office as a business address?"

"Course it is."

"Great. So, we're no further forward."

"Ain't there any more info about the company?"

"Err, give me a sec."

I click the link for the company page and I'm presented with a row of tabs: O*verview, Filing History, People, and Charges*. The first tab displays basic information about the company such as the incorporation date and nature of business. No help. The filing history tab would only be of interest if we wanted to check the balance sheet or confirm their accounts are up-to-date.

Optimism dwindling, I click the third tab: *People.*

"Yes!"

"What is it?"

224

"There's just one director listed for Folsom Property Holdings, and he happens to be called Fraser."

"Gotta be our man. What's his surname?"

"Raynott."

Clement doesn't respond, other than to stare back at me, ashen faced.

"What's the matter? This is good news, right?"

"Say the name again," he says in an uncharacteristically sombre tone.

"Raynott. Fraser Raynott."

The intensity of his stare is so profound I glance over my shoulder to check if there's anything or anyone behind me. There isn't, and I turn back to the same dumbstruck face.

"Clement? Are you okay?"

He empties the whisky tumbler and refills it with a triple shot. One gulp and another refill.

"Will you talk to me, please?"

"Raynott," he replies flatly.

Perplexed, it's my turn to employ a blank stare.

"I don't understand. What's the significance of the name Raynott?"

"The bloke who killed me … his name was Roland Raynott."

The first rule of counselling is to think before you speak. We are there to listen; not to judge, or cajole, or influence.

I take a sip of whisky and wait to see if Clement expands on his statement. Besides a few strokes of the moustache, he remains lost in his own thoughts. Seeing as I've already broken so many rules relating to professional conduct, I don't suppose another one will make much difference.

"Can I just get this clear, Clement? A man called Roland Raynott killed you?"

He slowly nods.

I'm too tired for this crap.

"It's all a bit of a coincidence, isn't it?"

"Except it ain't," he huffs. "It all makes sense now … that night by the garages. It weren't no accident you were there — I was supposed to meet you."

"Why?"

"So you'd lead me to Raynott."

"To what end?"

"I wish I fucking knew."

Sanity is rarely found at the bottom of a glass, but I'm willing to check. By the time I put my glass down, Clement is still in a semi-conscious state of bewilderment. I need to find some sense in all this madness.

"Okay, let's just suspend rational thought for one moment. When you were … murdered … Fraser Kingsland or Raynott was just a kid. I don't see how that has any bearing on our paths crossing. The man is a complete psychopath, but he didn't kill you."

"No, but his old man did."

"We don't know that. What evidence is there they're related?"

"How many times you heard the name Raynott before?"

"Well, never, but that's hardly evidence."

"You do your search thing then, Doc. Tell me how many people with the name Raynott live in London."

Keen to prove my point, I log-in to the same website I used to search for Kingslands. There are only two people in the whole of London called Raynott, and neither have the first name Fraser or Roland.

"Okay, I concede the name is rare but why do you think there's a connection?"

"Dunno. Sins of the father and all that, maybe."

Time to ask a question I've avoided asking several times on account it's ludicrous.

"If we are talking about the same man, do you think he's still alive?"

"I doubt it. He'd be in his nineties by now, and Roland Raynott was a snide fucker who drank like a fish, smoked like a trooper, and pissed off a lot of people."

"He sounds delightful. I see where Fraser gets his charm from, assuming you're right about his parentage."

"I am," comes the defiant response. "And if you think I'm

226

deluded, you should have met Roland Raynott. He thought he was Camden's answer to the Godfather. Bloke was a chancer, a bullshitter."

"Dare I ask why he attacked you?"

"He owed money to a car dealer. Bought himself a Jag on the never-never but failed to keep up with the repayments. The dealer paid me a pony to get the car back; so I did."

"It seems extreme; killing someone over a car debt."

"Bit more complicated than that. I nipped round his drum and while he was in bed sleeping off a hangover, I got the keys from his missus just as she was heading off to the shops."

"Right. Still makes no sense."

"I had to use a bit of persuasion."

"Oh, dear God. Don't tell me you threatened his wife."

"Nah, I ain't like that. I gave her a good seeing to in the back seat of Roland's motor."

"Good grief," I groan.

"I found out later he watched the whole thing from the bedroom window of their flat. Didn't have the balls to come down and do anything about it, though."

"So, you had sex with his wife and then repossessed his car?"

"That's about the strength of it, yeah. He took it kinda personally."

"Funny that."

"And, he beat the shit out of his wife."

"Oh."

"I put word around I wanted to have a chat with him about his behaviour. I've done some shitty things in my time, but I've never laid a glove on a bird. That ain't acceptable and I intended to teach the arsehole a lesson."

"And he thought he'd strike first."

"Yeah, but only a fucking coward would whack someone from behind with a cricket bat. That's the kind of low-life piece of shit Roland Raynott was."

"His son isn't much better; a right chip off the old block."

"Yeah, and that's why I reckon we bumped into each other that night. Raynott Senior might have got away with murder, but

I ain't gonna let Junior have one over me. This is now personal."

"And, knowing what you now know, how are you intending to deal with Fraser?"

"Dunno yet, but the goalposts have moved, Doc. This ain't just about you now."

Notwithstanding the lunacy of Clement's claim, his apparent desire for retribution creates a dilemma. I want Kingsland, or Raynott, or whatever his damn name is, out of my life for good. I want this over with. The question is: am I prepared to participate in whatever Clement now has in mind? It would be akin to driving a forty-ton truck, at speed, with no brakes. I'll be nothing more than a passenger; waiting for two immovable objects to collide.

It's not a decision I want to make, but I have to side with the lesser of two evils. That doesn't mean I have to abandon my principles totally.

"Just to be clear, Clement, I'm not willing to be part of any plan which involves murder."

"Who said I'm gonna murder him? I can't risk anyone dying … not again."

"Can I have your word on that?"

"No, 'cos I ain't in control of this, Doc. You're still not gettin' it, are you?"

"No, clearly not."

"This is all part of whatever fucked-up plan I'm meant to follow. I found you, we find Fraser, and I dunno what happens then."

"Yes, but I need to know what your revenge might entail."

"And I said I don't know yet."

"I'm not comfortable with such vagaries. I …"

"In case you'd forgotten," he interrupts, "that bloke already has you by the balls and unless we deal with him, you or your missus is in deep shit."

We've come full circle, and there's no point pretending my position is any less grave; regardless of Clement's new-found motives.

"Fine," I sigh. "We find Fraser, but I cannot condone any

228

physical retribution; particularly as that retribution is based upon a fairy tale."

"So much for an open mind," he scoffs. "What you want me to say, Doc? You think I should just forgive and forget?"

"No, I just want you to promise me one thing."

"I don't do promises."

"Okay, then assure me you won't do anything stupid until we've worked out if you're of sound mind. That was what I agreed to, and I'd appreciate you sticking to our deal."

"Alright," he says, begrudgingly.

"Thank you. Now we've got a name to work with what are the chances of finding him?"

"I dunno. He obviously ain't on the voters' roll so I'd need to ask around. Someone must know where he hangs out."

"When?"

"No time like the present."

He gets to his feet.

"Do you want me to come with you?"

"Nah. I ain't going to the library, Doc."

I'll readily accept the jibe if it means staying here.

"Fair enough. Shall we reconvene tomorrow morning?"

"I'll be round about nine."

With that, he marches out of the kitchen.

As the front door slams shut, I pour another glass of whisky. Is this what I've descended to: a man who drinks hard liquor on his own?

It's the first question in a process; a time of introspection. This is how it begins for the poor souls who sit across from my chair every day. One innocuous decision leads to another and, before you know it, your life is spiralling out of control. A grandmother innocently downloads a bingo app and, before she knows it, the bailiffs are at her door. A young woman agrees to a date and then wakes up to find she's a mother to two children and her Prince Charming is in prison for selling crack to schoolkids.

If I'd never agreed to meet Cameron Gail at The Duke, I wouldn't be here.

"You bloody fool."

Another gulp of whisky. I relish the burn as it detracts from my lament.

One bad decision is forgivable, but I've taken the wrong turn at every opportunity. I've become embroiled in a situation not of my making, but of my weakness. What was I thinking, making a deal with a psychopath to keep another psychopath at bay? I have metaphorically used petrol to put out a fire. Now, I can't see any way to escape. Trapped in a world of delusion and anarchy where the rules make no sense to a man like me.

I need to ground myself; find some semblance of normality in this madness. I grab my phone and call Leah.

"Hey, honey. How's it going?"

"I thought you'd dropped your phone down the loo?"

"Oh, I, um, dried it out. Seems to work fine now."

Lie upon lie upon lie.

"That's good."

"So, are you having fun? I miss you."

"I miss you too … and guess where I've been today."

"Err, no idea."

"A garden centre. It was brilliant."

"Seriously?"

"Yes, seriously. Don't sound so surprised."

"Sorry, I just didn't think garden centres were really your thing."

"You've never asked."

"Well, no."

"In fact, your dad says you told him I wouldn't be interested."

I make a mental note to thank my father. Grass.

"I'm glad you're enjoying it."

"Don't take this the wrong way, but it's rather nice being here without you."

"Oh great," I groan. "I called in the hope my wife might cheer me up."

"Why, what's the matter?"

Should I explain a man is threatening to either ruin me, or kill her, or that I've employed the services of a ghost to help? Decisions, decisions.

"Nothing. Ignore me."

"How's my surprise coming along?"

"It's … um, getting there."

"I'm looking forward to it, but …"

"But?"

"Would you mind if I stayed down here a few more days?"

"Not at all, although I'm surprised. I thought you hated spending time there."

"No, I hated you trying to sell the place to me. Your parents don't bang on about it every five minutes."

In the background, I hear my father's voice calling Leah's name.

"Oh, it's my turn. I'd better go."

"Your turn?"

"We're playing Scrabble."

"Since when did you play Scrabble?"

"Gotta go. Love you."

There's no opportunity to return the sentiment as my wife hangs up.

"Yes, love you too."

28.

God, why are you doing this to me? I can't even escape Clement in my dreams. I roll over and push my thoughts in another direction.

Not a dream. I'm sure I heard his voice in my head. Could I be the first person to contract insanity?

Reality crashes in. I sit bolt upright and open my eyes. It takes a second to work out where I am and what's going on.

I'm not insane, but why am I in the lounge? Slowly, memories leak back. Whisky, the phone call to Leah, more whisky. I remember lying on the sofa, listening to music and wallowing in self-pity.

I wish I'd just woken from a nightmare but no such luck. Nothing has changed and another day of awfulness lies ahead. For now, the crick in my neck and sandpaper mouth are of more immediate concern. I get up and traipse through to the kitchen.

Kettle on, I open the drawer in search of painkillers.

"Dammit!"

I now remember I had the last one a few days ago. My only chance of respite is caffeine.

With a mug of strong tea in hand, I sit down at the kitchen table and glance at the clock on the wall. It's just gone eight and it'll be another hour before Clement gets here. An hour before I know if he's learnt anything new about Fraser Raynott. If there's any consolation to this horror, it's that Leah will remain off the scene for a few more days. It's one less thing to worry about, but the list is still fairly comprehensive.

I finish my tea and as I'm about to head for a shower, the doorbell rings. For a brief moment I allow a positive thought to take seed. Clement is here early because he's got good news. That thought follows me down the hall to the front door. Keeping the chain on I open it a few inches. It's not Clement.

"Oh, um, Debbie. Morning."

The last person I expected to see is my colleague.

"Morning, David."

I remove the chain and open the door.

"What are you doing here?"

"I needed a word. Can I come in?"

"Sorry, sure."

She follows me through to the kitchen.

"Can I get you a cup of something?"

"A strong coffee might be in order, thanks."

"Coming up. Grab a seat."

Debbie accepts the invite and, once I've made her coffee, I sit down opposite. Another glance at the kitchen clock raises a question.

"Shouldn't you be on the way to the office?"

"That's kind of why I'm here," she replies awkwardly. "When I turned up this morning, Gerald was already there, along with three police officers."

"Oh, okay. Why?"

"I don't know, but he suggested I should make myself scarce for an hour. I tried to get an explanation but he would only say it's police business. Then, as I was about to leave, one of the officers emerged from your office carrying a computer. I presumed you'd want to know."

"What the hell do they want with my computer?"

"No idea, David. I was hoping you could tell me."

I wouldn't go as far as to say Debbie's tone is accusatory, but there's a definite undercurrent of concern.

"How long have we known each other, Debbie?"

"Four, five years."

"And in that time, have I ever said or done anything … anything at all which would suggest this allegation against me might be true?"

"No."

"I've always considered you a friend, and friends usually trust one another. With that in mind, I need you to trust me when I say I have done nothing wrong. Nothing at all."

"Why would the police take your computer, then? You know as well as anyone how that looks."

"I don't know, Debbie, but what I can tell you is I'm … I'm

having a few issues with someone who wants to end my career."

"Who would want to do that, and why?"

"It's best I say no more, not least because I don't want to put you in a position where your loyalties are torn again."

Only once I've finished the sentence do I realise the implication hidden in my words.

"Are you annoyed with me for reporting you?"

"Not at all. I understand your reasons for telling Gerald about my arrest."

"I am sorry."

"No need. I know you had the charity's best interests at heart."

"Thank you. I'd be lying if I said it hasn't been playing on my mind."

"Forget it, please."

She replies with a half-smile.

"Have you spoken to the police yourself?"

"About?"

"This individual who wants to end your career."

"It's complicated, and please don't take this the wrong way, but I'd rather not discuss it. I'm working on a resolution."

"I really hope you get it resolved soon — we miss you."

"Miss me, or need me?"

"Both. We're struggling with the workload."

"I wish I could help, but Gerald is a stickler for rules and he's the one who said I can't work until the police investigation is over. From what you've said, it sounds like they're getting desperate, taking my computer."

"I think they searched your office, too."

"Their choice," I shrug. "They won't find anything because there's nothing to find. Actually, it's probably no bad thing if it helps to clear my name."

"I hope you're right."

"About which part? Finding something or clearing my name?"

Her cheeks flush pink as she takes a sip from her mug.

"Sorry," I add. "I didn't mean to sound … it's been a trying week."

"I understand, and for the record, I hope they clear your name soon."

"Thank you."

Debbie then asks about Leah, and how she's coping with me getting under her feet. I assure her it's not an issue as Leah is visiting my parents. We then swap small talk before her hour is nearly up.

"Suppose I'd better get back," she says. "Before Gerald reports me to the committee for poor time-keeping."

"I'll see you out."

We get to the door and, just as she's opening it, a thought strikes her.

"Oh, you owe me lunch by the way."

"Do I?"

"Yes, we had a bet, remember?"

"You'll have to remind me."

"Do you recall we had a walk-in last week? The nervy young man who came in and then suddenly bolted out of your office after ten minutes?"

"Um, I'm … wait. Do you mean Cameron Gail?"

"That's him. Anyway, he came back in yesterday afternoon so you owe me lunch."

My heart rate suddenly peaks. I put my hand on the door to block Debbie's exit.

"This is important," I gulp. "I need you to tell me exactly what happened."

"Why?"

"Because Cameron Gail is the reason my career is on the line. He's connected to the man behind this false allegation."

She looks to the floor.

"I don't know, David. I'm not comfortable discussing clients when, you know, you're technically barred from work."

"Please, Debbie," I beg. "What's happened to me could happen to anyone, including you. If you want to protect the charity's reputation, I need to clear my name and Cameron Gail is key to that. Please."

"What do you want to know?"

"I need to know exactly what happened when he came in?"

"He wasn't in much of a better state than the first time. He asked for you and I told him you were on leave but I could book an appointment with another counsellor."

"And?"

"He kept mumbling on about a rehab course. I said there wasn't anyone free to discuss it but I could ask Mark to call him later in the day. I entered his details into the system …"

"His details?" I interrupt.

"Yes, the usual: full name, address, phone number."

"Can you remember those details?"

"Are you serious? I have enough on my mind at the best of times."

"Sorry, of course."

"But I can tell you Cameron had a real problem remembering much beyond his own name. He seemed vague about his address, and had to check his phone for the number."

"He had a mobile phone?"

"Yes, one of those cheap pay-as-you-go handsets, like dealers use."

It seems Cameron has got himself a budget replacement for his lost iPhone.

"Okay, okay. And you say he couldn't remember his own number?"

"Oh, err, no. I made a joke about no one remembering their own mobile number. He muttered something about the phone being new, as was his number."

"I need that number, and his address."

There's another glance to the floor.

"I can't give you his address, David. That's a sackable offence if I get caught."

"Debs, I'm desperate. Please!"

She considers my plea for a painstaking moment.

"You can have his number, but not the address. It's too risky for me."

"Even his number would be a help. I need to find him."

"I'll text it to you on one condition."

"Name it."

"It never came from me. I want your word on that."

"I swear on my life no one will ever know."

"Okay. I'll do it when I get back, assuming I'm allowed in."

It's completely out of character but I lean forward and plant a kiss on Debbie's cheek.

"You're a lifesaver, Debs, and I won't forget this."

"You'd better not. You already owe me lunch."

"If this helps to clear my name, I'll happily buy you lunch every day for a month."

"I'll hold you to that."

I wave her off and return to the kitchen. I'm too anxious to sit; preferring to pace up and down while I wait for Debbie's text message. I'm still waiting, still pacing, when the doorbell rings again. The kitchen clock suggests it is likely Clement on this occasion and I scoot down the hall.

The kitchen clock was right.

"Morning, Doc."

"Come in. I have news."

Clement follows me through to the kitchen and sits at the table. I can't contain myself.

"I have a lead on Cameron Gail's whereabouts."

"The chemistry kid?"

"Yes."

I relay the highlights of my conversation with Debbie.

"That ain't a lead. How does his phone number help?"

"I can talk to him. He knows more about Kings … Raynott's operation than most."

"He might, but ain't you overlooking another problem?"

"No."

"The Old Bill suddenly pitching up and searching your office. What are they after and who told them there was anything worth looking for?"

"Does it matter? They won't find anything."

"You sure about that?"

"Positive. I am innocent, remember?"

"You were innocent of raping that bird but that didn't stop the Old Bill arresting you, did it?"

"Well, no, but I don't see why searching my computer would …"

I don't as much sit on the chair as fall on it. Clement has led me along a path I have no desire to follow.

"Funny, ain't it, Doc," he continues. "Last night we go see some streak of piss who loves messing with computers, and the next morning the Old Bill are taking yours away."

"Oh, God."

"I ain't no expert, but could he have broken into your office and planted something dodgy on your computer?"

"He wouldn't have needed to break into my office. He could have just hacked the network."

"The what?"

"All the computers are connected to the internet, and if someone had the necessary skills, they could access the computers remotely."

"And done what?"

My phone chimes. I snatch it from the table in the hope the message is from Debbie. It's not.

It's the same number that sent the photo of Leah at the library, and there's another photo attached. The message is concise: *my employees are loyal, and it was only right we informed the police about your filthy habit.*

"What is it?" Clement asks.

"It's from Fraser. He's sent a photograph."

"Of?"

"I don't know, nor do I want to."

"Give it here."

He takes the phone and stares at the screen.

"How do I see it?"

"Tap the little paper clip icon."

He waves a sausage-like finger over the screen; eventually jabbing it with too much force. Then he squints.

"Ahh, fuck."

"What? What is it?"

"You don't wanna know, Doc."

"Is it bad?"

"It's a photo of a girl … early teens if not younger."

"I don't understand. Why would he send me a photo of a young girl?"

"She ain't got a stitch on."

I stare back at Clement in horror. His expression says it all; like he's caught wind of a noxious smell.

"That's fucking sick," he spits, turning the phone over and placing it on the table. "Why's he sending you nonce porn?"

"It's an example," I choke.

"Of?"

"Worst guess, it's a taste of what that arsehole Alex uploaded onto my work computer. That's why the police were at the office at the crack of dawn."

"What you saying? That kid could have put shit like that on your computer?"

"Yes, and a lot worse. It's a criminal offence being in possession of photos like that; one which carries a lengthy prison sentence."

My phone chimes again. It's probably Debbie, but I don't want to risk seeing the offending photo, and leave it face down on the table.

"I don't get why Raynott has done this," Clement then says, shaking his head. "What's to gain from fitting you up? It ain't gonna help him find that kid."

"No. Unless …"

I snatch my phone up and manage to swipe the photo away without looking at it. Then I open the second message. As I thought, it's from Debbie and contains a string of digits I hope are Cameron Gail's new phone number. I ring it, but I'm met with a generic message stating the caller is unavailable and I should leave a message. I slap the phone back on the table.

"Fuck. Fuck."

"I'm gonna guess you just tried calling the kid?"

I nod.

"You thinking what I'm thinking? Fraser has found him?"

"Why else would he do what he's done? If I'm right, and Alex has stacked my computer with God-knows what filth, the likelihood is I'll be locked in a police cell rather than searching for Cameron. And ... oh, shit."

"What?"

"My colleague said she entered Cameron's details into the system. If Alex hacked our network, he'd have been able to access the client files, including Cameron's. His address would have been in that file."

Clement strokes his moustache a few times.

"Shit. This is bad."

"What do you suggest we do?"

"There's only one person who can tell us what Fraser is up to."

"Who?"

"That grass. He's gonna wish he weren't born."

"Won't he expect us?"

"Dunno, and don't much care."

"Give me five minutes to get ready."

I dash off for a quick shower and return to find Clement staring out the window.

"Ready when you are."

He turns around and nods.

We set off on foot towards Camden; the streets markedly busier than when we made the return journey yesterday evening.

"How did you get on last night?" I ask. "Any luck finding information on Fraser Raynott?"

"Busted flush, Doc. I dunno how long Fraser has been using the name Kingsland, but no one I spoke to had heard of Raynott."

"That doesn't bode well."

"I ain't entirely given up. There's one person I reckon might dish the dirt on Raynott."

"Who?"

"One step at a time. Let's see how we get on in Camden first."

"Okay."

240

As we walk, a police car approaches from the opposite direction. It passes by at a pedestrian pace, and the officer in the passenger's seat stares straight at us. I look away.

I accept I've made several presumptions regarding Fraser Raynott's revenge but I've earned the right to be paranoid. For all I know, an investigator could be scouring the hard drive of my computer this very moment and, if they find what I fear they'll find, a warrant for my arrest won't be far behind.

We reach the corner of Plender Street.

"You alright, Doc? You're looking a bit pale."

"Is it any wonder? An uncorroborated rape allegation is one thing, but the repercussions of the police finding illegal material on my computer will destroy my life. I'll do time, and then I'll be on the sex-offenders register. I won't be able to get a job, period, let alone work as a counsellor. And then there's my wife, my parents, my sister … what will they all think?"

"We don't know what Raynott has done yet so put your pity on ice."

"Easy for you to say," I mumble under my breath.

We pass the nail salon and duck up the alleyway to the side.

"Have you considered how to get in the building if none of the neighbours are home?"

"We ain't gonna ring the bell this time. No warning."

He pulls a pin-like object from his pocket and steps up to the communal door. Thirty seconds of fiddling later, he opens it.

"How did you do that?" I ask, following him in to the lobby.

"Ain't rocket science. Now, listen up. When we get to his flat, I'm gonna kick the door in. You stay outside until I give the all clear. Understood?"

"But, what if anything happens to you? For all we know, Raynott might have stationed half-a-dozen men in the flat just in case we returned."

"Guess we'll know in a minute."

With no obvious concern, he turns and makes his way up the stairs. I follow because I have to; not because I want to.

By the time I reach the landing, Clement is already at the door to Alex's flat. He motions for me to stand up against the adjacent wall and puts his finger to his lips. A step backward and he raises his right leg. There's no warning as he suddenly propels his boot towards the mid-section of the door. The boot wins and the door clatters open.

Clement charges forward. To what, I don't know.

29.

There have been moments in my life when I've been genuinely scared; to the point I feared for my life.

Not long after I passed my driving test, I misjudged a bend and over-corrected the steering. I lost control and as the car spun around on the greasy tarmac. The rear nearside wheel hit the kerb and it flipped over. In that moment, I was scared. Genuinely scared.

Then, more recently, Leah and I were wandering through Borough Market in London, looking for a cheap place to have dinner. A fairly mundane Saturday evening then descended into chaos as three terrorists ran amok; indiscriminately stabbing anyone in their path. We were only on the periphery of the carnage but we saw the faces of those fleeing and we heard the screams of the victims. I can't recall how long we stood in stunned shock before we finally fled, but it was long enough to feel the grip of absolute fear. Eight people died, and many more were wounded that evening.

Then, of course, there was the confrontation yesterday – my first experience of being threatened with a gun.

Stood here now, outside a random flat in Camden, the fear is with me again. I know, because I'm paralysed by it. I hear the voices in the flat, the shouting, and then I hear two loud bangs in quick succession. Not as loud as a firecracker, but of a similar resonance, and not wildly different from the sound of muted gunshots.

I look towards the staircase to my right; the one we just climbed up. It's only eight or nine feet away but getting there would involve passing the door to Alex's flat. If, as I fear, someone inside has a gun, I'd be an easy target. However, if I stay here and that same person leaves the flat, they cannot fail to spot me.

Somewhere in the indecision I spare a thought for the man who just walked into a probable trap. There's nothing I can do for Clement, but I can survive long enough to seek justice. This is no longer about my reputation. This is likely a brutal, cold-blooded murder.

I look to my left, and the staircase at the far end of the landing, leading up to the next floor. There's no way out, but it does offer somewhere to hide, out of sight. Slowly, I risk a slight shuffle to my left. The floorboards groan at the sudden load.

"What you doing?"

My head snaps to the right at the same moment my bowels threaten an evacuation. Clement is in the doorway.

"Oh, Jesus," I gasp. "I thought you were …"

"Dead?"

"Yes," I gulp.

"Seems you can't kill a man twice, Doc."

"Patently. What happened?"

"Come see for yourself."

He beckons me to follow him into the flat. Unsure what awaits, I step through the doorway with some trepidation. Immediately, my concerns are realised.

"Recognise him?" Clement asks, pointing to the unconscious man lying prone on the hallway floor.

"Is that …. isn't he the same the guy who turned up at my flat that evening? The one you throttled?"

"Could be. Unfortunately, we can't ask him."

"Please, tell me he's not dead?"

"Nah. He's just having a nap."

"But, I heard … did he have a gun?"

"Yeah."

Clement dips a hand into his jacket pocket and pulls out a pistol; the barrel sleeved in a carbon-black cylinder — a silencer, I think. I stare at the pistol, then at Clement, and then at the guy on the floor.

"You didn't shoot him, did you?"

"Like fuck, but he tried to shoot me. I ain't a fan of guns, Doc, and this one is going in the nearest drain."

He slips it back in his pocket.

"You're bloody lucky, Clement. Thank God our friend there can't shoot straight."

"Yeah, thank God," he mumbles, rolling his eyes.

Putting aside the incompetence of Raynott's associate, we're here for a reason and there's so far been no sign or mention of that reason.

"Where's Alex?"

Clement nods towards the lounge door and steps over the unconscious obstacle. He then nudges the door open and scans the room.

"No sense playing hide and seek, dickhead," he calls out. "The longer you make me wait, the more you'll piss me off."

I edge up behind him. The lounge looks no different to how it looked last night, minus one weedy tech nerd.

"Five, four, three ..."

A figure slowly emerges from the side of the sofa; arms raised in surrender.

"Please," Alex whimpers. "Don't hurt me."

Clement strides straight over and punches him in the stomach. Alex immediately doubles-up although the impact appeared no more than a playful jab compared to what I've witnessed before. Clement then shoves him onto the sofa.

"What did I say to you last night?" he growls. "I warned you not to say anything about our visit, didn't I?"

"I ... I'm sorry," Alex pants. "I had no choice."

"No one likes a grass, sunshine. You ain't left me with any choice."

Clement turns to me.

"Do me a favour. Go down to the motor and fetch a pair of pliers and a roll of gaffa tape."

His order is followed by a discreet wink.

"Do you think we should give him a few minutes to redeem himself?" I suggest.

"He's already lied to us once. Think I'd rather cut his fingers off."

I step over to the sofa where Alex is now close to tears.

"I'm afraid there isn't much I can do to stop my friend here unless you're willing to tell us exactly what happened after we left last night."

He nods enthusiastically.

"But I should warn you, I'm an expert in dealing with people who lie, people who deceive. If I don't believe you, I *will* go down to the car and fetch those pliers. Are you going to cooperate this time?"

"Yes, yes! I swear."

It goes against my principles, but I can't deny how liberating it is to demand rather than placate; to enforce rather than enable.

"You've got five minutes," Clement warns.

"You heard the man," I add. "Tell us what you did when we left last night."

"I ... I told Mr Kingsland about your visit, and that the phone belonged to you. He went crazy."

"Define crazy."

"He threatened to break my kneecaps unless I made up for my mistake. I should never have allowed you to track the phone."

"And how did you propose to make up for your mistake?"

"I told him I had all the data on your phone, and I might be able to use it."

"For what?"

"He wants to find some guy called Cameron Gail, and Mr Kingsland said he might have a record at that charity you work for. I processed the IP data from your phone and used it to hack your office Wi-Fi network."

"And, what did you do while you were in our network?"

He gulps hard and murmurs something I don't catch.

"Say that again."

"I'm so sorry ... I didn't want to do it but Mr Kingsland insisted."

"Do what, Alex?"

"I buried a folder on the hard drive of your computer. It's not obvious, and you'd have to look hard to find it, but it's there."

"And what was in that folder?"

"Photos ... awful photos."

My worst fears and suspicions were correct — I don't need him to elaborate. Something inside of me then snaps, and before

246

I can stop myself my right foot kicks out and strikes his ankle hard.

"Arghhh!" he yelps, pulling his feet away in case I deliver another swift kick. "That hurt."

"Good!" I snarl. "Do you have any fucking idea what you've done? Not only have you likely destroyed my life, but your actions have potentially destroyed the reputation of a charity which has helped thousands of people. How do you think it'll look if one of their counsellors is found to have downloaded child porn on his lunch break? They'll never recover and Christ-knows how many people will suffer as a result, you stupid, stupid prick."

"I'm sorry … I had no choice."

The rage continues to bubble, and it's all I can do not to go full-Clement; at least not physically.

"You can shove your apologies. Give me one good reason I shouldn't go fetch the pliers for my psychotic friend here."

My psychotic friend intervenes.

"We need to find out what else he's done," Clement reminds me.

I unclench my fists and take a moment to compose myself.

"What else did you find while you were violating our network?"

"A file."

"Cameron Gail's file?"

He nods.

"And what did you find in that file?"

"Not much. Just an address, a phone number and a few notes."

"And did you give that address to your boss?"

"No," he whimpers. "I checked it first, and it was fake — a branch of Starbucks.

A mark of Cameron's rightful paranoia.

"What was the phone number?"

"I'd have to check."

"Well, go on then," I demand, my patience wearing thin.

He gets up and nervously makes his way over to one of the

laptops on the trestle table. After a few keystrokes, he reads out a phone number. I check it against the number Debbie texted me — the same number.

"That man has Cameron's new phone number," I say to Clement.

"Don't mean the kid will answer it."

"No, but I'm wondering what our tech wizard here might have done with it."

I turn back to Alex.

"I'm going to ask you a simple question and if I don't get an honest answer, I'll cut your fingers off myself, so help me God. Did Kingsland ask you to do anything with that phone number?"

Another nod.

"Well? What?"

"To track the phone."

"And did you?"

"Yes, to a street in Camden. It's difficult tracking a phone with just the number but I pinpointed a rough location."

The look on his face is too close to pride. It takes a Herculean effort not to slap it away.

"Are you saying Kingsland knows where the kid is?" Clement asks.

"More or less."

"And when did he find out?"

"Err, late yesterday evening. A few hours after you were here."

"To be clear, after we left last night you used the information on my phone to hack our office network so you could upload kiddie porn to my computer? Then, you accessed Cameron Gail's file, found his new mobile number, and tracked it to an address in Camden which you gave to Kingsland?"

He sniffs a few times and nods. I can't help myself and deliver another kick.

Clement then takes control of the situation; barely a second before my urge to kick Alex in the face becomes overwhelming. He grabs him by the arm and drags him back through the lounge door. I then hear what I presume is the bathroom door slamming shut. Clement returns without Alex.

"Think we need to take stock," he says. "I guess we know why Fraser stitched you up now — he's already got the kid."

"And what a great way of destroying my credibility. Even if I wanted to tell the police about Cameron, they're not likely to take the word of a man with a cache of illegal porn on his computer."

"You've been done up like a kipper, Doc. No mistake."

I flop down on the edge of the sofa and put my head in my hands. Now the rage is subsiding, the reality is kicking in.

"Christ, Clement. What the hell am I going to do?"

He sits down next to me.

"It's all or nothin' now. No half-measures, no pissing around playing nicely. It's either you or Fraser fucking Raynott."

"I appreciate the sentiment, but in practical terms, I ..."

I've seen grown men weep at my desk more times than I care to remember. I've never judged them, never thought them weak, but I've often wondered how low a man has to sink before he'll willingly shed tears in front of a virtual stranger.

Not wanting to find out, I pull a deep breath and wipe my eyes on the sleeve of my jacket.

"You alright, Doc?"

Neither the words nor the tone I expected; almost sympathetic.

"Not really."

"Try to look on the bright side."

"There's a bright side?"

"Nah. You're fucked, mate."

His retort comes served with a wry smile. Odd as it is, I find myself chuckling when crying would be a more appropriate response.

"Whatever is wrong with you, Clement, it isn't your sense of humour."

"Trust me: it's the only thing keeping me sane."

"The jury is still out on that prognosis."

"Ain't it just," he snorts.

The smiles fade and the moment passes. The gallows humour

offered a temporary distraction, but it's not brought us any closer to a solution.

"What are you going to do with Alex?" I ask.

"Don't worry. I've got a little plan for him."

"Care to share it?"

"In time, but we need him to do something for us."

"What?"

"Obvious, ain't it? If he can track that kid's phone once, why can't he do it again? It'll lead us straight to Fraser Raynott."

"A good idea, but I doubt he'd have let Cameron keep hold of his phone once they found him. It's probably at the bottom of a canal by now."

"Yeah, but you found out where your phone was, didn't you?"

"I found out where it was when Alex took it offline. We were just lucky it stayed in the same place."

"Gotta be worth a try, though?"

"In lieu of any other ideas, I suppose so."

"I'll go fetch dipshit. You tell him what he's gotta do."

"Why me?"

"He's scared of you."

"Don't be ridiculous," I scoff. "I just lost my temper a bit."

"You know what they say, Doc: a man angered by nothing cares about nothing. It's good to see you show some balls at last."

Clement heads off to get Alex. He returns a few seconds later and I get to my feet, ready for round two.

"Sit down," I order, pointing to the chair at the workstation. "We've got a little job for you."

Alex complies.

"I want you to locate that phone."

"I can't do that. Mr Kingsland made it clear what would happen if I let him down again."

"Okay, so I'll make it clear what will happen if you let us down. Find that bloody phone or we won't stop with your fingers."

I drop my eyes towards his groin. Tellingly, there's already a

250

patch of dark denim around his fly. The pang of guilt is quickly consumed by anger as I remind myself what Alex has done.

He turns and faces the screen.

"I'll be watching every keystroke," I warn. "You try messaging anyone and it's game over."

It takes less than a minute for Alex to establish the phone is no longer connected to the mobile network.

"It's switched off, which means I can't track its current location."

A thought occurs.

"Did Fraser ask you to track another phone, last week?"

"He did, but I only managed to locate it once or twice, for barely a minute each time. Perhaps the owner suspected it was being tracked and only switched the phone on when necessary."

"Let me guess: you identified two locations in Kentish Town?"

He nods.

I'd wager those locations were The Duke, where I met with Cameron, and my flat. That would explain how Fraser knew I had Cameron's original iPhone — until the battery died. Knowing the reason why I'm now in such deep shit does little to aid my escape.

"I want to know the last location of the phone you tracked last night."

He turns back to the screen without argument. Eventually, two long numbers pop up.

"That's the longitude and latitude," he confirms. "And the phone went offline at 11:22pm last night."

"Enter the coordinates into Google Maps."

He does as instructed and the screen displays a map of East London; a red pin marker just right of centre.

"I need an address."

"This form of tracking can't give you an address. It's not that accurate."

"A street, then."

"I can only give you an approximate location."

"Fine, just do it."

He zooms in on the map until the nearest street to the red pin comes into view: Decapod Street.

"That's definitely the last known location?"

"Yes."

I pull out my phone and take a photo of the screen. Then, I turn to Clement.

"Have you heard of Decapod Street?"

"I think it's out Stratford way."

"Stratford? Are you sure?"

"My memory ain't what it used to be, Doc, but I think so."

Neither is mine, but I do remember the garbled message Cameron left on Kimberley's phone, and he definitely mentioned Stratford. Not a point to discuss in front of Alex the Supergrass.

Now we have what we came for, it's time to decide what we do with said Supergrass. I instruct him to sit back on the sofa while I disconnect both his laptops.

"What are you doing?" he asks.

"These are coming with us."

"But … why?"

"Firstly, to stop you getting up to any other mischief. Secondly, as evidence."

"They cost a fortune, and Mr Kingsland won't …"

"Shut the fuck up," I snap. "After what you've done to me, do you think I care?"

As I pack up the laptops, Clement makes his own request.

"Gimme one of those phones," he says, pointing to a pile of basic handsets piled in a tray. No doubt burner phones for Raynott's army of dealers.

Alex hands one over.

"Just going for a piss," Clement says to me. "And then we need to get going."

I tuck the laptops under my arm and spot an iPhone on the table.

"That your phone?" I ask.

Alex nods. I snatch it up and drop it into my pocket.

"I need that," he whines. "Please, don't take it."

"You can't be trusted, and unless you've memorised Fraser's

252

phone number, you won't be tempted to tell him about our visit."

Clement returns.

"Ready?"

"Yep."

He steps over to Alex.

"If you want my advice, sunshine, pack a bag and get the hell out of here sharpish. Go somewhere you can't be found."

"Why?"

"'Cos a barrow load of shit is about to hit the fan. If you ain't away in the next twenty minutes, you'll be in its path."

We leave.

Back on the street, I confirm my thoughts.

"Shall we head back to my place? I need to put these somewhere safe and we can work out our next move."

"Good idea, and I need some breakfast."

We cover a few hundred yards of pavement when Clement pulls out the phone he liberated from Alex's flat. He then jabs the buttons and puts it to his ear.

"Police," he grunts.

"What are you doing?"

He ignores my question and proceeds to report a firearm being stored inside the toilet cistern of a flat in Plender Street, Camden. That done, he ends the call and drops the phone into a drain.

"I thought you were going to lose that pistol?"

"Changed my mind. If that kid ignores my advice, he'll have a few awkward questions to answer in about twenty minutes' time."

"Isn't grassing against your principles?"

"Usually, yeah, but sometimes you've gotta fight fire with fire. If that kid is sensible he'll already be packing a bag but if not, the Old Bill will keep him locked up while he tries to explain why there's a bloke spark out in his hallway and a shooter in his bathroom. Either way, he won't be helping Raynott for the foreseeable."

That's one pain in the arse dealt with, at least. The greater one, I fear, might not be so easy to deal with.

30.

Clement insisted we stop off at a convenience store for eggs and bacon; my attempts to purchase healthier options thwarted.

With a sense of déjà vu I place a plate on the kitchen table in front of him. Knowing the police could knock on my door any moment I have no appetite at all.

As Clement makes light work of his late breakfast, I sip at a mug of tea and stare at a digital map of Stratford on my laptop.

"I didn't want to say anything in front of Alex, but Cameron mentioned Stratford in his message to Kimberley."

"Oh, yeah. So he did."

Switching to street view the depth of our challenge hits home.

"It's a pretty built-up area," I comment.

"What is?"

"Decapod Street. Without a specific address we're up against it."

I spin the laptop around and show Clement the view of the street.

"See."

The coordinates Alex provided are at the junction of Decapod Street and Thornham Grove. Within thirty metres, there are rows of small industrial units on one side and a mix of apartment blocks and warehouses on the other. It's a typical urban vista and trying to identify a potential address looks near impossible.

"Can't we check like we did with dipshit's flat?" Clement suggests.

"Even if I had the best part of a hundred quid to check who owns every one of those properties, who's to say Raynott didn't simply lob Cameron's phone out of a car window while passing through? It could be in the gutter, or a drain, or anywhere. At best, this is a lukewarm lead."

"We've got the same problem, then — not enough info."

There is one option left but it's the least palatable.

"I'm wondering if now is the time to speak to the police."

"You serious?"

"We have Alex's laptops now as evidence I was framed."

"You know for sure they're evidence?"

"Err, I can check."

"Best you do that before you throw the towel in."

I get up and shuffle over to the side where I deposited the laptops. Opening the first one, I'm met with a password-protected screen. I open the second one and I'm met with the same obstacle.

"Well?" Clement asks.

"They're both protected by a password."

"Ain't that a surprise," he scoffs. "And I'm guessing that dipshit knows more about computers than you, or the Old Bill."

"Me, certainly, but I'm sure the police have experts who can bypass this kind of security."

"Alright, let's say they do. What will they find?"

"There's probably a record of Alex hacking the network at RightMind."

"Probably, or definitely?"

"I don't know."

"And what about that Cameron kid?"

"What about him?"

"Do you think Raynott just wanted a cosy chat with him?"

"Obviously not. We know exactly why he was so keen to find him."

"We do, and by the time the Old Bill gets around to working out what's on those computers, the kid could be dead and Raynott will have what he wants."

"Yes, but if I tell the police everything, surely they'll have to investigate. They'll find Fraser, and hopefully Cameron."

"Look at it from their view, Doc. They've got hard evidence you're a nonce, and if you turn up with some cock and bull story about Raynott without any evidence of your own, are they gonna take you seriously?"

"I have to try."

"It's a bloody big gamble, and if you lose, you'll spend a few years inside and everyone will know what you're doing time for

— you'll be a target from day one. Besides that, the kid will probably end up in a shallow grave, and every druggie in the city will be throwing cash at Raynott for his new poison. Face facts; there's only one person who can back up your story, and that's the kid — he's your evidence and we've gotta find him."

Every gambler I've ever met has come close to financial ruin because of their addiction. I stand to lose far more than just money, and Clement is right about Cameron. If I go to the police, I'm gambling with his life, and my own.

"I suppose we could head to Stratford and have a nose around," I concede. "It has to be better than sitting around doing nothing."

"I've got a better idea."

Whatever his idea is, I'm made to wait as Clement forks the final load of bacon into his mouth, washing it down with a gulp of tea. Eventually, he smacks his lips and gets to the point.

"Remember, I told you about that landlord I spoke to? His missus ended up with a face full of fag burns after he threatened to grass up Fraser?"

"Vaguely."

"His boozer was in the East End."

"So?"

"It can't be a coincidence, can it? Stratford is in the East End, the kid mentioned Stratford in his phone message, and we know his phone was in Decapod Street in Stratford. I'm wondering if Raynott has got a base there somewhere."

"You said he lived in Chiswick."

"Yeah, but you don't shit on your own doorstep. Makes sense he'd base his operation on the opposite side of town."

"I guess."

"But, there's no sense going over there and wandering the bleedin' streets hoping to catch a break. It'll take forever and we ain't got forever."

"What do you propose, then?"

"Somethin' I'd rather not do, but we ain't got no choice."

"Go on."

"We need to have a chat with someone who would know how

Fraser Raynott got where he is. Someone who knows what he's been up to all these years and maybe where he's based."

"And who might that someone be?"

"Reg Sutherland."

"Who's he?"

"An old mate of mine. There wasn't much that went on without Reg knowing about it. Always had his ear to the ground."

"You say that, past tense."

"I haven't seen him since … well, it's been a while."

"Okay, let's hope he can help. Do you want to use my phone?"

"What for?"

"To call him."

"That ain't gonna happen."

"Eh? Why not?"

"'Cos he probably went to my funeral."

I puff a tired sigh.

"Open mind, Doc. Remember?"

"Yes," I frown. "I'm trying."

"Reg lives in Holloway so it ain't much of a trek."

"How do you know where he lives if you haven't seen him … in a while?"

"I looked him up on the voters' roll in the library last month."

"Why?"

"To send a Christmas card."

"Did it cross your mind Reg might have wondered how he received a Christmas card from beyond the grave?"

"I didn't sign it, dickhead. I just said an old mate sends his best wishes."

"So, in between the assaults on drug dealers, you were writing out Christmas cards?"

"Yeah."

"You're a strange one, Clement."

"There's only Reg and a few others left. Won't be long before they're all gone."

He stares into his mug. I feel I should say something, but

what is there to say? His delusion is so acute he's mourning the loss of a life he never even lived. However, this could be a breakthrough moment as it's a chance to speak with one of Clement's acquaintances. God knows if this Reg Sutherland character can help us hunt down Fraser Raynott, but he could unlock the root of his friend's delusion.

"Okay, I'll go and see Reg."

I expected a little more enthusiasm, but he just nods.

"One minor issue, though — what do I say to him?"

"Just ask him about Raynott."

"Yes, but let's look at this from Reg's perspective. Some random guy turns up at his door with a raft of questions about a notorious local villain. Why on earth would he even open the door to me, let alone invite me in for a chat?"

"That ain't a bad point."

The moustache receives a stroke or two.

"You could say you're a journalist," he then suggests.

"I know as much about journalism as you do about counselling; nothing."

"I can give you a few pointers."

"With respect, Clement, what do you know about it?"

"Friend of mine was a journalist. I picked up enough from her for us to work with."

"Emma, by chance?"

"Say you're a freelancer," he continues, ignoring my question. "And you're investigating a historic murder."

"Right. Who's murder?"

He pauses for a moment and then looks me straight in the eye.

"Mine."

"Yours?"

"You heard me. If you say you're investigating my murder, Reg will talk to you. Say you've heard whispers about Roland Raynott, and that'll lead you on to Fraser."

"That is possibly the most insane thing anyone has ever said to me, and I've heard some ludicrous statements in my time."

"I don't doubt it, but you might learn something, Doc.

Something that'll help me as much as it helps you."

"Okay, it's your funeral."

"Again."

The doorbell rings.

"You expecting anyone?" Clement asks.

"No."

"Wait here."

He shoots out of his chair. I then hear heavy boots clomp down the hallway and the click of the front door lock. Seconds tick by and I can just make out mumbled voices but not what's being said. My heart rate peaks as indecision sets in. What if it's the police? Should I make a run for it? What if it's more of Fraser's goons here to retrieve Alex's laptops? I should definitely run. Then again, it could be Debbie or Gerald from work, or the postman, or just a neighbour complaining about the bins.

I get to my feet and decide on a compromise solution — I hide behind the kitchen door. The voices are still out of range but Clement isn't yelling, which must be a good sign. Drawing sharp breaths all I can do is wait.

Much to my relief, the door finally slams shut, and the reassuring clomps echo up the hallway. Clement steps back through the door just as I appear from behind it.

"Who was it?" I ask.

"Were you hiding?"

"Yes."

"Sit down."

We return to our seats at the table.

"Well? Are you going to tell me?"

"Yeah, but I don't want you to panic."

"There's a sure-fire way to make someone panic, Clement, and that's telling them not to panic."

"Alright. It was the Old Bill."

"Oh, God," I gulp. "What did they want?"

"Not gonna lie. They've got an arrest warrant with your name on."

My worst fear is now a reality — they've found Alex's

handiwork on my computer.

"Why did they leave? Surely they wanted to search the flat?"

"I told 'em you were staying down at your folks' place in the sticks somewhere. Said I was just looking after the place while you're away."

"Shit, this is bad. What if they turn up at my parents' house?"

"They ain't gonna find you, are they? It's bought us a day or two."

Suddenly, visiting Reg Sutherland feels significantly more urgent.

"We should go," I mumble.

"You might wanna hide them," he says, nodding towards the liberated laptops on the kitchen side. "If there is any evidence of what dipshit did, Raynott will want to get his hands on 'em."

"Yes … you're right."

"The question is: where do I hide them? You've seen how poky our flat is."

"Ain't you got a garage?" Clement suggests.

"Of course, if I can find the spare key."

I waste five frantic minutes searching through the kitchen drawers until I find it. I then wrap the laptops up in a towel and deposit them in a bag for life; one of the many my wife has accumulated in the last month alone.

"Set?"

"Yep. Let's go."

I put my coat back on and Clement follows me out the front door and down the path to the garage block.

"Here we are again," he mumbles. "Minus one piece-of-shit drug dealer."

"Sad as it is, he's likely fared better than I have over the last eight days, despite his injuries."

"I owe you one for stepping in when you did. Probably would have killed the fucker if you hadn't."

"Does that thought scare you?"

"Only three things scare me, Doc: boats, French food, and chicks with red hair."

"You're using humour to deflect. Everyone has fears."

"I don't, and that's the problem. Don't feel scared, don't feel pain, don't feel nothin'."

"Certain mental illnesses can dull emotion. It's not uncommon."

"So, you think I'm crazy?"

The troublesome padlock on the garage door offers an opportunity to consider an appropriate answer.

"I think, Clement, you're a complex individual."

"What's that supposed to mean?"

"In short, I can't say I've ever met anyone like you; either personally or professionally."

"Cheers."

"It wasn't necessarily a compliment, and to be honest, I'm slightly more concerned about my own mental health at the moment. And my liberty for that matter."

I tug the door open and search for a suitable hiding place for Alex's laptops and mobile phone. I settle on a space behind a pile of boxes containing Leah's long-forgotten stock.

"Sorted."

I close the garage door and lock it up.

"How do you wanna get to Holloway?"

"Tube?"

"Nah, let's get a cab. Best to stay off the streets as much as possible."

"Why?"

"You've got a short memory, Doc. You're a wanted man."

"Thanks for reminding me."

We traipse towards the main road and I'm forced to stand out of sight while Clement hails a cab. One eventually stops and I launch myself into the back like a celebrity avoiding the paparazzi.

The cab sets off and, once we leave Kentish Town, our conversation is limited to the traffic which is worse than usual. The driver comments about a burst water main somewhere by way of explanation. It's slow going and, as we turn into Hornsey Road, Clement loses patience as another queue of traffic forms ahead.

"Just pull over here, mate," he barks at the driver.

The driver obliges and Clement pays the fare. I step out onto the pavement. The big man follows and then surveys the area to gain his bearings.

"It's a few minutes' walk up the road," he confirms.

I glance around nervously. The area is noticeably run-down and if it weren't for Clement's presence, I'd be hailing another cab. Seeing as he is here, I need to ask him a question.

"This is possibly an odd question, but why don't you want to see Reg yourself?"

"You know why."

"Yes, but what if you're wrong and what you think happened, didn't? You must accept it's … actually, I can't even think of a suitable word."

"Insane?"

"Close enough."

"Alright, let's imagine I ain't lost my marbles. How would you react if, I dunno, Freddy Mercury knocked on your door?"

"I'd assume it wasn't him, on account he's dead. Logic dictates it could only be Freddy Mercury's doppelgänger. Besides, I didn't know Freddy Mercury so even if the man himself knocked on my door, I wouldn't be able to swear it was him."

"Maybe that weren't the best example. What if a dead relative knocked on your door, like a grandparent or an old teacher … someone you knew well?"

"I'd probably keel over in shock."

"There you have it, then. Reg is an old man now so how do you think he'd react to seeing me at his door? The poor old sod would probably have a heart attack."

"I suppose so."

We reach a corner and Clement comes to a stop outside a pub which, remarkably, looks less inviting than the God-awful pub we visited in Richmond.

"His flat is over there," he says, pointing towards a utilitarian block across the road. "Number six."

"Are you not coming over?"

"You want me to hold your bleedin' hand to his door?" He shakes his head. "I'll be in here when you're done. Good luck."

He pushes open the door to the pub and disappears inside.

Left alone on the pavement, I suddenly feel vulnerable: demoralised and vulnerable and close to beat. If a police car pulled up and took me away, I don't think I'd put up any resistance. However, the relief would be temporary. Hours of interrogation during which they might force me to look at the damning photos retrieved from my computer — a punishment in itself.

Just the thought of it is motivation enough. I've no choice but to keep going.

"God, help me," I mumble.

31.

With the traffic still at a crawl, I cross the road and approach the communal entrance to the flats. I pull open the door and step into the main hallway; the floor tiled and whitewashed walls no longer white. There's a set of stairs directly ahead, and the hallway extends to the left of it. I've no idea where flat six is so wander up the gloomy hallway; passing doors one to five. I reach number six and take a second to compose myself before ringing the bell.

I prepare my opening lines in my head, but all I can hear is Debbie's voice, saying what a terrible liar I am.

My thoughts are interrupted by the sudden thunk of a bolt sliding open. The face of an elderly man then appears at the edge of the door.

"Yeah?" he rasps.

"Are you Reg Sutherland?"

"Who wants to know?"

"My name is David Nunn and …"

"You from the council?"

"No."

"Social services?"

"No."

"Who are you, then?"

"As I was about to say, my name is David Nunn and I'm, um … a freelance journalist. I've been researching an unsolved murder that took place back in the seventies, near the Three Monks pub in Camden."

"What murder?"

"A chap by the name of Clement. I understand he was killed in an alleyway behind the pub."

He looks up towards the ceiling, and closes his eyes for just a few seconds, before fixing me with a stern glare.

"If you're gonna write anything bad about poor old Clem, you can piss right off."

"No, not at all. I'm only interested in potential suspects and one name keeps coming up — Raynott."

His eyes narrow and at the exact moment I expect him to slam the door in my face, he stands back and opens it fully.

Dressed in a pair of beige slacks and a maroon cardigan, Reg dresses like an old man but his shoulders are broad and he's the tall side of six foot. Even in his advanced years, I get the impression his bite is still as bad as his bark.

"Come in and close the door behind you."

I do as I'm told and follow him through to a dated but impeccably tidy lounge.

"I suppose I should offer you a cup of something," he says.

"I'm good, thank you."

"Sit yourself down, then."

As the old man lowers himself into an armchair I perch on the small sofa opposite. He reaches for a remote control and silences the television.

"Right … what was your name again?"

"David."

"Right, David. What do you wanna know?"

"Um, can I just go over what I've already established, and maybe you can fill in some blanks for me?"

"If you like."

"So, I understand you were good friends with the victim?"

"Yeah, thick as thieves we were. Clem was a few years older than me and I kinda looked up to him. He taught me most of everything I knew back then."

"Just so I can build a picture of what he looked like can you give me a description?"

"Tall, with dark hair, moustache, and sideburns. Built like a brick shit-house but sharp as a pin. Not a bloke you wanna mess with; that's for sure."

His description marries up with the man waiting across the road, but patently we're not talking about the same man.

"And the Three Monks was your local?"

"Yeah, for years."

"Can you remember what happened that night?"

"I can't tell you anything first hand as I weren't there. All I know is Clem left before closing time and someone whacked him round the head a minute later."

"Do you know what weapon the perpetrator used?"

"No idea. The police said it was probably a lump of wood, like a plank. They didn't have all the science on their side like they do these days."

"And what about suspects? No one was ever charged, I understand."

"Oh, there were suspects alright. Thing with Clem was … how can I put this … he had a lot of friends but a fair number of enemies too. I ain't gonna deny he could be a nasty bastard but deep down he had a heart of gold. If you were in trouble and needed help, you could always rely on Clem. Plenty of folks did over the years; me included."

"What about the name Raynott? I've heard it mentioned a few times."

Based upon his sour expression alone, I have an answer. Reg then elaborates.

"Arseholes the pair of 'em," he snaps. "Roland was the oldest, and then there was Eddy, his brother."

"Was Roland a suspect?"

"He had some bother with Clem in the weeks before he died, so yeah, fingers were pointed but there were no witnesses and no evidence. If it was Roland, he walked away scot-free."

"Do you know if Roland is still alive?"

"Couldn't tell you for sure, but I doubt it. He was older than me, older than Clem."

"I hear he had a son, Fraser."

"Yeah, that's right. Even as a nipper, he was a nasty little bastard and did a few years in borstal. Last I heard, he was running a protection racket and dabbling in drugs."

"You don't know what he's up to now, or where he lives?"

"Couldn't tell you, son. I met my Jeanie twenty years ago, and we moved down to the coast. Second wife, and a vast improvement on the first but … but I lost her eighteen months ago. I couldn't cope being down there without her so I moved back to The Smoke. It ain't the same town, but it's all I've known most of my life."

"I'm so sorry."

With some effort, Reg then gets out of his chair and shuffles over to a bookcase. He returns and hands me a photo in a silver frame.

"Our wedding day," he says, proudly. "She was a beauty."

I look at the photo of a couple in their early fifties, I'd guess. Reg was a handsome man back in the day and his wife as beautiful as he claimed.

"You're not wrong, Mr Sutherland. She's stunning."

I hand him back the photo.

"Now, I'm just waiting around to be with her again," he says. "Can't come soon enough."

Our conversation has taken an unexpected and sobering turn.

"You must miss her, terribly."

"Every hour of every day."

"My wife is away at the moment. It's only been a few days but I … sorry, it's not the same."

"Don't be silly, son," he replies, waving away my apology. "What I wouldn't give to be young and in love again. You cherish her and make the most of your time 'cos it comes and goes in a heartbeat."

"I'm trying."

Reg returns the photo to the bookcase and retakes his seat. I need to get back on topic.

"You mentioned Fraser was operating a protection racket. I don't suppose you know where he was based?"

"East End somewhere, I heard."

"Stratford, by any chance?"

"Could have been. His brother, Eddy, used to own a snooker hall out that way."

"Is Eddy still around?"

"Nah, I think he carked it some years back. Eddy was always too fond of the booze and last time I saw him, he didn't look a well bloke."

"Do you know what happened to the snooker hall?"

"I daresay Fraser took it over. Roland and Eddy were both

chancers but Fraser, give him his dues, had a head for business. Shame most of his businesses were bent."

"Sorry for the barrage of questions, but is the snooker hall still operating?"

"Couldn't tell you."

"I don't suppose you know which street it was on?"

Reg rubs his chin for a moment but it ends with a shake of the head.

"Sorry. It was a long time ago."

"No need to apologise. Are you aware of any other places the Raynott's owned in that part of town?"

"I think Fraser owned a bar, but that was demolished years ago. It was on the site they earmarked for the Olympic Games so he probably made a killing on it."

"Anything else?"

"Afraid not."

It seems I've reached the extent of Reg's knowledge as far as the Raynott clan are concerned. There is still one loose end I'd like to tie up before I leave.

"Regarding Clement: was he well known?"

"Clem? God, yeah. He became a bit of a local legend after he passed."

"In what way?"

"Folks were still mentioning Clem's name years after he died. Trouble was, those mentioning his name had never met the bloke, and the tales became more ridiculous. You know how it is?"

"I'm not sure I do."

"You've heard of the Kray twins, yeah?"

"The notorious East End villains? Yes, I have."

"Well, you shouldn't believe half the crap that's been written about them. Over the years, facts get twisted and myths are created. To a lesser degree, that's what happened with Clem."

"So, if I were to tour the pubs of North London, it's likely I might bump into someone who would know his name?"

It isn't beyond the realm of possibility that the man who clearly isn't Clement could have cobbled together enough information about this local legend to adopt a similar persona.

"Maybe, but I doubt you'd bump into anyone who ever met him. Sadly, there aren't many of us around now."

Reg's admission gives me an idea.

"You make a good point, and perhaps you can help me sort out those who really knew him from those who didn't."

"How?"

"I'd rather deal in facts than fiction; not least because I don't want to sully Clement's name. As you say, sometimes people pass on information second or third hand and it's never reliable, you understand?"

"Yeah, I understand."

"So, if I were chatting to a source claiming they knew Clement and they made certain statements about him, is there anything you could tell me which I could use to prove if they're telling the truth?"

"Not sure I'm with you."

"I'm after a nugget of information only his close friends would know."

Reg ponders for a moment and then chuckles to himself.

"Yeah, I know just the thing," he declares. "Bible club."

"Um, okay."

"It ain't what you think, son. The landlord, Dave, used to run a card school in a room at the back of the Three Monks. Obviously he didn't want the Old Bill or the brewery to know about it, so we all called it the Bible Club. If you wanted a place at the table, you'd ask Dave if there were any spots open at Bible Club."

"Seems an odd choice. Why not the book club, or poetry club?"

"Dave got the idea after he found an old bible stashed away in the attic. He used to keep it on the table, just in case the boys in blue ever dropped by unannounced. Dozy git thought it bought him luck."

"And did it?"

"Dunno, but one day someone nicked it so I suppose you could say it weren't that lucky."

269

"Did you ever find out who stole it?"

"Nah, and in truth, it disappeared around the same time Clem bit the dust. After that happened, we were all in shock and no one gave the bloody bible another thought."

"I see, and how many people knew about Bible Club?"

"A few dozen at most. Clem played now and then, and I used to have the odd game whenever I had some spare cash."

Interesting, as Clement had told me gambling is a mug's game.

"Was Clement much of a gambler?"

"Not really, on account he was a sore loser and lost his rag a bit too easily. I remember Dave telling me he took best part of a pony off Clem one night and he was properly pissed. Apparently he blew out an offer from the barmaid, Babs, downed a double scotch, and left the pub in a right huff. Sadly, it were that night Clem died. Never did get the chance to win his money back."

The memory of an earlier conversation with Clement surfaces. The specifics have been lost in the murk of recent events, but certain elements of that conversation do ring true with Reg's account. How that information filtered through to the man across the road is anyone's guess, but there's bound to be a plausible explanation. If Dave told Reg, he probably told scores of folk. Landlords do love spinning a yarn.

"Is Dave still alive?"

Reg shakes his head.

"As I said, son: there ain't many of us left."

I glance at my watch. I'd say twenty minutes well spent, but I'll only know how well when I take this information back to Clement.

With nothing else to say, I make my excuses and thank Reg for his time. At the doorstep, he asks if I can send him a copy of the article when it's published. I shake his hand and confirm I will, not that the article will ever be written, let alone published. Just another lie, but not on the same scale of lie my delusional friend is living.

I escape the block of flats and hurry across the road to the grotty pub. Fortunately, Clement is loitering at the bar directly

270

opposite the main door. He nods as I enter and says something to the barmaid. I amble up to the bar and a pint of lager arrives.

"How'd it go?"

"Interesting."

"Let's grab a seat."

We take our drinks to a table.

"Is Reg alright?"

"He's old. Seemed nice enough, though."

"Did you get anything out of him about Raynott?"

"I did."

"Well?"

I'm itching to test Clement on Reg's Bible Club disclosure, but now is not the time. There's far too much at stake to risk undermining his mental state before we've found Cameron; if indeed we can find him.

"Did you know Roland Raynott had a brother; Fraser's uncle?"

"Yeah, Eddy. Liked the booze and the birds. Fancied himself as a bit of a playboy."

His casual confirmation of what Reg just told me is a curveball. I expected Clement to shrug his shoulders in reply but somehow he's delivered a convincing response. How he knows is a question for another time.

"Did you know he used to own a snooker hall?"

"Ever heard the saying: before my time?"

"Yes."

"Well, in this case it's after my time," he says with a scowl. "How the hell am I supposed to know what Eddy got up to after I left the scene?"

"Okay, okay. I'm only telling you what Reg said."

"Alright, but do it without the questions."

"Sorry."

He knocks back a significant volume of lager and it seems to defuse his agitation. I relay what Reg told me.

"Apparently, Eddy owned a snooker hall and Reg thinks Fraser took it over after his uncle died."

"How does that help us?"

"The snooker hall is in Stratford."

"That's gotta be worth checking out. Whereabouts?"

"He didn't know but, if you give me a minute, I'll see what Google can tell us."

I tap my phone screen and wait for the results page to load. It doesn't reveal what I hoped for.

"There's no snooker hall in Stratford."

"Shit. Must have closed down. Ain't there a way you can find out?"

"Maybe. Give me a minute."

Most people assume Google is the answer to every question but Facebook has its uses. I open the app and search 'London, East End'.

"Got something," I murmur.

"What?"

"It's a Facebook group for, and I quote: to share vintage photographs, stories and memories of life in the East End."

"I understood about half that sentence. Just let me know when you've found something useful."

I click on the link and then use the search function to see if any of the twenty-thousand members have mentioned a snooker hall. The very first result is a photo of an imposing building with architectural similarities to an old cinema.

"Look at this."

I show Clement the photo.

"The Regency Snooker Club. Is that it?"

"I think so. Let me see if I can find out any more."

Returning to the post, I scroll down the comments to see if the location is divulged. Bridge Road is mentioned several times, and one comment offers a cursory history of the building; how it used to be a theatre, then a cinema, a snooker hall, and finally a nightclub. If the guy commenting is to be believed, the building hasn't been used for public purposes in almost a decade.

I relay the information to Clement.

"You wanna check who owns it now?"

"Okay."

I return to the Land Registry website and pay another three

pound fee to determine who owns the building on Bridge Road. My heart skips a beat when I open up the resulting record.

"It belongs to Folsom Property Holdings Limited."

"Fraser Raynott's company," Clement declares. "Looks like we've found his hideaway."

Buoyed by some positive news I'm already checking the location on Google to see how the building looks today. The resulting imagery is not so positive.

"The main entrance is completely boarded up," I groan.

"Let me see."

I lay my phone on the table so we can look at it together.

"What about the side, and the rear?"

Tapping the screen, we're able to skirt virtually down the side elevation of the building but the area to the rear — a car park, I'd guess — is enclosed by a high metal fence topped with razor wire.

"There doesn't appear to be any way in," I comment. "Unless you can get past the fence."

"Yeah, and that means no way out, either. No doors, and only a couple of small windows."

"Christ, it's like a fortress."

"I think that's the point, Doc. You could hold a firework display in there and no one outside would see or hear a thing."

Looking at the screen another thought occurs.

"Property prices in that part of town have risen more than just about anywhere. Why would a businessman like Fraser sit on a run-down building worth millions, unless …"

"Unless it had a greater value for his business operation."

I slump back in my chair.

"It feels like we've found the pot at the end of the rainbow, but it's empty. If Cameron is being held in there, there's no way of finding out, let alone rescuing him."

"We need to go check it out."

"What for? We can see there's no way in."

"No, we can't see from a tiny bleedin' screen. We need to go take a look."

"And what if Raynott spots us nosing around?"

"All the better. I let him walk away once, but he won't get a second chance."

A siren wails on the road outside and I just catch a flash of blue lights passing the window. It's a stark yet timely reminder I'm running out of time and options.

"How far is Stratford?"

"Tube station is only up the road and it's about twenty minutes or so from there."

"Best finish our drinks, then."

32.

Clement wasn't far wrong in his estimation. Half-an-hour after leaving the pub, we emerge from Stratford Underground Station.

"Bleedin' hell," he remarks. "What happened here?"

"What do you mean?"

"There weren't much of anything in Stratford; just slum housing and wasteland."

"The Olympics happened. They ploughed billions into regenerating the area."

Clement continues to stare open-mouthed at our surroundings while I check the location of Bridge Road on my phone.

"It's only a five-minute walk," I confirm. "Once you've finished sight-seeing."

"Yeah, alright."

After coaxing the mesmerised giant to follow, we make our way towards the High Street. Even I have to admit the area is architecturally contrary; the streets lined with contemporary buildings set to a backdrop of ugly tower blocks and high-level cranes. The gentrification of London's East End is still a work in progress, apparently.

As we close in on our destination, the bright, modern facades give way to grimy urban brickwork and Clement appears more at home. So much so, he starts a conversation.

"Did Reg have much to say about himself?"

"Not a lot, really, although he showed me a photo of his wife on their wedding day."

"He married?"

"Twice."

"Who'd have thought," he says wistfully. "Reg swore blind he'd never tie the knot."

"He moved down to the coast with his second wife."

"Why's he moved back to London, then?"

"She passed away and he couldn't stand being there on his own."

"Poor sod."

"I felt a little sorry for him, if I'm honest."

"Why?"

"I got the impression he doesn't have any family around, and he said most of his old friends have gone."

"You reckon he's lonely?"

"Desperately. He made some comment about wishing the end to come."

Clement lights a cigarette and takes a long drag.

"You said you feel sorry for him?"

"Kind of, yes. Who wouldn't have sympathy for someone in Reg's situation?"

"His situation ain't so different from mine, Doc," he replies, snorting smoke from his nostrils. "You wanna think about that."

I'm sorely tempted to bring up Reg's Bible Club and shatter this delusion once and for all but, with only a hundred yards to our destination, the timing is far from appropriate.

"I will."

The hundred yards pass without another word, and suddenly the building which once housed The Regency Snooker Club is in sight, on the corner of a one-way street. On first impression, the photos we viewed on my phone were a fairly accurate representation.

We cross the road and stop next to where the main entrance presumably once was, now hidden from view by eight-foot high hardwood panels. On each of the panels there's a sign warning of prosecution for trespassers.

Clement steps forward and presses his hands against one of the panels. He then turns and surveys the street.

"What are you thinking?" I ask.

"We ain't gettin' in this way without a chainsaw, and it's too open."

"And we don't know what's behind those boards. There could be a metal shutter."

"True."

With no luck at the front, we move to the rear of the building where a corrugated fence extends forty feet beyond the back wall to create a kind of compound or car park, accessed by two reinforced steel gates. There's no way to see what's on the other side and spirals of razor wire ensure no one is likely to climb up for a peek.

"That's that, then," I sigh. "Unless you fancy pole-vaulting over the fence?"

I'm joking, but even an Olympic pole-vaulter would think twice with the height of the fence and the prospect of snagging a testicle or two on the razor wire.

"Ain't looking good, that's for sure."

We plod back up the path alongside the flank wall which is virtually featureless. There are four small windows set in the rendered brickwork but the two at street level are protected by steel bars. Getting inside would involve an angle grinder and a dwarf; neither of which we have access to.

Suddenly, Clement comes to a stop. He bends down and studies the wall with all the intensity of an archaeologist.

"What's so fascinating?" I ask.

He takes a couple of steps back but remains focused on the wall.

"This used to be a theatre, and a cinema, right?"

"Apparently."

He then points towards the lower section of the wall where it meets the pavement.

"Look down there."

"At what?"

Frowning, Clement ushers me closer.

"See this line? That's the damp proof course, and it runs the whole length of the wall … or it should."

"Okay."

"Now, look here."

He squats down and points towards a three-feet wide section of wall where the cream-coloured render is flaking away and moss has taken root.

"There's no damp proof course in this section," he remarks, standing upright.

"An oversight by the builders?"

"Don't be daft. This place has gotta be eighty or ninety years old and any wall suffering from damp that long would be close to collapse. This section of wall was added within the last few years."

"You've lost me, Clement."

"Let me make this easy for you, Doc. Where's the fire escape?"

"Err, round the back I'd guess."

"There has to be more than one. Even back in my day cinemas had to have at least two or three, in different parts of the building."

I look down at the patch of moss and with the benefit of Clement's theory, it certainly looks the same width as a fire door.

"Oh, yes. I see what you mean."

"It's been bricked up, and it's a bodge job as there's no damp proof course; that's why the wall is plastered with moss."

"Why would Fraser have a fire escape bricked up?"

"Same reason he boarded the front. Only one way into the building, and one way out."

"At the back which is like Alcatraz."

"Exactly. If the Old Bill were to raid this place, they'd have to get through the back gates first, and then whatever security there is at the rear of the building. It'd probably take 'em an hour to get in."

"In which case, we're screwed."

"Don't be too hasty."

He squats down again and picks at the blown plaster. Several slices fall away to reveal a light grey material behind.

"Whoever did this used breeze block. Cheaper than normal bricks and quicker to build as they're much larger."

"Have you ever worked in the building trade?"

"Nah, but I've met a few builders over the years and I can tell you, a cowboy plugged this gap."

"Fascinating, but a wall is a wall and whatever it's made of, there's no way past it."

"That's where you're wrong," he replies. "If you swung a

sledgehammer at a normal brick wall, you'd likely break your arms. Breeze blocks, though, they're nowhere near as strong. A few heavy blows and you can break through 'em."

"Are you talking from experience or is this just theory?"

"I've swung a few sledgehammers in my time. Sometimes at walls."

"Notwithstanding your prowess with a sledgehammer, there are two obvious issues: one, I think someone might notice you hammering away at a wall in broad daylight, and two, there's bound to be an alarm."

"Alright, we come back when it's dark and there's no one around. First problem solved."

"And the alarm?"

"Doc, there's no door here. Folks have alarms on doors and windows, not walls."

"True, but there might be other kinds of security."

He leans up against the wall and folds his arms.

"Yeah, there might be," he admits. "And if we had a few weeks spare, we could afford to sit on our arses and look at other options. Or we could learn how to fly a helicopter and land on the bleedin' roof. But, we ain't got a few weeks spare, so it's this way or no way."

A frank and accurate assessment.

"Have you seen enough?" I ask.

"Yeah."

"Let's get back to the tube station. We can discuss how we might execute our nonsensical plan on the way."

Clement nods, and we set off.

"Do you have a sledgehammer?" I ask, as we cross the road.

"Not on me, but I can lay my hands on one."

"What else do we need?"

"A decent torch, and a few basic tools, just in case we need them once we're inside."

"If we get inside."

"We'll get in, don't worry about that."

"And what if the police turn up while we're snooping around?"

"That could be good news. If the kid is being held in there, or Raynott is using that place to run his drugs business, he's in deep shit if the Old Bill get a gander inside."

"I hadn't thought of that."

"You'll still be arrested for breaking and entering, but you'll probably just get a fine."

"A fine and a criminal record — great. There goes the last of my savings and my career."

"Better than serving time as a nonce, though."

"I should be grateful for small mercies, I suppose."

"Anyway, no point fretting about it. If luck is on our side, we'll get in, find the kid, and then you can take him and those computers to the police station — all your problems solved. If the Old Bill turn up, Fraser Raynott will be the one in handcuffs. It's a win-win."

"Maybe, but what about you?"

"What about me?"

"If we were to bump into Fraser, what have you got planned?"

"That's between me and him. No need for you to worry about it."

I shouldn't worry about it but, as we walk, on I find Clement's plight playing on my mind. It's an uncomfortable truth, but it feels like our arrangement has been a little one-sided in my favour, and maybe I've taken his help for granted. My positivity may be in tatters and hope is fading fast, but at least hope still remains and that's down to him.

"Listen, Clement. Whatever happens from this point forward, I want you to know I'm grateful for all you've done."

"I don't want your gratitude, Doc. You know what I want."

"Yes, I do."

"And?"

"And what?"

"You haven't said much about your little chat with Reg. Did he tell you I'm a figment of my own imagination?"

"No, he told me he was good friends with a guy called Clement. He then told me how that friend was murdered one

280

evening."

"Exactly what I told you, right?"

"More or less."

"But, you don't sound convinced."

"What I learnt is that there was indeed a man known as Clement. Admittedly, you bear several similarities to Reg's description, but it's no different from someone with long hair and a beard claiming to be Jesus."

"That's a stretch."

"Is it? Why would it be any more remarkable for the son of God to resurface than some random man in North London? Either way, the only possible explanation is one I don't think you're ready to hear."

"What? That I am losing my marbles."

"I didn't say that. This character — Clement — was well known. Judging by what Reg said, he became part of local folklore. If you look at it objectively, you could have heard all those tales and modelled yourself on that man … even taken his name."

"Is that what you think?"

"It doesn't matter what I think. It matters what led you to this point."

"Alright, I'm so deluded I've taken on the character of a bloke who died decades ago. That's what you're saying?"

"No, that's what logic and reason are saying."

"Does that happen? Can someone really be so fucked in the head they think they're a different person?"

"They can, in extreme cases. I mentioned Jesus because there have been countless individuals who've claimed to be the Messiah. Some of them have been just as convinced of their identity as you are of yours."

"Yeah, but I ain't pretending to be Jesus and you've been hanging around with me for what? Eight days? You must have an idea by now … do you think I'm a headcase?"

Now is not the time to admit I've considered him a headcase since the moment we met. However, it could be the time to test the water with what I learnt from Reg Sutherland.

281

"If I could prove your delusion is exactly that, just by asking a simple question, would you want to hear it?"

"The whole point of this is to work out if I'm mental, so yeah."

"Okay. You're sure?"

"Spit it out, Doc."

"Fair enough. What was the Bible Club?"

There's no immediate reaction to my question. Clement lights another cigarette, takes a drag, and then turns to me.

"Reg tell you about the Bible Club?"

"He did."

"Why'd he bring it up?"

"Because I asked him if there was a snippet of information only those close to Clement would know."

"Smart thinking," he replies with a thin smile, much to my surprise. "Wish I'd suggested it before you went to see him."

"Thank you. And are you able to give me an answer?"

"Yeah. Bible Club was a card school. We used to play in the back room of the Three Monks."

"Who organised it?"

"The landlord, Dave."

"And how did it get that name?"

"Dave's idea. He found an old bible wedged in the rafters when he was clearing out the loft. It gave him an idea for a cover story if the Old Bill ever dropped by. Used to keep it on the table during a game."

Three out of three. I'm not sure if I should be surprised or concerned.

"What happened to the bible?"

"Someone nicked it. Dave was convinced it was his good luck charm. Bastard took more than a few quid off me over the years, so who knows — maybe it was lucky."

Clement's recollection of events is almost perfectly in line with Reg's.

"So? Did I pass your test?" he asks.

"Four out of four. Well done."

His moment of jubilation fades as quickly as it arrived.

"Hold on," he then frowns. "I ain't a mug, Doc. I can tell by your face you still don't believe me."

"I'm not sure what you were hoping for but it's not definitive proof."

"Course it is. How else would I know about the Bible Club? Only a handful of people ever knew about it."

"Perhaps, but it doesn't prove you're the man Reg talked about for one simple reason."

"What's that?"

"It's impossible."

"So was flying once. Then some bloke built a plane."

"Yes, and he used science to work out how to make it fly, but we're not talking about science, are we? We're talking about a man dying and then waking up decades later. Bloody hell, Clement, can't you see why I'm still not convinced?"

We walk in silence for a good fifty yards before I get an answer.

"I get it, alright, but there's something I know that not even Reg does."

"What's that?"

"I know who nicked the bible?"

"Does that matter?"

"Yeah, 'cos I nicked it."

33.

We pass a pub and I utter a sentence I don't recall ever saying before.

"I think I need a drink."

Not waiting for Clement to concur or otherwise, I pull open the door and head straight for the bar.

"Two pints of your cheapest lager," I mumble to the young woman serving.

My companion joins me.

"Something I said?"

"We need to talk. I can't do this anymore. It's not fair on either of us."

The two pints of cheap lager arrive. I pay and usher Clement to a table. All I know about counselling, about mental illness, about dealing with fractured minds is now irrelevant. It's time for straight talking.

"I'm sorry, Clement, but there's no easy way to say this. I think you're suffering from a form of schizophrenia."

"You only think?"

"Yes, because I'm not qualified to diagnose your condition. As I've said all along, you need to seek professional psychiatric help."

"You really think I'm crazy?"

"I think your condition is deep-rooted and complex. We could sit here and talk for a week and I don't think we'd even scratch the surface of just how complex."

"So, nothing Reg said made one jot of difference?"

"Actually, it did, but not in the way you hoped. In my opinion, you're so obsessed with this Clement character, you've convinced yourself you are him. I think something awful happened in your life and your brain tried to block it out by adopting a new persona; switching your memories for false ones."

I'm met with a blank stare. Now I've started, I can't stop.

"I have to be honest with you, Clement. This charade is …

284

it's unhealthy, and I'm not helping you by playing along."

He reaches out and grasps his pint, raising it to his lips in a slow, measured movement. One sip and he returns the glass to the table.

"Who am I, then?" he asks.

"I don't know, but until you accept you're not who you think you are, you'll remain trapped in this purgatory, this delusion."

"Nah, you're wrong. I know who I am."

"Listen," I sigh. "You didn't die. Your name isn't Clement. Everything you think is real is just an illusion your brain has concocted to protect you from God-knows what. That's all there is to it, I'm afraid."

"I can give you names of people who would say different. Folks who'd say I ain't got a screw loose."

"Like Emma?"

The slightest shake of his head suggests not.

"Why won't you talk about her?"

"Nothin' to say."

"You can't keep running away from the truth, Clement. You need help, and I respect you too much to indulge this fantasy any longer. And, I'd bet that's exactly how Emma felt after you invited her to view a dead man's headstone and claimed it was yours. Is that why you don't want to talk about her — did she tell you to seek help too?"

"Did you not hear what I just said?"

I lean forward and place my hand on his forearm.

"I can only imagine how hard it is for a man like you to say you need help, but there's no shame in it. You've still time to fix this; to rebuild your life. All you need to do is open your mind to the idea."

He reaches for his glass again. This time, he drains it in seconds before getting to his feet.

"I'm going," he declares.

"But, we've got to talk about this."

"You keep chatterin' away, Doc. I've got shit to be getting on with."

"What could be more important than dealing with your

condition?"

"Getting hold of a sledgehammer, for starters. That's assuming you still want my help?"

"Yes, but …"

"Good. I'll come round your gaff about seven. Be ready."

He turns to walk away but throws a parting piece of advice my way.

"Oh, and Doc, I wouldn't make it obvious anyone is at home, just in case the Old Bill pop by with that warrant."

There's nothing I can do or say to stop him leaving so I sit and watch the door swing shut. It's not the first time someone has decided they'd rather not listen to my advice, and I've lost count how many clients have walked away in denial rather than face their demons. This time, it bothers me far more than it should, for reasons I'd rather not admit.

"Fuck," I mumble under my breath.

Left alone, a malaise sets in, helped in no small part by the sombre atmosphere. I let my eyes drift across the room to the few lone souls who, like me, appear weighed down by worry. We are the unlikeliest of kindred spirits. We're all sat alone in a run-down pub in East London, sipping cheap lager and wondering how we got here. Each of us has a tale to tell, but mine is surely the most tragic. The only other contender left a few minutes ago.

I finish my pint but decide against another. If I sit in this establishment any longer, the air of despondency will probably suffocate me. I get up and leave.

The journey home is marked by paranoia and trepidation. I've travelled alone on the tube hundreds of times but never have I felt so acutely alone. Clement, for all his faults, offered a reassuring presence. One way or another, it's unlikely we'll be taking many journeys together after today. Shit, I don't even know if he'll turn up later. Perhaps I should have held back and waited until the last possible moment before dropping my bombshell. Deep down, though, I know what I did was right. I hope, in time, he'll come to realise that.

It's a blessed relief to make it home and close the front door behind me. Out of habit, I'm about to call Leah's name but it catches in my throat before reaching my mouth. Never have I wanted a hug from my wife so desperately. About now, I'd give anything to sit down at the kitchen table and listen to her chatter away about her latest piece of tat, or yet another problem with the van.

I hang my coat up and traipse through to the kitchen. Inspired by my previous attempt to hide, I sit on the floor behind the door and prod the screen of my phone. It rings and rings. I'm about to give up when Leah finally answers.

"Hey, honey."

"Two phone calls in twenty-four hours," she replies in a jokey tone. "Are you checking up on me?"

"Not at all. I just wanted to hear your voice."

"Aww … is someone feeling lonely?"

Desperately, miserably so.

"No, but I do miss you."

"I miss you too. How are things?"

"All well here. Are you enjoying winter in Oxfordshire?"

"I'm enjoying the food, that's for certain. Did I mention we went out for afternoon tea yesterday?"

"No. Was it nice?"

"I've never had afternoon tea before."

"Have you not?"

"No, and I should divorce you for never taking me," she chuckles. "I thought I'd died and gone to sandwich heaven. And the cream scones … oh, my God … they were to die for."

It's lovely of my parents to keep Leah entertained, but it should be me taking my wife out for afternoon tea — if I'd ever thought of taking her.

"And you'll never guess what we've got planned for this afternoon. We're visiting an alpaca sanctuary."

"Oh, that's … different. I didn't know you had a thing for alpacas."

"They're so cute, don't you think?"

"I can't say I've given it any thought."

Leah continues to chatter away about alpacas, and cakes, and their plans for tomorrow which include a craft fair in Oxford and dinner at Dad's favourite pub — a former mill with oak beams and an open fire. I could listen to her all afternoon but she notices the time and apologetically ends the call.

With Leah heading off to swoon over alpacas, I'm left to feel sorry for myself in a dark corner of our kitchen. I've really not helped myself.

Eventually, I muster enough motivation to get up and I'm about to switch the light on when Clement's warning echoes in my head. I don't hold out much hope for our mission in Stratford later, but the moment I'm arrested, that's it. I'm done, finished, beaten. Avoiding the attention of the local constabulary is futile in the long run and I'm so tired of this. I need it over.

My hand hovers over the light switch.

"Tomorrow," I whisper.

For now, I need to focus on being invisible while keeping reality at bay.

With the bedroom being at the back of the flat, it's the best option for keeping out of sight. I draw the curtains, kick off my shoes, and hide beneath the duvet with my Kindle. The similarities to my childhood aren't lost on me. Many a time I'd hide under the blankets and read comics by torchlight. Reliving those days provides a strange sense of comfort. It's disappointing I might not get the chance to recommend my newfound strategy to clients suffering anxiety. I think it'd help.

Five chapters and my eyelids droop. Warm, comfy, safe; the right conditions for sleep. I'm too weary to resist.

My slumber is shattered by a pounding on the front door. I scramble from under the duvet only to find the bedroom is just as dark. How long did I sleep for? There's another bang on the front door, accompanied by a voice.

"Doc!"

The tension eases a little. It's not the police.

I get up and pad down the dark hallway to the front door. The big man on the other side looks particularly menacing, bathed in the half-light of street lamps.

"At last. What you been doing?"

"Um, nothing. I must have fallen asleep."

"I told you to be ready at seven."

I glance at my watch.

"Sorry, come in. I just need five minutes."

I'm about to turn and head to the kitchen when it strikes me Clement has not brought the promised sledgehammer.

"I take it you haven't got a sledgehammer up your sleeve?"

"Well spotted."

"Isn't that what you went off to do earlier?"

"Yeah, and I got one."

"Right, and where is it?"

"In the van."

"Since when did you have a van?"

"Since an hour ago. I didn't think it'd be sensible carrying a sledgehammer on the tube so I borrowed it from a mate."

"Oh, good. It'll be easier to get away when the police turn up."

"Have some faith, eh?"

Clement lumbers after me as I wander back down the hallway. Seeing as we don't have a fixed schedule and my mouth is fur-lined, I decide tea takes priority over getting ready to leave. Still concerned about a visit from the police, I switch on a decorative lamp Leah acquired but couldn't face selling.

"Do you want a cup of tea? I'm desperate, so it's not up for negotiation."

"Go on, then."

He sits down at the table. As I wait for the kettle to boil, I toy with the idea of resurrecting our earlier conversation. Clement gets in first.

"Been thinking about what you said."

"And?"

"And, I ain't happy about it."

"I'm sorry. I know it's not what you wanted to hear."

"That ain't what I'm unhappy about. I asked for your opinion, and you gave it. Fair do's."

"Okay, so what's troubling you?"

"The voice in my head."

"Oh."

"Is it normal?"

"Is it normal for those suffering schizophrenia to hear voices? Sometimes, yes."

"You reckon I should ignore it?"

"Depends on what the voice is telling you."

"Earlier, it told me about that bricked-up fire escape."

"Really?"

"Sort of. It ain't someone barking instructions in my ear. It's more like hints."

"How strange."

"Ain't it just. Seeing as you're so convinced I'm not right in the head, maybe you could explain it."

"I suspect it's just your subconscious mind at work. You probably glanced at the wall and noticed the moss, and your subconscious mind made the link."

I pour the tea and join Clement at the table.

"Are you saying the voice … it's like my brain talking to me?"

"In simplistic terms, yes. Your subconscious mind creates the thought and your conscious mind processes it as a voice. It's particularly common in children. Even in adulthood, people still do it."

"Do they?"

"It's like when you forget a name. After a while, you stop consciously thinking about it but your subconscious mind continues to work away. Then, all of a sudden, the name pops into your head; almost like someone told you."

"Yeah, but my voice comes and goes, and it ain't just reminding me of some bird I nailed back in '72."

"That, I'm afraid, is what differentiates those who are suffering mental illness and those who aren't. Your perception is skewed."

His moustache receives several slow strokes.

"Is this helping?" I ask.

"Dunno. It ain't easy being told you're mental."

"You're not mental, Clement. You're unwell and you need

treatment, that's all. There's no shame in it."

"Yeah, but there's shame in being locked in a padded cell."

"Now you're being ridiculous — no one will lock you in a padded cell or put you in a straitjacket."

"So you say. What if a quack takes one look at me and decides I'm fit for the loony bin?"

"Is that why you won't go see a doctor? Are you concerned what they'll say?"

He shrugs his shoulders.

"There really is no need for concern. If you sprained your wrist you'd go see a doctor, wouldn't you?"

"Guess so."

"Then why treat a mental illness any differently from a physical one? That's how you've got to think about it. You've got an ailment which needs treatment. It's as simple as that."

"But you can't help me?"

"I can't even help you with a proper diagnosis, let alone treatment. But, I can make you a promise."

"I'm listening."

"When this is all over, presuming I'm not locked up, I'll help you find suitable psychiatric care and I'll be there throughout your treatment. You don't have to do this on your own."

I take the slight tilt of his head as an affirmative nod.

It's only been five days since Gerald escorted me from the offices of RightMind but I'm already missing moments like this. Clement has barely taken his first step but he at least appears willing to acknowledge he needs help. Progress, no matter how slight, is progress.

Buoyed by a modest sense of accomplishment, I finish my tea and gather the other items Clement requested: a small tool kit and a torch.

When I return to the kitchen, he's staring into space.

"Are you ready?"

"Guess so."

"And you're okay?"

"I will be, when this bleedin' voice shuts up."

"What's it saying now?"

He looks up and draws a breath.

"Bible."

34.

It doesn't look like we'll be leaving the flat just yet.

"Is that it? Just the word bible?"

"Yeah."

"Does this have anything to do with our conversation earlier?"

"You tell me."

"You said you stole Dave's bible from the Three Monks."

"'Cos I did."

"You may have stolen a bible and it might have been from a landlord, and his name might even have been Dave, but it wasn't the one Reg mentioned."

"If you say so, but I know what I did."

"Go on then — tell me exactly what happened."

"Not much to tell. We played cards one evening, and I lost badly … dunno how much, but enough. After he cleared me out, Dave's missus calls him to the bar as a barrel needed changing so I swiped the bible from the table and stuck it in my jacket."

"Why did you steal it?"

"Just to piss him off, really."

"Were you intending to give it back?"

"Yeah, but I never got the chance."

"Why not?"

"'Cos fifteen minutes later, Roland Raynott whacked me round the head with a bleedin' cricket bat. That's why."

Once again, his story tallies-up with Reg Sutherland's. Could it be that Reg was relaying this tale to someone in a pub and, prior to his mental health deteriorating, Clement overheard it. It's just a guess, but Reg's tale becoming Clement's memory is a significantly more rational explanation than his.

"Do you know what happened to Dave's bible?"

"It weren't Dave's bible — it belonged to the pub. Some folks reckoned it had been hidden up in the loft for centuries. Who knows, maybe it belonged to one of those three bleedin' monks."

"Okay, what happened to the bible that wasn't Dave's?"

"Dunno, but four years ago I found myself in a bookshop. There was this bird there, scared shitless, and she was holding a bible that looked a lot like the one I nicked."

"Let me get this straight: you wandered into a bookshop and scared some poor woman with a bible in her hand?"

"I didn't wander in. I … I dunno how I got there."

"Overlooking that point, it was a bookshop, Clement, and bibles are books. Not only are there millions and millions of bibles in circulation, it'd be bloody strange not to find one in a bookshop, don't you think?"

"It was the one from the pub. I'm sure of it."

This is getting us nowhere and, if we continue, I'm likely to undo any of the progress we made earlier.

"Perhaps this is a conversation for another time. We should make a move, don't you think?"

"You asked."

And I really wish I hadn't. I switch the lamp off so Clement can't see my eyes roll.

As I shut the front door, I scour the street looking for the borrowed van.

"Where did you park?"

"By the garages."

We cut down the path and through the gate. A white van, slightly larger than Leah's has been abandoned rather than parked. Clement presses the button for the remote central locking and all four indicator lights flash.

"Cool, ain't it?" he says. "You don't need a key to open the doors."

I'm not sure if he's being sarcastic so I clamber into the passenger's seat without passing comment. Clement shoehorns his bulk into the driver's seat and turns the ignition key. Judging by the tone of the exhaust, I'd guess the van is long overdue a service.

"Who did you say you borrowed this from?"

"Just a mate."

"I presume your mate knows you've borrowed it?"

"Yeah, course he does. He weren't using it, anyway."

"Why not?"

"No MOT."

"Are you joking?"

Rather than answer, Clement jabs a button on the stereo.

"It plays compact discs," he yells over the sudden screeching of guitars. "Thought you might wanna hear some T-Rex."

I don't, but there's little chance of my objection being heard over the music. He then rams the gearstick into first and the van lurches forward towards the narrow lane which leads to the main road. We reach the junction and with only a fleeting glance to his left, Clement revs the engine hard and pulls out, narrowly avoiding the front end of a bus.

Within just half-a-mile I realise my mistake. What was I thinking? If there's one kind of driver you don't want to be seated next to, it's one with excessive levels of aggression and a reckless regard for personal safety. With the music blaring and the engine screaming, my vocal objections prove futile. All I can do is cling to the edge of my seat, close my eyes, and pray.

A journey which should have taken at least half-an-hour is mercifully over in twenty minutes. Lord knows how many speed cameras captured our sprint through the streets of London, but I'm glad my name isn't on the logbook.

Finally, we come to a stop in the one-way street next to the former Regency Snooker Hall; two wheels on the path next to our proposed access point.

Clement switches the engine off. Silence, at last.

"Christ almighty," I gasp. "That was horrific."

"You don't like T-Rex?"

"I was referring to your driving."

"We got here in one piece, didn't we?"

I reply with a frown and remove my seat belt.

"Shall we get on with this?"

We simultaneously exit the van and meet at the rear doors. Clement pulls them open to reveal the dark interior of the load space. He then hands me a luminous yellow vest like those worn by road workers.

"What's this for?"

"Put it on."

"Won't that draw attention?"

"Seems to be the opposite. Put one of those on and you're invisible — just another bloke doing a job."

"If you say so."

I slip the vest on as Clement then removes a stack of orange road cones from the back of the van.

"Cones?"

"Yeah, same reason as the vests. If it looks like we're supposed to be here, no one will pay us any attention."

"Where did you get them from?"

"Picked 'em up on the way to your gaff. They were just lying in the road."

Somewhere across town, I suspect a motorist is trying to excavate their car from a hole in the road.

Clement lays three cones either side of the path and puts on his own Hi Vis vest. He returns to the van and pulls out a sledgehammer.

"Let's do this. You got the torch and the toolkit?"

"Err, they're in the footwell."

"Go grab 'em."

I do as instructed as my fake workmate approaches the section of wall he intends to demolish. After running his hand from top to bottom, he appears to have identified the weakest section. I don't ask if the voice in his head offered advice.

A few rolls of the shoulders and he takes a firm grip on the sledgehammer. I stand well back as he positions his feet and lines up the first blow.

The sound when the hammer head strikes isn't as loud as I expected, but the result is catastrophic for the wall. At the point of ground zero a block-sized rectangular hole has appeared with a spider web of cracks splintering in every direction.

"Torch," Clement demands.

I step over to the wall and hand it to him. He points it into the cavity and smiles.

"Looks like a corridor, and I can't hear an alarm."

I'm too busy studying the hole to reply. I presumed it would take numerous blows to even chip away at the wall, but it seems Clement was right about the quality of the workmanship, or lack thereof. One blow, albeit a seismic one, was enough to pop the block straight out of the wall like a Jenga piece.

"Five minutes and we'll have a hole big enough to climb through."

He passes me the torch and suggests I retreat a safe distance. It's not a suggestion I'm likely to ignore.

It takes just eight more blows to form a serviceable gap in the wall. For Clement, it'll take a degree of contortion but I should have no problem squeezing through the hole.

"You got the toolkit?"

I nod.

"Come on, then."

Clement goes first and guides his left leg into the void. Once his foot lands on the other side he stoops down and squeezes his torso through the gap. I turn and check the immediate area before committing. No one around, and no wail of sirens in the distance. After passing the torch through to Clement, I copy his method and limbo into the darkness.

The silence on the other side is so absolute I can hear my heart thumping. I should be relieved not to hear the scream of an alarm or footsteps stomping through the darkness, but there's something disconcerting about the quiet.

Clement takes a few steps into the darkness and switches the torch on. We are indeed in a corridor and that offers two options for our next move.

"This way," he orders in a low voice.

There's no argument for left over right so I blindly follow.

We reach the end of the corridor and our only route forward is through a closed door. Clement switches the torch off and slowly pulls it open. The lack of light suggests there's no one at home; at least not in this part of the building. The torch is switched back on and we step through the doorway.

My eyes have little to do but my sense of smell is engaged by a dank, musty odour. Besides the stench, the air carries a noticeable chill.

Clement swings the beam of the torch through a wide arc so we can get some measure of our whereabouts. The vast, cavernous space can only have served one function — this was probably the main auditorium in the days the building served as a theatre and cinema. Now, it's just a shell; the seats long gone, and the raised stage in a state of neglect.

The torch beam settles on a door to the rear.

"What do you reckon, Doc?"

"It's as good a choice as any."

We follow the beam to the door and Clement switches the torch off before pulling it open. A squeaky hinge warns of our arrival. Again, we're met by darkness and again, the beam reveals much of nothing until it hits two sets of double-doors directly ahead.

"I think this is the foyer," I whisper. "Or was."

"Ain't seen a ticket in a long time by the looks of it."

We move into the centre of the space and Clement scans for exit points. There's another door back into the auditorium, two doors marked 'Gents', and 'Ladies', and a staircase where the beam loiters.

"Up?"

"Guess so."

We make our way up the wide staircase to a mezzanine with another door which turns out to be a storage room. Continuing up the stairs, we emerge onto a wide balcony overlooking the main auditorium. Another door leads to what must have once been a projector room.

"I've a feeling no one has been in here for years," I comment.

Clement steps over to the edge of the balcony and sweeps the beam across the empty space below.

"Don't make no sense," he mumbles.

"What doesn't?"

"Why go to the trouble of putting up fencing and barbed wire at the back? What's there to protect?"

"Nothing, apart from the building itself."

"Eh?"

"Perhaps it's meant to keep squatters out."

"Why the hell would anyone wanna squat in here when there are plenty of empty houses around town?"

"Squatting in residential properties is now illegal, but the law doesn't cover commercial property. Landlords go overboard with security."

"That explains the shop."

"What shop?"

"Don't matter."

He then leans forward and focuses the beam on an archway to the left of the stage.

"We should see what's through there."

"Is there any point?" I groan. "We were obviously wrong about Fraser using this place."

"It'll take two minutes."

"And every extra minute we spend trespassing is a minute closer to someone calling the police. Let's just get out of here while we can."

The oppressive darkness is not helping my spirits. This was my last hope and, although I knew the odds were not in our favour, the flame still flickered. Now, there is literally no light.

"Two minutes, and then we'll go."

"For God's sake, Clement. What's the point?"

"Gut feeling."

"Tell me it's not that bloody voice again."

"Come on."

He has the torch so I've no choice but to follow.

We make our way back down the stairs, through the foyer, and across the floor of the auditorium to the far corner. The archway, no wider than a door, has a curtain rail fixed to the top, but the curtain itself has probably rotted away in the dank air.

I follow Clement into a narrow corridor which appears to run parallel to the back of the stage. The grimy, pockmarked walls and bare floorboards suggest we're not in a part of the building the public ever got to see. The first, and most obvious, sight is a set of recessed fire doors directly ahead.

"I reckon they lead to that area at the back," Clement

suggests.

Stepping forward, he raps one of the doors with his knuckle. "Steel. Probably reinforced."

"Yes, to keep squatters out."

He turns the torch back to the corridor and presses on.

Halfway along, my patience and nerves are near exhausted. I'm about to suggest we leave when Clement comes to a sudden stop. He turns the torch towards a section of the left-hand wall, clad in wooden panels running floor to ceiling and each roughly five feet wide. The first one receives another rap of his knuckle. A dull thud echoes back along the corridor. He then raps at the second panel with the same result.

"What are you doing?"

"There's somethin' not right about this place."

"Yes. It's cold, damp, dark, and it smells like a blocked drain."

"I mean, it used to be a theatre, so where are the dressing rooms, and where'd they keep all the scenery and props?"

"Who cares? Maybe they had a temporary structure out the back. Can we please just go?"

The third panel receives a rap. This time, the resulting sound is markedly different from the first two panels; similar to tapping a hardback book and then an empty biscuit tin.

"There's a space behind here."

"So?"

"I wanna see what it is."

The panel is at least seven feet tall with a thick strip of wooden bead running along the top edge. Clement reaches up and runs his fingers along the top of the bead.

"Got something," he then grunts. "Like a latch."

Anyone less than seven feet tall would have the same view I do — basically, a view of nothing. Clement continues to fiddle until I hear a sudden clunk sound.

"Got it."

He adjusts the position of his hand and tugs the panel. The top part eases an inch away from the adjacent panel until Clement increases the force. Suddenly, the bottom section pops and the whole panel swings open like a door.

"Shit," I gasp. "I owe you an apology."

"Add it to the list."

Clement shines the torch into the open doorway. I step over to his side and, as I'm about to peer in, he moves forward into the darkness. A quick scan with the torch and he reaches towards the wall. The click of a switch and the space fills with light.

"Still wanna leave?" he asks.

"Admittedly, this is a positive development."

I step through the doorway and assess what Clement has uncovered.

"That answers one question," he says, nodding his head towards a huge, old-fashioned goods elevator. "And, it's gotta go somewhere."

Considering how poorly maintained the building is the last thing I fancy is a ride in an antiquated death cage. Fortunately, there's a set of stairs opposite the elevator.

"Someone put those panels up to hide this area," Clement comments. "Makes no sense for them to be there if they used to shift stuff between floors."

"I agree, which means whatever is down those stairs, it's likely Fraser doesn't want anyone finding it."

"We better go look then."

More cautiously than before I follow Clement down the stairs to another set of reinforced steel doors. Tellingly, there are three bolts keeping it firmly locked; positioned at the top, bottom, and centre. Clement slides each bolt open, and then carefully turns the handle of the right-hand door. As the door eases open, the scene beyond is as black as night, until Clement steps forward and switches the torch on.

I follow and pat the wall in search of a light switch. I strike lucky on the fourth pat and two rows of fluorescent lights flicker on.

"What the shittin' hell is this place?"

I've never stepped foot in one before, but I've seen enough photos to know what I'm looking at.

"I think it's a drugs lab, and I'd wager it's not for producing

301

the kind of drugs you'll find in a High Street chemist."

The room is at least forty feet square and equipped with all the apparatus required to produce illegal drugs on an industrial scale. Unlike the photos of other labs I've seen, there is nothing amateur about this set-up. Most of the equipment is polished stainless steel, including three huge cylindrical vats connected by copper pipes to a boiler. There's a rack of shelving spanning the back wall; neatly stocked with sacks of white powder and gallon-sized containers of fluid. The constituent components of crystal meth, I suspect.

"Raynott must have the market sewn up with this kind of opcration," Clement remarks.

It's an interesting observation, and one which leads to the primary reason we're here.

"Have you ever heard of the drug, crystal meth?"

"Nah."

"It's a huge problem in America, but thankfully it hasn't permeated the drug scene so much over here. The problem for suppliers is the market isn't huge and there are plenty of amateur meth labs around. I'd guess that's why Fraser was so obsessed with Cameron's drug — a highly-addictive narcotic no one else could supply."

"Evil bastard," Clement spits.

"I concur, but I think we've got him now. Once the police see this, they'll put Fraser away for a long spell."

"You think?"

"What more evidence do they need?"

"Do you know for sure this is being used to make drugs? Could be brewing ale for all we know."

"I've seen this kind of operation before, albeit on a smaller scale."

"Yeah, and I've met men like Fraser Raynott before. We need to find that kid — he's the only one who can tell the Old Bill what's been going on down here."

On cue, we both scan the space in search of any evidence that this is where Cameron Gail was being held.

"Clement, over there."

I point to the far side of the room towards a recessed fire door.

We make our way over and, on closer inspection, it appears someone has tampered with the door. The original locking mechanism is hanging upside down and three of the four screws designed to fix it in place are now missing. Ominously, the broken lock has been replaced with a steel chain, fastened by a padlock. Both items look like they're fresh from the shelf of a hardware store.

"Do you remember Cameron's voicemail message to Kimberley?"

"Bits of it."

"He said he was locked in, and I'm positive he mentioned a fire escape. Putting two and two together I think this is the fire escape he was referring to."

Clement is the first to spin around but I'm first to point towards the two doors to our right — one bolted shut while the other has a standard lock.

I take the lead and step over to the nearest door. I'm just about to unlock one of the bolts when Clement pulls me back.

"Don't go touching nothin', Doc. Dabs, remember."

"Dabs?"

"You were arrested last week. The Old Bill have got your fingerprints on file."

"Oh, good point."

After sliding the bolts across, Clement tugs the stiff door open. We're immediately hit by the unmistakable stench of shit.

"Jesus!" I spit, turning my head away.

Taking a second to inhale a breath through my mouth, I enter the room first, to find it's home to little else but a single bed; a young man in a t-shirt and jeans sprawled across it, face down.

"Cameron," I yelp, dashing over to the side of the bed.

There's no response so I kneel down and call his name again. Still no response.

"He's unconscious," I confirm.

I reach for his arm, and I'm about to shake him awake but the moment my skin touches his, I recoil.

"And he's … he's stone cold."

Clement edges over and places his hand on the back of Cameron's neck. He keeps it there for several seconds and then withdraws.

"I'm sorry, Doc. He's gone."

"What? No … he can't be. He's probably …"

"Trust me — the kid is dead."

35.

My mind fixes on the photo of Cameron and Kimberley; the happy couple I've only seen together on the screen of an iPhone. As distressing as it is to discover his cold corpse, I never really knew the young man. His former girlfriend will be grief stricken.

"You think Raynott killed him?" Clement asks, as we make a dignified retreat towards the door.

"Not directly. I fear he probably died at the hands of his own creation. Kimberley stressed how dangerous Kimbo is, or was now its architect is dead. I'm guessing Raynott used Cameron as a human guinea pig … until he escaped."

I take a final glance at the lifeless body. So many questions remain unanswered but it's a fair assumption that Cameron was brought back here last night after Alex tracked him down. It certainly isn't the resourced lab he was promised — more a prison.

"One consolation," Clement suggests. "Whatever shit that kid developed I doubt Raynott will be selling it on the streets now. Killing your own customers ain't good for business."

Theories aside, it's a tragic waste of a life, and of a brilliant mind. All Cameron Gail wanted was to help others; he didn't deserve to end his days locked in a basement, caked in his own faeces.

I pull the door shut.

"We have to call the police."

Clement strokes his moustache.

"Yeah, but I wanna check what's in there first."

His eyes shift to the adjacent door.

"I don't. I just want to get out of here … I need some air."

"It'll take five minutes."

"Clement, in case it has escaped your attention, there's a young man lying dead on the other side of that door — a young man we were supposed to rescue, remember?"

"What's your point?"

"You don't seem particularly bothered he's dead."

"Ain't much we can do about it, Doc, and it ain't our fault he's dead. You wanna blame someone, blame Raynott."

"Yes, but … God, I feel sick."

"It's just shock. Take a few deep breaths and you'll be alright."

A bizarre moment of role reversal but I take the advice. I've never seen a dead body before, let alone one belonging to someone I knew, and the experience is disconcerting beyond words.

"Please, can we just go?"

"No, 'cos this ain't over … not for me. I've gotta find Raynott."

"Can't you just leave it to the police? He'll get his comeuppance."

"There's no guarantee he will. He's probably got an army of lawyers who'll find a way to wrangle him out of this."

"An illegal drugs lab and a body? Come off it, Clement, there's more than enough evidence down here to put Raynott away for a long time."

"He could say he rented the building to the kid, and it was him who set all this up. He was the bleedin' chemistry expert, weren't he?"

"Well, yes."

"Think about it, Doc. Raynott's company owns the building, but I guarantee none of this gear can be linked to him. He's not an idiot."

I close my eyes and pull another deep breath.

"Somethin' else to consider," he adds. "Without the kid, your arse is still hanging in the wind. There's no one to back-up your story now."

A flurry of emotions continue to arrive and depart. The rush at discovering this place, and then the horror of finding Cameron's body. The shock still lingers but it carries an undercurrent of selfish consolation — an end to my plight and an escape from Fraser Raynott's clutches once the police catch up with him. Clement has now filled my head with doubts.

"We'll have a quick look, but then we call the police.

Agreed?"

"Yeah, yeah," he replies, already fiddling with the door lock. "Give me the toolkit."

I pass him the book-sized vinyl pouch containing a range of basic tools. It was one of the few useful items Leah found in her boxes of second-hand tat. He unzips it and extracts a screwdriver and a set of pliers.

"This'll only take a minute."

His estimate proved pessimistic as, thirty seconds later, the metal lock clunks to the floor. Clement returns the tools to the pouch and passes it back to me.

"Let's hope there's something in here worthwhile."

He opens the door and pats the inside wall, searching for a light switch. Another fluorescent light flickers on to reveal a room no larger than Cameron Gail's cell. I follow Clement in.

"Shit," he groans.

I've no idea what he was looking for, but the room contains just a desk, an office chair, a small couch, and a plain coffee table. The walls are painted an insipid shade of beige and the floor covered with carpet tiles. I'd guess it probably used to serve as one of the illusive dressing rooms Clement referred to earlier; now repurposed as an office.

"Shall we call the police now?"

"Hold up a sec."

The desk has three drawers and Clement tugs at the top one.

"Locked. Gimme the toolkit."

I hand it over and the lock receives the same treatment as the one on the door. Standing side by side, we peer into the first drawer. Disappointingly, it contains a few basic items of stationery: a hole punch, a tub of paperclips, a ruler, a pack of pencils, and a couple of biros.

The next drawer is of even less interest: two pads of paper and a mobile phone charger.

"Better get your phone ready," Clement suggests. "This ain't looking good."

He pulls the third and final drawer open and cusses under his breath. More items of stationery: a brass letter opener, a dog-eared notepad, and a now-obsolete sat-nav similar to the one my parents bought me after I passed my driving test.

"Fuck's sake," Clement snaps, slamming the drawer shut. "There's gotta be something in this bloody building."

"Um, what exactly were you hoping to find?"

"Anything that'll tell us where we can find Raynott."

I hadn't noticed the wastepaper basket at the side of the desk until Clement, clearly frustrated, boots it across the floor. Scraps of paper and an empty plastic bottle spill out. Still riled, Clement snatches the scraps of paper up, inspecting each one before tossing it aside. I presume he's hoping to find some tenuous clue to Fraser's whereabouts but daren't ask. Then, one piece of paper grabs his attention.

"Found something?" I squeak.

"Nah, it's just a number."

"A phone number?"

"Back in my day it was, but not now. There's just four digits — 2378."

"Could be a PIN."

"A what?"

"A personal identification number. It's used for paying in shops with a bank card or withdrawing money from a cash machine, or at least it was before contactless technology came along."

Clement shakes his head and shoves the slip of paper into his coat pocket.

"Bleedin' technology," he growls. "More trouble than it's worth."

He then makes a beeline for the drawer again.

"What are you doing?"

"Checking if there's anything in the notepad."

I find myself redundant as Clement thumbs through the notepad; the lines on his forehead creasing deeper with every page. With nothing else to do, I pick up the chunky sat-nav and reminisce about the journeys I took with mine during my teenage years. I press the button to turn it on and I'm greeted by the nostalgic digital drum beat; the manufacturers signature tune.

"What you gurning at?" Clement asks.

"Oh, nothing. I used to have one just like this."

"Bully for you."

"Trust me: it was a God-send as I had no sense of direction. Without it, I'd never have …"

I don't finish my sentence as a thought strikes.

"Never have what?" Clement asks.

"Found my way home."

I frantically prod the screen and I'm immediately reminded how painstakingly slow the device is. Working through the navigation menu, I finally find what I'm looking for — route history. Another prod and the page slowly loads. There's a long list of addresses but one of them leaps off the screen because it's in Chiswick and there's a tiny house icon next to it.

I show Clement and he returns a blank stare.

"I have a sneaking suspicion this is Fraser Raynott's sat-nav."

"Why's it stuck in a drawer down here, then?"

"Most modern cars have a sat-nav built-in, and every mobile phone has a navigation function so devices like this are pretty-much obsolete. I'd bet half the population has one of these stashed in a drawer somewhere."

Clement squints at the screen.

"What am I looking at?"

"Presuming it is Fraser's, this is a record of every journey he planned. And, as you can see, he's set his home address."

"You saying that address is Raynott's?"

"Didn't you say he lived in Chiswick?"

"Yeah."

"Well, then. On the balance of probabilities, yes, I think it could be."

"We need to see what it looks like from the outside before we waste time charging all the way across town. You can do that on your phone, right?"

I pluck it from my pocket and groan. The lack of signal is an annoyance, but it does answer another question.

"There's zero mobile reception down here. That's probably

why Cameron still had hold of his phone when he escaped."

"Not with you."

"You don't lock someone up with a mobile phone so they can call for help unless you know it's impossible for them to make a call."

"Why'd he bother letting the kid keep hold of it then?"

"Goes back to why Fraser was so desperate to get his hands on Cameron's phone. If all his research data resided on that phone, Cameron would have needed it to formulate the drug Fraser wanted so badly. Besides, even the brightest scientist needs the help of a computer — Fraser must have known that."

"A computer? You said the kid had a phone."

"A modern mobile phone is essentially a computer."

"Christ," he mumbles, shaking his head. "I can't keep up with this shit."

"I'll explain later."

We dash back up the stairs into the dark confines of the auditorium. I've just enough signal to google the address in Milnthorpe Road, Chiswick. From there, I navigate to the street view so we can inspect the exterior of what I hope is Fraser Raynott's home.

"It's a big detached house," I confirm, holding the phone for Clement to see.

"Look at the motor on the driveway — looks a lot like the one Raynott turned up in when we met."

I double-check, and there is a dark-coloured Mercedes saloon parked in front of the double garage.

"Why is the reg plate blurred?" Clement asks.

"Privacy, but even without knowing the registration, the odds look favourable. There are too many coincidences for this not to be Fraser Raynott's place."

"Yeah, you're right."

"What do you intend to do?"

"We need to move fast. If Raynott gets wind he's had a break-in, he could have the kid's body and all that gear moved in an hour or two."

"And, what about calling the police?"

"Call them on the way."

"To where?"

"Chiswick."

"Shouldn't we wait for the police to turn up first?"

"Only if you wanna be arrested for breaking and entering. Besides, once the Old Bill work out who the building belongs to, they'll send someone round to Raynott's gaff and anything could happen from there. At the moment, we've got the element of surprise on our side."

"I don't know, Clement. It seems a huge risk."

"Stepping out your front door every morning is a risk, Doc."

"Yes, but I rarely encounter unhinged, armed men on my way to work."

"Stay in the van, then. All I want is ten minutes with Raynott … that's all."

"Dare I ask what you intend to do with those ten minutes?"

"If you wanna walk away from this, you need evidence to back-up whatever is on those computers we snatched. I'm gonna gather some evidence from Raynott."

"That's the job of the police."

"They'll need a warrant and that takes time. We don't."

"And is that the only reason you're keen to chat with him?"

"Ain't gonna lie to you, Doc. I wanna find out where his old man is buried so I can go piss on his grave."

"And what if he doesn't tell you?"

"He will. If he doesn't, he'll pay for what Roland Raynott did to me."

"What you *think* Roland Raynott did to you. I don't wish to press the point, Clement, but your memories are an illusion and you need treatment. It'll be difficult securing that treatment if you're locked up."

"Maybe you're right, but I need to confront Raynott. I dunno why but …"

"But?"

"Don't matter."

"The voice?"

He nods.

311

"Have you considered the possibility that at some point in the past, you've had a run-in with Fraser Raynott?"

"Don't think I'd met the bloke until the other day."

"But you said he recognised you."

"I said it felt like he recognised me. Might have been wrong about that."

"True, but what if you have met before and your mind has suppressed the memories? It could be your subconscious mind is now misinterpreting those memories and leading you on this false path."

"Only one way to know for sure, Doc. We go and ask Raynott."

I don't have the energy to argue. I'm minded to let him go on his own and wait here for the police, but there's now more at stake than just my liberty. I owe it to Cameron to ensure Fraser Raynott sees justice, and I owe it to Clement to see this through.

"Seems you're not the only headcase. Come on."

36.

Debbie once told me the definition of insanity was attempting to drive from one side of London to the other. That advice isn't lost on me as we begin the journey from the urban East End to the leafy streets of suburban West London. The only saving grace is the time of day as it's now approaching eight-thirty in the evening and the traffic is noticeably lighter than it is during the day.

I wouldn't say Clement's reckless driving style has improved, but it lacks the maniacal urgency I experienced on the inbound journey, aided by the absence of glam rock music.

"Shall I call the police now?"

"Nah, not yet. Wait till we're about halfway."

"Which is where?"

"I'll let you know."

Conversation over, Clement returns to his own thoughts, as we enter the Limehouse Link tunnel.

"Anything you want to talk about?" I ask.

"Not really."

"Fair enough. If you change your mind, I'm happy to listen."

"There comes a time, Doc, where the talkin' ends and the doin' begins."

"I'm seeing that."

"What are you gonna do, when this is all over?"

"Do?"

"Yeah, with your life?"

"I'm not sure. The same as I did before this horror show began, I suppose. We'll see."

"You want my advice?"

"Considering how much of my advice you've had to endure, I suppose it's only fair."

"I'd suggest you get the hell out of this town."

"If only it were that easy."

"It's as easy as you make it. Tell your missus you've had enough and get on with it."

"She loves London."

"She probably loves you more, though Christ-knows why."

"Wow. Thanks for the vote of confidence, Clement."

"Anytime," he snorts. "Besides, this place ain't what it was. Dunno why anyone would wanna live here these days."

"You should tell Leah that."

"Nah, you should tell her. And I mean, tell her. Life's too short to waste being unhappy, Doc, and you don't need to be a shrink to know you're unhappy."

We exit the tunnel and it feels an appropriate moment to change the subject.

"Shall I call them now?"

"If it shuts you up, go ahead."

I'm about to make the call when Clement offers further advice.

"Can't they trace your phone?"

"Err, yes. So?"

"Report it anonymously. You don't want your name connected to that shit-show in any way, shape, or form."

"How am I supposed to ring them, then?"

He pulls his phone out and lobs it into my lap.

"It ain't registered to no one so use that."

"Okay."

"And just keep it brief. Tell 'em there's a drugs lab and a body in the basement. Oh, and mention the way in."

"Anything else."

"Nothing else, especially your name. Give 'em the basics then hang up."

I do as instructed and nervously make the call. It lasts less than thirty seconds.

"They're sending a unit over now."

"It'll take 'em ten minutes to get there and probably another twenty before the suits arrive. I reckon we've got at least an hour before they trace who owns the company on the title deeds."

Keen to inject a little urgency into our journey, Clement drops a gear and puts his foot down. With the River Thames to our immediate left, we tear through several amber traffic lights and slalom around buses and vans and any other vehicle which isn't breaking the speed limit. Several speed cameras flash and at one point my stomach spins as blue lights strobe behind us. Fortunately, it turns out to be an ambulance. Unfortunately, Clement decides it would be a good idea to tail it so we have a clear path. It turns right when we reach Embankment but we continue on the same frantic trajectory.

We just about avoid a head-on collision with a bus in Belgravia, nearly kill a cyclist passing through Earl's Court, and narrowly escape crashing into the back of a stationary truck in Hammersmith.

My nerves are in shreds by the time we reach Chiswick; not helped as the road widens to three lanes when we hit the Great West Road. Clement takes it as permission to put his foot down again.

"Where is it from here?" he asks.

"You don't know?"

"You're the one with the map."

"I'll check, but can you slow down, please? At our current speed we'll be in the West Country before I've had a chance to find it."

He eases off the accelerator and I'm finally able to unfurl my clenched fingers from the seat. I revert to the map I checked in Stratford and update our location.

"It's not far. The third turning on the left."

I receive a grunt in reply. He then, with a cursory check of the mirror, veers into the left-hand lane. Not for the first time on this journey a horn blares behind us. I decide I'd rather stare at the phone screen for the final few hundred yards.

"Next turning," I then confirm.

Clement swings the van into Milnthorpe Road and slows to a walking pace.

"How far?"

"Err, it might be easier to park up and check on foot. I can't see the house numbers in the dark."

The steering wheel receives a yank to the left and we mount the kerb. With both nearside wheels invading the pavement,

Clement cuts the engine.

"You're leaving it here? On double-yellow lines?"

"Do you think I give a shit about a parking ticket?"

He exits the van. Apparently not.

I get out the passenger's side and check the map again while Clement opens the rear doors.

"I hope you're not bringing that sledgehammer," I remark.

"Much as I'd love to, you've gotta use the right tools for the right job."

He strides over, a battered holdall slung over his shoulder.

"What's in the bag?"

"The right tools. Where are we heading?"

"By my reckoning, it's about seventy or eighty yards up the road."

"What number was it?"

"It's not a number — it's a name. Orange Blossom."

"Bleedin' hell," he groans. "That confirms it's Raynott's gaff."

"Does it?"

"Johnny Cash had a record called *Orange Blossom Special*. If I remember, it was fucking awful."

"I didn't like Raynott much before, but this obsession with Johnny Cash is really starting to irk."

"I'll mention it to him. Come on."

We walk side-by-side along the pavement, passing three large detached houses; none of which are the house we're looking for. The holly hedge fronting the third house ends abruptly; replaced by a brick wall at least six feet high with decorative iron rails running along the top. The length of the wall suggests the plot of land beyond is sizeable. It ends, only to be replaced by a pair of equally high wrought-iron gates and a slate plaque with two words engraved in gold letters: Orange Blossom.

The good news is we've finally found Fraser Raynott's home. The bad news is it looks impregnable.

"There weren't no gates in the photo," Clement remarks.

"They were probably open at the time, which is why we

didn't see them."

He stands back and appraises the challenge.

"Fuck's sake. Don't fancy climbing that wall, do you?"

"I've had a bad enough week without ending it impaled on a spike, thanks."

We should have guessed Raynott wouldn't scrimp on the security, but I had hoped our luck might hold out and there would be an easier route to the front door.

"What's that?" Clement asks, pointing to a silver panel of buttons recessed in one of the brick pillars.

"I'm guessing it's an intercom system; like a glorified doorbell."

"Why don't we just ring it then and say we're delivering a parcel?"

"Because it likely has a camera so the homeowner can see who's at the gates. I don't think Raynott is likely to invite us in, do you?"

He steps over to the panel and stares at it. Losing the will to live, I puff a long sigh and stare up at the house we've no hope of reaching. I can only see the first-floor windows but there are no lights on. For all we know, our foe might not even be at home.

"I think we've reached the end of the line, Clement. Shall we just go, and let the police deal with Raynott?"

He continues to stare at the pillar.

"One sec," he mumbles.

I step to his side and cast my eye over the panel. As I suspected, there's a camera lens at the top with a speaker just below. There's also a large button with a bell icon next to it; presumably the button to press if you want to announce you're at the gates.

"What's this for?" Clement asks, pointing to a numeric keypad in the lower section.

"Err, I'd guess it's for entering an access code. I think you can open gates like this with either a remote control or a code."

Slowly, he dips a hand into his pocket.

"A code like this?" he asks, holding up the scrap of paper he

317

rescued from a wastepaper bin forty minutes ago.

I shake my head.

"I doubt Raynott would have been so careless."

Clement returns his attention to the panel. Long seconds pass, and then he raises his right hand towards the grid of numbered buttons.

"What are you doing?"

"Following orders."

"Good grief," I groan. "Whatever that voice is telling you, you're wasting your time."

Undeterred by my pessimism, he glances at the scrap of paper.

"Two," he mumbles under his breath before pressing a button on the keypad.

"Four."

Another button receives a jab.

"Seven."

Then the third.

"Eight."

A slight pause, and the final press.

I take a few steps back, expecting an alarm to sound. There's no alarm, but there is the faint whir of a motor from both brick pillars.

Slowly, the gates sweep apart.

"Bloody hell," I gasp. "It worked."

"Must be our lucky day."

With the gates almost open, we're able to see what lies beyond. A paved driveway runs parallel to the right-hand boundary and leads all the way to a detached double garage some thirty yards away. Unlike the photo we viewed earlier there's no Mercedes parked up. To the left of the garage sits the mansion-like house in all its ostentatious glory. All but one of the ground-floor windows are dark.

"It doesn't look like Fraser is home," I remark.

"Perfect."

"Is it?"

"Yeah, 'cos it means we ain't gotta get inside the house. We can find somewhere to hide out and ambush him on the driveway when he returns."

"Somewhere?"

"Round the back."

"But, he could be hours."

"When you've waited as many decades as I have, Doc, a few hours don't matter."

The tone of voice and cold stare imply this is not a point of negotiation. With or without me, he's going in.

He takes a few strides forward and stops.

"You coming?"

There are many good reasons to say no, but there's one good reason to follow.

"I suppose we've come this far together."

With reluctance, I step past the gates and join my deluded companion on the driveway.

"Last chance to change your mind," he warns.

"Let's just move before a neighbour spots us."

Clement stays close to the neatly pruned hedge which runs the length of the right-hand boundary. If someone is at home and glances out of the window, our dark silhouettes should blend into the foliage. As we creep forward, the gates close behind us.

We reach the end of the driveway and there are two options for a route forward, either side of the garage. To the left there's a gate which appears to lead down the right flank of the house, or directly in front of us there's a narrow gap between the garage and the hedge. Crossing the driveway to the gate has to be the riskier option as we've no idea if the gate is locked, and there are two floodlights fixed to the front of the house, which are probably motion activated. Fortunately, Clement makes the same assumption and squeezes into the gap at the side of the garage. Only when I follow do I realise how tight that gap is.

"Might wanna breathe in, Doc," Clement whispers. "It's a bit tight."

He's not kidding. Following his lead, I'm forced to crab sideways with my shoulders pressed tight against the garage wall. Somehow I manage to shuffle all twenty feet without the hedge lacerating my face.

I escape to find Clement peering into near-darkness. There's just enough light pollution to make out the basic lie of the rear garden. They say crime doesn't pay but the landscaping and kidney-shaped swimming pool suggest otherwise. From what I can see, Fraser Raynott's garden is four times the size of my entire flat.

"Don't think anyone is at home," Clement remarks. "No lights on at all back here."

"What now? I don't fancy sitting by the pool; not in January, anyway."

"We wait."

"What if the police show up looking for Raynott?"

"They'll find the same as us — an empty house. They ain't gonna hang around."

"Let's hope not."

"Stop frettin'. It'll take 'em ages to search his building in Stratford before they send anyone here. For now, we've gotta find a decent vantage point."

With that, he turns and makes his way along the back wall of the garage. Upon reaching the end he takes a quick peek around the corner.

"This way," he hisses.

I follow, and we enter a walkway between the house and the garage; the gate at the end presumably leading back to the driveway. There are two ground-floor windows and a part-glazed door at the side of the house, but all three are dark. As Clement reaches the door he cautiously tries the handle.

"Locked."

"No surprise."

We move forward to the gate which is high enough to deter anyone from climbing over. In the darkness, I can just make out bolts at the top and bottom; validating our decision to edge up the other side of the garage. As unyielding as the gate appears, there's a quarter-inch gap running the entire length of the hinged edge, allowing a slither of light from the street to leak into the dark walkway.

Clement slowly eases both the bolts across and then peers through the gap.

"This'll do us," he says. "Better make yourself comfy."

My definition of comfy is being curled up on the sofa with a mug of hot chocolate. There is no comfort to be found lurking in Fraser Raynott's side-passage on a freezing January evening. The best I can do is sit down on the ground with my back up against the side wall of the house. I then hug my knees to my chest to retain body heat.

A glance at my watch: quarter-past nine.

Silent minutes pass and my mind turns to Leah. Having enjoyed a slap-up meal at Dad's favourite pub I bet she's now relaxing in an armchair next to a roaring log fire. Knowing Dad he probably bought a round of Irish whiskies. They're no doubt having a whale of a time whilst I'm sat here, cold, miserable, and still some way from salvaging a situation I never instigated.

"I don't know how much longer I can sit here, Clement."

"You wanna go sit in the van?"

"I want to go home."

"Just give it half-hour."

"And then what?"

Rather than answer my question he rummages through the holdall. I'm past caring what's inside.

His check complete, Clement's attention returns to the gap, without another word on my discomfort. I let my thoughts drift back to the scene fifty miles west; at a village pub in Oxfordshire. To torture myself further, I mentally run through the items on the menu, trying to guess what Leah would have chosen. Perhaps braised lamb shank in minted gravy, or pan-fried sea bass with triple-cooked chips. Then again, they serve an amazing beef wellington with crispy roast potatoes, or …

"Gates are opening," Clement spits.

"Eh? What?"

"There's a motor at the gates. Get ready."

Without shifting his view, he holds out the holdall by its shoulder strap.

"Take it," he orders.

I grab the strap and discover the bag is surprisingly light, which I take as a positive sign. At least it's not weighed down with hammers, wrenches, and other heavy-gauge instruments of torture.

"Is it a Mercedes?" I ask, scrambling to my feet.

He turns from the gap and, in the muted light, I can just make out his twisted smile.

"It is. Payback time."

37.

The Mercedes purrs to a stop and Clement places his hand on the gate handle. Besides the tick tick of a cooling engine and the thrumming pulse in my ears, it's deathly quiet.

Then it isn't.

The clunk of a German-engineered door mechanism followed a moment later by the sound of a car door slamming shut. Then a blip of the remote central locking being activated.

Clement continues to stare through the gap as footsteps stomp across the driveway. They reach the gate and continue on. Suddenly, the big man twists the handle and eases the gate open. I had expected him to explode from our hideaway but it appears stealth is the preferred option.

He makes his move.

By the time I've got my legs to function, Clement is already six feet beyond the gate, and moving silently up behind a figure in a dark suit, carrying a messenger bag. Then, as that man's attention turns to a bunch of keys, he momentarily looks to his right. I get just a glimpse of his face but enough to confirm Clement is about to pounce on the right man — Fraser Raynott.

Without warning, Clement swings out his right arm and grabs Raynott from behind in a choke hold. The messenger bag and the keys fall to the floor as Raynott tries to prize his assailant's arm from around his neck. From my position, I can't see his face, but I can hear him gasping for breath. Giving up on his first tactic my nemesis then tries swinging his arms backwards, as he desperately tries to land any kind of blow. He catches Clement a few times but the awkward angle strips the blows of any potency.

Finally, the wheezing stops and his legs buckle. Clement releases his stranglehold and Raynott's limp body crumples to the driveway.

"God's sake, Clement," I hiss, darting across. "Please tell me you haven't killed him."

"If I wanted to kill him, he'd be dead. He ain't."

He bends down and snatches the bunch of keys from the floor. They're thrown in my direction.

"Open the front door."

"What if there's an alarm?"

"We'll wake him up and tell him to shut it off. He won't be out for long so get your arse in gear."

Relieved I'm not an accessory to murder, yet, I fumble through the keys until I find one which looks most likely to open a front door. I then step past the sleeping Raynott and try to keep my hand steady as I slip it into the lock. It doesn't work.

"Hurry up, Doc."

I check the bunch again and try a second key. It turns with ease and I'm able to push the door open to reveal a dark hallway.

"Move!"

I spin around and jump to my left as Clement drags Raynott's flaccid body towards the door by his shoulders; the heels of his no-doubt expensive leather shoes scraping across the driveway.

"Grab his bag," Clement grunts.

I do as I'm told and snatch up the bag. The weight suggests it contains more than a few documents and a lunch box.

Joining Clement in the hallway I close the front door.

"See what's in there," he says, nodding towards a door on the left.

I shove it open and pat the wall in search of a light switch. Two garish chandeliers light up a room which, on first impression, has a style born of money, not class; Downton Abbey meets Kentucky whore house.

"It's the lounge," I confirm.

"Make sure the curtains are closed."

The room is huge and runs from the front of the house to the back. After depositing the messenger bag on a coffee table, I close the curtains at the front and then a set covering French doors at the rear.

Clement drags Raynott in and lies him face down on the deep, shagpile carpet.

"Pass me the bag, Doc."

I lift the strap over my shoulder and hand it to him.

"Err, you don't have pliers in there, do you?"

The holdall is unzipped and a length of blue rope extracted.

"Nah. Got a better idea."

He doesn't elaborate but sets about tying Raynott's hands together. The snoozing psychopath is then hoisted off the carpet and dumped into the nearest armchair. Clement then unbuckles Raynott's belt and pulls his trousers down to his ankles.

"What did you do that for?"

"You'll see. He'll come round in a few minutes."

"And then what?"

"We get your evidence. Where's his bag?"

"There," I confirm, nodding towards the coffee table.

Clement grabs the messenger bag and unzips it.

"It's a bleedin' computer."

"That might be just what we're looking for. If the gods are smiling down, it might contain evidence to clear my name once and for all."

"Like what?"

"Emails, for starters. Alex said he used encrypted email to communicate with Sleeping Beauty there. And, knowing what we know about his dubious business practises, I'd bet there's more than just a few incriminating emails on that machine."

Somewhat perplexed, Clement hands me the compact laptop. I rest it on the arm of the sofa and flip the screen open. I'm met by a standard Windows log-in page, with one noticeable difference from my antiquated laptop.

"It uses facial recognition to unlock."

"Come again?"

"If it doesn't recognise the user, it won't unlock."

It's an easy enough problem to remedy and I step over to the armchair. Holding the laptop in front of Raynott's face it pings a tone to confirm we've passed the security test. I return to the arm of the sofa and check the screen again.

"Oh, for God's sake."

"Now what?"

"A biometric check. It requires a fingerprint."

"Are you shittin' me?"

325

"Afraid not."

"Bring it over here."

Clement rolls Raynott over and, with some difficulty, we're able to press one of his stubby fingers on to the laptop's fingerprint reader. Again, it pings a tone to confirm we've passed the security check.

"Third time lucky," I mumble, as Clement rolls Raynott around.

One glance at the screen and I'm tempted to launch it towards the chandeliers.

"I don't bloody believe this."

"Let me guess," Clement groans. "We've gotta rub his bollocks on the keyboard and sing *My Way*."

"Worse. It needs a PIN."

"Like the gates?"

"Yes, but this PIN is five digits. The gate code was just four."

"Bugger."

"We could try it and add another number to the end."

"Your call, Doc."

He passes me the slip of paper and I enter the four digits and then add a zero. I hit the enter key and, rather than the polite tone we've heard twice before, the laptop sounds a negative beep. A message displayed in bold type confirms the device will be locked after two more failed attempts.

"Shit. If we enter the wrong PIN twice more, it'll lock and there's no hope of gaining access."

"Shame we told that computer dipshit to disappear. Could have done with him about now."

"I suspect that same dipshit set this up. Whatever information is stored on this laptop Raynott has gone to great lengths to ensure no one can access it."

"Guess we need to wake him up then."

Clement looms over Raynott and slaps him around the chops a few times. The slaps aren't hard enough to do any damage, but they're forceful enough to invoke a groan.

"Wakey, wakey."

Raynott's eyes blink open and shut a few times. One final

slap finishes the job.

"Whaddafuck!" he blurts. "Who …"

His immediate priority is getting to his feet but, with his hands tied behind his back and his trousers tangled around his ankles, all he can do is writhe in the armchair. He soon gives up when the reality of the situation dawns.

The confusion mounts when he glares up at Clement.

"You."

"Yeah, me … and I think you know my mate?"

"He does," I confirm. "On account he's doing his utmost to destroy my life."

Raynott glances in my direction but remains impassive; I'm no threat. He then turns back to Clement.

"Who the fuck are you?" he sneers.

"I'm your worst nightmare."

"You've got that the wrong way round, my friend. No one fucks with Fraser Kingsland and lives to tell the tale."

"Raynott, don't you mean? No one fucks with Fraser Raynott?"

"What you blabbering on about?"

"Cut the bullshit — we know who you are and we ain't got time to piss around. My mate here wants the code for your computer, and you're gonna give it to him."

"Am I fuck."

"Wrong answer."

Clement dips a hand into his holdall and removes a roll of gaffa tape. He tears off a strip and, after some futile resistance, slaps it across Raynott's mouth.

"Don't mind if I smoke, do you, Doc?"

"It's not my house."

It seems an odd time for a cigarette break but Clement lights up. He takes a long draw and puffs a cloud of smoke towards the stocky man in the armchair.

"I heard a little story about you, Raynott," Clement says casually, the cigarette dangling from the corner of his mouth. "What your crew did to the poor wife of some landlord in the East End."

327

He then squats down directly in front of the armchair.

"Do you remember?"

A vigorous shake of the head.

"Why don't I give you a little reminder?"

Clement carefully takes the cigarette between his thumb and forefinger, and moves it towards Raynott's inner thigh. It's a measure of how much I detest Fraser Raynott that I'm willing to watch on without a care for the man.

The red-hot tip of the cigarette gets within an inch of Raynott's milky flesh. His eyes bulge and his body stiffens but Clement remains resolute. I can't imagine what it takes to torture another human, but it surely can't reside in a sane mind. Unfortunately for Raynott, the man holding the cigarette isn't the right side of sane.

"Last chance. You gonna give us that number?"

Raynott responds with a scowl and a series of defiant grunts.

"Suit yourself."

I'm finally forced to look away as the stench of burning skin drifts across the room. Unfortunately, I can still hear Raynott's muffled screams. I wait until they die down before turning back.

Clement takes another long drag of his cigarette as Raynott whimpers in the armchair.

"How many burns did that woman have on her face?" Clement asks him. "Ten? Fifteen?"

Raynott screws his eyes shut.

"See, I'm a big fan of justice, especially the poetic kind. I've got a whole pack of fags in my pocket and if it takes an hour or two, we'll get through them. Every. Single. One."

He takes another drag.

"Unless you wanna tell me that number?"

Raynott draws a few heavy breaths through his nostrils, and nods.

"Knew you'd see sense."

The tape is ripped from his mouth.

"You're a fucking dead man," our prisoner gasps. "Fucking dead, I tell you."

"Yeah, yeah. What's the number?"

Raynott turns his rage in my direction.

"You better hope this fucker hangs around for the rest of your days as I'm coming after you, sunshine."

"Like you came after Cameron Gail?"

"Yeah, and I got my man in the end," he sneers. "You cross me and I never forget. That kid will tell you as much."

"That's not likely is it … now he's dead?"

"What are you talking about?"

The rage in his face drains away.

"Don't pretend you didn't know. You kept him locked up like a dog in that bloody basement, and forced him to take the drug that killed him."

"I … how do you …"

"We've just come from Stratford," Clement confirms. "Interesting old building you've got there. Sorry about the dirty big hole we left in the side wall."

"And I don't think I closed the door on the way out of the meth lab, either," I add. "My apologies."

Raynott stares up at the ceiling, perhaps considering his next move now we've revealed how much we know about his operation.

"I'll give you that number on one condition," he mutters.

"Go on."

"Once I've handed it over, you untie me and fuck off. I don't care if you take the bloody laptop with you."

"Fair enough." Clement turns to me and winks.

"1, 9, 6, 9, 5."

I tap the digits into the keyboard and the security screen immediately disappears.

"I'm in."

"Good. Now, you've got what you wanted so piss off."

"Oh, we don't want your laptop, Fraser," I reply. "I just need evidence to prove you set me up so I'm going to copy every file and every email on your hard drive and send them to the police."

"Do that, and you'll regret it. I'll make sure you …"

"Talking of the Old Bill," Clement interrupts. "We gave them a buzz on the way over; just to let them know about your

329

hideaway in Stratford. Can't have that kid's body lying around like that ... it ain't dignified. They're probably tearing the place apart this very minute and it'll only be a matter of time before they drop by."

Realising we've duped him, Raynott's skin takes on a pinky hue.

"What the fuck do you want?" he snaps. "Money? How much?"

"Money won't be much use to me if I end up in prison," I reply. "Have you forgotten? You set me up on a bogus rape charge and then had child porn installed on my work computer."

"Fine. I'll get that girl to retract her statement and my tech guy will remove all those photos."

"Doubt that," Clement snorts. "He's probably in Scotland by now after I had a stern word."

"But we have his laptops," I add. "As evidence."

Raynott's body language implies he no longer wants to chat. He's either simmering with rage or working through his ever-decreasing options. "How long you gonna be, Doc?"

"Five minutes."

"You crack on while I make myself comfortable with our new friend."

Clement then grabs another armchair and drags it across the carpet so it's directly in front of Raynott's. He sits down and stares at him.

I don't know what his plan is, but I'm more interested in securing evidence to prove my innocence and implicate Raynott. With that task in mind, I open the file library and check the contents of the documents folder. It contains twenty individual folders, each with dozens of spreadsheet files; even criminals need detailed accounts, it seems. A cursory glance at a few of the spreadsheets confirms my theory and I upload the entire folder to a file sharing service I can access later.

Then, I switch to his emails. A quick search returns rich rewards — an email in which Raynott instructs Alex to dump 'kiddie porn' onto my computer.

I upload all the emails to the same file sharing service. The process itself only takes a few minutes thanks to Raynott investing in a high-spec machine.

"All done," I confirm. "I've now got copies of all his documents and emails."

"You're so dead," Raynott spits.

"Talking of dead," Clement says. "Is your old man still around?"

"I'm not telling you anything more until you tell me who you are."

"Don't matter."

"Yes, it does. I know you. I'm sure of it."

Clement puffs a deep sigh and reaches into his pocket. He then lights another cigarette, takes a drag, and positions it between his thumb and forefinger again.

"I'll ask you one more time," he says, sitting forward in the armchair. "Is your old man still around?"

Raynott stiffens in his seat and relents.

"No, he's dead."

"When did he die?"

"Three and a half, maybe four years ago. I don't keep track."

"Month?"

"What is this? Who cares when he died?"

"Month?"

"I don't know. March, April."

Clement pulls another long drag.

"Funny he should cark it about the same time I came back."

"Hilarious," Raynott spits, unaware of the delusional context.

"Did he suffer?"

"What?"

"You heard. Did he suffer?"

"How would I know? We weren't exactly on speaking terms so go ask the bloody staff in the care home."

"What was he doing in a care home?"

"The hokey-fucking-cokey. What the hell do you think he was doing in there … dying."

"Of what?"

"Of being old. He had a couple of strokes and the third one

finished him off."

Clement gets to his feet and slowly paces up and down the room. With every step his mood appears to darken. As he passes in front of the fireplace for the third time, he suddenly snatches a vase from the mantelpiece and hurls it towards the wall opposite. It explodes into a thousand pieces.

"Jesus Christ," Raynott yells. "You have any idea how much that cost?"

His answer comes by way of a backhanded slap across the face.

"I don't give a fuck. Where's his grave?"

Still smarting from the slap Raynott sucks air across his teeth.

"I can't remember," he hisses. "Edgeware way."

"Specifically?"

"I don't know. I paid for his care home and made sure he had a half-decent send off — a damn sight more than the sanctimonious old tosser deserved."

"Why?" I interject.

"Why what?"

"Why didn't he deserve more? He was your father."

"None of your damn business."

Clement turns and grabs a porcelain figurine from the mantelpiece. It meets the same fate as the vase.

"That was a one-off," Raynott whines. "Ten bloody grand it set me back."

"Count yourself lucky I didn't ram it up your arse. Answer his question."

"What? I ... what's this got to do with anything? You've stitched me up, alright, so take your questions and fuck off."

It seems Raynott is stupid, stubborn, and evil in equal measure. Another backhanded slap is duly administered.

"Fuck!" he seethes, shaking the sting from his cheek.

"Answer him."

Raynott slowly turns his head in my direction and spits. The globule of saliva misses my shoe by six inches.

"Sod this for a game of soldiers," Clement says, before

reaching into the holdall. "I ain't got the patience."

He pulls out a carving knife and holds it up to the chandelier; inspecting it like a surgeon might inspect his instruments before theatre.

"Err, Clement. What are you doing?"

"I tried being nice but it ain't working. Gonna cut his toes off."

I turn to Raynott. His demeanour is now markedly panicked.

"Whoa," he gulps. "Just hold on a sec. No need to do anything hasty."

"It might be a good idea to answer don't you think?"

"Fuck's sake. What do you want to know?"

"I asked why your father deserved a son who abandoned him in a care home, and has clearly never visited his grave."

"And I told you — he was a hypocrite and a sanctimonious old tosser."

"He was a fucking coward," Clement snorts.

"Yeah, and a drunk, and a wife-beater, and a thief, and a good-for-nothing excuse for a father. And they say the apple don't fall far from the tree, so if you're wondering why I'm the way I am, go buy a Ouija board and ask my old man."

Unexpectedly, the two men seem in complete agreement.

"Why was he a hypocrite? Did he frown upon your hideous business practises?"

"He found God, apparently. Started preaching on about how I'd live to regret my deeds, and I should seek forgiveness while I had the chance."

"Perhaps you should have listened."

"Like I didn't. The bloody idiot kept ringing me day and night, saying he could feel … what was it … a presence looming, or some shit like that."

"A presence?"

"I don't know; like the Grim Reaper, I suppose. He said it was too late for him, but I could still take the righteous path. I reckon he had dementia; the crazy old bastard."

Clement suddenly drops the knife as if the handle has become super-heated. Then, he moves zombie-like towards the

333

armchair and lowers himself down.

"Bottle of pop and a bag of Salt 'n' Shake crisps," he says in a low voice.

Puzzled, Raynott looks up at me for an answer. I shrug and he returns his gaze to Clement.

"What you on about?"

"I remember now. We have met before."

Raynott's frown deepens.

"And it all makes sense."

I don't recognise Clement's disconnected tone of voice, much less his wide-eyed expression. My concern mounts when he begins chuckling to himself.

"How did I miss it? Dickhead."

"Clement? You okay?"

He ignores my question and sits forward.

"How old were you, Raynott? Couldn't have been more than four or five, I reckon."

"Eh?"

"Your old man took you into the Three Monks a few times; made you wait in the corner while he played the fruit machine. Remember?"

Raynott's lower jaw drops but no words follow.

"Dave, the landlord, felt sorry for you. Gave you a bottle of pop and a bag of crisps, didn't he?"

Raynott swallows hard, his eyes now wider than Clement's.

"How … how do you know?"

Clement leans further forward until there's only five feet of tense air separating their faces.

"You were waiting for your old man on a Thursday afternoon. He was playing the fruit machine and gave you an earful when you disturbed him, didn't he?"

"Uh? I …"

"You waited in the corner, by the jukebox, snivellin'. Remember?"

Raynott's face, which was red from the slaps, has lost all colour.

"There was a big bloke, weren't there? He took pity and said

334

you could choose a tune. Think hard, Raynott — can you remember what that bloke looked like?"

In an instant, some colour does return to Raynott's face, albeit a bluish hue.

"Now, what was it you chose?" Clement continues, stroking his moustache. "Let me think."

As the big man ponders, the man opposite is struggling for breath, his eyes now bulging.

"That's it," Clement declares. "Benny Hill, *Ernie, Fastest Milkman in the West*."

Raynott gasps but manages to rasp a handful of words.

"How could you know … no … it's impossible …"

"All coming back to you now, is it? Most of the regulars thought your old man was a wrong'un but little Fraser, he weren't a bad nipper. You could have taken another path but nah, you didn't. You followed in his footsteps and kept on going to become the proper evil bastard you are."

I watch on, dumbstruck, like I'm in the audience of a two-hander play with compelling dialogue but an implausible plot. However, the acting on display is Oscar-worthy.

To confound the situation further Raynott starts sobbing.

"Seems we've come full circle," Clement says. "Me here, you snivellin'."

"Please," Raynott coughs. "I'm not … I'm sorry …"

Clement gets to his feet and looks down upon the wreck of a man before him.

"I should thank you, really 'cos now, I know. I ain't no one's saviour — never was."

With Raynott now visibly shaking, Clement bends over him; his features hardened, stern.

"You ever read the bible"

Impossible to say if his head shake is through fear or to confirm in the negative.

"Romans 6:23," Clement says flatly. "For the wages of sin is death, but the gift of God is eternal life."

He pauses a beat then continues."

"You've been taking wages that ain't yours to take. Now, it's time to face your judge."

Petrified, Raynott lurches back in his chair; his eyes rolling, his breathing shallow and irregular. It's no act.

"Shit, Clement," I yelp. "I think he's having a heart attack."

The big man turns to me and shrugs.

"I can't watch him die. That wasn't part of the plan."

I make a move towards the armchair, intent on practising my rusty first-aid skills, but Clement steps in the way.

"Nothin' you can do, Doc. He's as good as gone."

"But, this isn't right."

"It ain't our place. Not yours, not mine."

"No, wait," I plead. "You said no one would die … that's what you said."

"I said I wouldn't kill no one, and I ain't. He's gonna die because he's an evil piece of shit … just like the others. I understand now."

On cue, Raynott convulses in the chair and gargles a deep, gasping cry. Then, every muscle in his board-like body appears to fail simultaneously. He flops back and his head lops to the side; his eyes glassy, empty.

Three men in the room: all inert but for drastically different reasons. From the silence, my mind fixes on the rhythmic ticking of a clock. I glance at the fireplace to the source: an ornate brass carriage clock. It promptly stops.

38.

It would be easy to assume there are two dead men in Fraser Raynott's lounge. One in an armchair, and one perched on the edge of the coffee table, head in hands. That second man isn't dead; more a state of stunned paralysis as his mind struggles to process the barrage of questions.

"Oi!" a voice barks.

I look up. Clement is in the process of pulling Raynott's trousers back into position, having already removed the rope binding his hands together. He then drags the second armchair back to its original position. Apart from the fragments of china and porcelain on the carpet near the wall, the scene looks perfectly normal; no hint of the preceding madness.

"Get your arse in gear, Doc. We gotta go."

I stand up and avoid looking at Raynott's bloated corpse. Not because I feel any guilt for his demise, but because his dead eyes are staring in my direction.

Clement makes his way to the back of the room and squats down by the curtains. He stays there for a moment and then strides back to pick up the holdall.

I'm about to ask what he was doing, but it becomes obvious when light flickers from the floor by the French doors. The flames quickly begin to eat their way through the heavy fabric.

"What the hell did you do that for?" I gasp.

"Nothing like a fire to destroy evidence."

"Evidence?"

"There won't be any trace we were ever here. The Old Bill will think it's down to one of his rivals."

"What about Raynott? You can't just leave him here to … it's not right."

"Ashes to ashes, Doc. Come on."

With the flames already licking at the decorative cornice, further discussion would be unwise unless I wish to join Raynott in the afterlife. Still dazed, I follow Clement out to the hallway.

"How do we open the gates?" Clement asks.

"You ask that now? *After* starting a fire?"

I scan the walls and spot a control unit by the front door. Dashing over to it, I press a button with a gate icon above.

"Gates open, I think."

We leave the house and sneak back down the frost-dusted driveway.

The road itself is quiet and, being close to eleven o'clock, many of the neighbouring houses are in darkness. They're in for a rude awakening when the fire engines arrive; assuming anyone is awake to notice the Raynott residence is on fire.

Back at the van, Clement tosses the holdall over the driver's seat and gets in. I take a final glance up the street to double-check there are no witnesses to our departure. All is still in the cold night air.

Moments later, we're heading away on the Great West Road. Clement's driving is as erratic as the inbound journey but there are fewer vehicles on the road to worry about; not that I don't have more pressing matters to discuss with him.

"Listen to me: you urgently need psychological evaluation."

"You think?"

"I know, Clement."

"That's it, then. I'm certifiably mad, am I?"

"You're stark-staring insane, and I don't need a doctorate in psychology to work that out. You just stood there and watched a man die … and what the hell was all that nonsense about the Three Monks?"

"You heard Raynott. Explain it, if you can."

"No, no way. I'm not being led down that path because there are plenty of ways you could have known about what happened that day. Let's talk about your sudden epiphany."

"My what?"

"The realisation you're here to do God's bidding, like some kind of celestial hit man."

"Told you, it makes sense."

"In your head maybe. For those of us not living on planet Clement can you explain how you reached that ridiculous conclusion?"

"Straightforward, Doc. I thought I was sent back to, dunno, do good and make penance for my wayward behaviour in the past. I got it wrong. I was meant to see the wrong'uns to a place where they'd be judged."

"Unbelievable," I groan. "Now you're saying you've killed people because it was God's will?"

"Fuck's sake," he snaps back. "Do you ever listen? I ain't killed no one, and I sure as hell didn't kill Raynott."

"Not directly, perhaps, but we might have saved him if you'd have let me administer CPR."

"Do what?"

"Resuscitate him. I could have saved his life."

"And what makes you think he deserved saving? Gimme one reason … just one."

"Because … because …"

I'm still trying to think of a valid reason when we approach a roundabout way too fast. The van sways left and right as the tyres squeal, but somehow we make it to the other side.

"Can't think of one," Clement crows. "Can you?"

"He had a right to live; the same as anyone else."

"And what about that Cameron kid? Didn't he have a right not to be locked up and force-fed his own fucking drugs?"

"Of course he did, but two wrongs don't make a right."

He shakes his head.

"That's where you and I differ, Doc. You think you can save everyone, but some folks … well, they're just plain bad, beyond saving. All I did with Raynott, and every other evil piece of shit, is help them on their way. They made their choices."

"But you were the common denominator."

"I know."

Rather than look at the road he turns to face me.

"That's why I was sent back. To guide these arseholes to a place they can't do any harm."

"How heroic," I mumble under my breath. "And deluded."

"Believe what you like. I know who I am, and I know my place now."

There is no sense continuing the conversation. There's even

less sense trying to help Clement, I fear. Events over the last hour have only cemented his delusion.

With the man beside me now beyond help, and a pressing need to quell my frustration, I focus on my own situation. The files on Raynott's laptop should be ready for me when I get home. The question is: once I've had a chance to scan them thoroughly, what do I do with any evidence I uncover? I can hardly tell the police how the information came into my possession without incriminating myself.

I'm pulled from my thoughts as the van suddenly lurches to the right.

"Wanker," Clement shouts, while pressing hard on the horn.

"Who?"

"Taxi driver. Pulled out without indicating."

I choose not to point out the hypocrisy of his statement and return to the problem in hand. The more I think about it, the more I wonder if I even need to hand the files over considering the situation with Raynott — I no longer need leverage against the man attempting to destroy my life, on account his life is over. I just require proof I'm innocent. For that, I have Alex's laptops and they should contain the same email exchanges as those on Raynott's laptop, along with a digital record of Alex's hack on the RightMind office. That should be evidence enough to clear my name regarding those horrendous images.

Then there's just Chantelle Granger's allegation.

It's certainly a concern, but nowhere near as much as the images. There's no evidence, but I'd rather it went away with no further scrutiny from the police. I think it's safe to assume Miss Granger was not a willing participant in Raynott's plan; no more than Cameron or Alex. His modus operandi involved heavy use of the stick, rather than the carrot. The stick, like the man, has been destroyed so perhaps she'll retract her statement now the threat has gone. I guess it's also safe to assume the queue of liars ready to levy false accusations against me will quickly disperse without Raynott to orchestrate their campaign.

Now the shock of watching a man die has eased, the cold, hard benefits of that man's death are finding their way home. As

Clement suggested, cutting the head off the snake is a sure-fire way to avoid a fatal bite. Not the ending I envisaged, but it is a definitive ending. And Christ, I needed this chapter of my life to end. As for the next chapter that's a question for tomorrow.

For now, I'd like to wallow in nothingness; to sit back, close my eyes, and let my mind unwind.

As we pass through Shepherd's Bush, Clement accelerates hard to beat an amber light. The constant jerking left and right, and back and forth, is no aid to sleep. I conclude it'd be easier to doze on a rollercoaster and, instead, stare out of the window.

The vista opens up as we reach Westway: a three-lane carriageway heading east towards the heart of the city.

Eventually, three lanes merge into two and the scenery becomes increasingly claustrophobic as we hit the Edgeware Road. The traffic is light but the streets of London are never empty. Even at this hour, there are deliveries to be made, passengers for the night buses to shuttle around, and taxis ferrying tourists from the West End to their hotels.

We pass the statue of Sherlock Holmes, Madame Tussauds, and St Marylebone Parish Church, which looks nothing like a traditional church. Then again, St Marylebone is nothing like a traditional parish, in my eyes at least. The church has no steeple or rickety lychgates, there's no quaint little pub on the edge of a green, no cricket pavilion or village hall. No summer fete or Christmas fair, no homemade strawberry jam or Morris men. No rolling fields, no oaks, no elms, no silver birch. No deer, no badgers, no hedgehogs. In short, there is nothing here I love apart from one woman, and this damn city nurtured the creature who threatened to take her away from me. I loathed Fraser Raynott and yes, perhaps a tiny part of me is glad he's dead, but the city which created him lives on; churning out more of his ilk and an endless stream of victims. Crime, drugs, broken lives — the circle continues.

I've had enough.

Clement suddenly takes a sharp left turn. It's a relief to see the road ahead is clear. A few hundred yards of empty tarmac on the final leg of our journey. Five minutes from home. Five minutes from my bed.

A heavy boot presses down on the accelerator, and the engine screams until a new gear is selected. I glance across at the speedometer: approaching forty miles-per-hour. With Clement taking advantage of a clear road, I look towards the horizon and the BT Tower comes into view — torch-like, reaching up into the night sky and adding to the haze of light pollution.

A bright white light flashes in the corner of my right eye. I glance towards the opposing lane; towards a flatbed truck emerging from a side street some hundred yards away. As it straightens up after the left turn, the driver indicates to turn immediately right, across our path. I expect him to wait for us to pass before making that turn. Either the driver doesn't see us, or he's playing a high stakes game of chicken, because suddenly the truck cuts across our lane.

Clement has no choice but to hit the brake pedal hard. At the same time, he yanks the steering wheel to the right, to avoid hitting the truck side on. I don't know if our dilapidated van is fitted with traction control, but if so, it does little to change our direction of travel as the tyres lose grip on the icy tarmac. Frantically, Clement whips the steering wheel in the opposite direction as the van's rear end fishtails to the left.

I brace for impact knowing the back of the van is about to swing into the rear end of the truck. The impact never comes. God only knows how we missed it, but I catch a fleeting flash of the truck's taillights in the side mirror. As my eyes then flick frontwards, the relief is short-lived. Our van is now a rogue waltzer car; spinning and sliding across the glassy road surface. Light zooms from left to right as my stomach heads in the opposite direction.

Out of control, the van continues to spin as Clement grapples with the steering wheel while revving the engine in the hope one of the front tyres gains traction and pulls us into a straight line. As terrifying as our predicament is it's not the first time I've been trapped in a spinning vehicle. There's no comfort in knowing what to expect.

Suddenly, one of the front tyres snatches at the tarmac and

the van lurches forward. The cabin fills with the stench of burning tyre-rubber and the windscreen fills with an image I've barely time to process: a flight of concrete steps, narrower than the width of our van, with a waist-height brick wall either side. A slight change of angle and light reflects from the polished steel handrails running both sides of the steps. I brace for impact again knowing we're about to come to a sudden, violent stop.

With my eyes closed and every muscle taut, I await our fate.

39.

When it arrives, the impact is brutal. The seatbelt bites, but it does little to prevent my face smashing into the hard plastic dashboard. No airbags, no protection.

With the intensity of a white-hot branding iron, the pain arrives. Coloured orbs of light explode from the back of my eyes while fragments of the shattered windscreen rain down. The air is forced from my lungs; replaced with a mixture of petrol fumes and brick dust.

Then there is stillness.

I'm conscious and aware of my surroundings. Not dead, that much is obvious as the dead feel no pain — I've plenty of pain. I wheeze a shallow breath and assess the extent of my injuries. Difficult to know where to start. Ground zero is around the bridge of my nose and spikes up towards my skull; nauseating, sharp. Then, my chest, shoulders, and back; bruised, tender. The fear ratchets up a notch as I try moving my head. A cramp-like spasm erupts from the base of my neck.

"Shiiiit!"

Whiplash? Please, let it be just whiplash. I send a message to my right hand, and three fingers tap at my thigh. I then send a similar message to my feet and I'm able to move my toes. The panic eases a fraction and I allow my eyes to flicker open. The scene steals a breath. Seconds ago, two separate entities existed: a white van and a brick wall. Now, those two entities are entwined as one. The van no longer has a bonnet; now a mass of buckled metal interspersed with chunks of brick. It's impossible to say where the dashboard ends and the carnage begins.

My attention then switches to another part of the decimated structure. A part which has dramatically shifted position but retained integrity — the tubular steel handrail. Now at a near-horizontal angle, it protrudes like a spear from the debris and extends past the windscreen boundary, past the dashboard, and beyond the steering wheel.

"You alright, Doc?" a voice rasps.

Tortuously, I turn my head to the right. It hurts like hell, but there's no repeat of the previous spasm.

"Clement?"

I have to blink several times to decipher what I'm looking at. Still, it doesn't quite compute. The steel handrail has made its way beyond the driver's seat towards the van's cargo bay. What I can't comprehend is how it is bypassing the driver. From my vantage point, it looks almost as if it's tucked under Clement's armpit, but unless the impact has damaged my perception of depth, the distance is every kind of wrong.

I risk leaning forward a shade to gain a better view. Clement doesn't move and continues to stare blankly ahead. My new position explains why he's not moving — the shaft of silver steel is not under his armpit but perforating his chest just below the collarbone.

"Oh, fuck! Oh, fuck!"

Concern for my own wellbeing is washed aside as a wave of panic crashes.

"Don't fret, Doc."

"You've got an inch-wide pole sticking out of your chest. What the hell am I supposed to do other than fret?"

"Wouldn't mind a smoke. They're in my pocket … bit awkward for me to reach 'em."

For a brief moment, I consider his request. Common sense then kicks in.

"A naked flame and petrol fumes aren't a great mix. Besides, you need an ambulance … and the fire brigade."

I edge a hand towards the pocket of my coat.

"What you doing?"

"Phone," I wince. "Just need to …"

"You need to get the fuck out of here. Now!"

"I'm going nowhere."

My fingertips brush the phone bezel. If I adjust my position a fraction, I should be able to snatch it.

"Doc, it ain't up for discussion. Get out of the bloody van."

Pincer-like, my fingers latch on to their target and I slowly extract the phone. It's an awkward, pain-ridden extraction, but I get a grip on it and swipe the screen. Clement grabs my wrist.

"Just 'cos I'm skewered like a bleedin' kebab, don't mean I can't snap your wrist. Call who you like but do it thirty yards from here."

"Clement, please. You're seriously injured. We don't have time to argue over where I make the call."

With obvious discomfort, he slowly turns his head. Not quite enough to face me, but a sufficient angle for his eyes to lock on mine.

"Don't matter about me," he says; his voice now scratchy as much gravelly. "I ain't got a missus to look after. You have."

"Please. Let go of my wrist so I can make the call."

"I'll only let go if I've got your word. You gotta get out of this van, Doc. I'll beg if I have to."

I look into his eyes; the same eyes I once described as empty, dead. Now, they're pleading.

"Okay. I'll get out, but promise me something."

"What?"

"You won't die while I'm making the call. Please."

"You know I don't do promises, Doc. Besides, if I go, it'd be kinda fitting to leave this way."

"What? Why?"

"Long story."

"You can tell me on the way to the hospital."

"Yeah, maybe."

He releases his grip on my wrist.

"One last thing," he coughs. "I never told you but, that bible I took from the Three Monks — Roland nabbed it after he whacked me. If you ever find it, do me a favour and put it back where it belongs."

"Err, how do you know he took it, if you were supposedly dead?"

I can't even begin to imagine how much pain he must be in, but somehow he finds a smile.

"Just a niggling voice in my head."

I roll my eyes and reach for the door handle. Opening the door itself proves a painful, arduous task, but it eventually pops

346

open. I turn to release my seatbelt.

"I'll be seeing you, Doc."

"Just remain calm. Don't move, and don't you dare light a cigarette."

"Thirty yards, remember?"

"Yes, yes."

I muster a reassuring smile and limp away from the van. Thirty steps is all I can manage. I feel sick, disorientated, and cold … so bloody cold. Must be shock, or concussion, or both. I lean up against the side of a bus shelter, and I'm about to dial 999 when a figure bounds up to me; a black guy in a jacket similar to the one lagging our immersion tank in the airing cupboard.

"Bruv, you okay?"

"Err, no. I need to call an ambulance."

"Already rung them. You know your face is proper mashed, man?"

"Is it?"

"It's a horror show, and you got the shakes somethin' bad."

He then unzips his jacket and drapes it around my shoulders.

"You need to sit down, bruv, before you fall down."

He takes my arm and guides me to a bench in the bus shelter.

"Thank you," I mumble wearily, my eyelids suddenly lead-like.

"Don't you go falling asleep. That ain't good if you're concussed."

"Are you a doctor?"

"Nah, man," he chuckles. "My mum, she loves that Holby City. Learnt all my first-aid watching that show as a kid."

A squally breeze suddenly kicks up and the young man huddles himself. The breeze carries a welcome sound: a siren.

"Meds will be here in a tic," the young man says. "Just keep talking to me."

"What's … what's your name?"

"Noah."

"Like the ark, right?"

"Yeah, like the ark. Ain't heard that one before."

"Sorry."

"Don't be sorry, man. It's all cool. You know what it means, my name?"

I try to shake my head, but another sharp spasm cuts it short.

"It means, rest comfortably."

I look up at Noah's kindly face and just as I'm about to mumble a response, a glimmer of flickering light snags my attention. I turn to the left.

"Oh, no … no … no!"

The van is now alight; flames and tendrils of black smoke billowing from the compacted steel carcass that was once the engine bay.

"My friend," I gasp, trying to get to my feet. "He's … he's in …"

My legs don't cooperate and I stumble towards Noah. He manages to keep me upright and I'm guided back to the bench. As my backside lands on the cold plastic, a cacophony of sirens sound and the entire scene pulses with blue light. A fire truck and an ambulance pull up to the kerb near the stricken van. Again, I try to get up, but Noah is having none of it.

"Nah, man. You ain't going nowhere till the meds check you out."

"But … but, my friend … he's still in the van …"

His eyes widen.

"Stay here."

The young man sprints towards one of the firemen who is already unwinding a hose from the side of the truck. Frantically, Noah points in my direction, and then waves his arm towards the van. The fireman nods, and yells an order to the other three members of the crew who are only just exiting the truck. Two of the crew make straight for the van, but barely a second later, they're stopped in their tracks as a ball of fire erupts from the engine bay, consuming the cabin.

As the two firemen duck down to avoid the fireball, I lurch forward.

"Clement!"

I manage six or seven steps when a paramedic steps into my

path.

"Sir," he says, firmly. "You're injured. We need to take a look at you."

"I, but …"

Distraught doesn't come close to describing my emotional state. Another paramedic arrives and the two men guide me back to the bench.

"What's your name, sir?"

I ignore the question and duck my head to the side to see what's happening with the van. The fire crew already have a hose aimed at the base as clouds of thick black smoke belch upwards. The high-pressure jet of water quickly snuffs the flames to reveal the charred remains of a van. Then, as quickly as it erupted, the inferno subsides.

One of the firemen then cautiously approaches the driver's door and peers in. It would be beyond hope of hopes to think Clement might have survived, and the fireman's lack of urgency as he traipses over to his colleague tells me all I need to know.

I slump back against the Plexiglas wall of the bus shelter.

The paramedics prod with more questions I neither hear nor care to answer. I think I mumble my first name, but that's as far as my mind is willing to engage. All I can think about is Clement, and his horrific last moments. Is there any worse way to go than being trapped in a burning vehicle, conscious of the flames lapping at your ankles? How is it fair that a man like Fraser Raynott can shuffle off with chest pains and a gasp, while a man like Clement — decent, honourable, loyal — is taken in such barbarous circumstances? There can be no God because surely no God would consider this justice.

My physical pain is consumed by the emotional. It aches with such savagery I can scarcely catch a breath. When I think it isn't possible to feel any more wretched, my chest begins to heave and the torment reaches new heights. Shutting my eyes, I try to block out the horror, but the acrid smoke-filled air and taste of blood and tears keep the reality rooted. I can now see why some of my clients sought death as a means to end their own hell.

"David. David."

I ignore the voice until a hand lands gently on my shoulder.

"Can you hear me?"

I swallow hard and open my eyes, expecting to see a paramedic. It isn't a paramedic with a hand on my shoulder but a man wearing a bright orange tunic trimmed with fluorescent strips; his face shadowed by a white helmet.

"David? I'm Watch Manager McGee from Kentish Town Fire Station."

I stare up at the man, not wishing to hear what I know he's about to tell me. The worst words anyone can ever hear.

"I just need to ask you a few quick questions before the paramedics treat your injuries. Is that okay?"

"Whatever," I mumble.

"I understand you were in the van when it crashed. Was there anyone in the back?"

"I … the back? No."

"Are you sure?"

"Positive. Just me and Clement."

"Who is Clement?"

"The driver. He was … there was a pole stuck in his chest …"

"And where is he now?"

I close my eyes and wait until another wave of nausea passes.

"He's in … he couldn't get out. He's still in the van."

Watch Manager McGee glances at the nearest paramedic; a look of confusion.

"David — there's no one in the van. My colleague said there's a metal pole piercing what's left of the driver's seat, but there's definitely no driver."

"What? That's impossible. Check again."

"Sorry, but it looks like your friend fled the scene."

"He wouldn't, he couldn't. You're wrong … he could barely breathe, and … and, he must have lost so much blood. I'm telling you now; there is no way Clement could have got out."

The fireman bends down and looks me straight in the eye.

"Dead or alive, there is no one in that van, David. No one."

SIX WEEKS LATER ...

40.

Once again, I'm asked to wait. The receptionist offers me a seat but I decline, and stress I'm unwilling to wait more than two minutes. She scuttles away to relay my message.

Precisely one minute later Simon Crawshaw-Smith appears.

"Hello again, Mr Nunn."

The smarmy estate agent holds out a hand. He receives a bunch of keys rather than a handshake.

"We've cleaned the flat," I confirm. "As per our tenancy agreement."

"Very good."

"When will our deposit be refunded?"

"I'll need to organise a final inspection before the deposit can be released. We're very busy at the moment but I should be able to fit it in within the next couple of weeks."

"Couple of weeks?"

"Yes, and then it'll be another week or two before our admin team can process a bank transfer."

"So, it could be up to a month before we get our deposit back?"

"Give or take," he replies, with the smuggest of smiles.

I take a step forward, invading his personal space.

"See that telephone on your desk, Mr Crawshaw-Smith?"

"What about it?"

"If that deposit isn't in my bank account within the next three days, I'll come back here and shove it so far up your arse you'll require colonic irrigation to make a call. Do you understand?"

"I … how dare you. I won't be threatened."

I take another step forward so my nose is only inches from his.

"I'm not threatening you, dipshit," I growl. "I'm promising you."

"Understood," he gulps. "Three days it is."

"Thank you."

I turn and stride away, delighted in the knowledge I'll never have to see Crawshaw-Smith's face again.

Out on the street, I'm greeted by a blue sky. It's an unseasonably mild day for late February; so much so, I've swapped my winter coat for a denim jacket. I turn and make my way to the second destination on my list.

I'm no longer an employee of RightMind so I have to tap on the door when I arrive. Debbie looks up from her desk, smiles, and skips over to the door to let me in.

After a slightly awkward hug, I decline an offer of tea, on the grounds I've a lot to do today.

"I'm so glad you called in, David," she beams. "I really wanted to see you before you left."

"Ditto, which is why I'm here."

I remove the rucksack from my shoulder and unzip it.

"I've got something for you."

Debbie appears puzzled when I hand over a plain envelope.

"What's this?"

"Open it."

She carefully tears open the envelope and slides her fingers inside.

"Oh, David," she then giggles. "I was only kidding."

"A promise is a promise, Debs."

A fifty pound Greggs voucher isn't everyone's idea of the perfect gift and it doesn't come close to repaying my former colleague. If she hadn't turned up at my flat that morning and let slip about Cameron Gail, I'd now be staring at the inside of a prison cell. I owe her a lot more than a few dozen sausage rolls; which is why I suspect she wanted to see me this morning.

"Thank you. I appreciate it, David."

"You're more than welcome."

Unable to contain her apparent excitement Debbie then claps her hands together.

"I have some incredible news," she says.

"Really? Do tell."

"We received a huge donation yesterday — nine hundred thousand pounds!"

"Wow," I gasp. "That's amazing."

"Isn't it just? It'll help us recruit at least three additional counsellors, and it buys us more than enough time to find a new tenant for next door."

"I'm so pleased, Debs."

"So am I," she gasps. "I'm not a religious type but I've been praying to the man upstairs that a miracle might come our way. We're in such desperate need of extra funding."

"Seems those prayers were answered."

"They were. It's just a shame we can't thank our benefactor for their generosity."

"Oh, why not?"

"The donation was made anonymously."

"Well, whoever they are, I'm sure they're just happy knowing their money will help so many people."

"I hope so."

I know so, and after a few minutes of small talk and a parting hug, I leave the offices of RightMind for the final time.

Continuing on to my next destination, I pass the familiar parade of shops offering products and services to the residents of Kentish Town: groceries, haircuts, carpets, Indian food, and funerals. In early January, I'd had no reason to use the services of a funeral director, and I still haven't. However, I did send them a sizable contribution towards the cost of Cameron Gail's funeral — a funeral I attended ten days ago.

In the preceding days I'd agonised whether or not it was right to go.

Looking back, perhaps I could have done more, but who's to say the outcome would have been any different? It was Cameron who darted from my office during our first meeting, and it was Raynott who sent those two men to hunt him down at The Duke that evening. Two brief meetings, which ended prematurely. I never really had the chance to build a relationship with the troubled young man. Still, the guilt gnaws away.

At Cameron's funeral, I have to confess I did my best to avoid Kimberley Bowhurst. I felt almost as much guilt for letting her down as her former boyfriend. Then again, maybe she's

355

carrying her own sack of guilt around. Could she have gone to the police? Should she have let them hear Cameron's garbled message?

Truth is: we all make decisions and we all have to live with the consequences. Sadly, the consequences of Cameron Gail's decisions meant he never got the chance to live with his.

If there was any semblance of positivity, it came in a brief conversation with Alan Whiting — Cameron's former tutor at Oxford. He caught up with me just as I was leaving the cemetery, and he asked if I knew a date for the inquest into Cameron's death. I didn't have an answer. Scientists aren't renowned for emotional ebullience, but losing such a gifted young student had clearly left a mark on Dr Whiting. After confessing his own guilt for not persuading Cameron to continue his studies, the doctor disclosed how he intended to deal with that guilt — the continuation of Cameron Gail's research into a treatment for multiple sclerosis.

I could have asked him how he intended to do that, but I already had a strong inkling. Four weeks ago, I received a call from the manager of a charity shop. Unbelievably, she'd located an iPhone in a box of household tat — one which fitted the description of an iPhone I'd been searching high and low for. Once I'd charged it, and more in hope than expectation, I tried to guess Cameron's password. It took one attempt: Kimbo. I found what I hoped to find and anonymously emailed an entire folder of research files to Dr Whiting.

On the subject of files, two days after the accident, I paid a visit to our local police station. I handed over Alex's phone and laptops, and confirmed they'd been left at my front door together with a printed confession letter. It detailed exactly what the laptops had been used for and how the perpetrator couldn't live with the guilt. I don't know if Detective Greenwood believed my tale, but he sent the laptops away for examination. A few days later, he called to confirm they'd found evidence of a hack on the RightMind network. Unfortunately, he had no idea where the owner of those laptops had disappeared to. Apparently, the police were already keen to find him to discuss a pistol found at his former flat.

More importantly, though, during that same call Detective Greenwood also confirmed Chantelle Granger had withdrawn her allegation.

There were, however, other questions posed by the detective. I responded to every one of them with the same response: no idea. Those unanswered questions related to links between the owner of the laptops and a recently deceased resident of Chiswick. Apparently, that resident had been on the radar of the Organised Crime Division for several years, but they'd never been able to find hard evidence of his illegal activities. Not that it mattered, but they found plenty of evidence at a disused snooker hall in Stratford, along with the body of a young man locked in a basement. Seeing as their chief suspect has already been tried by a higher power, and his punishment administered in the form of a fatal heart attack, Detective Greenwood confirmed they're unlikely to pursue their investigation.

That is just as well.

I suspected the enhanced security protocols on Fraser Raynott's laptop had been installed for good reason, and I was right. In amongst the folders and files I copied, I found details of an offshore bank account in the Cayman Islands. In total, Raynott had squirrelled away over six million pounds, which I'm in the process of redistributing to good causes, thanks to the idiot recording his log-in credentials in a file.

The prospect of playing Robin Hood came after days of soul searching, and after I learnt the cost Fraser Raynott paid for his life choices. He never married or had children, and I can't deny it was pleasing to discover my nemesis was the last in the Raynott bloodline. As I saw it, the police had no idea of his offshore account; the only proof residing on a laptop destroyed in a fire. I unearthed further reassurance amongst Raynott's emails, specifically those from a highly qualified financial expert who confirmed just how untraceable his client's money would be. Besides, I've gone to great lengths to ensure the individual who redistributed that money is equally untraceable. Surprisingly easy if you do the right research and use the right software.

It seemed only fair I should be compensated for what that man did to me. Of the six million pounds, I have invested three hundred thousand in a two-bedroom cottage near Oxford. Situated on the outskirts of a lovely little village; it's a perfect forever home. There was, however, the minor detail of persuading my wife as much.

When Leah returned from my parents, I had a lot of explaining to do. Firstly, I had to explain my injuries. The hospital only kept me in for observation after the accident — my injuries limited to concussion, whiplash, and a broken nose — but my face was a bruised and swollen mess. It wasn't the surprise my wife expected. I told her I'd been involved in a road accident, but I didn't share the exact details of that accident. To her credit, Leah adopted the role of nurse and for the first time in our marriage, she looked after me. At that point I realised I've been underestimating my wife for far too long; treating her like a victim.

Lesson learnt.

During my convalescence, I spent days on the sofa, browsing Rightmove to keep my mind occupied. In fact, I did everything I could to avoid thoughts I knew I'd have to confront at some point. On the fourth day, after Leah returned from Oxfordshire, I bit the bullet and showed her the details of the cottage I hoped would sway my argument.

Actually, I had no intention of putting forward an argument or even discussing the subject. I told her straight: I'd had enough of London and we were moving. In a final and ironic lie, I told her I'd won a sizeable sum on a lottery scratch card.

Her reaction proved unexpected.

Five days without me or my controlling ways, as she put it, Leah returned with a completely different attitude towards the county of my birth. I owe my parents because they were instrumental in changing her view. I suspect Dad also mentioned how deeply unhappy I'd become living in London. I endured a lengthy lecture from my wife about not looking after my own mental health, and to my astonishment, she insisted we view the cottage as soon as possible.

That is why we are no longer residents of a poky flat in Kentish Town. Leah is currently saying her goodbyes to friends and acquaintances before we head down to Oxfordshire this afternoon to pick up the keys to our new home. And once we've settled in, I need to make a definitive decision about my career in counselling. I don't know if I still have the same enthusiasm I once possessed, but maybe a few weeks of fresh air and serenity will restore that enthusiasm. We shall see.

For now, I've got one final place to visit.

I reach the fringes of Camden and double-check our meeting place and the time. I'm early, but I'd like the opportunity to sit and work through my own thoughts.

Another few streets and my destination comes into view: The Brewmaster Coffee Shop. I cross the road and take a moment to study the exterior. I doubt most people would notice, but there are still a few hints to the history of the premises. The main door is sited on the corner, and there's a set of solid timber doors embedded in the pavement; giving access to a cellar no longer used to store beer, wine, or spirits. As I approach the door I can't help but glance towards the alley running down the side. Just a glance, but it sends an icy shiver down my spine. I hurry inside.

Mid-morning, and it's fairly quiet. There are perhaps seven or eight other customers dotted around the tables and a few more sat on stools. Besides a couple of middle-aged women chatting in the corner, all the other customers are staring at digital devices. It's a far cry from the scene which would have greeted me if I'd wandered into this building forty or fifty years ago.

I walk up to the counter and order a tea. A bearded guy processes my order and a three quid cup of lukewarm piss is duly served. I'm just about to pay when I hear the clack of heeled shoes behind me.

"David?"

I turn around to a middle-aged woman with short blonde hair.

"You're early too," I smile. "It's lovely to meet you, Emma."

I'm not in the habit of hugging people I've never met, but on this occasion, it feels appropriate. I may have never met Emma Hogan but we've talked at length on the phone. In fact, if it wasn't for Emma, I think I'd have completely lost my mind six weeks ago.

"So, today's the big day, then?" she says.

"It is. No more London. I can't say I'll miss it."

"I was born and bred here, but I can't deny it wears you down after a while."

"I'm probably being harsh. I am leaving with a few fond memories."

"But mainly awful ones," she chuckles.

The jovial smile quickly fades as she drinks in our surroundings.

"This is it then? The infamous Three Monks."

"Yep, once upon a time."

"That's how all good stories start; with those words," she says, wistfully.

"True. It's just a shame they don't all have a happy ending."

I've heard Emma's story, and it didn't end happily. However, today is a chance for closure; for us both to embrace our respective journeys with a big man decked in double denim.

Emma orders a coffee and we sit at a table near the window. She starts by picking up on a conversation we had three days ago.

"Have you heard anything more from the police?"

"Only to say they've closed the investigation. Lack of resources, apparently, but I think we both know why."

"They don't believe you?"

"No, and I can't say I blame them. I wouldn't believe me."

"That's that, then," she sighs.

"In fairness, they checked seventeen different cameras in and around the scene of the accident. It's not as though our friend was easy to miss, but every one of those seventeen cameras managed to. As far as the police are concerned, there was only ever one person in that van. Fortunately, I suppose, they can't prove I was the one driving."

"Because you weren't."

"Indeed, but I'm not sure the police would believe my alternative explanation."

I'm still struggling with the truth myself, and I know Emma has endured a similar conflict for months. We share a look which implies I'm not far wrong.

The door opens, and a conservatively dressed man enters the coffee shop. I look across as he scans the room, and our eyes meet. I get to my feet as he approaches.

The man offers a handshake.

"It's great to finally put a name to the face, David," he says, warmly.

"You too, Bill."

Like Emma, William Huxley has his own story to tell. I've heard it, and we've chatted at great length. It was Emma who first got in contact with the former politician after our mutual friend mentioned Bill during a conversation. It seems he was initially reluctant to talk about his experience — not surprising when you consider Emma's profession — but he relented when she turned up at his home on the Isle of Wight and refused to leave. There's still a lot I don't know about Emma, but I do know she's a spirited, feisty individual. I can see why a certain person fell for her.

Bill returns from the counter with a cup in hand.

"This used to be a pub, right?" he comments.

"It did."

"Shame it still isn't. I could murder a cold Chablis about now."

"Patience, William," Emma grins. "We'll find a nice pub when we're done. I think we'll all need a stiff drink by then."

"And maybe a toast," I add. "To an absent friend."

They both agree with a solemn nod.

We swap small talk for five minutes, and Bill appears keen to chat about his charity. He's a minute into explaining his expansion plans when the door opens again. I look across and recognise the woman in the doorway. Not because we've ever met, but because I've seen her face on a poster in a bookshop window.

She wanders over.

"Are you all early, or am I late?"

"We're early," Emma replies. "It's lovely to see you, Beth."

The two women then embrace before Beth turns to Bill.

"How is the subject of my second novel doing?" she chuckles.

"Couldn't be better, thanks. More importantly, how's the third coming along?"

"I'm getting there, with Emma's help. It should be with my editor by late spring."

"Good to know," Bill replies. "I'm looking forward to reading Cliff's next adventure."

"Sorry for the spoiler, but I think you already know how it ends."

"I do," he nods, glancing across at Emma.

Beth then turns to me and I receive an unexpected hug.

"I guess you're the latest member of our exclusive club, David?"

"The latest, but sadly the last, I suspect."

The reason we're all currently in a Camden coffee shop together is because Beth Baxter once owned a bookshop. That, and a particular book she inherited. Seemingly itching to establish if that book has resurfaced, she gets straight to the point.

"Can I see it?" she asks, nervously.

"Of course."

We all re-take our seats and I delve into my rucksack. I extract a padded envelope and peel the flap open.

"Here you go."

Beth dips her hand into the envelope and slowly pulls out an old bible. A tense hush descends on the table as she inspects the cover and then flicks through the pages to the end.

"Dear, God," she gulps. "I ... I can't believe ..."

We await a verdict. A single tear offers a clue to that verdict.

"Is it the same bible?" I ask.

Choked with emotion, the best Beth can do is nod.

When Leah returned from Oxfordshire, after she'd got over the shock of her husband's battered facial features, an inevitable question arose: how did we get on with her stall? I had to confess I wasn't in a fit state to run a bath, let alone a stall, but I made amends by insisting I help her the following Saturday — primarily because I didn't want all her junk coming with us to Oxfordshire. She agreed, and on the Friday I felt fit enough to assist in her stock selection.

Midway through that process, Leah asked me to sift through the crates of books she'd acquired at the last market, and to select those I thought would be most saleable — my wife is not a big reader. I discounted several in the first crate and opened the second. In that crate, I unearthed no less than a dozen copies of Fifty Shades of Grey and several paperbacks by authors I'd never heard of. Right at the bottom, I found a bible.

Initially, I wondered if it might have some value — being old and beautifully made — so I flicked through the pages to check the condition. Like Beth, I physically gasped when I stumbled upon six lines of handwritten text in the back.

O child of need, who shall be thy steed?
To carry thou on, tho hope be gone
The light to see, with words for thee
For once thou speak, thy steed thou seek
O Heavenly alchemy;
blessed thou shall be.

Frantically, I scoured my mind in search of a moment someone could have slipped the bible into the crate without either Leah or I noticing. There was only one suspect, but I'm one hundred percent positive that suspect never had the opportunity. The bible had been in the crate since the day Leah brought it home.

That moment — stood in the lounge holding that old bible — I also shed a tear. There was nothing left; no plausible excuse even the most militant agnostic could cling to. The truth, even when it's near impossible to accept, is the truth.

There and then, the last of my lingering doubts left the room.

Emma reaches across the table and squeezes Beth's hand.

"Are you okay, hun?"

"I'm not sure how I feel, to be honest. It's my job to find the right words but there just aren't any."

"No," Bill says. "There aren't."

A woman with wild silver hair approaches the table.

"I'm guessing one of you is Emma?" she asks.

"That'd be me."

Emma stands up and shakes the woman's hand. She then introduces herself to the rest of the table. Sian is the proprietor of the coffee shop and she received a phone call from Emma last week; a phone call which would have sounded crazy to anyone but a former hippie like Sian.

"I'm ready whenever you are."

We stand and follow Sian through a door to the side of the counter. Two flights of stairs later we assemble at the bottom of a narrow staircase leading up to the attic.

"I think it's wonderful, what you're doing," Sian coos. "So few people believe in the spiritual these days."

The reason four random strangers are at the bottom of a narrow staircase in a Camden coffee shop is because all four of us want to fulfil one man's final wish. That one man has impacted all of our lives beyond reason, beyond hope, and it must be said, beyond sanity. Four lives changed forever, and the life of one dead man in double denim … well, who knows.

Beth and I head up the stairs first, followed by Emma and then Bill.

Thankfully, the attic has a boarded floor and a single bulb emits sufficient light for us to conduct our task. I don't know how old the building is, but the stale air and near-ethereal silence would befit a medieval chapel.

We stand in a tight circle with Beth holding the bible.

"Now we're here, I'm not sure what to say."

"I took the liberty of preparing a few words," Bill says. "Once a politician, always a politician, I'm afraid."

The look of relief on Beth's face is obvious; as it is on Emma's. Even though this was my idea, I hadn't thought beyond this moment, so I'm only too happy for Bill to take the lead.

"Clement," he begins. "I hope, wherever you are, you can hear these words. The reason we're all here today is because of you; not simply to honour your wishes but because you've left an indelible mark on all our lives. I think I speak for all of us in saying that our lives would be markedly different today if we'd never met. You brought hope when we'd all lost hope, you gave us strength when we were at our weakest, and you left us with the greatest gift any man could bestow — the gift of belief. There is … there is …"

His voice breaks.

"Sorry," he croaks. "This is tougher than my maiden speech in Parliament."

"It's okay," Emma says softly, placing a hand on his shoulder. "Take your time."

The former politician draws in a deep breath and continues.

"There is one thing I wish I'd said to you, before you left. I wish I'd told you how blessed I felt, to have known you. You were, and will always be, our guardian angel. Rest in peace, my friend."

Bill bites hard on his bottom lip while Beth and Emma are both struggling to keep their emotions in check. The lump in my throat threatens to choke as my eyes water.

Beth hands me the bible.

"It's right that you do it."

I daren't reply for fear of losing it. Instead, I take the bible and run a hand across the cover. I have to blink the tears away in order to do what I came here to do. A few steps to my right, I reach up and gently tuck the old bible behind the nearest rafter.

"Job done, Clem," I just about murmur.

Time passes, and the four of us just stand motionless, staring up at the bible. I suspect each of us is processing our own thoughts and our own memories. Perhaps, though, we're all asking the same questions; those that no one can truly answer.

We've all talked at length — to each other, and collectively — and we've all tried to make sense of our individual experiences. Even now, together, I don't think we're any closer to understanding the truth about Clement. I wonder if we're meant to. Whoever he was, or whatever his motives, there's every chance the man will remain a mystery; a miraculous, denim-clad, beer-swilling, cigarette-smoking, straight-talking, physically intimidating, politically incorrect mystery.

I, like my new friends, will never forget the man who gatecrashed our lives and changed them forever. And, I hate to admit it, but God, will I miss him.

"I don't know about the rest of you," Bill says, breaking the silence "but I could murder a drink."

"Count me in," Beth replies, a slight tremble in her voice.

I concur and all three of us turn to Emma.

"I'd love a proper drink but I'll settle for an orange juice."

She places a hand on the significant bump protruding from her midriff.

"I don't think Junior would appreciate me swigging pints like his Daddy."

THE END

Before You Go…

I genuinely hope you enjoyed reading Clement's latest adventure. If you did, and have a few minutes spare, I would be eternally grateful if you could leave a (hopefully positive) review on Amazon. A mention on Facebook or Twitter would be equally appreciated. I know it's a pain, but it's the only way us indie authors can compete with the big publishing houses.

Stay in Touch…

For more information about me, my books, and to receive updates on my new releases, please visit my website: www.keithapearson.co.uk

If you have any questions or general feedback, you can also reach me, or follow me via…

Facebook: www.facebook.com/pearson.author
Twitter: www.twitter.com/keithapearson

Printed in Great Britain
by Amazon